2, 1 ,

For Page

THE HINDENBURG LETTER

Danke Schöen

Roger L. Conlee

Roza.

Pale Horse Books

Library of Congress Control Number: 2008940610

ISBN: 978-0-9710362-7-7

Cover Design: Mark A. Clements
Author Photo: David Friend Productions
(www.DavidFriend.com)

www.PaleHorseBooks.com
www.RogerConlee.com

For Erin, Kelley and Doug,

the joys of my life

CHAPTER ONE

Jake Weaver was engaged to a terrific woman, had a good job on one of Old Man Hearst's top newspapers, and the future spread out before him like a wide sunny boulevard. So why was he strapped to a cold steel table in a Gestapo dungeon?

The weasel-faced man bent over a storage battery and fondled the toggle switch. He'd snapped an electric cable to Jake's ear with some kind of spring clip. Another to his arm. With a demonic grin he said, "I do not really give a damn who you are or what you say. Have you noticed how much I enjoy my work?" Behind him, hooks, straps and chains hung from rough concrete walls.

The whip-cut on Jake's face burned hot and his ribs ached as if they'd been whacked with a ball-peen hammer. He glared hatred at Weasel Face, but the bastard merely smiled.

Jake's tongue felt fat and spongy. "Listen," he managed to croak, repeating his oft-told lie, "my name is Hans-Karl Vogel. I am a Swiss—"

His eyes dancing with pleasure, Weasel Face flicked the switch. Jake's body bucked against his bindings. Searing pain scalded his every nerve ending. Then, thank God, it was over. *Thank God.*

"Now, *Herr* Vogel—or whoever you really are, you must give me something. Give me something, my little toy."

"Look," Jake murmured, "I have a wife . . . kids . . . in Zurich. Please, don't do this."

"Ah, a family man. That is really so nice." Weasel Face bent over and glared at his captive from close range, his fetid breath filling Jake's nostrils. "You will tell me what I wish to know, Herr Vogel. You will talk. And not about your *Frau und Kinder*. Oh, dear me, how I do enjoy my work." And his maniacal laughter filled the room.

Weasel Face walked back to the battery and fondled the toggle switch.

Jake had gotten himself into a lot of scrapes over the years and had made his share of mistakes, some of them whoppers, but nothing compared with this, nothing. He figured he would be a long time dead before anyone back home would ever know what had happened to him.

He squirmed against the strong bindings that pinioned him to the table. It was no use. With each movement they only grew tighter. The walls seemed to be closing in. His torturer laughed his demented laugh yet again.

If only Jake had never received that letter, that damn letter Rolf Becker managed to sneak to him from Nazi Germany. Was that four weeks ago? Five?

Weasel Face threw the toggle switch.

CHAPTER TWO

"Oh my God, they killed Uncle Dieter." The Germans executed his uncle!

A month before, Jake was sitting at his desk in the city room of the *L.A. Herald-Express* when he opened the letter. He knew right off who it was from. The simple code in which it was written took only minutes to decipher. It ripped into his consciousness like a bullet between the eyes. Uncle Dieter, the man who'd been more of a father to him than his real father, *was dead*.

Jake's hand, still clutching the letter, shook like an aspen leaf. For a moment he was oblivious to the fact that he was surrounded by rowdy voices, ringing telephones and clattering typewriters. Slumping back in his chair, he tossed the letter aside and cradled his head in his hands. Could this be a mistake? he wondered. No, the sender was a good reporter, never got his facts wrong. This was no mistake. Oh my God, he thought again. *Oh my God.*

"Hey Jake," called Gracie Pike, one of the Society writers. "You okay?"

He didn't answer. Minutes passed before he picked up the letter and re-read it.

The last time he'd seen Uncle Dieter had been back in '35. His uncle had flown across on the *Graf Zeppelin*, then reached Louisiana by train. Since the death of his wife Marta in 1930, Dieter had been kind of a lost soul. One reason he'd treated Jake like a son was because he and Marta never had kids of their own.

It was during Dieter's visit that Jake had got the job offer from L.A.'s *Herald-Express*. His father had said, "Don't go out there to that wicked place. You'd be a thousand miles from your mama and me. You're doing fine right here. Besides, you might not be good enough for a big-city newspaper." *Thanks for the vote of confidence, Dad.*

Dieter had taken Jake aside and whispered, "You do it, boy. You *are* good enough. You must seize this opportunity." As usual, Dieter was the more astute of the brothers.

The letter felt cold, seemed to chill Jake's fingers. Questions swirled. Why had Dieter been executed? He was no lover of Hitler and it would be just like him to get involved in a resistance movement. Or to start one.

Jake recalled—this must have been in 1933 or '34—Dieter telling him that Adolf Hitler, the new chancellor, was a small-minded xenophobe who would not be good for Germany. His bluster about restoring the country to its former greatness was dangerous jingoism. The army should get rid of him. Had that belief become Dieter's death warrant?

The letter had come in a large gray envelope adorned with postage stamps bearing pictures of stern-looking old kings. And a big, purple-inked Stockholm postmark, 27-10-42, with a crossbar on the stem of the seven. October 27, 1942.

Inside the envelope was a smaller one containing the letter from his friend Rolf Becker. Getting information out of Germany was tough these days. Downright dangerous, in fact. Rolf, a reporter in Berlin, must have smuggled the letter to a trusted contact in neutral Sweden for forwarding to America.

What a risk Rolf had taken. Had Uncle Dieter's death put him in danger, too? Were the Gestapo or the SS aware that Dieter had known Rolf?

Jake was part of a large old German family, one wing of which had emigrated to America before the Great War. The original name was Weber but it got changed to Weaver in a foul-up at Ellis Island. When Jake was growing up in Baton Rouge, German was spoken in the Weaver home as much as English.

He set the letter aside, reached for the mug of coffee on his desk and took a sip. It had gone cold. He thought about the day he and Uncle Dieter had spent at the state fair in Shreveport—this was shortly before Jake had left the paper in Longview, Texas, for the job in L.A. Jake had practiced his German on Dieter at the fair, and his uncle said his vocabulary and pronunciation were excellent. And now that good man was dead. Jake's heart felt weighted down. He shook his head. Very slowly.

He put the coffee mug down on his desk. Anger still churned inside. Okay, he told himself, here's what I have to do: get into Nazi Germany somehow. Right now, in the middle of a world war, and get to the bottom of this. His fiancée, Valerie Jean Riskin, wouldn't like it. Making her understand wouldn't be easy.

Jake considered himself the best military reporter in L.A. Lately, he'd been working on a fascinating story, just the kind W.R.—meaning Hearst—liked: the Nazi plot to kidnap Walt Disney. It had led him in some surprising directions.

Getting to the bottom of the Disney thing and wrapping up a hell of a story, Jake thought, was almost reason enough to sneak into Germany. Finding the bastards who killed Uncle Dieter and getting his revenge—that was *more* than enough.

CHAPTER THREE

With one foot up on his battered old desk, Jake rummaged through a pile of notes that his mind wasn't really on.

He'd never been particularly vengeful, although he'd once beat the hell out of a seventh grader he caught robbing a little kid of his lunch money at Our Lady of Mercy. The little kid was Jake's next-door neighbor. Although Jake was only a sixth grader at the time, nobody did things like that to his friends, not if he could help it. Now he found himself itching to do worse, much worse, to whoever had ordered Uncle Dieter killed.

Jake wondered what his fiancée, Valerie, would say about this lust for revenge. He was planning to discuss this with her tonight. Valerie Jean Riskin was a tool designer at North American Aviation and one of the best things who had happened to him—as he liked to put it—in 1942.

He'd met Valerie six months ago while running down a story. Jake had fallen for the attractive widow right away. He knew he was no Tyrone Power—medium height, ruddy complexion, reddish hair—but, miracle of miracles, she'd felt the same about him. The immediate magnetic charge had cut both ways.

Five months later, he'd said, "How about lunch, or dinner, or getting married?"

She'd said, "Okay."

Valerie was bright and clever and always had good ideas about his work. Yes, he would talk over his latest brainstorm with her at dinner tonight in her Inglewood apartment.

Another idea popped up. He was acquainted with Steve Early, President Roosevelt's salty press secretary. He'd had several contacts with Early while working on stories. Jake looked at his watch. 11:20. That would make it 2:20 in Washington. Early might be back from lunch by now. And sober? One could hope.

So, what the hell. Jake placed a call and surprisingly got Early on the line in only three minutes. Jake told him the whole thing, his pursuit of the Walt Disney story, his friend on the *Deutsche Zeitung*, and the dastardly Nazi execution of his revered uncle. He threw in "dastardly" because he knew it was a word FDR used. This was a long call, and Jake tried not to think about the phone bill. He hadn't reversed the charges; that would be pushing it.

"Won't be easy," Early said after Jake described his burning need to get into Germany. "Still, the boss might go for it. That kind of damn fool cloak-and-dagger stuff appeals to him. Maybe I could fix it for you to meet with him."

An audience with FDR! "That'd be fine, Steve," Jake said. "W.R. would like that."

"Old Man Hearst doesn't cut much ice with the boss these days. Burned too many bridges over the Wagner Act. Appreciates his support for the big move-out of the Japs, though," Early said, referring to the forced relocation of Japanese-Americans from their homes near the coast.

"I'm not looking for the president's approval," Jake said, "but meeting with him would be swell. It'd be nice to know if he thought this wasn't too bad an idea, him knowing Putzi Hanfstaengl and all." Hanfstaengl was a man who now figured in Jake's theories about Walt Disney.

"I'll hang it on the clothes line and let you know what happens," Early said.

Jake hung up and put a few fresh teeth marks in the yellow copy pencil he was holding. On the radio over in the sports department, someone was singing, *I've Got a Gal in Kalamazoo*. Tex Beneke, or maybe Ray Eberle.

His thoughts turned to Berlin and Rolf Becker. His friend had been there, what, four years now? He'd taken that job in early '38, around the time Hitler seized Austria. Jake wondered what it was like being a reporter over there these days, the propaganda ministry telling you what to print every day.

Rolf Becker had been born in Germany, but he'd moved to America and become a newspaperman like Jake. They'd grown close while working together on Hearst's *Herald-Express*. Chasing hot stories, fast women, and cold booze.

Then in the late Thirties Rolf got a tempting job offer from the *Deutsche Allgemeine Zeitung*. Rolf was fascinated with the crazy goings-on in the new Germany. He'd always been drawn to danger and on top of that he felt some kind of spiritual tug from the land of his birth. He said, why not take this offer and see first-hand what it was all about over there under the Nazis? After awhile, his curiosity satisfied, he would come back to the States.

So Rolf went off to Berlin. But then Germany invaded Poland, Europe fell into war, and he was stranded.

The *Deutsche Zeitung* once had been mainstream and first-rate, respected internationally, much like New York's *Herald Tribune*.

When the Nazis came to power, they forced many newspapers out of business, especially those owned by Jews. They cowed others into becoming publicity mills for the New Order, but they allowed the *Deutsche Zeitung* to continue because they thought it made them look good to the rest of the world. The paper was intimidated, of course, but its coverage of Nazi triumphs was restrained in comparison with the bald propaganda spewed forth by the others.

Jake wondered how he could get a message through to Rolf.

Brushing the thought aside, he hauled himself to his feet and ambled to the managing editor's office.

"Johnny," he said, sticking his head in the door. "Got a minute?"

The wall bore a poster of a pretty Marine with a finger to her lips. The caption read, "Silence Means Security."

Jake replayed the long-distance conversation he'd just had. When he finished, John Campbell shook his head and said, "You crazy-ass Texan—"

"Loozy-ana, Johnny, Loozy-ana."

"Whatever. Texas, Louisiana, it's all the same. Well, I'll tell you, Jakey boy, W.R. just happens to be in town. He and Miss Marion are at the beach house for a few days." Beach house? Their Santa Monica mansion had a hundred and ten rooms and something like fifty baths. "He's gonna stop in tomorrow. Let's us have a little talk with him about this."

Even at the age of seventy-nine, Hearst popped into the city room at least once a month. Jake marveled that W.R. still kept close tabs on his papers, despite his amazing social life and the years spent building his ostentatious castle up the coast.

Hearst had been looking for sensational headlines to sell papers all his life. "What's the *Mirror*'s banner?" he would say, referring to the afternoon competitor, the *L.A. Mirror*. "Beat the *Mirror*, gentlemen, always beat the *Mirror*."

They usually did beat the *Mirror*. The *Express* had the largest circulation of any daily in town, even the morning *Times*. With typical Hearst bluster, this fact was proclaimed boldly every day in the masthead.

Jake felt the Old Man's advice wasn't very good, that he'd learned to write a news story better in ten years than W.R. had in half a century. Still, Hearst was a good boss and fun to talk with.

Jake hoped Marion Davies would come with him tomorrow, as she often did. Miss Davies was a sharp cookie, not a bit high-hat, and she exerted a calming influence on the mercurial Old Man. She was W.R.'s spouse in all but name, because his real wife, the once lovely Millicent Willson, now a proud old woman, refused to grant him a divorce.

Some disagreed, but Jake thought Miss Davies was a fine actress, especially in comedy roles. Her career would have fared better if W.R. hadn't butted in, trying to make her the world's greatest star. Hearst's constant meddling must have angered her.

Jake knew about anger. It had crawled into bed with him last night and rolled out with him again this morning.

Okay, so somehow Uncle Dieter had run afoul of the Nazis. But why hadn't they just thrown him in a concentration camp, as they'd done with those brave Lutheran ministers who'd refused to stop preaching the Gospel? The bastards didn't have to *kill* him.

Jake looked down and found his fists clenched exactly as they were when he'd coldcocked that seventh grader twenty-five years ago.

CHAPTER FOUR

Jake called and made an appointment to see Walt Disney. Then, seated at his desk, he popped a stick of Beech-Nut gum in his mouth, doodled on coarse gray copy paper, and mentally rehashed that whole kidnap business. After much digging, he'd convinced himself the reason the Nazis wanted to nab Disney was so they could exchange him for Ernst "Putzi" Hanfstaengl. That was such a peculiar name, plus hard to say, that Jake merely wrote "H" in his notes.

An early crony of Hitler's, the German-born but Harvard-educated Hanfstaengl had fled for his life back to America after a nasty falling-out with the Nazis. "H" knew too many deep dark secrets about Hitler and his crowd, and they wanted him back.

"H" had briefly been Hitler's foreign press chief. Maybe he knew the truth about the mysterious death of Hitler's niece and mistress, Geli Raubal, in 1931. The dangerous truth could be that Hitler had had her killed, or had killed her himself. The Munich police were convinced of Hitler's involvement, but Nazi pressure had silenced them.

A New York and then Berlin society boy, Hanfstaengl had helped Hitler in his rise to power. He knew plenty about the Führer, and the Nazis wanted him badly. Now he was a guest in the White House, of all things, an unofficial adviser to FDR on Germany. Safest place he could be. But with the kind of leverage the Nazis would have with Walt Disney in their clutches—Mickey Mouse was loved all over the world—they'd have a better way to smoke him out.

Jake always found the meetings with Disney interesting. When he'd first approached the famous animator, the chain-smoking creator of Mickey Mouse had pretended to shrug off the warnings. But Disney had taken them seriously, had even hired a former L.A. cop to bodyguard him and his brother Roy, the bean-counter of the operation.

Jake's thoughts turned to his father. He wished they could have been closer, but he'd often clashed with the man, a case of too much offspring rebellion. Always with guilt, Jake sometimes wished Dieter, who had more warmth and charisma, had been his father instead. A sharp needle of that guilt stabbed him now.

It was Dieter who'd first tipped him off to the Disney thing. Dieter had cabled him from a Danish town just over the border, apparently reasoning that the Gestapo wasn't watching messages from occupied Denmark as closely as those from Germany proper. The cablegram read:

YOU KNOW HOW I MAKE PREDICTIONS MOST SILLY STOP SYMPHONIES CONDUCTOR COULD LEAVE PODIUM SUDDENLY FOR EUROPEAN TOUR STOP ADVISE OUGHT-OH LOOK INTO THAT STOP HOPE WELL STOP LOVE, RETEID

Jake had puzzled over that for a long time. The first and easiest thing to figure out was that RETEID was Dieter spelled backwards. It took him longer to put the words silly and symphonies together. The early cartoons that made Mickey Mouse a star were called the Silly Symphonies. The "conductor" of course was Walt Disney.

But then a week passed before the rest clicked into place. ADVISE OUGHT-OH LOOK INTO THAT. It finally dawned on Jake that Otto was the name of a German restaurant in Culver City, named for Otto von Bismarck. It was a hangout for Germans and German-Americans and, Jake soon learned, anti-American plotters. The place lost a lot of trade during the London Blitz when being

German became damned unpopular. After Pearl Harbor, desperately trying to stay afloat, the owners changed the name to *The George* and hung a portrait of George Washington in the lobby.

So Dieter's cablegram was saying, "Walt Disney could suddenly be whisked off to Europe, and you know who controls Europe. You'd better look into the restaurant Otto." Which of course Jake did.

An hour later, he knocked off for the day and went across the street to the Continental, the scruffy saloon that served as watering hole to newsmen, con artists, pool sharks, and workers from the L.A. trolley barns and nearby van and storage company. A yellow neon sign in the dirt-streaked window read BREW 102.

He met Charlie Root for a shooter, as he did every couple of weeks in the off-season. Root had hooked on as player-manager of the Hollywood Stars' Pacific Coast League ball club after his career with the Chicago Cubs had played itself out. He left tickets for Jake whenever he asked.

Like all ball clubs these days, the Stars were feeling the talent pinch caused by the war. Uncle Sam wanted able-bodied young men to carry rifles, not baseball bats. So Root, at forty-three, while managing an assortment of vintage ex-major leaguers and hopeful kids fresh out of high school, still pitched every fourth or fifth day.

A mist of tobacco smoke hung inside. On the jukebox, some orchestra, Tommy Dorsey maybe, was playing *Tangerine*. Jake found Root at the bar, a glass and a bottle of Old Granddad in front of him, deep in conversation—or argument—with Shaker, the bartender.

"Hi Cholly, hi Shakes," Jake said, slipping onto the stool next to Root. Shaker was wiping a glass with a damp towel.

"This guy keeps arguin' with me about the Babe," said Root with a jerk of his head in the barkeep's direction. "Hell, it was me who was pitching—I oughta know. Shaker here didn't see nothing but a fuzzy newsreel, coupla weeks later."

Jake knew Root was referring to Babe Ruth's "called shot" in the

'32 Series, when he supposedly pointed to the centerfield bleachers before belting a home run into them.

"Gimme an Eastside, Shaker."

"What, no hooch?"

"Nah, I'm having dinner with Val, gotta be reasonably sober." Jake turned and prompted Root. "So? You were the pitcher."

Root sighed like a dying bagpipe. "I'll tell you both one last time, then I'm never gonna mention it again, understand? Sick and tired of this damn subject."

He threw back a gulp of whisky with a quick jerk of hand and head. "Okay, the Babe is being rode something fierce by our boys. Them Cubs are mean bench jockeys. The Babe yells something like 'Shut your yaps, fellas,' and points at the dugout. He never points to centerfield. If he does, Katy bar the gate, I'm knocking him on his ass. God knows I've drilled guys for less. Jake, you saw what I did to that big Wop with the Seals this year—couldn't sit down for a week after that. I'm sure as hell not gonna talk about the Babe calling his goddamn shot anymore, 'cause he never did. Period. The End. Get up and leave the theater. Get me?"

Shaker put a bottle of beer in front of Jake, while Root shook a Wings cigarette from his pack and fired it up. The door opened and a gorgeous blonde sashayed in, her wavy locks almost covering one eye, a good imitation of Veronica Lake's hairdo. She was glued into a snug white blouse.

"New dame over at the van and storage," Shaker explained longingly.

"Holy smoke, look at that front porch on her," Jake muttered.

"Down boy," Root said.

"Only looking, Cholly. I'm engaged to the greatest gal in the world. She's made a hell of a difference in my life."

"You fell big this time, Jakey."

"Yeah, I sure did."

Jake had been married a few years back to a cocktail waitress when he'd been a rookie reporter in Texas. He always called the short-lived marriage to Dixie Freitas his biggest mistake. His gaze sliding back to Root, Jake knew he was still keyed up about going into Germany, but it wasn't something he could talk about with Charlie or Shaker. So he steered the conversation back to baseball. What was it like working for Bob Cobb, things like that. Cobb, who owned the Brown Derby restaurants and had invented the Cobb salad, also owned the Hollywood Stars.

Shaker walked off to take care of a new customer at the other end of the bar.

Root leaned forward and stared at Jake for a long, disconcerting moment, then said, "I know that look. What are you up to?"

"Whatta you mean?"

"There's a certain look when a guy's betting on a game, or is gonna swing through a bunt sign. You're up to something; whatcha got cookin'?"

"Nothing, just the same old stuff. You're imagining things, Cholly."

"Bullshit. But okay then, keep your damn secrets. Just make sure you're at the opener come April." Jake hadn't missed a Stars opening game since '39.

"Sure, you bet."

"Promise? You're our good-luck piece."

"Damn right, Cholly. I'll be there."

If he wasn't chained in some Nazi dungeon or lying seriously dead in an unmarked grave outside Berlin.

Driving to Valerie Jean's apartment in his Chevy Ridemaster coupe, Jake thought about the state fair eight long years ago. At the end of that special day, Uncle Dieter had hugged him tightly and said, "Jacob, I love you like a son."

Though Jake was just a nickname, Dieter had picked up on it and, like a proper old German, had formalized it into Jacob. Jake's actual name was Raleigh Ashford Weaver.

And I love you like a father, Jake had thought in silent reply. Now, as bleak anger raged anew, he hated himself for not having said it aloud.

Suddenly he couldn't drive. Tears blurred his eyes. He pulled over to the curb along Florence Avenue and pounded his fists on the steering wheel. "I love you, Dieter, *mein Held*," he whispered, using the German word for hero. There were so many things he should have said to that fine old man. Fine old man who'd lost his life defying the Nazis.

He didn't know how long it was before the storm inside him spent itself and he could fire up the car and drive on to Inglewood.

He finally reached Valerie's street and, wonder of wonders, found a parking space four doors down. Even with gas and rubber rationing, there were more cars in L.A. than places to put them. Valerie's apartment was one of a cluster of stucco, tile-roofed cottages arranged in a U-shape around a small courtyard. The November days were short and the blackout was in effect. The place was as dark as his mood as he passed under a large, wrought-iron archway and headed for Apartment Three on the left side of the courtyard.

At thirty-two, Valerie was five years younger than Jake and taller than him when she wore heels. He didn't mind—he liked that look. The only woman tool designer at her plant and one of the few in America, she had a crop of silky black hair, an angular face with stunning cheekbones, and large blue eyes that always turned his knees to rubber. They had planned a January wedding, a few weeks after Christmas. Hadn't set a date yet. Nothing elaborate, just a few friends.

She opened the door a couple of seconds after his knock, saying, "Well if it isn't the Kid himself." Her pet name for Jake was the Louisiana Kid. He often called her Sweets.

Those big azure eyes smiled at him and his knees did their rubbery thing. After a long, warm kiss, she took the bottle of chenin blanc he handed her with an "Oh, thanks." He put his coat and hat on a chair and followed her to the kitchen, which was filled with tasty warmth from the oven.

"You can help with dinner," she said.

He sniffed. "Something smells great."

"We're having chicken with potatoes O'Brien." Valerie had been shedding her small-town Midwestern customs since arriving in L.A. One of the ways was by taking a culinary class at night school.

"Potatoes O'Brien? I think I used to play football with Potatoes O'Brien when I was a kid."

Valerie made a face. "Good thing I'm not serving corn. You've got too much of that already. Now slice some mushrooms and help with the sauce, Raleigh Ashford."

Reaching for a knife, Jake said, "Yeah, yeah. I never shoulda told you my whole name. Mom went a little crazy when I was born."

"Don't belittle those family names. I think they're dignified."

"Oh, sure."

"They are! Anyway, I'm roasting the chicken with a curry baste. That's what you smell. Remember when all I could do was fry chicken and chops? Steaks, too, except you can't get good beef these days." She pulled a corkscrew from a drawer and handed it to him. He did the honors on the wine bottle, snipping the foil and popping the cork while Valerie produced two crystal goblets.

During the next hour and a half, while they finished off the wine and food and rinsed the dishes, they talked about what they would do for Thanksgiving dinner, and the home they hoped to buy near La Brea and Washington. Jake intended to sell his little house in Compton—the neighborhood was slipping—and West L.A. seemed a good compromise between their work locations, his downtown, hers out by the L.A. airport at Mines Field.

Then Jake slipped in his bombshell. He slowly and carefully described the letter from Germany, his bitter reaction, his conversations with his managing editor and Roosevelt's press secretary, and his determination to sneak into Germany and do something about it.

He thought Valerie did a good job of covering up her surprise and something else—disapproval?—with thoughtful questions. She knew about Dieter but hadn't been fully aware of the closeness between him and Jake.

He didn't have Rolf Becker's cryptic letter with him but at her urging he recited it from memory.

"Heavy dark rain the other day; much thunder and lightning. Dieter heard Mendelssohn's Opus 103 in A minor. It brought tears to my eyes and an ache to my heart. The piece was conducted by Siegfried Schaeffer."

Jake said, "I found out that Opus 103 was Mendelssohn's *Funeral March*. When I added that to 'tears' and 'ache in the heart' and 'Dieter,' it could mean only one thing. 'Siegfried Schaeffer' took a little longer, but then I realized he was telling me Uncle Dieter had been rubbed out by the SS."

Valerie was quiet for a moment, her brow scrunched in thought. At last she said, "I believe you've got it right. The SS must have killed him. I'm so sorry," she said, and softly stroked his hand.

After a moment, she asked, "So you're really serious? You definitely feel you must go?"

Jake nodded grimly.

"Then how will you get into Germany? What are your ploys?"

"I don't know, Sweets. Haven't worked out a plan yet."

"What help can you expect from the president?"

"Don't know that either. Have to wait and see."

"Well, see what Hearst has to say about it. I won't stand in your way. I want you to love me, not resent me."

Then it dawned on Jake that what he'd seen in her eyes was fear. Her husband had been killed in a car crash in Illinois. She must be terrified. What a thoughtless dope I am, he told himself. Losing a second man would be really tough on her. Should have seen that right away.

Their lovemaking that night seemed more intense, more urgent, than usual, that Valerie's whole body was communicating a desperate concern for him. He found that both heartening and humbling.

Later, snuggling against him, she placed a hand to his cheek and whispered, "We'll get married in late winter then . . . after you get back."

He knew that even though she was worried, she would never say "*if* you get back."

"Right, we sure will, Sweets."

If he wasn't chained in some Nazi dungeon or lying seriously dead in an unmarked grave outside Berlin.

CHAPTER FIVE

The *Herald-Express* was on South Trenton Street just below downtown. When he arrived there after spending the night at Valerie's—he hoped her landlady hadn't seen him sneak out—Jake went first to the wire room. He did this every day to check the AP, UP and Hearst's INS for war news. A copyboy was tearing stories off churning machines and hanging them on the wall where long sheets of teletype paper dangled from spikes like uneven gray tapestries. Occasionally a bell would ring four times on one of the machines, signaling that a bulletin was coming in.

The world situation looked a little better. The Allies had landed in North Africa and the Vichy French had stopped resisting after firing a few shots to satisfy their honor. Far to the east, Rommel was retreating across Libya after the British had bloodied his nose in a big battle at a railroad stop in Egypt known as El Alamein. Deep in Russia, the Germans were having all sorts of trouble taking the key Soviet town on the Volga, a place called Stalingrad.

On the home front, war production was finally swinging into high gear. It looked to Jake as if 1942 might end more cheerily than it had started, three wretched weeks after Pearl Harbor.

Hearst came into the newsroom a little past noon, without Marion Davies. The old Victorian entered like a benevolent monarch, chatting with reporters and editors, always using their last names preceded by a "Mister" or a "Miss." Jake found him, though still tall and erect, looking gray and careworn with dark circles under his eyes.

He stopped at Jake's desk and clapped him on the shoulder before giving him a sturdy handshake. "Mr. Weaver, how is my favorite bloodhound? That was a splendid job on the Halsey story. A wonderful beat for our papers." He'd told Jake the same thing at least twice before.

Two months earlier, Jake had gone on a three-week assignment to Guadalcanal. One of his stories accurately predicted the firing of the Navy's South Pacific Area commander and his replacement by William "Bull" Halsey, a contentious old warrior. Jake had smuggled the story past the censors in the seabag of a wounded Marine sent to California for treatment.

"When that ran two days before the official announcement it was a triumph for our papers," Hearst said, "and didn't do your reputation any harm either."

After chumming around in the city room, Hearst spent ten or fifteen minutes with managing editor John Campbell in his office. Then Campbell emerged and summoned Jake with a wave that spilled ashes from his cigarette.

They were drinking coffee from thick mugs. "Want some of this battery acid?" Campbell asked. Jake said sure and Campbell went to the door and shouted, "Boy," whereupon a copyboy, the sleeves of his white shirt rolled up, trotted over and was told to fetch more coffee.

Jake listened to the Old Man hold court nostalgically, rambling on about some battle or other he'd fought with Joseph Pulitzer and his *New York World*, his big rival in the heyday of yellow journalism, now thirty years gone. Then he dissembled about his late friend Teddy Roosevelt, "that great American who had more guts than McKinley, Bryan and Wilson put together." Jake felt as if he'd stumbled into a time machine.

But the time machine jerked to an abrupt halt in the present. "What about this Guadalcanal thing, Mr. Weaver?" Hearst demanded. Jake told him the end of the long, bitter campaign was in sight. The Japs were being thrown far back from the American airfield and the

U.S. would soon have the island secured.

"North Africa?"

"Our troops are green and the Limeys are laughing at us. But we're starting to push through the mountains toward Tunisia. It'll take awhile, but we'll eventually get Rommel penned up between us and Montgomery."

"Eventually, hmmph. Too damn slow if you ask me. What about this L.A. boy, Patton?"

"He's a good tank commander, sir. Very aggressive. I think he'll be okay."

"I hope so. Be good for the paper if some L.A. boys like Jimmy Doolittle and George Patton won this war, wouldn't it?"

"Be good for everybody, sir."

"What are you working on now?"

Jake outlined the Walt Disney story, as he'd done before, and then went on to tell about Uncle Dieter and the cryptic letter from his friend Rolf Becker on the *Deutsche Zeitung*. Hearst's eyes widened. While Jake laid it all out for him, the boss nodded with clear interest. Hearst said that he knew Putzi Hanfstaengl, that years ago Putzi had owned an art gallery in New York which he and Mrs. Hearst had patronized. "Later, in '34 I think it was, when he was back at the family home in Munich, Putzi showed us around on one of my trips to Europe."

The Old Man was actually acquainted with Hanfstaengl! Jake hadn't known that. He filed that away as possibly useful information.

Hearst shot questions.

"You speak German? . . . Steve Early is going to get you a meeting with Roosevelt? . . . This Rolf fellow lives in Berlin and writes for the *Zeitung*? . . . He used to work for us? Oh yes, he did, Becker, I recall the name now . . . He meets on a regular basis with Goebbels and the propaganda ministry? . . . You really believe you can pull this off, Mr. Weaver?"

Hearst leaned forward now, his tie loosened. He was buying it, Jake knew. The man who'd pioneered color comics and Sunday supplements. The man who'd founded the International News Service. Who'd sent battalions of reporters into Cuba and almost single-handedly fomented the Spanish-American War. Who'd made Teddy Roosevelt a national hero. Who in vain had sought the nomination for president. This was just his cup of tea.

"So," Jake concluded, "I've just got to do this. Got to go into Germany."

Hearst stared at him for a long moment, then at Campbell, who said, "Well, Chief, what do you think of Jakey boy's idea?"

The Old Man took a sip of coffee and returned his gaze to Jake.

"No," he said. "It's out of the question. I positively forbid it."

CHAPTER SIX

That afternoon when Jake called Valerie at North American, she said, "You sound down, Sailor, something's wrong." In the early Thirties, Jake had had a brief hitch in the Navy before becoming a newspaperman.

"No, everything's fine," he fibbed. Darn, this woman was perceptive.

"We hadn't made plans for tonight," she said, "but do come over. Please. Or else I'll come to your place. I can tell we need to be together tonight."

So here he was in Inglewood again. Jake loved fine dining and her curried chicken had been a success last night. Tonight, though, was a step down, Jake having brought tamales and tacos from Juanito's, a Mexican dive he fancied, and bottles of a local beer. Valerie made a green salad to go with them.

She listened as Jake rehashed his meeting with Hearst. "And what happened after Hearst said 'positively not?'" she asked while setting out plates and napkins on the white-enameled table in her kitchenette.

Jake pulled out a chair for her. "I argued my case brilliantly, of course, but he stuck to his guns."

"Pretty formidable guns."

"Yeah. Hundred-caliber at least. He said he wasn't the gambler he was in his younger days, 'specially with another man's life. He once sponsored a trans-Pacific flight and two fliers got killed. He said he wasn't ever gonna let that happen again. Then he gave me a sob story about all the money he lost in the Thirties and what a drain that San Simeon monstrosity is."

"He didn't say monstrosity, did he?"

"Nah, and neither did I. I reminded him what a whopper this could be for the *Express* and the news service." Jake paused and took a swig of Aztec beer. "He said no, I was too personally involved and there was a good chance I wouldn't come out alive."

Valerie touched the back of his hand. "He could be right, you know."

"He said maybe Rolf could smuggle out some stories and that would be just as good. We'd label them as from our secret source, our mole deep inside the Nazi Reich. Cause a great sensation."

"That's not a bad idea."

"But it is, Sweets." He set the bottle down. "See, they'd find out who was writing those, the Gestapo would. They'd pour a lot of resources into that, and Rolf could end up just as dead as Uncle Dieter."

Valerie put a hand to her mouth. "Oh, right. I hadn't thought of that. Much too risky to ask of your friend Rolf."

"Yeah, that's what I told the Old Man. In the end, though, he still wouldn't budge about my going. Said I could go there after we win the war, find out then who did what to Dieter."

Jake figured that if and when the Germans lost—and there was no guarantee on *that*—those efficient bastards would cover up crimes like that, destroy all the records before the Americans could come marching in.

"I'm so sorry," Valerie said. "I know this is a big disappointment." She was trying to sound empathetic, but he knew her heart wasn't in it. She didn't want him to go. Period. She *loved* him, for God's sake. He finished his taco in silence, vaguely aware that Jo Stafford was singing something on the radio.

Later, after clearing the table, they talked for awhile about the wedding. Jake's city editor, Gus Dobson, would be best man and

Valerie's friend Pauline Hyatt, the matron of honor.

Jake couldn't keep his mind on any of that. He was thinking something else. How could the Old Man stop him from going? Fire him? Hell no, if he did that his hotshot military writer would just hook up with the competition. The *Times* would take him in the blink of an eye. Wouldn't they?

"What are you thinking?" Valerie said. "You've got that look on your face."

"Jesus, you and Charlie Root, think you're such mind readers."

"Charlie Root? Oh, right, your buddy, the Stars' manager. He can tell when you've got something up your sleeve, too, can he?"

"There's nothing up my sleeves, Sweets, just these hairy old arms that love to hold you."

Valerie smiled and leaned close to kiss him.

"Oh, there's one other thing," he said after she pulled away. "Almost forgot. Steve Early called back this afternoon from the White House. FDR wants to see me. It's all set up for next week."

"But if you're not going to Germany—"

"Still a great opportunity, Val, an exclusive interview with the top man. Johnny Campbell loves it. Hearst will, too."

"Yes, there's that," she said, unable to hide the concern in her eyes.

CHAPTER SEVEN

At the gate of Disney's Buena Vista Studio in Burbank, Jake had to show his ID to a soldier instead of a civilian guard. He knew the government had commandeered part of the studio and had Disney's people producing training films and patriotic shorts, but this came as a shock. The government hadn't taken over any other studios.

Was Roosevelt sore at Disney for some reason? Disney certainly wasn't un-American, throwing his resources into these wartime projects. He'd even taken a big tour of South America for the cause of Pan American solidarity against the Nazi threat. And, of course, to ballyhoo *Snow White and the Seven Dwarfs* while he was at it, but who could blame him for that? Just good business.

Jake walked through manicured lawns to Disney's office, one of a cluster of one-story, sand-colored stucco bungalows comprising the studio. Some were free-standing, some connected by breezeways. The number of khaki-clad GI's milling about depressed him. The place had the look of an occupied country.

"Please have a seat," the secretary said. "Mr. Disney is some-where on the grounds. I'm sure he'll be here shortly. But uh . . ." She stopped midsentence with a nervous little smile that might have meant "Oh dear, he's double-booked himself again."

That's when Jake noticed that someone else was waiting, too. One of two chairs in the small anteroom was occupied by a slender man of fifty or more with high Slavic cheekbones, a suit of European cut a few years out of style, and a polka-dot bow tie. His rimless glasses gave him the look of a skinny Ben Franklin.

Holding tightly to a sheaf of papers, the man gave Jake a shy glance and said, "Goot mornink."

"How do you do?"

"Quite vell, tank you." As if reluctantly, he added, "Mit Mr. Diss-ney you haff bis-ness?"

"Yes. I'm a newspaper reporter. And you?"

"Yes, I too mit Mr. Diss-ney haff bis-ness." The man looked away, his ration of small talk apparently spent.

Jake's antenna went up. This guy sounded Russian. Was Disney making a film for the Reds? Jake didn't think much of the shifty Soviets, who'd invaded Finland, then taken half of Poland as Hitler's bedfellows, before the Germans changed all that last year by invading Russia. Suddenly the Commies were loyal and trusted friends of the U.S. and Britain. Sure, and would you like to buy a bridge?

Jake smelled a story. Maybe Roosevelt felt the same way about the Russians and didn't trust Disney. Maybe that was why the Army had moved in.

He thought about all the strange possibilities here. And the contradictions. He'd always known Disney to be a right-winger, anything but a communist sympathizer.

Minutes passed. Disney was always running late. Still silent, the other man gripped his papers in his left hand; they looked like maybe sheet music. The fingers of his right hand flittered momentarily as if playing a piano.

Jake's musings turned to the original tip about the kidnap plot that came from Uncle Dieter.

The outer door began to open and Jake heard a slushy cough. The slim figure of Walt Disney appeared. He wore a tan cardigan, pleated gray slacks and white-and-black wingtips. His face bore a tidy little mustache. He looked grouchy, deep scowl lines in his forehead, but he quickly transformed himself when he saw he had visitors. A broad grin lit his face and he magically became the peppy, fatherly, creative genius.

"How good of you to come," he said—but to whom?—as Jake and the European with the bow tie sprang to their feet. The answer came in less than a second as Disney grasped the other man's hand with a hearty shake.

"Come in, come in, my dear fellow. I hope I haven't kept you waiting long." He put a hand on the man's shoulder and guided him toward his office. Before closing the door, he looked back and seemed to see Jake for the first time. The hassled look flashed across his face before the boyish grin returned.

"Awfully sorry, Mr. Weaver, I seem to have forgotten." He tapped his forehead with his index finger. "Can you give me thirty minutes? Take a look at our workshops. Gabe here can show you around."

"Sure," Jake said, "that's all right."

Gabe, the ex-cop turned bodyguard, had slipped into the room behind Disney.

"Awfully sorry," Disney repeated as he closed the door.

Jake walked across the lawn with Gabe to another low building, one lined with large windows. Inside, animators and illustrators sat at upward-angled tables, with daylight streaming through the windows.

Gabe turned Jake over to a man who introduced himself as Norm Ferguson, who proceeded to show him around.

"The boss forgot you, didn't he?" Ferguson grinned knowingly. "Asked you to give him half an hour."

Men and women were drawing cute little pigs, dogs with floppy ears and sad eyes, mischievous ducks with near-human faces. Jake saw a sketch of Grumpy, one of the Seven Dwarfs. His face looked just like Disney's had in those two quick flashes before he'd covered it with his trademark grin.

They paused at a table where a woman worked on a drawing of a four-engine bomber. "We're making an animated film for the Army called *Air Power*," Ferguson explained.

In the next cottage, which was kept much darker, men ran film through a Movieola, stopping occasionally to scrutinize certain frames. In a third building, painters in stained smocks worked on a movie backdrop, an ocean scene with a desert island, roiling surf, and realistic cloud formations.

When the tour ended, Jake said, "Thanks a lot. Never saw the inside works before. Quite an operation."

As Jake reached the office, the man in the bow tie was just emerging.

"I am sorry to haff delayed you. You are newspaperman, yes? I like you should call me. Let me giff you number for where I am stayink. One week more I am being here." He extended his hand. "My name is Sergei Prokofiev."

Jake felt his mouth drop open.

CHAPTER EIGHT

Now what was this famous composer doing here? Jake puzzled, as he re-entered Disney's office, and why did he want Jake to call him? What did he know?

He wasn't going to ask Disney the second part of that question. Prokofiev's body language and secretive tone had said "keep this between us."

Sketch pads, a coffee mug filled with colored pencils, scattered papers and letters, and a nearly full ash tray cluttered the drawing table that served as Disney's desk. Some tacked-up storyboards covered one wall.

A two-foot-high enameled statuette of Mickey Mouse sat on a credenza behind him. Donald Duck appeared nowhere. Jake had heard that Disney didn't much care for Donald Duck because he'd become too popular. His first meal ticket, the mouse, would always be his favorite.

"Sorry to keep you waiting," Disney said, waving Jake to a chair and taking a drag on his cigarette. "Did you get to meet Maestro Prokofiev? I plan to make a film of *Peter and the Wolf,* his great operetta or suite or whatever you call it. I've had my mind on this project for some time now. A natural for animation."

"Sounds swell, Mr. Disney."

"Prokofiev loves the idea. Can you imagine? He just turned all the music over to me"—he gestured at the sheet music lying on the table—"and wouldn't even discuss payment. Said he doesn't care about that, but of course I'll see that he's properly compensated. Say, this is all off the record. I don't want this in print yet, although I guess my film work isn't exactly your beat anyway."

"Don't worry about that," said Jake, who never played dirty with his sources.

"Just wanted you to know why I kept you waiting," Disney said.

Jake plunged into the kidnap thing. Had Disney seen any strange people following him or hanging around? Had Gabe the bodyguard noticed anything? Several more questions of that type. Jake had come up with nothing new in months. Maybe the Nazis had given up. Some stories just don't pan out. He was riveted now on Uncle Dieter's demise and what was behind it. On Hearst's refusal to let him go to Germany. And now Prokofiev, and why he wanted to see Jake.

"Did you see my shops?" Disney asked.

"Sure did, very interesting, but I couldn't help noticing there seems to be some tension in the air. Is it the Army presence?"

Disney frowned. "That, and a lot of things. Hell, these ungrateful bastards"—he suddenly stood and threw out his arms—"going on strike, unionizing. We used to be a happy little family around here."

This abrupt soul-baring before a near stranger was disconcerting.

Jake recalled the bitter strike that took place before the war when Disney employees had been organizing. After Disney waged a staunch fight against the union, and lost, it was whispered that he'd become a changed man, nursing an angry sense of betrayal.

"I once imagined I was Peter Pan, the flying boy who never grew up. Not anymore." He fell silent for a moment and took his seat again. "I just hope *Peter and the Wolf* pans out."

The quiet lingered, Disney obviously embarrassed.

Jake ventured a few more questions but they yielded little, the interview more or less a bust.

Disney looked at his watch and it gave Jake the opening to break it off. As he rose to leave, Disney said, "I'm sorry about sounding off like that. I guess I'm a bit on edge these days."

"It's the war, Mr. Disney. We're all a little on edge."

"Yes. Keep me informed, then, if you learn anything new."

"Sure will, sir."

Jake believed good reporters didn't let grass sprout beneath their feet so, next day, he was having coffee with Sergei Prokofiev in a downtown hotel. "You are known for breaking—is that the word?— the big stories, *da*?"

"Sometimes, when I get lucky."

"Modest you are being, surely. Now then, I haff some information that in USA must be made known. This I think you can more better do than music critics with whom I have acquaintance."

"Possibly, sir. What kind of information is it?"

"You do not know the name Paul Hindemith?"

"You mean Hindenburg?"

"No, no, Paul Hindemith. Is no relation to old field marshal. Paul Hindemith is fine composer and also Berlin teacher of the music. Also he is mine friend." Prokofiev scanned the room and dropped his voice to a whisper. "He tell me one of his young pupils of the piano is build big rocket that maybe bomb London, bomb Moscow, maybe also New York."

"New York?"

"So he say."

That would be a hell of a weapon, Jake thought, if it had a big warhead. Unstoppable, if it had enough range. "How do you know this?"

"Hindemith tell me."

"When? How? You're a Russian—"

"Please, no, I am of Ukraine."

"Ukrainian, I see, sorry. But your country's at war with Germany. How did—"

"In Berlin I see Hindemith, before the Germans they attack USSR. In April of last year it was."

"A year and a half ago. If he was developing a rocket weapon then, it's much further along now."

"So you see, this, it is important."

They both stopped talking as a waiter came and refilled their cups. A minute passed in silence. Prokofiev stirred some cream into his coffee.

When the coast was clear, Jake said softly, "But why tell me? You should tell the War Department."

"This I try. In Washington I see a colonel. He is condescend to me. Say 'Yes, yes, thank you, we take care of it.' I think he not be serious. He not even write note. So, the Army I try. I permit see only a *kapitan*. Same thing. Pretend interest, but not believe."

"I cover the military, I know the type. Some of these deskbound officers are pretty lazy. Also, they get lots of tips from civilians that are pretty harebrained."

"Harebrained?"

"Fantastic, worthless."

Hurt clouded Prokofiev's eyes. "Without worth? This you believe too?"

"Oh no," Jake said quickly, "I follow up lots of things the military wouldn't touch." Hell, on the face of it, the Disney kidnap plot looked more harebrained than a rocket weapon. Those Germans were great engineers. "But rockets can't fly thousands of miles, can they?"

"Hindemith pupil say maybe this one can. In testing it has fly fifteen miles high. Engine has great force. Say it can fly much higher."

"*Jesus*. Must have some kind of powerful new propellant fuel. Who is this piano student anyway? What do you know about him?"

"Is scientist, not yet thirty, big strapping fellow. Is from wealthy Prussian family. Is genius inventor, not care about politics, is much determine to see big rocket be success."

"Young guy, you say?"

"Yes, von Braun his name. Wernher von Braun."

CHAPTER NINE

Jake dreamed that night of huge black rockets shrieking down on American cities from above the stratosphere. He kept running around, trying to catch them in his arms before they hit. He couldn't. The first explosion threw him in the air and tore away his pants. He floated back to the ground, where he ran around, his manhood exposed, trying in vain to catch the others. It turned out to be one of those rare times where later every vivid, humiliating detail of the dream remained etched in his mind.

The next day at the paper the images still disturbed him. He was thinking about a piano student named Wernher von Braun, and of trying to catch big rocket bombs with his hands.

The desks in the city room, except those in the editors' offices, sat out in a big open space among fat, load-bearing pillars. Jake's was close to Society's bullpen—he called it the Henhouse—where the women always gabbed too damn loud. Sticking a finger in his free ear when talking on the phone played hell with note-taking.

He'd made up his mind about going to Germany. He would defy Hearst and let the chips fall wherever they damn well might. He scribbled away on his notepad. *Clippers not flying, steamships not running. How get into Germany? . . . Through Switzerland? If so, how reach Switzerland?* Which was completely surrounded by Axis territory. *Go through Sweden? . . . Across occupied France via Spain?* He had a contact in Madrid, a guy he'd interviewed during the Spanish Civil War.

Suddenly he realized that Gracie Pike, over in the Henhouse, was talking with Marion Davies on the phone. The Hearst papers all had their gossip columnists, or sob sisters. The most famous was Louella Parsons on the morning *Examiner*, sister paper of the *Herald-Express*. The less known Gracie Pike thought she was better than Parsons, and on some days she was. Marion Davies, a great source for column tidbits, often called the sob sisters, or vice versa.

"Yes, Miss Davies," Gracie said. "Greer Garson? Uh huh. At Romanoff's. Cobalt blue cocktail dress." Gracie scribbled away. "Okay, thank you so much, Miss Davies . . . What? . . . Jake Weaver? Yes, I think so." She looked over at Jake and clamped a hand over the voice piece.

"Jake!" Gracie could have been heard on Pico Boulevard a block away. "Come over here. Miss Davies wants to talk to you."

Good. He always liked talking with Miss Marion. Wonder what she wants?

"Gracie, you're so genteel," he said as he walked over to Society. The phones had recently been upgraded with extensions and those new-fangled hold buttons, and Gracie could have transferred the call, but she probably didn't know how. She couldn't even change a typewriter ribbon. "Get an earful, girls," Jake said. "You'll enjoy this. Probably wants to meet tonight at our secret hideaway."

Jake took the phone and said "Hello."

"Why, Mr. Weaver, what a naughty idea. I'd be delighted, but just where *is* our secret hideaway?"

"Uh, golly, Miss Davies . . ." Marion Davies always did light comedy best, but darn that Gracie; took her hand off the phone too soon.

"You're blushing, aren't you, Mr. Weaver? I can almost see that red face of yours through the phone line."

"I believe you're right, ma'am. I'm sure sorry—"

"About what? Don't you think I have a sense of humor? I'm flattered that you make cracks like that to the news ladies."

"Well, uh, thanks . . . I think."

She laughed. "Now, Mr. Weaver, I understand you met with Willie yesterday and that he shot from the hip. Gunned you right down. He told me about it last night. I agree with him, of course; it's much too dangerous. But I also know how it is to feel to the very marrow of your bones that you just *have* to do a certain thing. I once wanted to kill Norma Shearer. Wanted to *kill* her. She got a role I was *perfect* for. Oh, I'm sorry, that's not at all the same . . . Now, your uncle—"

"Was a very special man."

"You loved him like I do my Willie."

She was the only person Jake knew who referred to Hearst as Willie. "Yes, that's so," he said.

"Do you really think you can get in there, find out what you need to know, and get safely out again?"

"I've got a chance, ma'am. You see, I speak German and I was there a few years ago. I have a good idea of the layout, the geography, how the trains run, that sort of thing."

"And you have a friend there? One of Willie's former reporters?"

"Yes, Rolf Becker. He would help me, and I could help him. You see, it's not just about my uncle. I've got some other leads to follow up. Stuff this country needs to know about."

"It would be lovely to bring those awful Nazis down a peg. But what if Willie doesn't change his mind?"

"I'd go anyway, ma'am." Jake paused, looked around and wondered what the Society gals thought about his half of this conversation. "Yes, I'd go anyway."

"I believe you would, Mr. Weaver, I believe you would. If it comes to that, *promise* me you'll be as careful as you possibly can."

"That I'll certainly do. I've grown pretty attached to this old rear end of mine." Gracie Pike, who'd been hanging on every word, reached over and gave that old rear end a squeeze. Jake tried not to yelp.

"What was that?" Davies said.

"Nothing, nothing."

"Well, I can understand your need to find out about your uncle, for your own peace of mind. About these other things, as far as I know, you've never failed yet, on any of the big stories you've gone after. Willie calls you his favorite bloodhound."

"That's flattering ma'am. I try."

"I'll speak to Willie then. I really will."

"That's not necessary, Miss Davies. Please, no, this is my business."

"Oh, I think it *is* necessary. I will do it, Mr. Weaver."

"Well, thanks, but—"

"Now where is our secret rendezvous again?"

Jake's rendezvous that night was at Valerie's apartment.

"What's this?" he said as she handed him a large box from Buffum's with a big pink bow attached. "It's not my birthday. Too early for Christmas."

"Open it and see."

Jake undid the box, drew away some tissue paper, and pulled out a gray woolen overcoat. "Aw, gee."

"It can get cold in Washington these days, and even colder in Chicago," Valerie said. "I know what November can be like back there. We can't have the Louisiana Kid freezing to death."

"That's great, Sweets," he said, giving her a hug. "Thanks. That old raincoat of mine isn't all that warm."

They began telling about the events of their day. Valerie said she'd made some drawings for a modified tail assembly for the B-25H.

"Speaking of tail assemblies," Jake said, and then told her about Gracie Pike squeezing his ass.

Valerie reached behind him. "Like this, Sailor?"

"Uh, no, you do it much better."

CHAPTER TEN

The Army DC-3 labored skyward from Grand Central Air Terminal in Glendale, circled twice for altitude, then, or so it seemed to Jake, barely cleared the towering San Bernardino Mountains. Once the mountains gave way to desert, he was able to relax and read, having brought along several newspapers and a couple of books. He read all the dispatches from North Africa first.

He started William Shirer's *Berlin Diary* before the plane touched down at North Platte, Nebraska, to refuel. Jake hoped the CBS broadcaster's account of life under the Nazis would be enlightening.

The book described Germany's cynical efforts in the late Thirties to maintain a good image around the world. Now, Jake thought, after snatching Poland, bombing the hell out of London, and unleashing their panzer hordes against their own ally, Russia, they didn't give a damn anymore. Hitler had crossed the Rubicon. Now it was win or else, all or nothing.

Jake finished the book a few hours later, just before the DC-3 began its bumpy descent into Chicago through layers of angry November clouds, ending its thirteen-hour journey for the day.

After checking into the Blackstone Hotel, he called Bill Stoneman, the *Chicago Daily News*' military writer, and made plans to meet for a drink.

Powdery flurries of snow feathered the air as he walked to the Headline Club on East Wacker Drive. His breath pushed forth in gray plumes of steam and he was grateful for his new overcoat.

He found Stoneman waiting inside the club. The heat was on, thank you very much, and somewhere in the back a pool game clattered. After settling in and ordering their drinks, Stoneman gave him a serious look. "So you're on your way to a meeting with FDR?"

"Yep. Four o'clock tomorrow."

"Steve Early set it up?" Stoneman looked envious.

"Yep."

"You old bulldog, you must have something up your sleeve to wangle a personal pow-wow with Roosevelt. What are you up to?"

"Nothing special."

"Baloney. You've got to be working some angle."

Holy cow, Jake thought, Charlie Root, Valerie, and now Stoneman. Am I that easy to read?

"Well, ask the mighty one about these convoy losses on the North Cape run to Russia. A lot of Illinois corn and pork's going into the drink, the way those U-boats are clobbering hell out of the Limey transports."

They talked about the North African campaign, expansion of the Great Lakes Naval Training Center, mutual acquaintances in the newspaper game, and Stoneman's dislike of J. Edgar Hoover, whom he called a publicity hound, "a Keystone cop." The one subject Jake avoided was his determination to go to Germany.

Two hours passed like minutes. When Jake stood to go, Stoneman said, "I still want to know how you pulled this off. You got something on Steve Early?"

"Only my dazzling charm and brilliant powers of persuasion, Bill."

"Bullshit, but just remember, FDR's jovial grandfather image is a front. He's as shrewd and cunning as they come."

Jake took a cab back to the Blackstone, even though it wasn't far. It was colder than a witch's tit in January.

That night he dreamed of huge black rockets shrieking down on

American cities from above the stratosphere. His pants got blown off again. What would Siegmund Freud make of that? he wondered as he boarded the DC-3 at Midway Airport in the morning for the final hop to Washington.

Jake had never seen Washington from the air. As the plane descended on its approach leg, the Mall and the Capitol sprang into view through a sprinkling of clouds, then the Washington Monument, like a huge gray spike, the White House, and the Lincoln Memorial. He felt like a schoolkid on a field trip. Gazing down on all these famous symbols, he was suddenly glad that his family had moved to this big, rambunctious country. Then the broad Potomac spread below him and the plane thudded down at the little airport on the Virginia side.

As he hopped down the portable stairway at the plane's rear door, a tepid breeze washed over his face. Hmm, warmer than Chicago, he thought as he made his way to the taxi stand out in front.

Jake found the Willard Hotel crowded with men in business suits and military uniforms. The war felt more real here than back home, even though L.A. teemed with soldiers and aircraft workers. This was the hub of it all, the nerve center of a great war machine that was still gearing up.

There was just time to check in, brush his teeth, slap some bay rum on his face, and change shirts. Then he walked the two blocks to the White House, just beyond the Treasury Building.

A white-helmeted MP at the east gate found his name on the visitor list and passed him through. After he signed the official usher's book, press secretary Steve Early met him and they passed down a long corridor to an anteroom just outside the Oval Office. Early introduced him to Grace Tully, the president's private secretary.

Jake and Early talked for several minutes, then a haggard little man in a rumpled gray suit emerged. Jake recognized Harry Hopkins, the director of Lend-Lease and the president's top adviser.

Early introduced them and Hopkins said, "I've seen some of

your wire stories. You and Dick Tregaskis wrote some good stuff from Guadalcanal. That scoop on Admiral Halsey caused quite a flap with the Navy. How the devil did you pull that off?"

Hopkins didn't wait for an answer. "The chief is ready for us," he said. "Let's go."

"Break a leg," Early said, and Jake gave him a little wave as Hopkins led the way into the Oval Office. Jake took off his hat. Only six days since getting Rolf's letter and look where he was now.

The office, its walls painted a soft yellow, was larger than he'd imagined. He saw tall fanlights above each window. Although he seldom got stage fright in the company of powerful men, he felt a twinge of uneasiness.

The president wheeled his chair from behind a big, cluttered desk and pushed himself forward to greet him, a gesture Jake found touching. The conveyance was more like a kitchen chair on wheels than a hospital wheelchair.

"Good to see you, Mr. Weaver," the president boomed in his hearty radio voice, extending a hand. Dark circles underscored the eyes on his famous face. The graying hair was thin, the eyebrows an untrimmed hedge. He wore a white shirt and a bow tie with blue polka dots.

"And you, sir," Jake said, taking the hand. Above slack, wasted legs, FDR's upper body looked strong and the handshake was a bone-crusher. "Please call me Jake, Mr. President. Mr. Weaver is my father."

"Ha ha, that's grand." The president's eyes twinkled behind the iconic pince-nez glasses. "Mr. Weaver is his father. I very much like that, don't you Harry? Jake it is, then. Well, have a seat, Jake." He rolled himself back behind the desk and picked up a fountain pen.

Jake sat in a guest chair in front of the desk and put his hat in his lap. Hopkins plopped down on a nearby sofa.

"I've read some of your stories. They're quite good indeed," the president intoned in his Harvard accent. "You seem to have a knack for digging out things our military would prefer that you hadn't. A regular snoop. My old friend W.R. Hearst must be very proud of you."

Old friend? Jake wondered. The president must have caught that, for he said, "Your employer has fought me on a lot of things, but he's also backed us on a few. He's much more my friend than that old devil Colonel McCormick." The president shook his head in irritation. Jake knew the *Chicago Tribune*'s publisher hated the New Deal and everything FDR stood for.

"I was quite pleased that Mr. Hearst dropped his isolationist stance and got on the bandwagon after Pearl Harbor."

"Didn't everyone, Mr. President?"

That drew a presidential laugh. "Almost everyone at that, Jake."

"In any event, Mr. Hearst sends his best regards, Mr. President." Which was a white lie. "He and I both thank you for agreeing to see me."

"You're quite welcome. Now, Steve Early has briefed me, Harry too, on your uncle. I'm very sorry to hear about that. You have the condolences of Mrs. Roosevelt and myself."

"Thank you, sir."

"Now about your going into Germany. Extremely dangerous. Right into the lair of that horrid madman, eh? Tell me about it."

Jake did. He gave a concise airing of his story about Uncle Dieter and Rolf Becker. Then he stopped and narrowed his eyes. "Now there's something else you need to know, Mr. President. Sergei Prokofiev—"

"The Russian composer. Mrs. Roosevelt and I like his work very much indeed."

"Yes, sir. He told me the Germans are developing a rocket bomb that may be capable of hitting London or even New York from a great altitude."

"A rocket? That could reach New York? Good God, Harry, have you heard anything like that?"

Hopkins sat up, tired eyes suddenly bright, and said, "No sir."

"How does Prokofiev know this?"

"He saw a friend of his in Berlin, a music teacher, before the Germans invaded Russia. This man said that one of his pupils headed up the German rocket program. A man named von Braun, supposedly a young genius."

"Harry, see what Army intelligence knows about this." Hopkins went to a small table across the room from the president's desk and picked up a phone.

"High altitude, you say? We've had an inkling of a radio-guided flying bomb, basically a pilotless airplane, but nothing along these lines."

"Prokofiev says it has gone fifteen miles high in tests and might be capable of going much higher. It would plunge down on a city almost from outer space." Jake worried that he was starting to sound like one of Hearst's over-dramatic news stories.

"My word, there would be no way to defend against such a thing." The president spun the fountain pen between his first and second fingers like a baton, then looked up at Hopkins, who was returning to the sofa. "Anything?" he asked.

"Not right offhand, Mr. President, but they'll get back to us."

The president placed a cigarette in a long holder and lit it with a kitchen match. When he clamped it in his mouth at a jaunty angle he looked exactly like his newsreel shots. "You're quite certain that you want to attempt this?" he asked Jake.

"You sound just like my fiancée, Mr. President, but yes, I do. I'm not going to let the bastards get away with this. Pardon my language, sir." What's the matter with me? Jake scolded himself, using city room vernacular in this place.

"A real vendetta, eh? Infiltrating Germany would be quite an undertaking." The president stopped and seemed to mull something over. At last he said, "But you could certainly do us a great service if you could learn more about this rocket bomb. And of course achieve your own ends as well. You'd need some good papers, very good papers."

Get papers for me? Jake sat dumfounded. He remembered Bill Stoneman's warning about FDR's guile.

"The British," the president continued, "might help us with those papers. They're better at that sort of thing than we are. We're setting up an OSS operation in Switzerland"—Jake knew about the Office of Strategic Services, America's new spy organization—"but it's quite embryonic. You'll have to go through Britain. You speak German, is that right?"

"Yes sir. My parents were born over there." He figured the president knew this.

"*Und ihr Freund, Herr* Becker, he could help you?"

"You speak German yourself, sir?"

"Very little I'm afraid. I took two years at Groton a very long time ago."

"Well, I think Rolf could help, sir. Naturally I'm not familiar with his present situation."

"Naturally . . . Well, if you can spy for Mr. Hearst you can certainly spy for your Uncle Sam," the president said with a hearty but surprising laugh. Jake didn't see anything funny about this.

"You would contact the British on my behalf, sir? And help me get into Germany?"

"It's certainly a possibility, Jake, especially if you can do all of us some good in there." The president looked toward Hopkins. "Maybe he could even do something about Putzi's letter, Harry. That could be most useful."

"Maybe," Hopkins said noncommittally.

Letter? Jake had no idea what they were talking about.

A buzzer sounded and the president looked at a brass nautical clock on his desk. "Oh my, the time does fly," he said, flipping a toggle switch on a small black box. "Yes, Grace . . . Yes, I know my 4:30 is waiting. I'll be with him in a moment."

The president flipped the switch again and said, "I'm sorry, Mr. Weaver, I must see the secretary of commerce, but we need to talk more about this. Can you come back in an hour?" It was a command, of course.

Be a spy for the president? Jake felt dizzy. This was all moving so damn fast.

"Of course, Mr. President."

"Good. I'll see you at"—he glanced at the clock—"just after 5:30 then."

Harry Hopkins knew his boss well. Although the friendly tone of voice hadn't changed a bit as the reporter had been dismissed with FDR's usual cordiality, a slight something in the way he'd cocked his head, had clued Hopkins.

So he wasn't surprised when the president said, "Harry, what do your instincts tell you about this fellow?"

"Seems like a pragmatic, get-the-job-done kind of guy."

"Does he strike you as honest?"

"I suppose so. Why?"

"Well, there's all that German background of his. And then I've never trusted Willie Hearst as far as I could throw Primo Carnera. Have the FBI find out what they can about him. Has he had any contact with the German-American Bund? Does he have any overseas bank accounts, that sort of thing."

Hopkins nodded and went to the phone in the back of the room.

CHAPTER ELEVEN

A White House usher led Jake to the press secretary's office. When the president had used the words infiltrate and vendetta, it slapped into hard focus the enormity of this crazy thing he was planning to do.

Compared with FDR's, Steve Early's office was a closet. It had only one window. Open newspapers covered most of the desk.

Early, talking on the phone, motioned Jake to a chair. When he hung up, he grinned and said, "How'd it go?"

Jake recapped most of the meeting for him.

"Well, well, I told you the boss likes cloak-and-dagger stuff."

Jake asked if Putzi Hanfstaengel was staying in the White House.

"Nah. He's interned under guard at a house over in Virginia." Hmm, Jake thought, I'd heard wrong about that.

"Why?" Early asked.

"Well, Hearst knows him, and maybe he could give me some useful dope on my going into Germany."

"His advice would probably be 'don't go.' He's a strange duck, that guy. International playboy, fell in with the Nazis in the early days. Supposedly even helped Hitler write *Mein Kampf.*"

"No kidding? From what I hear, that's junk writing, an amateurish hodge-podge."

"I guess he had a little pull with the publishers, being a dictator and all." Early laughed hoarsely. "FDR tried to read a translation, but gave it up. Anyhow, he'd probably okay your seeing Hanfstaengl. Want me to ask?"

"Sure."

The phone rang. Early answered and said, "Yes, Grace . . . Oh, really? Sure, I'll tell him. Thanks."

Early hung up and gazed appraisingly at Jake. "Well, old friend, you've really stirred up something. The chief wants you to stay for dinner. Instead of 5:30, he wants to see you at 6:30."

"Dinner? My God, I don't have any clothes, just this suit I'm wearing."

"That'll be fine. He doesn't dress for dinner unless he's got some special guests."

Jake laughed. "Which I'm not."

"Hell, you know what I mean, heads of state, royalty, stuff like that. We've got a couple of extra offices where you can wait, read the papers, take a nap if you want. Or else you can run back to your hotel for a little while."

"No, I'll wait here, Steve. Don't want to take a chance on being late."

The phone jangled again and Early answered. "Yes, Mr. Hopkins . . . Yes, he's here . . . Okay, I'll tell him . . . Yes sir." Early hung up. "Hopkins says to tell you the Army doesn't have anything on a big German rocket. What the hell is that all about? You didn't mention any rocket."

"I don't know if I should say."

"Come on, Jake, you owe me big."

Jake knew that was true, also that Early couldn't release anything about the rocket without FDR's okay. "You're right, sorry." He told him what Sergei Prokofiev had said.

Early whistled. "Jesus, fella, you're really in the soup now." He stared at Jake for a moment, then got up and said, "Well, Mr. Information, let's find you a place to relax."

He took Jake into a nearby room, which had a small oak desk

with a typewriter and phone, and a threadbare loveseat against a wall. "Make yourself at home. You want some coffee or a drink? I'll send someone in."

"Thanks. I could use some coffee."

Early left.

The office was stifling, so Jake stepped to the lone window and raised the sash. Cool air flooded in. He stood there gazing out toward the Washington Monument. The short November day had gone dark and the great obelisk stood unlit in the purple gloom. Still, a few lights shone here and there. He was surprised to find wartime Washington dimmed out, not fully blacked out.

Jake flinched as a huge web of lightning crackled over the Mall, lighting the monument for an instant as if a great flashbulb had gone off. A clap of thunder split the air, the concussion thudding in his ears.

For some reason, as he backed away from the window, he thought about his promise to Charlie Root to attend the Hollywood Stars' opener in April. The word "infiltrate" popped back into his mind and a shiver stole up his spine like Pete Rieser taking an extra base. Would he be able to keep that promise to Root?

"Pardon me, sir."

Jake jumped and turned. A black steward in a white coat and white gloves stood in the doorway. "Mr. Steve said you might like something, sir?"

"Some black coffee would be fine, thanks."

"Very good, sir. Thunderstorm like this be most unusual in November," he said as he turned and left.

Jake sank down on the loveseat. Rain began pelting down outside but he left the window open, the crisp air as nice as a March breeze off Santa Monica Bay.

He had a habit of mentally putting his reporter's notes in order whenever he had time to kill. He thought about Putzi Hanfstaengel. He tried to remember everything he'd dug up on the wealthy

German-American. Born in Munich, the guy's full name was Ernst Sedgwick Hanfstaengl. On his American mother's side of the family he was a cousin of Civil War Union general John Sedgwick. After his childhood in Munich, Putzi was educated at Harvard and later owned an art gallery in Manhattan, where art collectors William Randolph and Millicent Hearst got to know him.

He returned to Germany just after the First War and got involved with the Nazi movement and its fiery leader. As a well-connected member of the international set he gave Hitler a touch of respectability in certain circles, plus considerable financial support. Putzi had actually composed some of the brassy Nazi marches.

Jake also wondered what the president had meant when he'd mentioned "Putzi's letter."

"Here we are, sir." The steward had returned. He placed a tray on the edge of the desk near Jake. It contained a china cup, a silver spoon, and a ceramic carafe. Jake wondered, do you tip these guys? No, that'd probably be insulting.

"Thanks."

The man gave a small head bob and departed. Jake poured some coffee and took a sip. It was darn good. His travels the last two days had been wearing and the shot of caffeine was welcome, his adrenaline having ebbed since meeting the president. He took another drink and wondered what brand this was.

His thoughts turned back to Putzi Hanfstaengl. "H" had shown Hearst around Germany in 1934 when the Old Man and his entourage visited Europe. And he no doubt was the one who'd arranged the infamous meeting between Hearst and Hitler. Hearst had been royally pissed off when the U.S. and German press published a photo of him leaving Hitler's Chancellory.

The hoodlums around Hitler never took to Putzi. Too refined for their tastes. According to Steve Early, they played a bizarre joke on him, putting him on a plane and telling him he'd been ordered on a dangerous mission behind the lines in the Spanish Civil War. Scared to death, he was flown around Germany for a couple of hours, then let out back where he'd started. That's when he vamoosed out of Germany. Fast.

Now here he was, stashed a few miles away in Virginia, supposedly an adviser to FDR on the Nazis.

Jake drank some more coffee. Wait a minute. Something else just occurred to him. Putzi was just about Roosevelt's age. Maybe they'd been at Harvard at the same time. Maybe they'd known each other as students. Hmm, wouldn't that be something.

There were so damn many interconnections. Everybody knew the man but Jake.

CHAPTER TWELVE

When he was ushered into the Blue Room, Jake was greeted by a tall woman about his own age with a long, plain face. "Hello there, you must be Mr. Weaver. I'm Anna Roosevelt, your fellow Hearstian." She stood beneath an ornate chandelier and a gilt-framed painting of James Monroe. "Father will be along in a moment."

Jake knew Anna Roosevelt and her husband ran the *Seattle Post-Intelligencer*, a Hearst paper. He took the hand she offered. "Right, I'm Jake Weaver, fellow Hearstian." The Roosevelts' eldest child looked quite a bit like her mother, but less homely, he thought unkindly, and her smile was cheery. She wore a brown, high-necked, short-sleeved dress.

"Your work is quite good. We've run many of your stories off the wire," she said, then quickly shifted gears. "There will be six of us for dinner. Mother is at an Army hospital or *somewhere*. May I offer you a—"

A side door Jake hadn't noticed swung open and a white-coated butler wheeled the president in. "Ah, there you are," Roosevelt boomed. "I see you've met my dear Anna." His daughter bent over him and they kissed cheeks, one of her hands resting on a presidential shoulder.

As if finishing his daughter's thought, he said, "May I offer you a drink, Jake? I make a tolerably good martini."

"That's fine, Mr. President, if you're having one."

"Indeed I am. By the way, Anna dear, our guest is to be called Jake. He maintains that Mr. Weaver is his father. Isn't that grand?"

Anna Roosevelt smiled, apparently agreeing that was grand.

The butler wheeled the president to an ornate but low-slung sideboard laid out with liquor bottles, mixes, glasses, and a silver ice bucket beaded with water droplets. The butler gave a small bow and left, and the president busied himself building a pitcher of martinis.

Jake knew that Anna Roosevelt often came east and served as White House hostess when her mother traveled. Her tone when she'd said her mother was off somewhere, and the way she'd greeted FDR, told him she was a daddy's girl.

"Here we are, my dear," the president said, turning and offering her a glass. "And for you, Jake." He raised his own glass and said, "What shall we drink to, then?"

"Victory," Jake suggested.

"Right as rain, old top. That's just the thing." He raised his glass. "To victory."

"Victory," Jake and Anna Roosevelt said together.

Jake took a sip. A bit too much vermouth. "That's excellent, Mr. President."

"Thank you. I do enjoy a good martini after a hard day, and Hitler and Tojo have certainly given me some hard days recently." The president frowned and put down his glass. "Say, Jake, I like first-hand accounts from those who've been at the front. Tell me about Guadalcanal as you see it. That's been a hard, slow campaign."

"Yes sir, it has, but we're winning. The Japs underestimated our strength and fighting ability. They've reinforced piecemeal and the Marines have chewed up and spit out every one of their counterattacks."

"Chewed up and spit out. Marvelous. That says it so much better than the official communiqués I get from the Navy."

"What happens after we take Guadalcanal, Mr. President?"

"This is secret, Jake, but we'll march up the Solomons and knock out their big base at Rabaul on New Britain."

"Mr. President!" a male voice admonished. An admiral had entered the room, with shoulders full of stars, a chest full of ribbons. He tossed a peaked cap laden with gold braid on a side table.

"Oh, Bill," said the president, "I think we can trust this scribe here to keep our confidences. Jake, may I present Admiral Leahy, chairman of the Joint Chiefs? Bill, this is Jake Weaver, one of W. R. Hearst's finest reporters."

Leahy shook hands rather coldly. "How do you do, sir," Jake said. Leahy looked him up and down as if inspecting a newly minted ensign. Jake hoped his tie wasn't crooked.

"I must caution you, Mr. Weaver, to keep to yourself anything you hear tonight of a strategic nature."

"Scout's honor," Jake said, holding up a hand as if taking an oath. He'd met several flag officers, some pompous and superior like this one, others just regular guys. Never grovel was his rule, don't play the junior officer.

Anna Roosevelt backed him up. "A fellow Hearst journalist would never harm the war effort, Admiral."

Thunder rumbled distantly and raindrops drizzled down a window. It was a dark and stormy night, Jake thought with a quick internal grin.

The president wheeled himself to the sideboard and poured a martini for Leahy. "Here, Bill, you have some catching up to do." Leahy took the glass and the president turned to Jake. "Anna's been here for a couple of weeks, taking a break from the fourth estate."

"When I get back," his daughter said, "I may offer Jake a job. We could use him on the *P-I*."

"I wonder if Willie Hearst would approve such a thing," Roosevelt said. "And then too Jake might prefer the night life in L.A." He winked and Jake felt acutely embarrassed by this glib small talk.

The president lifted his martini glass and said, "Let's drink to West Coast journalism." The others dutifully raised their glasses.

Leahy, with a stare as sharp as a knife, said to Jake, "I appreciate the assurances, but I'm still thinking of your premature story about Admiral Halsey."

"Sir, I dig up whatever I can to make a good story. If I can scoop somebody, so much the better." Jake couldn't help it, had to stand up for himself, even if they threw him out on his ass. "You," he continued, "were about to announce Halsey taking Ghormley's command anyway. I beat you by only two days. That jeopardized nothing. I won't write what the president just said about the Solomons, or anything else that would harm the cause or help the enemy."

"Well said," the president put in. "I think that settles it then, don't you, Bill?"

"Of course, Mr. President." Leahy's free hand was a fist.

Grace Tully stole into the room, leaned down and whispered something in FDR's ear.

"Thank you, Grace, and thank Harry for me," he said with a mere flicker of a glance at Jake, who wondered what the hell that was all about. As Grace Tully left quietly, Jake once again flashed on Bill Stoneman's warning about the president's guile.

Anna Roosevelt took Jake's arm and deftly drew him away, leaving her father and Leahy alone to huddle in quiet conversation. Had FDR given her some kind of signal?

She pointed out the satin drapes, paintings and assorted trappings on the other side of the Blue Room. "That lovely crown molding was personally selected by Elizabeth Monroe, who decorated this entire room after the fire."

"The War of 1812," Jake said. "Damn British firebugs."

"Yes, burning the White House was a foul act."

"Well, Mrs. Monroe had excellent taste," Jake said, wondering what the president and the admiral were talking about.

Before long a butler in the ubiquitous white coat came in and said, "Dinner is ready, Mr. President."

"Let's be on our way then. We're waiting for one more, but I'm sure he'll be along shortly. Traffic has been just horrid lately." The butler wheeled the president out the door, down the corridor and into the State Dining Room. Anna Roosevelt followed, trailed by Leahy and Jake.

A tall, pretty woman in black satin and pearls stood near the table.

"Jake," the president said, "may I present Princess Martha of Norway. She and her lovely children are staying with us for awhile. This is Mr. Weaver, one of Anna's fellow journalists."

"Your highness," Jake said with a respectful nod of his head.

"Oh, none of that now," she replied with an elegant little hand flutter and a pleasing accent. "I am just a war refugee to whom you Americans have been very kind."

The table, which could accommodate many times more, was set for six with place cards at each plate. The crystal sparkled and a blue presidential seal adorned the white china.

"I'll be sitting on the president's left," Anna Roosevelt said to Jake, "and the princess on his right. You'll be next to me, opposite Mr. Hanfstaengl."

CHAPTER THIRTEEN

Hold the first course another few minutes," the president said, and the butler nodded assent. "Bring the martini pitcher in here if you would and give everyone a little bonus."

Glasses filled, the president looked around and said, "What shall we drink to this time?"

A tall, tan, smiling man entered the room at that moment and said, "To our great leader, Mr. Franklin Delano Roosevelt, of course."

So this is my "Mr. H," Jake thought, sizing him up. He was resplendent in a tailored silk suit with a glistening white handkerchief peeking from his chest pocket.

"No, no, Mr. Hanfstaengl, that won't do at all," said the president. "We shall drink to our good friend and comrade in arms, Winston Churchill."

"Winston Churchill," they all chorused.

When the toast had been drunk, the president said, "Putzi, I believe you know everybody here but one. Say hello to Jake Weaver, one of Willie Hearst's top correspondents. Jake, this is Ernst Hanfstaengl of Harvard, Manhattan, Germany and various points in between."

"Very pleased to meet you," Hanfstaengl said.

"Likewise." Jake shook the man's large hand.

Everything about this odd cosmopolitan, his confident manner, his diction, his highly polished Italian shoes, his manicure, bespoke smoothness—*now*. Jake would love to have seen him squirming aboard that plane back when the Nazis—vicious prank—had pretended they were going to dump him into the middle of the Spanish Civil War.

"Mr. Hearst is an old friend of mine," Hanfstaengl said. "I've sold him a painting or two in my time. Please tell him I said 'Siss Boom Bah.'"

All the guy needs is a raccoon coat, Jake thought. He almost replied "Boola Boola," but remembered that Boola Boola was Yale's, not Harvard's. "Er, sure," he said, noticing that the admiral's eyes looked darkly unimpressed by this man in his fifties playing the Harvard cheerleader. Leahy, military through and through. No room for humor. Too bad.

"Well, then," the president told the butler, "I believe we're ready for some salad."

Dinner proceeded interestingly enough, the president asking Leahy questions about the war, Anna Roosevelt making small talk, Hanfstaengl alternating between flippancy and insightful comments, Princess Martha hanging on the president's every word. Jake nodded a lot.

Jake, who splurged whenever he could on fine meals in places like Chasen's and Perino's, found the strips of flank steak, served with sauce-drenched noodles, overcooked. He liked his wine and his meat red. As he forked a piece into his mouth, the president glanced at him, seemed to read his mind and said, "Not a gourmet meal, is it, Jake?"

Thankfully not expecting an answer, FDR said, "You know, the food here was superb when my Cousin Teddy was president. He had a Swiss couple by the name of Martin. Mar-*tahn*," he added, giving it the French pronunciation. "He was head butler and she was the cook. Such marvelous meals. But I suppose we're lucky at that, managing a few scraps of beef when so many have none at all. Anna here thinks the White House should be rationed just like everyone else. Ha ha."

Anna Roosevelt muttered, "Oh, father."

Dessert consisted of waffles topped with whipped cream and chocolate sauce. After it was cleared away, Anna Roosevelt and the princess excused themselves, and the others returned to the Blue Room.

Now there would be Man Talk. They situated themselves around a blazing fireplace and a butler brought in four enormous cigars on a silver tray. I like a good cigar, Jake thought, but my God, these look like railroad ties.

The president picked one, removed the band, and sniffed it regally. "Fine Havanas. Thank you, Bill, for getting this valuable cargo safely through the U-boat blockade." He laughed at himself again.

Leahy muttered, "He knows they came by plane," the closest he'd come toward levity.

After the stogies were fired up, Jake said the Blue Room was beginning to resemble its name.

FDR laughed, then turned serious and said, "You won't find good tobacco like this in Germany, Jake." Hanfstaengl's brows arched.

The butler returned with brandy snifters and a full crystal decanter. He filled the snifters, serving the president first, then the others. He placed the decanter on an end table next to Roosevelt, stoked the fire, and left.

The president looked at his three guests and began to describe Jake's plan to infiltrate enemy territory. Leahy frowned. Hanfstaengl leaned forward and listened, wide-eyed.

"Jake heard from Sergei Prokofiev, the Russian composer, that Germany is developing a high-altitude rocket weapon with potentially great range. Could bomb London, perhaps even . . . well, I hate to think of it."

Leahy grimaced as if to say he shouldn't speak of such things in front of Hanfstaengl, but the president went on. When he paused to drag deeply on his cigar, the admiral turned to Jake and commanded, "A composer? And just how would he know this?"

"A piano student in Berlin was the lead engineer on the project. The guy's piano teacher told Prokofiev, before the Nazis attacked

Russia and he had to scram."

"If there's any truth in that, the scientist is a loose-lipped fool."

"Apparently he's not political," Jake said, "and very proud of his achievements."

"Yes," said Leahy, "scientists tend to be like that. We have to work hard to keep the lid on some of our own egghead hotshots."

Jake gazed into the flames dancing in the fireplace. What covert projects have *we* got going? he wondered. He'd heard something about secret experiments with uranium.

The president said, "Perhaps if Jake really does pursue his perilous undertaking, he could learn more about this rocket for us."

Leahy's dark look seemed to say, "Oh sure, this nobody reporter spy for us inside the Third Reich?"

Jake had been thinking that if he really could gather information on the rocket he'd be doing something meaningful in Germany, something beyond his personal craving to exact some family revenge.

The president went on to other topics. North Africa, where supply problems, bad weather and stiff German resistance were playing hell with the drive on Tunis. Shipment of B-17s to the new Eighth Bomber Command in England for the planned air offensive against Germany. "All of this is off the record, Jake."

"Absolutely, Mr. President."

Republicans in the Senate were holding up a mineworker safety bill. "Henry Wallace needs to crack the whip on those scamps." Jake knew that was just talk. The vice president presided over the Senate, sure, but had no pull with the Republicans.

"Churchill," the president went on, "wants us to meet in Casablanca in a couple of months to further define our war strategy. And that is most definitely off the record." A burning log popped loudly as if to emphasize the point. "What do you think of the idea?"

When no one answered, Jake wondered if he was expected to.

The president looked right at him.

"I believe it would be unprecedented, sir, a sitting president leaving the country in wartime."

"Precisely why I should go. It would be a grand gesture, make quite a statement, Allied unity and so forth."

"It would be good for morale, Mr. President," Jake offered.

"That it would, and I would certainly enjoy a nice sea cruise, too."

And so it went, the president pouring refills from the decanter and tossing out juicy political morsels that Jake couldn't and wouldn't touch.

At one point, while the president was saying something about Vichy France to Leahy, Hanfstaengl leaned toward Jake and said quietly, "May I have a word later in private, Mr. Weaver?"

Surprised, Jake said, "Sure."

As the fire began to burn low, Jake sneaked a peek at his wristwatch. Eleven-ten.

Fifteen minutes later, the president yawned and said, "Well, gentlemen, it's been a grand evening." Knowing he was dismissed, Jake stood and so did Hanfstaengl.

"Bill, if you have a minute more," the president said to Leahy, fitting a cigarette into his holder, the cigars long dead.

Jake moved toward the door. "Thanks very much for the hospitality, Mr. President." He made a motion across his mouth as if zipping his lip.

The president smiled. "Precisely. Say, old top, you'll be hearing from Harry Hopkins in the morning. I hope you're staying on another day."

"Of course, Mr. President."

In the corridor, Hanfstaengl caught up with Jake and said, "Will you please breakfast with me tomorrow, Mr. Weaver?"

"Sure." Knowing Hanfstaengl was living across the river in Virginia, Jake wondered if Putzi was spending the night in the White

House.

"Fine. I'll call on you at your hotel, if that's all right. Which is it?"

"The Willard."

"Splendid. I think room service would be best. Nine o'clock all right?"

"Fine, nine o'clock it is."

In the Blue Room, the president said, "Bill, I had the FBI check on this Weaver fellow and it seems he's all right. No arrests, no foreign bank accounts, no links to the America First Committee or the Bund, nothing like that. I'm going to help him get into Germany, in a very hands-off way, of course."

He caught Leahy's look.

"Look at it this way, Bill, it might be useful to us, that rocket and all. If he uncovers some valuable intelligence, swell, good for us. In the worst case, if he blunders badly, well, Willie Hearst has one less reporter, but what's that to us? We don't know the man."

"I see what you mean, sir," the chairman of the Joint Chiefs said to his commander-in-chief.

Outside, the rain had stopped, the night now clear and frigid. Jake hunched deep into his new overcoat as he walked back toward the hotel, Pennsylvania Avenue's sidewalks glistening from the rain. The city around him slumbered in darkness.

He glanced up at a cold sweep of stars like sequins shimmering on black satin. He spotted Orion the Hunter, a favorite constellation first pointed out to him years ago by his Uncle Dieter. The thought warmed him for a moment, but then exhaustion struck. He'd been on his guard for hours, before the president of the United States, no less. His day had started nineteen hours ago at the Blackstone Hotel in Chicago. It felt like a week.

CHAPTER FOURTEEN

Breakfast arrived at Jake's room ten minutes after Putzi Hanfstaengl did. Coffee, juice, toast and eggs, scrambled for Jake, over easy for Hanfstaengl. Jake signed the bill and handed the kid a Liberty half-dollar. "Thank *you*," the boy gushed.

Hanfstaengl wore a charcoal blazer with a sporty gold ascot at the neck of a wide-collared blue shirt. Jake had put on a fresh shirt and tie to go with the only suit he'd brought. Before his guest arrived, he'd called the airport and delayed his departure a day.

Hanfstaengl thanked Jake for seeing him and Jake said, "Not at all." After all, he'd been wanting to meet this man.

As they attended to their breakfast, Jake got the warning he'd expected that Germany was a very bad place these days and that his plan was foolhardy. "But if you are going"—Hanfstaengl leaned forward, brushed a toast crumb from his lip and looked directly into Jake's eyes—"I left there in some haste. Because of the nature of my departure, I left something important behind and I would be immensely grateful if you could retrieve it for me."

Had somebody slapped a sign on Jake's back saying, LET ME BE YOUR ERRAND BOY IN NAZI GERMANY? Jake put down his coffee cup, certain that his face said no. "I've got something else to do. And now Mr. Roosevelt has asked me to see what I can find out about this rocket bomb. I don't see how I can—"

"I could pay you a nice finder's fee. It would mean a great deal to me."

Although Jake had had a good night's sleep, he suddenly felt very tired. *Why did I ever have to get that letter from Rolf?* he asked himself. Jake had information of his own to pry out of this man, but right now he just wanted him to leave. He knew he'd have to hear him out, though, friend of FDR's that he was.

"I'm not interested in a finder's fee," he said. Even though his paycheck as a newspaper reporter was pretty modest, he didn't want any palm oil from this man. "But tell me more, Mr. Hanfstaengl." As if the guy needed prodding. Jake supposed he'd be asked to fetch something from a lock box in some Berlin bank.

"The item is quite small; you could put it in your pocket," Hanfstaengl said, gesturing left-handed with his fork. "I could have left it in my safe deposit box"—*I knew it*, Jake thought—"but my former friends have surely cleaned that out." *Oh!*

"What is this item, exactly?"

"A sealed envelope. I shouldn't say more."

"You'd better if you want my help."

Hanfstaengl's face clouded, taken aback, but just for an instant. He leaned forward and said, "Yes, you're quite right, you'll need to know. If Mr. Roosevelt trusts you, I certainly shall. It is a letter that von Hindenburg wrote, before his death, to Hitler. It spells out his wishes on the form of government the old president wanted Germany to establish after his death."

Jake had never heard anything about this.

"Hindenburg was much revered. He was a field marshal in the last war, you know, a national hero. Now, in 1934, he knew he was dying. Ostensibly, he and Hitler shared power at the time, Hindenburg as president, Hitler as chancellor. He knew Hitler planned to take total control after he died, combine the two offices and make himself Führer."

"And this deathbed letter tells Hitler not to do that?"

"It says that Germany should establish a constitutional monarchy, not a bogus republic with Hitler ruling by decree."

"Hindenburg should have gone to the press," Jake said, "made that letter public."

"Yes, because of his great prestige, it could have been crippling to Hitler's plans. It was the mistake of a senile old man. His last will and testament, which said nothing about this, was published but the letter was kept private."

"And Hitler kept it that way," Jake supplied.

"Yes, and made himself dictator."

Jake put down his coffee cup. "How did you get possession of the letter?"

"He showed it to a couple of people, Vice Chancellor von Papen and me. I 'borrowed' the letter, promising to return it."

"You were close to Hitler, is that right?"

"Yes. He trusted me in those days. My family's prominence gave him some credibility. For a time, he was smitten with my sister Erna. Thankfully, nothing came of *that*. I even composed some music for Hitler, sad to say now. When he asked for the letter back, I told him that I had destroyed it for his own good, so it couldn't fall into the hands of his enemies."

"And he accepted that?"

"His exact words were, 'Good, I would have done the same. But if I ever learn that you are lying, it will be very bad for you.'"

"That must have had you shaking in your boots."

"It did, but I swore with a straight face that I had burned it."

"Soon after that you broke with him, is that right?"

"Not immediately. I was still under the mesmerizing man's spell." Sadness darkened Hanfstaengl's eyes. "But I did finally see the light. In any event, the letter is now in the possession of a certain woman. It will be a bit tricky getting to her, but I'm sure a resourceful reporter such as yourself can manage it. I'll give you a note to hand her, so she'll know to trust you. The tricky part is that she is married."

"Married?"

"Yes, to a rather public figure. This man is very promiscuous.

The lady and I became, well, intimate."

"So she got back at the creep through you."

"I prefer to think that the lady was simply overwhelmed by my considerable charm"—he grinned—"but there's probably an element of truth in what you say. She despises the scoundrel but has to keep up the pretense of a happy family in the eyes of their adoring public and, of course, the party."

"Family?"

"Yes, they have several small children."

Any of them yours? Jake thought. "Why didn't you bring this letter with you?"

"I had entrusted the lady in Berlin with it for a few days while family business took me to Munich. Then, as I mentioned, I suddenly had to leave in haste and unfortunately I was still in Munich. I telephoned her and she promised to safekeep it for me, saying I would surely be back when the madness calmed down and German life became more normal. We all thought that would happen, that the Nazi extremes were just a passing phase."

Hanfstaengl folded his napkin. "But then the madman invaded Poland, and now I fear I will never see her again. From this all-out struggle she will emerge either as one of the queen bees of a mighty German empire or the piteous consort of a despicable little prisoner of war."

"Holy smoke," Jake said, hunching forward. "Just who is this lady?"

Hanfstaengl paused long, sipped some of his coffee and then seemed to stare at a thought hidden somewhere deep in the cup. He looked up at Jake and said at last, "Magda Goebbels."

Jake dropped his knife. *The wife of Hitler's propaganda minister?*

CHAPTER FIFTEEN

Jake exhaled sharply, discovering he'd been holding his breath. He recalled pictures he'd seen of Joseph Goebbels' tall, blond wife.

Hanfstaengl said, "I can have the message delivered here this afternoon, along with their address in Lanke."

Jake had a vague notion of where Lanke was, northeast of Berlin, he thought.

"Herr Goebbels is never there during the day. Not terribly often at night, for that matter. He usually stays in his townhouse on the *Wilhelmstrasse*, near the Chancellory."

"I'm not taking any letters to Frau Goebbels," Jake spouted. "It's a cinch I'll be searched when I enter Germany."

"Oh, quite right, how stupid of me. I'll think of something you can tell her then, some word or phrase that will tell her you've come from me. Let me see . . . ah, I have it. Tell her that *Jucken* sent you."

"*Jucken?*" Jake questioned. "Itch?"

"Yes, she said she often got the itch to have me, you see."

Oh Jesus, let me out of here, Jake thought. What he said was, "I'm not making you any guarantees, Mr. Hanfstaengl."

"I understand. Do what you can."

Proof that Hindenburg wanted Hitler out, that he wanted Germany to restore the monarchy. What a story that would be. Pulitzer Prize stuff. But right now Jake had more pressing things to deal with.

"I've got some questions for you," he said, suddenly speaking German.

Hanfstaengl's eyebrows arched appreciatively. "*Ja?*"

Jake proceeded to ask about security measures in Berlin, whether the trains, buses and trams were still running, and how was his German?

Hanfstaengl said it was quite good, though *mit etwas Akzent*, with a bit of accent. He'd have to be careful, but he could probably pass as a Czech or an Austrian.

Or an American, Jake thought darkly. He told himself that, among other things, he'd have to remember to hold his fork with the left hand in the European manner. Then he asked about ways of getting out of Germany.

"My knowledge isn't very current, but I believe that ferries still run to Sweden from Rostock. Your papers would be examined quite closely, of course, and you'd need a very good reason for your exit."

Jake switched back to English. "So you've kept mum about subjects like Geli Raubal."

Hanfstaengl's eyebrows shot upward. "You know of Hitler's niece?"

"Sure, and like some other people, it wouldn't surprise me if Hitler killed her, or had her killed."

"I have nothing to say about that."

"But you know something, or have an educated opinion."

"I have nothing whatever to say. I am quite serious about the danger to my family."

Then, as if he had a great need to unburden himself, Hanfstaengl said, "I thought that under the National Socialists, Germany would undergo another great renaissance, in the tradition of Goethe, Frederick the Great, Bismarck. At first the renewed energy and confidence—after defeat, depression, hunger—was inspiring. But at the end of the day, how wrong I was. Those small-minded, nihilistic bourgeoisie are not enlightened leaders, but simply the petty destroyers of a great culture they can neither understand nor appreciate." His voice began to catch. "These fools are tearing it to shreds. How could I have been so blind? Imagine, killing the crippled and feeble-minded." He slowly covered his face with his hands and murmured, "I should have seen through them at once. Why ever did I go back? Better I'd stayed in New York."

After a long moment, he dropped his hands and slumped back in his chair. His face slackened into deep lines and grooves. Jake knew he was about fifty-five but right now he looked seventy.

These couldn't be easy things for a Harvard aristocrat to admit. "A lot of people were fooled," Jake said.

"Furthermore, I believe the Nazis want to kidnap me."

Wouldn't be surprised, Jake thought. Remove a potential source of embarrassment. Maybe that's why they want to nab Walt Disney, so they can swap him for Putzi. Even with that bodyguard around, Disney would be a lot easier to lift than this man under the president's care here in buttoned-up Washington. FDR would give up Hanfstaengl in a minute to rescue the hugely popular Disney from the clutches of the Huns.

"Did you hear what I said?"

"Yes, kidnap you. I guess to make sure you keep zipped up about these things you might know."

"Precisely."

"I hope the Secret Service is keeping a good eye on you then."

"Better than you know, Mr. Weaver."

"Well, let me take down Magda Goebbels' address, just in case." Jake was a reporter, after all. It could make a great story.

The phone jangled a few minutes after Hanfstaengl left. Jake jumped, took a deep breath and answered on the third ring.

"Harry Hopkins, Mr. Weaver. The president asked me to call. Can you come over to the White House? I have some information for you."

"Sure. What time?" he asked the president's top adviser.

"As soon as you can. Right now be convenient?"

"Sure. I'll see you in ten minutes, Mr. Hopkins."

Harry Hopkins had a cluttered office, larger than Steve Early's but much smaller than the president's. A painting of Thomas Jefferson and a photo of FDR hung on a wall; the window looked out on the Rose Garden, now bleak in late autumn. Hopkins looked tired and care-worn, with dark circles under his eyes much like the president's. His tie hung loose at his neck.

Jake turned down Hopkins' offer of a cigarette. His host lit one for himself.

"The chief wants you to go to London," Hopkins said. "The British can help you with ID and papers, as well as transportation into Germany."

"They'll get me in there?"

"Yes, the MI6, their spy outfit, has ways of inserting agents into Germany."

There was that word again. *Spy.* "And do they have ways to get them back out again?"

Jake thought Hopkins' expression said he had no idea. "I'm sure they'll have some notions about that."

Notions? Great. What have I gotten myself into? Jake thought for the hundredth time in the last two days.

When Jake said nothing to that, Hopkins threw in, "The chief can't order you to go, but will you do this for us? Info on that rocket would be valuable and the Hindenburg letter could make for some powerful propaganda. The government will give you all the help it can."

Which Jake knew would be nothing at all once he was inside Germany. But without Hearst's backing, the trip would wipe out his meager savings. However, with Uncle Sam picking up much of the tab, he could swing it. And the resolve to avenge his uncle burned as hot as ever.

"Mr. Hopkins, I'm putting all my cards on the table. First, I'm going, and it's to see about my uncle, get some satisfaction there. Then, second, I'll try to find out something about the rocket, but I could come up empty. Third, that letter. So there it is, those are my priorities, in that order. Knowing that, if you guys still want to send me to England, okay, I'm in."

Hopkins inhaled deeply on his cigarette, then slowly blew the smoke from his nostrils. "I like your candor," he said at last. "Okay, I think the chief will buy that. I'll let you know soon as possible. If it's a go, I'll send you the instructions on whom to contact in London, when, where, all that." He snuffed out his cigarette in a Grinnell College ashtray. "The president will send a message to Hearst. You'll want to go home, tie up loose ends and make preparations."

Update my will, Jake thought morbidly.

"Then we'll fly you to England on one of the bombers we're ferrying over there."

"Jake Weaver the spy."

Hopkins laughed. "I guess so."

"Damn, did I say that out loud?"

CHAPTER SIXTEEN

The plane refueled in St. Louis, then stopped for the night at Kirtland Field in Albuquerque. Jake hadn't heard from Harry Hopkins before leaving the capital, but he was sure he would, and soon.

The airline hotel's lobby was crowded with Air Corps cadets from the field. At the desk, Jake found a message waiting for him from Old Man Hearst, who'd called from Wyntoon, his estate in northern California. Jake went to his room, pulled off his shoes, and returned the call.

"Mr. Weaver, good, I'm glad I caught up with you. I had a call from our great white father and he says you can do us some good over there." So Hearst had got word of the president's reply before Jake. "What all happened in Washington?" the Old Man asked.

Jake gave an account of his experiences at the White House, omitting Putzi Hanfstaengl and Magda Goebbels.

"Well, I still don't like the idea, you understand, but under the circumstances I'm dropping my objections. In these times one can't very well buck the commander-in-chief. I understand you'll first go to London. Send us a story from the U.K., a color piece, what London looks like these days, the mood of the people and so on."

"I'll do that, sir."

"You be careful, Mr. Weaver, very careful."

"I plan to, sir."

When Jake walked into the city room the next afternoon, three days before Thanksgiving, a telegram awaited him. "CHIEF BUYS IT STOP STAND BY STOP HOPKINS."

Jake read it twice, then slumped into his chair and rubbed his eyes. A moment later he called Sergei Prokofiev's hotel.

"Maestro," he said when he got Prokofiev on the line, "this is Jake Weaver."

"Mr. Weaver, yes. You have been able, with the information I give to you, to do something?"

"A bit, yes. I was wondering if you have an address in Berlin for Wernher von Braun?"

"No, but he is at Physics Department, *Universität Unter den Linden*. Why?"

"I can't really say, sir."

"I see, yes, secrecy, it is important. He is nice boy. I would not wish him to be harm."

"I'm sure he won't be, sir. Unter den Linden University, that's in Berlin, isn't it?"

"*Da*, on street of same name, Unter den Linden."

"Great, thanks very much, sir."

"Not at all, my friend. Germany must be defeat."

When Jake hung up he saw Claudette Colbert over in the bullpen talking with Gracie Pike. The actress looked small and pretty in a tangerine-colored dress, he was thinking, when John Campbell, the managing editor, stalked over and called him into his office.

Campbell shut the door and said, "I thought I was running this newspaper, but oh no, I find out it's you and W.R."

"Huh?"

"Mr. Hearst told me to put you on paid leave for three, four weeks, maybe even a month."

"Four weeks *is* a month, Johnny."

"Smart ass." He threw a pencil to his desk so hard it bounced two feet in the air. "How the hell am I supposed to make budget, doing things like that? And who's going to cover your beat around here?

What the hell is going on?"

"Come on, Johnny, let's go across the street to the Continental. I'll buy you a beer."

In Valerie's apartment that night, Jake recounted his meetings with President Roosevelt, Harry Hopkins and Putzi Hanfstaengl. She listened with a mix of fascination and anxiety. Valerie seemed intrigued and yet frightened by Hindenburg's letter to Hitler. "Don't you dare go near that Goebbels woman. Just forget Hunstrangle or however you say it. You'll be in danger enough without trying to bring out that letter."

Mentioning that Claudette Colbert had been in the office distracted her, but not for long. How was her hair done? Was she prettier in real life than on-screen? Jake said short, kind of curly, and no.

The next day, an Army major called on Jake at the *Herald-Express*, causing stares and whispers around the city room. The major said he was from the Army's rocket testing center in New Mexico, and he understood Mr. Weaver might soon be in a position to learn about Germany's rocket program. He had a list of questions the Army would like answered.

Exactly where were the Germans testing? Some location in Germany or in one of the occupied countries? What kind of fuel was being used? A solid propellant? Some combination of liquid chemicals? Gasoline, liquid oxygen, hydrogen peroxide? What kind of oxidizer? Jake asked what oxidizer was.

"The oxidizer," the major said with a sigh as if Jake were obtuse, "is a substance which supplies the oxygen that ignites the fuel, makes it burn. Might be nitrogen tetroxide."

On it went. The rocket's dimensions. Payload. Range. Launch platform. What other rocket uses were they studying? Defensive ground-to-air rockets that could knock down Allied bombers? RATO.

What was RATO? Jake wanted to know.

"Rocket Assisted Takeoff, to get big planes airborne faster. Are they working on that?"

When the major had exhausted his list, he looked around the messy city room, then at Jake's cluttered desk and the notes he'd taken as if to say, "What the hell could this ignorant reporter possibly find out for us?"

Jake wondered that, too. "I'll see what I can do," he said lamely. After the officer left, he endured a buzz of questions and teasing.

Jake and Valerie pooled their food-rationing stamps and were able to buy a small turkey for Thanksgiving. Valerie went all out, roasting the bird and preparing the usual trimmings: stuffing, cranberry sauce, mashed potatoes and gravy. Jake, who'd brought wine and the salad fixings, helped out, slicing vegetables and handing her utensils.

While the turkey cooked, Jake sniffed the air and said, "Yum, smells almost as good in here as you do."

Valerie didn't respond with her usual flirtatious smile. In fact, she never once called him the Louisiana Kid and remained uncommonly quiet through dinner. Jake knew why. He was leaving on Sunday and she hated the whole idea. Feared for his life. Her late husband's death was bad enough. She sure as hell didn't want to lose another man.

They'd been through it all before, though, Jake's strong bond with his uncle and his determination to go, so they didn't discuss it further. As a result, they sat through a few long, uncomfortable silences.

Jake practiced with the fork in his left hand, tines pointed downward. When Valerie noticed, she looked about ready to cry. He switched back to eating American style.

After they cleared the table and washed the dishes, aware of her melancholia, Jake gave her a hug and suggested, "Let's take a ride and see our new house." It wasn't exactly their new house, not yet, but they'd put in an offer and were waiting to hear.

In West L.A., he parked his Chevy coupe at the curb in front of the Craftsman house on Sycamore Avenue. Seeing it cheered Valerie a bit, lifted some of her gloom. She gazed at the house, white with blue trim and a small, neat yard, and said, "Maybe we could put up a picket fence. Wouldn't that look nice?"

"Sure would, Val. Picket fence. Let's do it."

Her frown returned. "*If* we get the house."

"We will, Sweets, we will."

After lovemaking that night, she clung tighter to him than ever. He wished he could think of something to say that would help.

He lay there awake, thinking about the telegram he'd got two days ago. A Western Union messenger had delivered it to him at the paper.

Jake had told the boy to wait, tore open the yellow envelope and read from the strips of teletype paper glued to a flimsy sheet:

REPORT MAJOR BAILEY 9 AM SUN 28 NOV MARCH FIELD RIVERSIDE STOP DEPARTURE 10 AM STOP CONFIRM STOP SEE BALLARD AT EMBASSY LONDON STOP I AM CONTACT HERE STOP CAN MESSAGE ME THRU EMBASSY TIL DEPART ENGLAND STOP BEST LUCK AND GOOD HUNTING ME AND CHIEF STOP HOPKINS.

Jake took a pencil and scribbled a reply. OFF I GO INTO WILD BLUE YONDER STOP WEAVER.

CHAPTER SEVENTEEN

Jake had never been so cold in his life, freezing his ass off here at the North Pole. Goose Bay, Labrador, wasn't exactly the North Pole but it might as well have been. On final approach to this bleak outpost in morning sunlight, the pilot had called into her intercom, "This isn't the middle of nowhere but you can see it from here."

The cold, bouncy, seventeen-hour trek had started in Riverside, California, with a stop at Chanute Field in Illinois to refuel and change crews. Without a bombload, the B-17E had a range of well over three-thousand miles, so only the one stop was needed. That's where three Women's Airforce Service Pilots, WASPs, had taken over.

One of them, a freckle-faced, brown-haired youngster, said, "Hey gals, we've got us a passenger. Hope he's not nervous about women drivers." She smiled at Jake and said, "Mr. Weaver, is it? I'm your chauffeur for the northeastward hop to Goose Bay." She introduced the copilot and navigator, and said, "If you want a view, just crawl into one of those empty gun turrets and bundle up."

Dusk was falling over barren Illinois cornfields as the bomber took off. Once it reached cruising altitude, Freckle-Face called occasional wisecracks over the intercom. "What's a nice boy like you doing in a place like this?" Things like that.

At one point, she said, "Before crossing the Atlantic, a full crew, gunners and all, will take over this crate. Us gals will have to turn around and deadhead back. You see, they don't trust mere women over the Atlantic in their precious planes. The male crew will have their guns armed and a few bombs aboard. You can't tell when a German U-boat might take a potshot at you with its deck gun. If that happens, the B-17 will counterattack and try to sink the bastard. A woman, of course, would burst into tears and probably crash her plane."

"The hell she would." Jake forgave the bald sarcasm—she was feisty and a fine pilot, his kind of woman.

As the plane had droned through the night, Jake, bundled in Army blankets, had used a flashlight to review notes from his meetings with the Army rocket guy and Putzi Hanfstaengl.

Now here he was at this snowy outpost at the edge of the continent, warming his hands over one of three oil-burning stoves, surrounded by young Canadian and American officers. Milling among them at the stoves, the women fliers took the flirting and teasing in good humor, giving as good as they got. A Victrola started playing *Jeepers Creepers*. Hoots and hollers broke out as Freckle-Face began jitterbugging with a Canadian.

Jake knew the two nations had jointly built this stark new base, consisting of three long runways and a collection of rounded metal huts and assorted buildings of fresh, unpainted lumber. He'd seen the Canadian flag, the Union Jack in the upper left quadrant, whipping straight out in the icy wind.

Departure from Goose Bay was in five hours, so Jake was given a bed in the officers' quarters, a Quonset hut divided into small rooms by tin walls, where he could nap for awhile. He fell into a deep sleep.

When he woke up, he learned he wouldn't be continuing on that B-17 after all. An Army captain had rescheduled him on a Royal Canadian Air Force C-54 Skymaster. Jake knew he should have felt relieved, but was actually disappointed. No action, no bomb runs on enemy U-boats. Fool that I am, he thought.

Before long he was airborne, seated on a bench bolted to the fuselage, surrounded by lashed-down crates. Wonder what's in those? he asked himself. Artillery shells, machine guns? He peered out through a tiny window at the cloud-covered North Atlantic. Just before night fell, he caught a stunning sight: an iceberg, shining brilliant white in a narrow shaft of sunlight through a gap in the winter clouds. He then spent some time by flashlight re-reading and memorizing the Army's questions about German rockets. He wasn't going to bring that list, or anything like it, into Germany.

One of the last things Valerie had said to him popped into his mind. "You'd damn well better come back to me, Jake. I'll be waiting for you." He was damn well going to try.

Hours later, the copilot roused him from slumber and asked if he'd like to ride in the cockpit awhile.

"Sure," Jake said, and he began to thread his way forward past the cargo and the navigator. Soon, strapped into the copilot seat, he fell into conversation with the pilot, who all the while scanned the sky, his eyes sweeping right to left and back again.

Clouds glowed pink in the early dawn. "See anything, let me know, eh?" the pilot said. "We're a bit more than an hour out. A proper course would take us directly over Ireland, but they're bullheaded neutral, you see, so we must dogleg round a bit. Actually just a few miles off Cork now, fairly close to the spot where the Germans torpedoed the *Lusitania* in the last war." Jake looked down at the dark, empty sea and thought about its many secrets.

"Bloody hell!" The pilot jerked the yoke, driving the plane down and to the right. Jake was thrown hard against his leather harness. A shadow blanketed the cockpit. A loud roar. A huge four-engine plane passed overhead. Looked like a giant vulture. Jake saw the Maltese crosses of the German air force on its wings.

The C-54 jinked left and right. "What the hell," Jake shouted. Blood rushed to his head. Ominous orange tracer shells spun toward them from a rear gun turret. Clouds bucked and jumped at the pilot's wild evasive maneuvers.

The ocean beneath them twisted this way and that. *Ping ping*

ping. Shells hitting the left wing. Chunks of aluminum jumping and spinning away. Jake's fingers gripping tight to the sides of his seat. He knew that wing contained important things, fuel lines, control cables for flaps and ailerons, stuff like that, stuff that made this plane fly.

"Jesus," he muttered. *I'm back in the war.*

The gray German plane droned onward, the tracers beginning to fall short. It veered to the right and soon was out of range.

Jake let out his breath. "What the devil was that?"

The pilot pulled the plane back to straight and level, cast a huge sigh, and said, "That, my Yank friend, was a Focke-Wulf Condor, long-range German recon bomber."

Condor? Perfect, Jake thought.

"They patrol the Atlantic searching for targets they can radio to their U-boats." The pilot stared at the left wing, trying to assess the damage. "Nice chap, eh, firing on this unarmed transport. Came on us at six o'clock, where we're blind. Got a few hits on us."

"Why didn't he stick around and finish us off?"

"He's probably low on petrol. End of his run. He was on a heading of about one-four-zero, so he's hustling his bum back to occupied France . . . Oh, balls, he got number two engine. See it smoking there?" He flipped a switch. The prop stuttered a moment, then came to a stop. "Tough to maintain altitude on three-fourths power. Afraid this is going to be close."

That's three, Jake told himself. Five years ago he'd survived a crash landing and this year a Japanese naval shelling on Guadalcanal—now this. How many lives did he have left?

The copilot pushed past the navigator and touched Jake's shoulder. "Sorry, have to chuck you out now. Both of us needed to nurse this baby home." He slapped the pilot on the back. "Nice flying, Hughie."

On his bench again, Jake became acutely aware they were flying lower and slower. No action? Ha! The pilot's words rang in his ears. "Afraid this is going to be close."

Jake recalled the time when he and a friend, trying to fly to Tijuana in a small plane, had made a crash landing in a citrus field north of Oceanside. One of those in a lifetime was enough for the Louisiana Kid, thank you very much.

At long last, rolling green fields, sectioned off by hedgerows, appeared below. He saw a city off in the distance, unmistakably London. He spotted the famous landmarks, Big Ben and the Tower Bridge, standing defiantly after all the hell of the Blitz they'd been through. An array of tethered barrage balloons, floating in the air like little gray sausages, accentuated the fact that this was a city at war.

A few minutes later, the trees and fields tilted. Jake grasped the bench with both hands to keep from sliding, and the plane bumped down on a military airfield. He was two days from home and just a few hundred miles from Nazi Germany. "Nice flying, Hughie," he said softly.

CHAPTER EIGHTEEN

Savoring his first good look at London, Jake took his time getting to the U.S. Embassy, walking up Park Lane from his hotel. His room was small, the toilet paper hard and rough. To his left, a sandbagged anti-aircraft battery marred the beauty of Hyde Park, the gun's snout pointed at the dull gray sky like an accusing finger.

Across the street two bombed-out buildings sagged. One had been a stately Georgian mansion. They were cordoned off by wooden barricades and watched over by elderly men in Home Guard uniforms.

The Blitz had left its mark everywhere. It looked as if twenty-five percent of the buildings were damaged if not burned out altogether. And yet, the occasional whole block stood unscathed. Thank God the nightly raids had stopped. Now the Luftwaffe had its hands full in Russia, where the Germans—couldn't happen to a nicer bunch of guys—were getting their noses bloodied at a big factory town on the Volga.

Londoners bustled about beneath the unpromising sky. Young women pushed perambulators or carried grocery sacks, and quite a few pedaled bicycles, no doubt because gasoline was scarce. Older men and women strolled along with their umbrellas and canes. No young men. Jake knew where they were. North Africa, ships at sea, air bases.

Ah, there came the embassy, a couple of blocks over, near Grosvenor Square. The American flag fluttering above it looked awfully good. So did the two starchy-stiff Marines guarding the entrance. Jake identified himself at the reception table and was told Mr. Ballard was expecting him. Second floor, third office on the right.

Ballard, plumpish, about thirty, wearing black-rimmed glasses, offered his hand. "Mr. Weaver, hello, good to meet you. The White House has asked us to extend every courtesy. Care for some coffee?"

"Sure. Black, please."

Ballard motioned him to a guest chair and picked up his phone to order the coffee. Then he sat and handed Jake an envelope. "I'm instructed to tell you to meet with a Colonel Freeborn of British Military Intelligence at 4 p.m. today. They're in Whitehall, not far from here. You'll find the address and other particulars all there."

Jake took the envelope and nodded.

"If you need anything at all while you're in London, I'll be happy to oblige."

"I may need to send a message to the White House."

"Nothing easier. Just let me know. It will go in the diplomatic pouch, which we fly to Washington every day."

A young woman came in with two cups and a carafe on a tray. She filled the cups and left. Jake sipped some coffee while Ballard busied himself with cream and sugar.

"If you're going to be here a couple of days or more, I'll be glad to make some suggestions. Would you like theater tickets, anything like that?"

London theater, still going on despite the bombing. He'd enjoy that. "Sure, very nice of you."

"We can give you a lift down to MI6."

"Thanks, Mr. Ballard, but I'd like to walk it."

Colonel Freeborn looked like a scholarly sort. Mid-fifties, bald as a gourd and, Jake guessed, a veteran of the First War. He'd look at home in front of a classroom at Cambridge.

"Mr. Weaver, right," he said by way of greeting. "Splendid." A framed photo of an oval-faced, middle-aged woman sat on a credenza behind his desk and a picture of King George VI hung on the wall, beside a map of Western Europe with colored pins stuck into it. Freeborn wore a dark blazer and striped tie.

"This will be rather a change," the man was saying. "My section normally run double agents, chaps who spied for the Germans but whom we've uncovered and, ah, persuaded to work for us. Send the Jerries false information, don't you see. Your case is quite different. Your government would like us to provide cover and get you into Germany. No sending of intelligence. That about it?"

"Yes sir."

"Right then, I should say you look to be about five feet, nine inches and a bit over eleven stone. Sorry, one-hundred-sixty pounds."

"Pretty close, sir."

"Well then, we've had a spot of luck. Your hair's all wrong, of course, reddish brown, but that's easily handled. I say, would you like some tea? Something else?"

"No thanks, I'm fine. You want to dye my hair?"

"Yes, a shade of dark blond, with your permission, of course."

Jake laughed. Dye his hair? That would be something. "Now what's this about luck?"

"Ah yes, Hans-Karl Vogel, a Swiss businessman with German papers, transit documents, passport and so on, died here the other day, poor chap. Sudden heart attack. He was about your size."

So they wanted Jake to impersonate this Vogel. That explained the hair. He leaned forward in his chair. "This heart attack was natural?"

"Oh, completely. We had no cause to tamper with the poor fellow. We've had the local police and the press keep his demise quiet. His belongings remain at his hotel, and we can have his clothing tailored to fit you. Shouldn't take much, same general size and all. We can snap your photo and create a new passport."

"If I'm going to impersonate this Swiss guy, what kind of business am I in?"

"Jolly good. Well then, you represent a Zurich firm, *Schätzen*, that manufactures stamped metal products, Jerry cans, motorcycle seats, mess kits, die-casting parts, that sort of thing. As a neutral, you can sell these products to both the Germans and to us. Quite legal for a firm in a non-combatant nation, many examples of that. Sweden sells ball-bearings to each of us, put their economy in a pickle otherwise."

"Do I make anything that can be used on a rocket? Couplings, fasteners, anything like that?"

Freeborn's eyebrows seemed to grow. Damn, Jake had just broken one of his cardinal rules: Don't volunteer information. This guy didn't need to know about Prokofiev and von Braun.

"Hmm. That I don't know, but we can look into it. Now, how does all this strike you so far?"

"I'll have to think about this. For one thing, I don't know if my accent can pass for Zurich Swiss. I've been told it might sound Austrian or Czech. "

"We've language specialists who can listen to your German, make a judgment on that."

"Good idea."

"We can do that straightaway if it suits you."

Jake nodded and Freeborn picked up the phone.

A Captain Speidel soon appeared. After a conversation in German, the captain said, "You learned your German from Berliners, am I right?"

Jake nodded.

"Even so, your accent doesn't sound North German, and that is good. Watch your 'ch' and 'g' sounds, make them a bit sharper. All in all, I should think the Zurich cover will work for you."

Freeborn said, "Thank you, Speidel, that will be all for now," and gave Jake a questioning look.

"Okay then, if he's satisfied, I guess I'll try to be Hans-Karl Vogel."

"Splendid. We'll book the tailoring for tomorrow, then, if you like, snap your picture wearing the poor bloke's things, and produce the passport."

"A good passport?"

"Oh, quite. I assure you it will appear most genuine to even the fussiest German official. Now, we have information on his firm with which you can familiarize yourself. Also some personal details. Religion, family, so forth. We keep a close eye on neutrals doing business with both sides, don't you know."

"I can imagine." *I've got a lot of homework to do,* Jake told himself. "Tell me, was this guy a German- or French-speaking Swiss?"

"Both, but German was his native tongue."

"Good. My French stinks."

Freeborn granted him a little smile. "Right then, any questions, Mr. Weaver?"

About a million, colonel. "What about Vogel's family? Won't they tell the Germans he's missing?"

"One of our forgers will prepare a letter to his wife, saying his business in England requires him to stay a bit longer."

"You think she'll buy that?"

Freeborn put his hand to his head and ran it through the memory of his hair. "The man traveled quite a bit, was often away for extended periods. I should think she's accustomed to such delays. Our forgery people are quite good. We have samples of his handwriting, you see, even one of his letters. Should buy you some time, eh?"

"Wouldn't a telegram be safer?"

"The Jerries play hell with that. Telegraph lines run through occupied France, you see, while conventional post is flown in from Portugal on Swiss planes."

"I see. Hey, maybe I could hitch a ride on one of those mail planes myself."

"Sorry, strictly forbidden. Swiss crews only, no passengers. We're still working on how to get you into Germany. Ever make a parachute jump?"

Jake's heart just made one. "God, no."

"We could give you some jump training, but it may not come to that. Your eventual destination is?" Freeborn asked with a stare that said he wished he knew more about this mysterious American.

"Berlin."

"Ah." Eyebrows rose. "I think then you shouldn't need to make a jump. Bit tricky but by other means we may be able to put you on the ground north of there, somewhere along the Baltic."

Jake pictured a submarine.

"I'll have more for you on that in a day or so. I know you're probably in a rush to be getting on with this, but we must first take all precautions, make the necessary preparations. We even have a current German rail timetable for you."

"No kidding? You people are pretty thorough." Roosevelt had said the Brits were better at this than the Americans. Looked like he was right.

"Thoroughness is the key, yes. We've had some experience, and success I might add, in deceiving Jerry over the years."

Jake was starting to feel better about all this.

"Of course in this game, despite all precautions, there's always the unforeseen."

Until he had to go and say that.

That night Jake took a long walk that ended at the Fortune Theatre in Covent Garden. With the city blacked out, he'd promptly bumped into a lamppost, but his eyes adjusted and soon he could see a lot by moonlight. Ominous BOMB SHELTER signs loomed everywhere in the gloom. He was saddened to see air-raid damage to the Houses of

Parliament, part of its roof blasted away, the whole edifice surrounded by an entanglement of barbed-wire. Scaffolding indicated repairs were underway. Happily, though, Westminster Abbey and Big Ben's tower stood unscathed.

Settling into his seat in the theater, Jake twisted his program. He remembered the time at the movies—a Ray Milland film?—when Valerie was making small circles on his earlobe with her index finger the way she did. That always aroused him. A woman behind them had leaned forward and asked her to stop; it was blocking her view.

Jake smiled, but other thoughts nesting in his mind came forth unasked. What if the forged letter didn't fool the Swiss wife and she alerted the Germans? Why had he mentioned rockets to Colonel Freeborn? Would he be able to find Wernher von Braun and, if so, what could he say to him? Above all, could he learn who killed Uncle Dieter and why? He hoped his old friend Rolf could help with that.

A gunshot. Jake jumped. So did three hundred others. The play had started with a bang—cute—and the curtain rose to reveal a dark and eerie manor house. The Agatha Christie play, *Peril at End House*, featured her Belgian detective, Hercule Poirot. The actors and scenery were good and Jake lost himself in the production for the next two hours. Just what he'd needed. In the end, Poirot adroitly solved a series of murder attempts on the pretty young mistress of the mansion. After the curtain calls, the sound system played *God Save the King* and everyone stood.

Valerie would have enjoyed all this, Jake thought, as he stepped out onto the dark street.

CHAPTER NINETEEN

Freeborn had been right. Vogel's clothes fit well, with only some minor alterations. After the fitting, Jake was shown down a hall to a small barbershop. All this took place in Freeborn's building, not in public shops as he'd expected.

A cheerful woman in a white smock shampooed his hair, then cut it, styling it a bit shorter. "This will look proper where you're going," she said. On her radio, Vera Lynn was singing *We'll Meet Again*. The melancholy lyrics brought forth wistful thoughts of Valerie.

Next came the dye job. When it was done, the woman handed Jake a mirror. Some stranger with a head of dark blond hair stared back at him.

Now he was back in the colonel's office. Freeborn wore civilian clothes, brown tweed suit, white shirt and a regimental tie adorned with some kind of crest. The calendar on his desk read December 1. This time Jake accepted when asked if he'd fancy some tea. He preferred coffee, but English tea was pretty good, too. Valerie liked tea, and it gave him a sense of connection.

"Your passport will be ready tomorrow," Freeborn said. "You've been brushing up on Herr Vogel, have you?"

"Spent two hours on it last night." The personal effects had included an identity card and a motorcar driving permit, worded in German, French and Italian. Jake said, "I've got a son and daughter, I see."

"Right. Best you keep after it, log as much to memory as you can." He picked up an unlit pipe, then put it back down. "Now then,

I believe you said something about rocket accoutrements the other day."

Damn, Jake knew that chicken would come home to roost.

"We're aware the Jerries are working on the A-4, a rocket that supposedly can reach beyond the stratosphere. I shan't pry into your business, mind you, but if you happen to learn anything about that, where they're testing, anything at all, his majesty's government would be ever so grateful, you know, Allied unity and all. We've been quite generous in sharing information with you Yanks, the cavity magnetron for radio detection and so on."

What could Jake say? These people were giving him some immense help, and he knew the U.S. and Britain were sharing all kinds of secrets.

"It's unlikely that I'll learn anything, but if I do, I'll be glad to tell you."

"Good show."

Jake offered a small grin. "Anything new on getting me in there?"

"Yes, seems I misspoke yesterday on landing you north of Berlin. That's out. We have a small reconnaissance aeroplane, the Westland Lysander, that's able to fly beneath their radar. I thought that it could do the job, land you on a beach near Rostock, don't you see, but unfortunately it hasn't the range to get there and back. Submarine? Different problem. It's virtually impossible to slip past Denmark and enter the Baltic. Very narrow strait there, much too dangerous. But we've some other options for you, none of them without risk, of course."

"Of course." Jake drank some of his tea, willing his hand not to shake.

Freeborn raised one finger. "The Lysander can fly you to France, where the Resistance have set up a secret landing ground on a remote heath. From there, you could go by train." He raised a second finger. "We can place you in neutral Portugal and, again, the trains. Long journey, that, many frontiers to cross." A third finger went up. "Or we can put you in Switzerland, whence one of our agents can spirit you by boat at night across the *Bodensee*, Lake Constance to us"—he stood and pointed it out on his wall map—"to Friedrichshafen on the Würtemberg side. No border frontiers to cross. I should think that's your best choice."

Why the lake? Jake wondered. Why not go around to the land border? Then his question answered itself. If Vogel often crossed the border near Zurich, the German guards there might know him by sight.

"How would I get to Switzerland?"

"Bomber Command can fly you there."

"From Gibraltar?"

"No, from here. It's closer, actually."

"But can you land in a neutral nation?"

"The Geneva Convention permits a belligerent ship a short stay in a neutral port for emergency repairs. The same principle applies to aerodromes. We can effect a problem with a petrol pump, gyrocompass or some such thing."

"You've done this before?"

Freeborn put his elbows on the desk and made a steeple of his hands. "Twice, I believe. The first was actually legitimate. A motor was going dicky. The second time was a ruse, bringing in an agent. The Swiss aren't keen on it, and we don't wish to abuse the privilege, raise suspicions and so forth. But I think we should be able to pull this off once more. The Germans and Italians have done this as well. It's a bit of a game."

Some game, Jake thought. "How did your agent get away from the plane? Don't the Swiss have guards at their airports?"

"The aeroplane is pulled into a hangar for repair. The Swiss don't watch it for hours on end. They usually satisfy themselves that the repair has been started, lose interest, then nip off for a pint, something of that sort."

Jake didn't know much about the Swiss army, only that they had great knives. "Before I met up with you folks, my idea was Spain or Portugal. Switzerland sounds better. I'd like to try that."

"Thought that might suit you. I should think, then, that we'll place you aboard a pathfinder, the de Havilland Mosquito. These precede a bombing raid, mark the target with incendiaries. When that job's done, it can veer off and make its 'emergency' landing at the Zurich aerodrome."

Jesus, Jake thought, I'm going on a bomb run?

Freeborn caught his look. "We've yet to lose a pathfinder Mosquito, Mr. Weaver. They fly at 31,000 feet, where the German ack-ack can't reach them."

There's a first time for everything, Jake thought. The Mosquito was built of wood, to foil radar. He knew that. I'm going on an air raid over Nazi Germany in a wooden plane, he told himself. Valerie would love that. Her words echoed in his mind. "You'd damn well better come back to me, Jake."

Something else occurred to him. Vogel's firm was located in Zurich. Better get in and out of there fast. Wouldn't do for the phony Vogel to be unmasked on his home turf.

"I was wondering," he asked, "how you get your diplomats in and out of Switzerland. Surely not by bombers using this tactic."

"Prior to last month, we were able to send them by rail across unoccupied southern France, but since our invasion of French Algeria the Germans have seized all of Vichy France. It's a problem we're still working on . . . Anything else at the moment then, Mr. Weaver?"

"I have an American bank draft I want to convert to German currency. Can you help me get some Reichsmarks?"

Freeborn lifted his phone. "Richards, find out if foreign exchange at Barclays still have German marks, would you? . . . Oh, they do? Splendid. Make an appointment with the proper chap there for our Mr. Weaver, that's a good fellow."

Soon after that was arranged, the meeting ended. Freeborn

offered his hand and said, "Come round again tomorrow. Half ten suit you?"

"Half ten?"

"Sorry, ten-thirty I believe you say. Should have something from Bomber Command by then."

That evening, after keeping the bank appointment to collect a supply of German bills, Jake went to a pub in the Strand to eat. He found the robust atmosphere of the little place appealing. As he perched himself on a barstool, a music-hall tune clamored from a radio above the bar.

"We're going to hang out the washing on the Siegfried Line. . ."

The fare was skimpy, a cheese sandwich and chips, but the thick, tepid beer wasn't too bad. Cold would have been better.

Jake dug into the *London Times* with the curiosity he always had for local papers when he was away from home. Headlines trumpeted the Afrika Korps' retreat in Libya after Montgomery's victory at El Alamein. In fact, with the Germans bogged down at Stalingrad and Rommel's failure to take Suez, most of the stories were optimistic. Winston Churchill was quoted as saying, "This is not the end. It is not even the beginning of the end. But it is, perhaps, the end of the beginning."

"Got that right ruddy Rommel on the run, eh, mate?" an alliterative voice said. Jake turned to the man on the next stool, who'd apparently been peeking over his shoulder. His appearance—threadbare coveralls, dirty fingernails on rough hands, reddish face, salt and pepper hair—screamed working stiff, longshoreman maybe.

"Sure looks that way, friend."

"Say, you a Yank then?"

Being a Louisianan, Jake wasn't wild about being called a Yank, but what were you gonna do? "Right, I'm here on a newspaper assignment."

"Done met a few of your flying corps, but you're the first oy've seen outta uniform."

"Glad to be first at something. Jake Weaver's the name." Extending his hand.

"Bertie Bigby, motor mechanic." More alliteration. Shaking Jake's hand.

"Tell me, Mr. Bigby, what was it like around here during the Blitz?"

"None o' that Mr. Bigby now. Me mates calls me Bertie."

"Okay, Bertie, and call me Jake. The Blitz then?"

"Bloody awful, them Nazis"—he pronounced it Nazzies—"comin' over every bloody night. The explosions, the fires, the bloody shrapnel fallin' over hell an' back from our own ack-ack. People packed like sardines into the tube stations to save their ruddy necks."

"How'd you fare personally?"

"Our little flat, out in Hoxton you see, me and the missus, we was lucky. Two places hit on our street, but not ours."

"Glad to hear it." Jake took a drink of his lager, put the mug down, saw it was almost empty. "What do you think about the war now, at this point?"

"Diff'rent thing altogether. We got 'im now, bloody old Adolf. After bombin' hell out of us the way he did, chasin' us outta France, bloody U-boats killin' our lads at sea. He's about to get his, he is, and about time."

"How do you mean?"

"Couldn't take Moscow, now the Bolshies got 'im bloody well tangled up out there; gettin' his arse whipped in Africa too; our air boys bombin' his ruddy cities."

Bertie finished his beer. Jake signaled the bartender for another round.

"That's true, Bertie, things are looking up, but there's a lot of fight left in that war machine of his. Remember, he still controls most of Europe and all its resources."

"True enough, Jake, but old Adolf's bit off more'n he can chew this time. He'll bleedin' fall, him and his ruddy Nazzies."

Bigby's troubled eyes belied his words. Looked to Jake like he was trying to convince himself.

"Them seventy million Krauts won't stand for gettin' whipped on two fronts, losin' thousands of their lads like that, all for bloody nothing. They'll throw their blasted Führer out on his bloody arse, that lot will."

"And what happens then? A new government makes peace?"

"Summat like 'at."

The bartender placed fresh mugs in front of them.

"Thank you kindly, mate. Cheers."

"My pleasure, Bertie. So then, you don't believe we'll— your people and ours—eventually have to make a landing on the continent?"

Bigby seemed to sag into himself. He stared at his hands as if he'd never seen them before. At long last he said softly, "Oy was there, Jake. The Somme, Nineteen and Sixteen. Bloody lucky to come out wit' me life. You wouldn't believe the things oy saw, the things oy done. Still have bloody nightmares, oy do, after all these years. Still jump like a scared bloody kitten when one of me motorcars backfires."

He put a hand on Jake's arm. His eyes seemed to plead. "Me only boy's in the army. We don't need no bloody invasion of bloody France. Oy prays on it every bloomin' night."

Jake went to the Reuters office that night and cabled a story to the *Herald-Express*. He wrote of the high morale of the English. Their good-natured attitudes. The repairs they were making of bomb damage. Food shortages resulting in meager fare in their cafés and pubs. A plethora of bicycles and of military uniforms. Lukewarm beer. He also touched on their anxieties about fighting in mainland Europe, the black memories of their terrible losses there twenty-five years ago.

* * *

Sirens began to wail outside Jake's room as he was getting ready for bed. Couldn't be an air raid. Those had stopped, hadn't they? He went to the window, pulled back the heavy blackout curtains and raised the sash. Looking down from his perch on the fourth floor, he saw people scurrying about in the moonlight, rushing toward the subway entrance across the street.

A whistle shrilled and an angry voice shouted, "Kill that light, you bloody fool." A silver-helmeted air-raid warden down below seemed to be looking right at him. Oops. Damn! Jake ran across the room, knocked over a chair, and punched the light switch.

He remembered the notice posted on the back of the door. "In the Event of Air Raid, Walk Rapidly to the Basement Shelter, using Staircase, not the Lift." He didn't do that. As if drawn by a Lorelei, he returned to the window and gazed out. He heard the drone of airplane engines, and soon the "crumph" of distant explosions. The damned Luftwaffe was back.

Searchlights began to comb the sky with blue-silver strings of light. Ghostly barrage balloons and puffs of smoke appeared and disappeared in quick flashes as the lights probed the heavens. More explosions. Then a glow appeared off to the east. Fire.

Jake stood frozen, fascinated. Never find the stairs in the dark anyway, he rationalized. Orange and red tracer shells from groundfire soared up into the night. Reaching their apex, they burst into bright sparkles of light. Suddenly he saw a spectral twin-engine plane caught in a cone of searchlights. Bomb doors hung open beneath a long, slender fuselage. The doors swung up and closed and the plane jerked sharply to the left, escaping the tentacles of light.

More concussions thudded at his eardrums. The glow in the east grew brighter. Fire must be spreading. Shrapnel from spent ack-ack shells began to clatter down on the street and rooftops. A bitter stench of smoke and cordite permeated the air. Minutes passed and gradually the drone of engines died away. The distant thunder stopped. Eventually, the sirens sounded a long, steady, one-note tone. The all-clear.

Jake stepped back and wiped his forehead with the back of his hand. Holy Moses, he'd just witnessed a German air raid.

He'd written his story too soon. Have to write another tomorrow.

CHAPTER TWENTY

As he walked in a biting wind to his meeting with Colonel Freeborn, Jake looked for signs of fresh damage from last night's raid. Saw just a little. He felt less groggy, his body adjusting to the time difference.

London looked good to him. He'd never before considered that a landscape of stone and concrete, with few trees, could look appealing. He paused at Downing Street, an unimposing cul de sac. Number 10 stood just a few steps away. This seat of empire was guarded by exactly one middle-aged soldier wearing the British Army's inverted soupbowl tin helmet. Strange place, this England at war. Jake pictured Winston Churchill in there, chomping on a cigar, talking strategy with some field marshal.

He reached MI6 minutes later. When Colonel Freeborn waved him to a chair, Jake said, "I thought the Germans had stopped bombing London, that their bomber fleets were all in Russia."

"Oh rather, but they keep a few in France, bring them over occasionally to sting us a bit, remind us we're still the enemy. They're not big raids."

Hmm. It had seemed big enough for Jake, and certainly was for whatever unlucky Londoners lost their lives last night.

Unconcerned, Freeborn said, "Bit of a change, Mr. Weaver. Bomber Command won't risk our sending a Mosquito into Switzerland. Vice Marshal Harris is afraid the Huns might pinch it somehow. Got a bit cross with me, actually."

Jake swallowed hard. This went all the way to Bomber Harris, the stormy chief of Britain's bombing force?

"So, you'll go in one of the regular aeroplanes in the bomber stream."

"Stream?"

"Right, Bomber Command sends its planes in a long stream, not in mass formation as you Yanks do. Helps avoid collision at night, don't you see. The stream extends for miles."

Should have known that, Jake told himself.

"They've something laid on for tomorrow night," Freeborn said.

Jake cringed inside. So this was it, he was going tomorrow night, and smack dab in the middle of an air raid. Ack-ack, searchlights, night fighters, the whole nine goddamned yards.

Jake knew the Brits' Bomber Command and the U.S. Eighth Air Force, now just getting organized, hoped to bomb the hell out of Germany, maybe even effect victory without much ground fighting. Also, that the results so far were dismal. The British had tried daylight "precision" bombing with disastrous results. Their losses were so heavy they'd switched to nighttime "carpet" bombing. Pathfinder planes ignited fires in a German city, then the main bomber force followed and indiscriminately pounded the place. Jake could see no difference between that and the Nazis' much-scorned Blitz of London. The problem was, if the pathfinders missed, so did everyone else. He knew these raids had achieved virtually no disruption of German arms production. Maybe they would, eventually. Maybe.

Freeborn handed him his new identity card and passport. The Swiss coat of arms, a white cross inside a red shield, was embossed on the cover of the passport.

He flipped through it, saw his picture, familiar and yet not, with that new hair style. Blotchy entry and exit stamps from various European nations, in black and purple ink, smirched several pages. "Some of our best work," Freeborn said, "even down to the actual paper stock used by the Swiss."

Yeah, these people were thorough. No wonder they'd built such an empire, tottering though it might be at the moment.

The printed name, Hans-Karl Vogel, though no surprise, still jarred him. He'd have to get used to being that man. He turned to the identity card. It bore a slightly different face shot, also from yesterday's photo session.

"The bomber," Freeborn was saying, "will be pulled into a hangar—one of ours, by the way—BOAC. When the Swiss guards leave, or if they fail to inspect in the first place, simply walk off and take a taxi to the *Bahnhof*, the railway station. Take a seat on the third bench back from the ticket window. A man will approach and ask, in German, 'Do you have the time, my good man?' He'll say exactly that."

Jake got out his notebook, at which Freeborn's brows arched into black checkmarks. "Don't worry, I'll memorize this tonight and burn the paper."

"Splendid. At this point then, you glance up at the big clock and respond exactly, 'The clock here is wrong?' Do you have that?"

"The clock here is wrong?"

"Just so. This will be Mid-Wicket, one of our agents. He'll take care of you."

"Mid-Wicket?"

"It's a cricket position. We never use these chaps' real names."

"Okay, fine, I'm in Zurich and I find Sticky Wicket"—which Freeborn didn't find funny. "Now, you had some notions on getting me out of Germany?"

"Just coming to that." Freeborn consulted a notecard. "We suggest going by train back to the Swiss border. Simplest all round. But if you should have an emergency in Berlin, go to Number 84 *Marburgstrasse* in the Schöneberg district. A woman, quite striking but for a broken nose, will answer the bell-push. Tell her, again in German of course, 'Excuse me, I am looking for the *Volkspark*. Can you direct me?' Use exactly those words. Do this at precisely 3 p.m.

Central European Time, on any day except a Sunday. She will answer, 'The one on *Lessingstrasse*?' and show you in. Have you got that?"

Jake looked up from his notebook. "Yep, *Lessingstrasse*. And she is?"

"Tapestry, again one of ours. Tapestry is German and was over here spying for the *Abwehr* when the war began. We turned her. She wasn't fully cooperative at first, but when her husband, a flier, was killed in the air battles here in the summer of '40, she grew more enthusiastic. She's become most reliable and is quite anti-Nazi."

"Okay, I've got all that. Mid-Wicket, big clock, Tapestry with the bad nose, 3 p.m. except on Sunday."

Freeborn said he would have Jake's clothing pressed and waiting for him. "Right then, do destroy those notes, won't you? And give us a hand with that rocket if you can. Oh, we'll post the letter to Frau Vogel tomorrow, saying you've been delayed. And that should about do it, I think. Be here at half eight in the morning. We'll see that you're motored up to Dalton."

"Dalton?"

"Right, RAF Station Dalton, a bomber field in Yorkshire. Bit of a drive for you." Freeborn stood. "Good luck, Mr. Weaver. His majesty's government wish you all the best." They shook hands. "Cheerio then."

Wearing Vogel's clothing, Jake went to St. James's Library that afternoon and read everything he could find on rockets and their components, anything that Schätzen Products' Hans-Karl Vogel could talk about with Wernher von Braun.

Later, he wrote a letter to Valerie and a shorter one to Harry Hopkins. He told his fiancée that things were going well, that the British were cooperating. That he loved her and missed her. That he was glad he'd soon be her husband.

He considered asking her to call Charlie Root and tell the Hollywood Stars' manager that he'd keep his promise to be at opening day in April, but thought better of it. Root knew nothing about all this and would wonder why he wasn't calling himself.

To Hopkins he merely wrote, "The British have been more than helpful. Thanks for smoothing the way for me here. I'm off soon." Then, in a moment of whimsy, he added, "I shall return." *And not in a pine box, I hope.*

Jake walked to the embassy for a last meeting with the State Department guy. He gave the letters to Ballard and asked him to put them in the diplomatic pouch to Washington. "This personal letter to L.A.—they can mail it for me, I assume."

"Of course. They do it all the time for our staff."

"Well, thanks for everything, Mr. Ballard. I don't know if I'll be seeing you again." He shook the man's pudgy hand.

"It's been my pleasure, Mr. Weaver. Best of luck now."

In the day's fading light, Jake left the embassy and took the Underground to Westminster Station. He strolled past the damaged Houses of Parliament, stepped out onto Westminster Bridge and crossed the Thames, busy beneath him with barges and other boat traffic.

He sat on a bench on the south embankment and gazed at the great city. Just visible as dusk descended, the Union Jack fluttered unsubdued on several rooftops, a scene probably centuries old. This likely would be the last night he'd ever spend here. He thought about Valerie and how far he was from home and friends. He closed his eyes for a bit and then Big Ben began bonging out the time. One by one, five sublime, melodic peals washed through the gathering darkness, then echoed richly for a moment on the cold air as if they too were reluctant to leave.

CHAPTER TWENTY-ONE

He rode to Yorkshire with three young airmen in a drab gray Range Rover. One of them drove and all of them smoked and bitched about the ruddy this and bloody that. Mile after mile on mostly narrow roads, they passed fields of cows and sheep, hedge rows, bundled-up locals on bicycles, a few small towns and villages.

Five hours after leaving London, they finally pulled into Dalton, a rough, sprawling air base not unlike the one at Goose Bay, Labrador. The sentry at the gate checked the airmen's IDs, confirmed that Jake was the Mr. Weaver he expected, wrote something on his clipboard, and waved them through.

After the long drive, Jake thought getting out to stretch was almost as good as sex. To him, the frosty wind sweeping off the North Sea was sweet as a kiss after that smoke-filled old Rover. How about that? He was getting used to England's winter weather.

A long column of four-engine bombers lined the far side of the field. Avro Lancasters, Jake thought, noting their twin tails. Several service trucks were there, and mechanics bustled about, fussing with engines, cowlings, ailerons and machine guns.

A pink-cheeked young officer trotted up. "Hello there, I'm Flight Lieutenant Maxwell, Number 420 Squadron. You must be the important Yank."

"Yank yes, important no," Jake said, grinning and holding onto his hat the way he'd done in the Chicago winds a week ago. And what a week it had been.

"I'm the pilot of *O for Oliver*," the youth said, "best old Hallie in the whole bomb wing."

"Hallie?"

"Right, the Halifax, that's what you're looking at over there, Handley-Page Halifax heavy bombers." Jake was thus enlightened about his next mode of transportation. *So much for Lancasters, you brilliant military writer.*

Maxwell shook hands, picked up Jake's satchel and gestured toward one of the huts. "I'm to take you in tow. Come on then, this way."

The kid looked like he could be a junior at Catholic High in Baton Rouge."Mind if I ask how old you are, Lieutenant?"

"Twenty-two when I flew my first mission in April." Maxwell winked and added, "About thirty now."

"Yeah, I guess all this would age you in a hurry. How many missions you have now, Lieutenant?"

"Max. Call me Max, sir. Tonight's will be our twenty-fourth sortie in old *Oliver*. I'm to see that you get a good meal, well, a meal at least, attend our briefing if you like, and have yourself a little kip."

"Kip?"

"Spot of sleep. Nap, I believe you say."

"Thanks for the translation . . . So . . . you know where I'm supposed to be going tonight?"

"Oh yes, we're to deliver you"—Maxwell looked around, then lowered his voice—"to Zurich. You're the important American, ah, spy, might as well say it. No sense beating round the bush, eh?"

"Spy yes, important no."

"Ha. All you Yanks are important to us, help us beat the Jerries a bit faster, now you're on board."

"I hope it works out that way, Max."

"Our crew were chosen, as we've done this once before. I'm familiar with the field at Zurich, the landing patterns and all that.

You'll love *O for Oliver."*

"How do you find that field at night? Do you follow a radio beam or something?"

"No, it's all visual. Navigator gets us close, then we look for their beacon, alternating green and white light. Only bright beacon in that part of Switzerland." He stopped and looked Jake in the eye. "Only my crew know about this. At the briefing, should you care to sit in, you'll just be an American observer, no other explanations."

"Fine, and yes, I want to be there."

"Splendid. Ready for a spot of lunch then?"

"You bet." Jake was famished.

Feeling full if not satisfied after a meal of boiled ham, potatoes and cabbage, Jake walked with Maxwell to a Nissen hut of corrugated steel. He was introduced to the rest of *O for Oliver*'s crew, the flight sergeant navigator, bomb-aimer, flight engineer, wireless operator, mid-upper gunner and rear gunner. They were small men and young, some of them still teenagers. All but one shook hands cheerfully. That one, the rear gunner, displayed a small grimace and walked off. Doesn't like the idea of taking me to Switzerland, Jake told himself. Can't say I blame him.

Walmsley, the wireless operator, said, "You'll be squeezed in next to me, sir. Be ruddy cramped in there, but I'm sure we'll manage."

"Let's go then, lads," Maxwell said. "Getting on to briefing time."

Rows of wooden folding chairs faced a curtained wall in a large smoky auditorium. An officer holding a long pointer stood on a platform in front of it. Jake settled in with the rest of the crew, about halfway back, beneath a low ceiling with exposed wood beams and hanging lights. Maxwell took out a pack of Woodbine cigarettes, offered one to Jake, who shook his head, no, then lit one for himself.

"Right, all here then?" the briefing officer said. He nodded to a sergeant at the side of the platform, who pulled a drawstring and opened the curtains to reveal a huge map of western Europe.

"Gentlemen, this will be a long one," the officer said. "Your target tonight is Stuttgart." He pointed to the city in southwest Germany. "Heavy industry there, armaments works, machine-tool and aircraft engine factories. Normal easterly departure over the North Sea, usual rendezvous and assembly areas. Cross the Dutch coast here, near Leeuwarden." He pointed to the map, where red tape marked their route. "Try to get you in there just beyond the worst of the enemy's coastal flak belt. Once past that, you'll turn south-southeast on a heading of one-six-zero. Avoid the flak concentrations at Essen and Mannheim"—pointing again—"then buzz on to Stuttgart. Reach the target approximately two a.m., Central European Time. The pathfinder squadron should have a good bonfire going for you. Tonight's flare markers will be yellow."

"The colors change each time," Maxwell whispered to Jake.

"Make your bomb run at 19,000," the officer continued, "drop your eggs, turn west by northwest and run like hell for home over France and Belgium." Not us, Jake thought, exchanging a look with Maxwell.

The officer went on for several minutes, giving details Jake couldn't follow. B flight, C flight, battle order. Looking around, he saw pilots and navigators taking notes or consulting their own charts.

"Bomber Command has another attack on for tonight," the guy was saying, "to Hannover. Should keep some of the night fighters away from you."

"Oh sure," someone snorted.

"Now to the weather. Looks a bit off but acceptable. Here's our meteorologist." The officer stepped aside and a thin, bespectacled man took his place.

"Low pressure forming over the Alps, I'm afraid." He pointed. "Chance of snow in the target area by morning but you should be okay, get in and out well ahead of it. Southeast winds over the target.

Expect some thin altocumulus over target as well, at about 12,000 feet, nothing much to worry about. Should see the fires clearly. The winds associated with the approaching front should give you some tail push going home, perhaps get you back a bit early."

Next to Jake, the navigator whispered, "Right, but bloody head winds going in, the silly burke. No picnic, this."

"Any questions, gentlemen?" the meteorologist asked.

There were several. Moon, wind speed, icing conditions.

"Waxing moon, bit more than a quarter full."

"Great for the Kraut night fighters," the flight engineer muttered. "Bloody bad for this lot."

"Low in the west when you hit the coast, but down well before you reach target."

"A bit better, that," the flight engineer admitted.

When the questions finished, the briefing officer returned and said, "That's it then. One hundred-twenty-two planes tonight." Jake knew the Brits' much-ballyhooed thousand-plane raids were rare, most attacks being smaller. "Takeoff commences at twenty-one hundred. Good hunting, lads."

As the room emptied, Jake went to the huge map, checked the scale of miles, and figured that Stuttgart was about a hundred and forty miles from Zurich, flyable in less than an hour.

Leaving the hall, he saw ground crews wheeling bomb trolleys toward the flight line. Women drove most of the tractors. They towed carriages loaded with dark green cylinders, tiny propellers on their snouts and sharp tail fins on their backsides. Death warrants for a lot of Germans. Across the way, opened bomb bays beneath the planes waited for them like the mouths of hungry sharks.

Maxwell led Jake into a Nissen hut and showed him to a small walled-off bedroom. His satchel stood beside the bed. It was 4:40.

Jake asked about the German night fighters. "It's what they call their *Himmelbett* system," the young pilot said. "Rather new development. They've outfitted some Ju88 squadrons with their new

Liechtenstein airborne radar, with forward antennae mounted in the nose. Ground controllers guide them close enough to our stream for the 88's to pick us up on their own radar. Nasty business, but fortunately they've only just begun putting it into effect. We've encountered just a few so far."

Lips pursed, Jake slowly shook his head.

"Meanwhile, our science boys are working on ways to jam that radar. They'll come up with something. Nothing to worry about, sir. I'll leave you now; get a couple hours of shuteye if you can. I'll rouse you in plenty of time, catch a sandwich, show you how to get into your flight suit, all that."

"Flight suit?"

"Oh yes, fur lining, quite necessary. Bloody cold up there. You can change back again on board once we're in the hangar in Switzerland."

Jake knew it would be tough to change in the confined space on the plane. "Could I just wear it over my clothes?"

"Be bulky as hell, sir, but keep you warmer at that. I'll see if I can scrounge one large enough to do the job."

Maxwell left. Jake took off his shoes, stripped down to his underwear, and plopped onto the bed. Battling all kinds of unwelcome thoughts, he tried to fall asleep.

He woke with a start. He'd had some bad dreams, but couldn't remember them, just knew they'd been bad.

He got up and dressed, then slipped his German rail timetable and the forged passport and identity card into the inside pocket of his jacket. He stuck Vogel's billfold, containing the Swiss driver's license and a supply of Reichsmarks, in a pants pocket. He also had a few Swiss francs.

Satisfied that he'd memorized everything—the addresses, the words he was to say to Mid-Wicket and Tapestry, his notes on rockets—he tore the papers into tiny bits. Then he flushed them down the toilet. It took three flushes to do the job. "Damn British plumbing," he muttered.

Maxwell had found a flight suit big enough to fit over Jake's clothes. Soon, in a large locker room, the pilot helped him squeeze into it. Jake had been fumbling with the various buckles and straps. Once the suit was on, he felt he weighed a ton, a very warm ton. As he moved about like a drunk penguin, Walmsley, the wireless operator, laughed. Valerie would laugh, too, he thought.

Maxwell handed him some fur-lined flight boots. "You'll have to wear these, sir, otherwise your feet will freeze. Hope these will fit. Have to pack your shoes, I'm afraid."

The rear gunner, the boy who'd been unfriendly when introduced, flashed him a hostile scowl. Jake took him aside. "You have a problem with me, pal?"

"Too bloody right I do, mate. These missions are too flipping dangerous without you lot putting the touch on us for a lift to ruddy Switzerland. Just ducky, have to spend a day with them cheese mongers, then fly home all alone."

Yeah, not being accompanied by friendly planes would be frightening in enemy air space, but Jake didn't like this twerp talking to him like that.

"'Cause of you we're carrying one less 250-pounder."

"The damn thing," Jake said, "might not have gone off anyway. The RAF gets lots of duds. Fifteen percent of your bombs never explode."

"Get stuffed, mate. You're a dud yourself, so why don't we just drop you out, good an' proper, 'long with them others."

Jake held up his hands, palms outward. "Look chum—"

"Button it up, Jigger," Maxwell snapped, approaching with a parachute in his hands. "Take your animosity out on the Jerries, eh? Now shake Mr. Weaver's hand."

The gunner hesitated, then lowered his eyes, gave Jake a limp handshake, and skulked off.

"Don't mind the sergeant rear gunner," Maxwell said. "Jigger's fairly new to this crew, bit of a problem. Doesn't know a jot about tact. I'd transfer him out, but the squadron's short of experienced men just now. Before we got him, his plane took some hits and he was wounded. Still has a piece of shrapnel in his leg. He rides all alone in the rear, tough job you know." Maxwell's face paled slightly. "It's nerves, Mr. Weaver. We're all afraid, he just shows it more," an admission that did nothing for Jake's morale.

Quickly self-assured again, Maxwell said, "Now then, let me tell you about *O for Oliver.* Four lovely Rolls-Royce Merlin engines. Cruises at 240 miles per, can push up to 270 in a pinch. Ollie's a reliable old bird. We'll be fine tonight."

"Thanks, Max. I really am sorry for the trouble I'm putting you all through."

"Don't give it a thought. Now then, this is your parachute. I'll show you how to fasten it on, though you don't wear it on board. Just keep it close to hand." After showing Jake how to use the parachute clips, he handed him a chocolate bar. "A little nosh for later," he said. Then, in a louder voice, "Off to the lorry, lads. Time to saddle up."

They filed out into the cold night, toward trucks waiting to take them to the flight line, Jake waddling along carrying his satchel and parachute. Somewhere out there in the dark was a machine which, piloted by a man fifteen years his junior, admittedly scared, was about to take him to Nazi Germany. Venus shone brightly in the western sky.

"God save the King and our ruddy crew," the wireless operator said.

CHAPTER TWENTY-TWO

O *for Oliver* spent half an hour climbing, circling, jitterbugging about in the black sky to join up with other Halifaxes, visible only by small blue lights on their tails. At last the bomber stream that would stretch for miles as it approached the continent of Europe was assembled. It seemed a miracle to Jake that all these explosive-laden planes avoided disastrous collision while forming up in the dark.

Most of the crew were packed close together in the front of the cold, quivering plane. The flight engineer—Americans would say copilot—sat beside Maxwell at the controls. The navigator squeezed in behind them, his charts, slide rule, protractor, ruler and other paraphernalia spread out before him on a fold-down tray. A tiny amber light illuminated them. This, plus a faint glow from the instrument panel in front of Maxwell, formed the only visible bits of light.

Behind the navigator, Jake had crouched beside the wireless operator as instructed. Crouched as best he could, that is, with all the bulk he wore, his parachute and satchel wedged beside him. In front of the pilots, the bomb-aimer's head made a faint silhouette behind his plexiglass bubble. The mid-upper gunner perched above and just behind Jake while Jigger, the cranky rear gunner, sat far in the back, quite invisible.

Jake could see little except the ghostly backs of the heads in front of him, and the occasional bright star through the nose glass. Finding their way through this ink-black sky seemed another miracle. Maxwell had sure been right about the cold. It was attacking Jake's every neuron.

A buzzing sound crackled in his headset, then Maxwell's voice said, "Go to oxy, lads. Climbing to 21,000 now."

Walmsley showed Jake how to clamp his oxygen mask to his face, and he began to inhale sour, rubbery-tasting oxygen. Made him a bit giddy at first, but soon the rich stuff made his breathing easier.

The strong purring of the Merlin engines reassured him. On takeoff, Jake had liked the throaty baritone of these Rolls-Royce engines, similar to the sound made by the Porsche Uncle Dieter had driven. More pleasing to the ear than the growl of a B-17's Pratt & Whitneys.

Some time later, the intercom crackled to life again, startling him. He'd been dozing a bit. How much time had passed?

"Lights up ahead," Maxwell said. "Getting close to the coastal flak belt. On your toes, lads." Jake snapped alert.

"Permission to test guns?"

"Right, go ahead."

Jake heard a whirring sound as the turrets powered up and rotated, then a brief clatter as the Browning .303 machine guns fired. A few shell casings dropped down on his left shoulder, surprising him. They came from the mid-upper gunner, his feet dangling just above Jake's head.

Through the bomb-aimer's glass blister, he saw far-off searchlights panning the sky and, silhouetted against them, several bombers in a crooked but forward-moving line like a connect-the-dots game. He also saw what looked like a tiny fireworks show in the distance. He knew what that was, and it was slowly growing larger. He hoped the briefing officer was right about their being able to slip around the worst of the flak.

The searchlights slowly drew closer, their blue-white fingers windshield-wiping the sky as if saying, "We'll find you, we'll find you, we'll find you."

Dreadful minutes passed. Through the forward glass, he began to see what looked like orange and red blobs floating lazily upward. When each one stopped, it hung in the sky for a second, then burst in a dazzling sparkle of crimson, orange and yellow. Christmas trees of hell.

Soon Maxwell said, "The flak is not as thick as it looks, Mr. Weaver. They're not able to shoot up this whole big sky." An unpleasant grunt answered that. Must be the rear gunner. Shut up, Sergeant, Jake thought.

Then they were in it. The bomber began to bounce. Jake heard the thud of explosions and felt them, too, vibrating through the plane's thin aluminum skin. He hadn't prayed much since that Japanese battleship attack on Guadalcanal, but he found himself doing it again. "If you're up there, God, please watch over this crew. They're good people . . . but I guess you know that."

Walmsley lowered his oxygen mask for a moment and gave him a wink and a grin. Jake, wearing heavy gloves, answered with a thumbs-up. A twenty-year-old encouraging a man almost old enough to be his father. Yeah, these were good people.

A bright flash. Thunderous boom. The plane shuddered, cockpit snow-blind bright for an instant. Fliers' heads frozen in that flash of light. The plane jerked wildly, as if kicked by some giant mythical horse, throwing Jake against one of the metal ribs of the fuselage. He sat there stunned.

How could they possibly survive this, the heavens convulsing in an Armageddon of explosions? He never should have come. He was going to die. "I'm sorry, Valerie," he whispered.

But the plane soon straightened out, the intercom buzzed, and Maxwell's tinny voice returned. "A close one that time, gentlemen, but we're okay. Almost past this lot now. Old Oliver took us through worse last time, actually."

The blasts and flashes tapered off and eventually stopped altogether. Again Jake heard only the reassuring resonance of those Rolls-Royce engines, purring along flawlessly as far as he could tell.

That's four, he told himself. Got five lives left, have I?

He felt the plane turn toward the right, no doubt heading south-southeast as he recalled from the briefing.

Maxwell came back on, saying, "We'll be over the old Fatherland in about ten minutes. Everybody look alive now. The night fighters will be up soon." So much for feeling reassured.

These are brave boys, Jake told himself, going through all this several times a month. He doubted that he could do it. In fact, he was giving thought to backing out, quitting altogether. He could just tell Maxwell to forget about Switzerland and stay in the bomber stream all the way home.

But no, at this point it would take more guts to do that than to go ahead. How could he explain to Harry Hopkins, President Roosevelt, Colonel Freeborn? And he would humiliate himself in the eyes of this crew, convince these Limeys that their allies across the Atlantic were soft and gutless. Only Valerie would be pleased, but even that would be hollow—she might always wonder about his courage in other situations yet to come. No, he couldn't chicken out now.

The plane droned onward. Over the intercom, the navigator gave Maxwell occasional course corrections as they doglegged around the heavy flak concentrations in the industrialized Ruhr.

The only time Jake had come to this country before had been on the German ocean liner *Cap Arcona* in 1930, New York to Hamburg, five days. Little different travel arrangements this time.

Now he couldn't make out a single star through the bomb-aimer's glass. Must be cloudy out there. How much longer to Stuttgart, he wondered, when the navigator called out, "Forty-five minutes to target, Flight Lieutenant. Right on course."

Soon turbulence began to jolt the plane and Maxwell said, "Getting some rough head winds, lads. That snowstorm may be approaching faster than expected."

"Bloody met man," someone griped. "Never gets it effing right."

Oh great, Jake told himself. How can we land in Switzerland in a snowstorm? Maybe the bomb run would be called off. What then? Would they jettison their bombs on some dairy farm or a vineyard and head for home? With him still on board?

"NIGHT FIGHTER," the rear gunner screamed. "Bloody night fighter, seven o'clock." The plane dived and Jake's stomach stayed behind. "Firing on *G for George* right behind us." The turrets buzzed as the gunners switched on their power.

The plane corkscrewed right, left, down, and up, like riding huge swells in a storm at sea, Maxwell not giving the enemy an easy target. Jake heard the staccato slap of machine-gun fire over the engines' screams of protest.

Now a rattle of gunfire sounded *inside* the plane. Chunks of metal popped down on Jake's shoulder. They'd been hit. No, wait, these were shell casings from the mid-upper gunner as he fired a burst at the German.

"He's gone past," the rear gunner yelled. "Shot the bloody hell out of old *George*'s right wing. Two motors on fire. They're starting to jump."

"They all getting out?" Maxwell urged.

"Saw three, maybe four. Can't see now, too flipping dark. Can't see nothing. Plane fell off right fast."

"Pray God they all made it," Maxwell said. "Poor blokes, their address will be Stalag Something or Other starting tomorrow."

"Must've been one of the good Krauts," the navigator said. "He only fired on the motors."

A different voice volunteered, "A lot of these bloody bastards shoot up the fuselage, Mr. Weaver, try to murder us all."

"I hope those guys are somewhere else tonight," Jake replied.

"Amen to that, sir."

Several minutes crawled by with no further attacks. Maybe the briefing officer had been right, that the RAF raid on Hannover was drawing most of the night fighters.

Jake thought about the young men who'd jumped into the blackness from their unlucky plane. He hoped they all got out, hoped they'd be rounded up quickly by people in uniform. He'd heard grisly tales of downed fliers murdered in rage by civilians who'd been through too much bombing. Airmen carried pistols. German farmers had rifles, shotguns and pitchforks.

In the dim light from the navigator's table, he noticed three or four small round stains on the left arm of his flight suit. He hadn't seen those before. The suit had been clean when he'd put it on. Like a fat raindrop, another one suddenly appeared. *Jesus*. The mid-upper gunner—Jake had forgotten his name—was bleeding.

"Upper gunner," he called. "Can you hear me?" No answer.

"Mr. Weaver, what—"

"He's been hit, Max. He's bleeding."

"Pull him down out of there, Mr. Weaver."

"Okay."

Jake got up on his knees and reached. The gunner was slumped back, his head lolling against the plexiglass. In the bad light, Jake thought he saw a jagged hole in that glass. He got his hands on the boy's thighs and tried to pull him off his perch, a small iron saucer like a tractor seat. He didn't budge. *Oh, strapped in.*

"You getting him down, Mr. Weaver?"

"Working on it." His gloved hands groping awkwardly, he finally found the harness clasp and yanked it open. The gunner plopped heavily down into Jake's arms and the two of them fell into a clumsy tangle. Almost face to face, he saw a gash in the boy's leather flight cap, slick with blood.

"He's down now, Max."

"Good. Walmsley, take over. Grab the med kit, see what you can do."

"Right, Lieutenant."

"Mr. Weaver, we need that space you're in. Go up and take over Archie's gun position."

Jake unplugged his intercom connection, tugged himself up and wriggled his fanny onto the little iron seat. He'd been right, the plexiglass bore a sharp hole, icy air whistling loudly into the turret. Resting one hand on the butt of the machine gun, he groped around till he found the gunner's intercom plug, which had pulled loose when he was yanked down. Jake plugged himself into the middle of a busy dialogue. "Give him a hand, navigator."

"Right."

"Got a cut on his forehead. I'll hold a plaster against it. May be concussion."

"See if you can revive him," Maxwell said. "We've some smelling salts in the med kit. Alternate those with oxygen. Don't let him want for oxy very long."

"Right, sir."

Jake fingered his own oxygen, glad to find it still in place, the bottle hanging at his throat.

"Mr. Weaver, you're our mid-upper gunner. If we're attacked again I'll power up your turret from here. Can you fire that gun?"

"I think so. The firing lever's practically in my lap."

"Good. If it comes to that, lead the fighter. Don't fire at him, fire ahead of him."

"Okay. There's a bullet hole in the glass up here. The night fighter hit us at least once."

"Could have been one of *George*'s gunners, you never know. Lot of stuff flying around up here. We'll tape up that hole when we land. Afraid you'll have to put up with it for now."

Well, Jake told himself, I'm an RAF gunner, something new for my resumé. He suddenly remembered that his parachute was down below somewhere, maybe underneath the wounded gunner. *Jesus Christ and General Jackson.*

"Archie's awake, sir, and the bleeding's almost stopped."

"Fine. Put some antiseptic on that gash and bandage it up. We'll get him to a doctor in Switzerland."

"Six minutes to target, Lieutenant. How's the weather?"

"No worse. Lot of cloud cover, but I think we'll be able to see the glow through the clouds. Those magnesium markers burn awfully bright. Ready then, Sheffie?" Apparently addressing the bomb-aimer.

"Ready, sir."

So these young men, following orders of older, wiser men, were about to drop tons of high explosives through a layer of cloud with no aiming point but a murky glow of light three miles below them. How could they hope to hit the munitions plants that were supposed to be their targets? Maybe they couldn't even hit Stuttgart at all. Maybe that glow down there was Würzburg or Heidelberg, or a bonfire out in a potato field.

Was this the meticulous, scientific warfare of the 20th century so many had written about? That he himself had written about? Orville Wright, look what they've gone and done with your sublime invention.

"One good thing about the clouds," Maxwell said. "Searchlights can't find us. Okay then, going to bombing altitude, 19,000." Jake felt the plane drop a bit.

"There, I see the glow, sir."

"Tally ho, then. It's your aeroplane, Sheffie."

"Starboard, sir, a bit starboard . . . more, more starboard . . . hold it, that's fine. Steady now." From his perch, Jake couldn't see the bomb-aimer, but he pictured him leaning down and peering into his Blackett bombsight.

Jake saw a frightening spectacle, those lazy streaks of light climbing again, swimming through the cloud layer, hanging, then erupting into brilliant, multicolored starbursts. The flak seemed to burst at exactly this altitude. Concussions began to vibrate through *O for Oliver*'s outer skin. The plane started bouncing like a kid playing jump rope, but still somehow managed to plow on through that lethal sky.

"Twenty seconds," called the bomb-aimer. "A bit port, sir, just a touch . . . fine, that's it. Bomb doors open." Even colder air whistled into the plane. Despite wearing an oxygen mask, the tart taste of smoke and cordite hit Jake's nostrils and mouth. Same thing he'd smelled on Guadalcanal, where it had meant death and fear and craziness. Meant the same thing here.

"Five, four, three, two . . . ordnance away."

The plane lurched upward as two tons of weight fell away. The bomb doors swung up and closed with a thump. Brilliant explosions continued to burst about the plane. It skipped and jumped even crazier. Jake braced himself against the gun mount. With the bomb bay closed, he was soon breathing cleaner air.

"Mr. Weaver," Maxwell called, "the explosions and fire down there create a vortex of heat, a whole new weather pattern. We're riding that heat squall now. It's quite normal."

"Uh huh," Jake managed. Sudden heat meeting snow clouds meant what, thunderstorms?

A moment later, the plane turned to the left. They'd attacked from the northeast, so this must be south, heading for Switzerland. Leaving the bomber stream had to be a tricky maneuver, the danger of midair collision great. His muscles tensed, stretched tight like the skin on a kettledrum. He saw a couple of dark, winged shapes streak past at a sharp angle.

Before long, the flight grew less turbulent and the flashes of light disappeared.

How many old men and women and kids were dead or maimed back there? Doctors, teachers, dance performers?—he recalled that Stuttgart had a renowned ballet company—all because these people had let a mad clown named Hitler seize control of their country.

Well, that's five lives, or is it six? Jake had lost count, had no idea how many he might have left.

He was glad nothing bad had happened crossing the bomber stream.

That luck didn't hold.

The flight engineer's voice buzzed onto the intercom. "Number two motor's doing a bunk, Max. Running all out of sync, RPM's down. Oil pressure's off."

"Sort it out, Lenny. Fix it."

"Trying, Max. Fuel mix buggered, carburetor possibly icing."

"Lenny, we've got to synchronize the Merlins. It's vital." Desperation in Maxwell's voice. Jake remembered him saying, 'We're all afraid.'

O for Oliver was shaking again. The engines no longer sounded like Uncle Dieter's smooth Porsche, more like a ratty old Chevy with a blown muffler.

"Weather's going all to hell too," Maxwell said. "That sodding snowstorm's found us."

Despair shrouded Jake. Now that they had a real reason to land there, Zurich might be impossible to find. How could they ever see its flashing beacon?

He fought the urge to ask Maxwell what he was going to do. Obviously the pilot was trying to work that out right now.

For the next several minutes Maxwell and the flight engineer were the only ones who spoke, trying everything they knew to solve the problem. Jake pictured them, ghostly in the light of the instrument panel, pivoting and nodding as they manned the controls and discussed their options like surgeons over an operating table.

A tight fist of tension settled over the rest of the crew. Jake felt it like a physical reality, like the plaintive wail of a blues saxophone at a bayou funeral. This plane was in trouble and everyone knew it.

CHAPTER TWENTY-THREE

"Okay, bugger this, I'm shutting it down," Maxwell said at last. "Best thing all around. Three motors pulling together will drive us better without a fourth trying to shake the bloody wing off." Soon the ratty old Chevy became a Porsche again, but singing an octave lower, like going uphill. "How's the fuel?"

"More than half remaining, skipper. We can make it home. Tail winds will help. If we can't make base, we can surely reach a field in East Sussex."

"Right, but we may not be able to keep altitude. I'm not keen on flying low and slow over occupied France, lot of enemy guns there. Maybe Gibraltar?"

"No sir. Too far and against head winds. We'd never make Gib."

"You're right, of course you're right. But I don't want to risk going down in France."

A thought bolted into Jake's mind. *We're somewhere over southwest Germany, and I'm just extra weight. These boys would have a better chance without me.* He sometimes got a rush of unreasoned brilliance like this, often resulting in his biggest scoops.

He thought about his parachute, down below somewhere. "Maybe I'll just bail out, Max," he offered recklessly. *What am I thinking! What am I saying?*

"And lose my mid-upper gunner? No, Mr. Weaver . . . Gordon, get us to Switzerland."

"Please, Max," Jake protested. "Don't do that."

"Mr. Weaver, you're needed here. I'm not doing this for you, I'm doing it for Archie. He needs a doctor."

Jake respected that—this young man was a good commander. The rear gunner interrupted the thought. "You bloody daft?"

"Shut it, Sergeant Gunner, or I'll have you on report. I'll not limp this aeroplane across three-hundred miles of enemy territory on three motors with a casualty on board. Navigator, Switzerland!"

"Yes, sir. Take a heading of, ah, one-niner-five then. Forty minutes or so."

"Thank you, Gordon." Calmly now. "Here's the plan, lads. We'll go to Switzerland, circle for awhile and search for clear air. This storm has to blow past to the north. We'll stay over the Swiss plateau this side of the Alps. Nights are long now, but we'll see first light before long. We'll find Zurich or some other field"—his most reassuring voice now—"and have us all a nice rich Swiss breakfast."

"Bloody hell."

"Sergeant Gunner, not one more word."

Except for the drone of the engines, silence descended over the plane.

After awhile, the navigator said, "Over Switzerland, sir. I make us close to Zurich."

"Thank you, Gordon. Still bad visibility. Can't see a ruddy thing down there. We'll keep at 18,000 ... if we can. Wouldn't want to tangle with the Eiger or Matterhorn, eh?"

The wireless operator touched Jake's foot. When he looked down, Walmsley lowered his oxygen mask and gave him a reassuring grin. Jake made the "V for Victory" sign with his first two gloved fingers.

"How's Archie?" Maxwell asked.

"Bloody groggy, sir, but conscious."

"Good, try to give him some water."

Jake thought about his contact, Mid-Wicket, and the big clock at the Zurich railway station. *Probably have to stand you up on this one, fella. Hope you don't wait there all night.*

A couple of tense hours later he felt the plane slow down and begin to descend. Pressure popped in his ears and he removed his oxygen mask. "Landing gear down," Maxwell was saying. "Flaps down. That snow doesn't look to be very deep. Let's hope whatever's beneath it is firm."

The pitch of the engines changed and the wheels bumped into position. Through his glass canopy, Jake saw what looked like a white pasture rising up to meet them. Where the devil were they? The plane thudded and bounced a couple of times, then reeled into a skid. Maxwell fought the yoke but the slide worsened. A roostertail of white powder showered across the plexiglass. Then, with a vertigo-inducing spin, metal groaning in protest, the plane skidded completely around facing the other way—and stopped.

Jake's head had smashed hard against the glass, pushing out the breath he'd been holding. Now in the dim light of early dawn he could make out a large wooden shed with a steep, snow-covered roof. This was some little country airport—couldn't be Zurich. He also spotted a billowing flag, a white cross on a field of red.

"Any of you chaps know how to yodel?" Maxwell said. The pilot shut down the engines. Soon Jake heard the hatch swing open. Cold air flooded in. "Here comes some bloke on a tractor," Maxwell said. "Hope he speaks English. Best stay put, Mr. Weaver."

Maxwell hopped down and Jake saw the word OLTEN in white block letters on the side of the building. Olten was a town near Basel, wasn't it? Jake had been studying maps of Switzerland and Germany the last few nights.

He rubbed the knot forming on his head, then slipped down from the turret and squeezed past Walmsley and his patient. Moving close to the open hatch, he found that Maxwell and the Swiss were having trouble communicating.

"What do you want here, *Englander*?" the man demanded in Swiss German, his breath blowing steam with each word. "You do not belong here."

"Sorry, no *spreche* the *Deutsch*. We need a doctor and have to work on one of our motors." Maxwell pointed to the number two engine. "Motor *kaput* and we have an injured man. Do you understand?"

Jake had to help. He got himself to the open hatch. In his flight suit, he looked like one of the crew, so he showed himself to the man on the tractor, who wore a ski cap, thick woolen sweater and heavy gloves. The tractor had a snow scoop mounted in front. "We are sorry to inconvenience you," Jake called in German. "This is an emergency. We have a wounded man in need of medical care. Our presence here is legal under the Geneva Convention."

Maxwell gaped at Jake in surprise.

"*Ach so?*" Ski Cap said.

"We also need to fix one of our engines," Jake continued. "We'll leave as soon as possible. What's the condition of your runway?"

"It is turf grass, covered by three centimeters of snow. It will melt soon."

"*Danke*. Now please call a doctor."

"Ask him how long the runway is," Maxwell said.

The answer was a thousand meters. Jake translated and Maxwell thought a moment, then said, "Hmm, I make that more than twenty-five hundred feet. Okay, if it's a good sunny day and the snow melts, we can make it up off this grass—*if* all four motors are pulling."

"All right," Ski Cap said. "Make your damned repairs and get your English asses out of here. I shall have to report this."

"Of course, but please hurry and call a doctor."

"All right, all right."

"*Danke schön, mein Herr*," Jake said to the man's retreating back.

Soon Maxwell, the flight engineer and the bomb-aimer, perched on the left wing, had the cowling off the balky engine and were fussing about in there. Jake hopped down and waddled about in his bulky gear, looking around and working the worst of the kinks out of his muscles. Other crewmembers did the same, all but Walmsley and the injured Archie. It was a crude airfield, the big shed serving as a hangar. Three biplanes were tied down between the shed and a small tin hut. Canvas covered their engines and open cockpits. He saw no radio antennae, only the flagpole and the windsock.

Before long, a small black coupe drove up and a young man popped out carrying a black bag.

"*Herr Doktor*," Jake called. "Over here. We have a man with a head wound."

The doctor, looking surprised to hear a British flier speaking German, hurried to the plane and pulled himself aboard.

As the sun rose, so did the temperature. Jake estimated that it was above freezing, probably pushing forty degrees. A wall of clouds to the northeast, remnants of the snowstorm, grew ever more distant.

Minutes later, a police car drove up, a green and white Citroen. Jake didn't want to be seen by cops, so he edged into the shadow of the hangar. Two uniformed officers piled out and one strode to the plane and addressed Maxwell, interrupting the work. The cop was almost out of earshot, but Jake could tell he was speaking English. They must have been communicating okay because Maxwell didn't call Jake over to help. Good. He wasn't interested in talking to cops. The other officer approached the plane, where the doctor stuck his head out of the hatch and spoke with him.

Jake walked around behind the long, deep shed and saw a tree-lined road leading toward some distant rooftops and church steeples. The town of Olten. Lumps of snow were falling from spruce trees. In a fenced field across the road, cows pawed at the wet ground and grazed inanely, ignoring him.

Jake made a slow circle around the building. When he got back to the runway side, the police were driving off. "Everything okay?" he called to Maxwell.

"Yes, Mr. Weaver. They said they'll report our presence to the Air Ministry. Even if they try to intern us—which I doubt—I'm taking off at dusk, if Archie is fit. I'll not buzz across France in daylight."

He looked up at the flight engineer, who was still on the wing with a wrench in his hand. "Think that's it then, Lenny?"

"Right, Max. Air lock in the fuel line. Should be able to bleed it off right quick, then we can test the motor."

Maxwell nodded and stamped his feet here and there, checking the firmness of the runway, where random patches of grass showed through the thinning snow cover. Then he did a walk-around, inspecting all the plane's exterior surfaces. The bomb-aimer perched on top of the fuselage, taping the hole in the gun turret.

The doctor jumped down and told Jake, "I have stitched up and dressed the head wound and given him some medication for pain. He suffered a concussion. He will be all right, but keep him quiet—and awake."

Jake translated for Maxwell, who gave a huge grin and said, "Splendid news."

"And how am I to be paid?" the doctor asked.

"Send your bill to the British Embassy in Bern," Jake improvised.

Maxwell's grin widened. "Spot on," he said.

"Very well. They had better pay. I shall have to report this, you know." The doctor reprising Ski Cap's earlier remark.

Jake said, "Of course, *vielen Dank*," and they shook hands. The man made for his car and drove off.

Ski Cap had parked his tractor beside the wooden hangar and disappeared inside. No time to waste, Jake told himself. Go now. He climbed back into the plane and peeled off his boots and the cumbersome flight suit. He patted his parachute and said, "Glad I didn't need you this trip, old pal."

The rear gunner had crawled into the bomb-aimer's bubble up front and was glaring at him. Jake opened his satchel and removed his shoes. While putting them on he winked and said, "Have a safe flight home, Jigger. Long life to you." He tossed his satchel to the ground and jumped down. He shook his head and smiled when he heard the words "right turd" issuing behind him.

Spotting Maxwell standing beneath the twin tails, Jake waved and said, "Thanks for everything, Max. I'm gonna shove off now while old sourpuss is out of sight."

"If that's what you think best. Sorry about Zurich. I'm glad we met, Mr. Weaver. Best of luck to you."

Jake said, "You're a great pilot. Win the war now, my friend," and loped past the hangar toward the road. When the airport was a couple of hundred yards behind him, he opened the satchel and put on Hans-Karl's overcoat. He reached down, scooped up a handful of snow and held it for a moment against the bump on his head. Then he readjusted his hat at a proper angle and continued on toward the town.

If Olten was close to Basel, as he thought it was, then he would enter Germany at Basel. It was on the border west of Lake Constance. It was unlikely any German guards there would know Vogel by sight. Hans-Karl surely crossed the border close to Zurich, which was many miles from Basel.

Jake thought about the men he'd just left behind. He tried to picture Jigger at the age of thirty. A used-up bitter little man, old before his time, grumbling in his cups at a third-rate pub. "Oy was there, mate. Nineteen and Forty-two. Bombin' bloody Germany. The things oy saw, the things oy done." Jake knew he'd remember the crew of *O for Oliver*, even that troubled rear gunner, the rest of his life.

However long that might be.

CHAPTER TWENTY-FOUR

Jake walked about half a mile and had reached the outskirts of Olten when a teenage girl approached on a bicycle. She stopped and said, "Are you all right, *mein Herr*?" He must have looked a sight, this stranger trudging through a dusting of snow at the side of the road carrying his satchel.

"*Ja,* it's just that I lost my way in the storm last night." Realizing that must sound pretty implausible. "I need to reach Basel. Is there a bus or train?"

"Both. Buses go four or five times a day, trains twice, I believe. The *Hauptbahnhof* is not hard to find"—she turned and pointed—"straight ahead about half a kilometer to *Martin-Distelistrasse*, then one block to the right."

"*Danke schön, Fräulein.*"

The pretty town had lots of trees, half-timbered buildings, steep roofs with dormers, flower boxes beneath windows, and Christmas decorations draped above the streets from lampposts. Jake found the *Bahnhof*, bought a ticket for the noon train, then went into the railway hotel to change clothes, have the ones he'd worn all night pressed, and get a meal. The chocolate bar he'd eaten on the plane was long gone from his rumbling stomach.

Remembering to use his fork with his left hand, tines turned downward, he ravished a breakfast of eggs, bacon, thick slices of toasted Italian bread, and rich, black coffee. He doubted he'd get such good fare in wartime Germany. As he ate, he thought about the British agent he was to have met last night in Zurich and wondered what he would report to London.

When he stepped out onto the street, Jake gasped at what he saw and ducked back into the doorway. Led by Lieutenant Maxwell, all but two of the crew of *O for Oliver* hiked into town, probably also in search of a hot meal. They must have got that engine running. To be seen as acquainted with these Englishmen wouldn't do, not here.

The flight engineer wasn't with them. He must have drawn the short straw and been left behind to watch the plane and the injured gunner. Hope these guys get safely back to Yorkshire tonight, Jake thought.

By early afternoon, Jake was in Basel after a short train ride. Searching for the border after leaving the *Badischer Bahnhof*, he found himself in the old flagstoned market place, which was decked out with holiday shopping kiosks and cheery decorations. Stately Gothic and Renaissance buildings of stone and brick surrounded the square. Admiring the buildings, he thought, good for these people, staying out of wars.

Soon afterward, north of town, he reached the Upper Rhine and a bridge leading across to Germany. The Jura Alps rose bleak and gray off to the left. He passed the Swiss guard post and hesitantly walked out onto the bridge.

"My name is Hans-Karl Vogel; I am a Swiss businessman," he coached himself. "My name is Hans-Karl Vogel; I am a Swiss businessman. My name is Hans-Karl Vogel; I am a Swiss businessman."

Ahead, the scene on the north riverbank was a stark contrast to the cheerful square he'd left behind. His gut tightened at the sight of the black and red swastika flag fluttering above the guard booth. He thought the heavy, intertwined lines of the swastika could be nothing else but a double cross.

A lowered bar blocked the way and two men milled about in greatcoats of field gray, carrying rifles and wearing the heavy, flaredin-back German helmets seen in so many newsreels. One man was older than Jake and the other looked to be about sixteen. They shuffled about, stamping their feet and rubbing their gloved hands.

Well, here we go, Jake told himself, reaching into his jacket for his passport and identity card. My name is Hans-Karl Vogel; I am a Swiss businessman.

A third man, fortyish, wearing glasses and a mustache, stepped from the booth which, candystriped red and white, comically resembled a fat barber pole. He approached Jake. "What is it you want?"

Jake held out his passport and identity card and said, "I am Hans-Karl Vogel of Schätzen Products in Zurich. I have business appointments to keep in Germany."

The mustachioed guard took them, gave the passport a quick glance, then scrutinized the identity card closely, comparing the photo with Jake's face.

"Where is your vehicle, Herr Vogel? A salesman on foot in these December winds?"

Damn good question. "Bad luck, it broke down in Basel. I'll have to make use of your excellent rail system. They give me a lousy '36 Fiat to drive. With my seniority you'd think I could get a BMW."

The guard laughed. "With my seniority, I too should rate a BMW, but on my pay I must get along with a mere Volkswagen. Quite reliable, though, but small and noisy. Of course, these days who can get enough *Benzin* anyhow?"

Jake nodded.

Mustache squinted. His expression changed. "Why do you cross here? You are not close to Zurich."

"I had orders to fill in Basel."

"And how am I to know you are who you say you are?"

Jake gave his best good-guy grin and said, "Well, *mein Freund*, you have my identification and my picture. Some of your countrymen are waiting for needed supplies which I can get for them."

"So you say. Perhaps we should call Schätzen Products and ask about you."

Jake cringed inside. Got to make this sound good. "They would laugh and say, 'That's old Hans-Karl all right, never know where that vagabond will turn up.'"

Jake saw a snow-dusted Volkswagen parked off the road a few yards beyond the guard post and remembered passing a filling station a block or so from the bridge.

"Say, friend, perhaps I could get you a few liters of *Benzin*, eh?"

"You would do that?"

"*Ja,* why not? Making deals is what I do. I'm hours behind schedule anyway."

"Hmm." Mustache studied Jake's face and rested a hand on his Mauser rifle, absent-mindedly or threateningly Jake couldn't tell.

"Well, Herr Vogel," he said at last, "that would be kind of you." He opened a gloved hand to show it was empty. "But I have no Swiss francs."

"*Ist kein Problem.* Maybe one day you'll do me or one of my countrymen a good turn."

"And you can put it down on your expense account," Mustache said with a knowing grin. He shrugged. "All right then, go and fetch me a tin of *Benzin* if you will." He handed Jake his passport and identity card.

Fifteen minutes later the sun was weakening and wisps of fog began to swirl as Jake returned, his deal made, lugging a can of gasoline. He'd persuaded a Swiss guard to return the can after the German had emptied it.

Old Mustache reappeared and Jake handed him the gas. Reaching into an overcoat pocket, he also produced a chocolate bar and a pack of State Express cigarettes. "You might like these as well, my friend."

Mustache took them, examined them for a moment, then stiffened and declared, "You are under arrest, Herr Vogel."

Jake froze. The teenager, standing a few feet away, snickered.

Jake had blown it, bribing this guard. His stomach churned. What now? A concentration camp?

Technically, he hadn't yet entered Germany. He glanced back toward the Swiss guard post eighty yards away across the bridge. Would he be shot in the back if he made a run for it?

But Mustache laughed heartily, then pulled himself together and said, "My little joke. Oh, the look on your face, if only you could see it."

Third-rate comedian! While Jake tried to get his heart started again, Mustache reached down and swung the guard-bar upward. "Welcome to the Third Reich, *mein Freund. Sieg Heil,* " he added with a quick, sloppy Nazi salute.

It was all Jake could do to answer with a mild "*Sieg Heil,*" hating himself. No salute.

"Erich, give our friend a lift to a hotel or the Bahnhof in Lorrach, wherever he wants to go."

The boy clicked his heels together. "*Jawohl.*"

"*Danke* for the *Benzin,*" Mustache called as Jake and Erich trudged toward a battle-gray *Kübelwagen*. Welcome to the Third Reich indeed. They walked several yards, a thin coating of snow crunching underfoot on the macadam roadway.

"Wait!" Mustache called. "Come back." Jake and the kid stopped and looked around. "*Kommen Sie hierherr,*" Mustache repeated.

As Jake walked back toward the guard booth, the man said, "I am going to call your company in Zurich after all."

CHAPTER TWENTY-FIVE

Just to be on the safe side," Mustache said. "Schätzen Products, was it?"

Jake's throat tightened. He nodded gloomily. "I assure you it's a waste of your time."

"Probably so, but I have not held this job for nine years by being careless. I will detain you just a few minutes more."

Further resistance would only worsen the situation, make Jake look guilty of something.

Inside the booth, Mustache barked orders into a phone. "International call. Zurich. Schätzen Products . . . How would I know the exchange, *Fräulein*? What are you being paid for?"

Jake listened fearfully. A cottony swirl of fog riffled through, turning him even colder. In this game, there's always the unforeseen, Colonel Freeborn had said.

"Personnel department, *bitte* . . . The Reich Border Authority, *Südwestlicher Sektor*." Mustache hummed quietly for several seconds. "*Ja*, excuse me, *mein Herr*, do you have a Hans-Karl Vogel in your employ? . . . I see . . . *Ja*, he is here . . . *Ja, einen Moment*." He leaned out of the booth. "Vogel, they want to talk to you."

Just what he'd been afraid of. Mustache stepped aside and Jake went in and took the phone, his hand shaking. "*Ja*?" he croaked in falsetto.

"Vogel, what *im Himmel* are you doing there? You are supposed to be in London."

"Change of plans." With feigned hoarseness.

"What do you mean, change of plans? Are you all right? You sound strange."

"Cold. I have a cold. Big new order. I will explain later." His back blocking Mustache's view into the tiny hut, Jake disconnected with his finger, but didn't put the mouthpiece down. "Oh, you need to know this minute, do you? Well, it's a very big new order in Berlin . . . Of course, sir, I will get there quickly as I can, but you know that miserable old Fiat went *kaput* again. Call for it at that garage we use in Basel. Now I have a train to catch. I will call from Berlin. *Wiederhören.*" He set the mouthpiece in the cradle and stepped outside.

Mustache looked at him. "All right then, Herr Vogel, it is good to be sure about these things." He stamped Jake's passport and said, "You may go now. And take care with your cold . . . Erich!"

The youngster clicked his heels with precision and again led Jake off toward the army vehicle. Had he pulled it off? He had no idea what Vogel's voice sounded like—back when he had a voice. No, it couldn't have worked. That guy in Zurich would think about it, realize the voice and accent were all wrong, then call Vogel's hotel in London. What then? Jake could only hope Colonel Freeborn had covered that potentiality and given the hotel some story to tell.

The boy started up the *Kübelwagen*, pulled onto the road and ran through the gears.

Worrying about this won't do any good, Jake told himself. Just forget it and be pleasant, don't transmit your jitters to the kid. "Are you in the army or the police or what?" he asked.

"Hitler Youth," the boy said proudly. "On my next birthday I will become a private in the Wehrmacht."

"Is that what you want?"

"*Ja*, of course, it is my duty to the Fatherland."

"Where will you go, to Africa or maybe the eastern front?"

"After my training, the eastern front, I hope. I want to kill Communist Russians, many of them."

"I hear the eastern front is tough duty."

"Lies, all lies, that we are having difficulties there. Just propaganda from the *beschissenen Tommis*. The Führer says we will take Stalingrad, close the Volga, and force the damned Bolsheviks to surrender."

"I hope so," Jake lied.

He noticed the sidearm holstered at the boy's waist. Jake had done some pistol shooting with cop friends at the L.A. police range. This pistol was smaller than a Luger. Jake wanted to ask about it, but didn't. Keep it simple, he told himself.

Well, here he was in Germany for the second time in his life. The first time had been almost thirteen years ago, when the country reeled under the worldwide Depression, and wild political turmoil was spilling over into street fighting. The occasion of that first visit had been the memorial service for his Aunt Marta near Berlin. Jake had been twenty-four. He'd never been down here by the Black Forest. The fall colors must have been beautiful a month ago.

After a couple of miles they reached Lorrach. An anti-aircraft battery, much like those in London, stood in an empty lot at the edge of town.

Night was falling. Swastika flags mixed incompatibly with holiday decorations in the *Marktplatz*. Little Christmas shopping huts had been erected here, as in Basel, adorned with evergreen boughs and bright glass balls.

Jake asked to be dropped at the Bahnhof.

Saying *"Auf Wiedersehen, danke und viel Glück"*—good luck— Jake entered the station and got out his timetable. Old men and women occupied wooden benches and a few soldiers milled about carrying duffel bags. Going on or returning from furloughs, no doubt. Many looked to be in their late twenties. Must have signed up shortly after Hitler came to power. A couple of them had weary faces and hard vacant eyes. Unmistakably veterans.

If Jake was reading his timetable right, he could take a train from here to Freiburg, then change to one bound for Stuttgart. That sent a chill snaking through his bones—they'd just bombed Stuttgart— where he'd change again for Berlin. He would reach Freiburg at 21:20 if the train ran on time. He could take a room there for the night and arrive in Stuttgart tomorrow in daylight. He wondered if the Stuttgart Bahnhof was still standing.

It must be dark outside now. Wonder if *O for Oliver* has taken off and headed for home. It would be morning in L.A. Valerie was probably getting to work at North American about now. That Vera Lynn song began running through his head. *"We'll meet again, don't know where, don't know when . . . ."*

Looking around cautiously, Jake walked to the ticket window. Was anyone following him or staring at him? At the window, the agent said the train would be crowded and no compartments were available. Jake didn't mind riding in a second-class coach to Freiburg, which wasn't far. He found that he could buy a ticket all the way to Berlin. The agent prepared it, neatly printing by hand all the times and train changes.

Jake paid and thanked him, slipped the ticket into a pocket and went to a news rack, hoping to find the *Deutsche Allgemeine Zeitung*, his friend Rolf's paper. No luck. There was only a small Lorrach daily and the *Voelkischer Beobachter*, the Nazi party paper. The headline, possibly dictated by Joseph Goebbels himself, read RUSSIANS RETREAT AT STALINGRAD.

In London, the word had been that the Germans had overextended their supply lines and were close to being trapped there by hordes of fresh Red troops. Jake, the amateur strategist, thought they'd be stupid not to fall back from Stalingrad and establish a more stable front.

He put the paper down, refusing to spend money on that Nazi rag. Seeing Goebbels' newspaper triggered thoughts of the propaganda minister's wife Magda and Putzi Hansfstaengl. He didn't really know if he would attempt to honor Putzi's request to try to fetch

Hindenburg's letter to Hitler. Uncle Dieter, Wernher von Braun and Rolf Becker would come first. He recalled that Rolf used to complain that Jake was too bossy. It was the only thing they'd disagreed on. Jake had felt he'd been tutoring, just trying to make him a better reporter, as he did with others on the staff.

The benches were crowded. He found a seat beside a man who was both very fat and very foul-smelling. Jake sat and thought about all he'd been through in the last hour and the lies he'd told to Old Mustache. He felt a growing confidence in his German. He discovered that, despite the anxiety, the constant dancing with danger, he got a perverse pleasure from his role-playing, in this portrayal of another person. God, he was weird.

Suddenly the stinking fatso said, "Did you hear, the *verdammte* English terror raiders bombed Stuttgart last night."

"Is that so? Much damage?"

"Not much, the radio says, and the *Tommis* lost thirty percent of their airplanes."

Jake hadn't seen a single plane hit over Stuttgart but that didn't mean they'd got away clean. He hadn't been able to see much.

"Good." Getting to be a pro at lying.

"They hit a hospital, though, killed many helpless patients." That was possible, Jake knew, but more likely a propaganda lie.

The train was announced. He got up and made his way to the gate amid a throng of others.

As the train lumbered along between Lorrach and Freiburg, a man in a stark black *Schutzstaffel* uniform—the SS—followed up the aisle behind the rail agent who was punching tickets. He stopped, glared at Jake with distrustful eyes and blurted, "Are you German?"

"No, I am Swiss."

"Passport and identity card." The man shot his hand out impatiently. He examined them closely, compared the photos with Jake's face, and fired off a string of harsh questions about his reasons for being in the Third Reich. Jake willed himself not to sweat or shake as he answered.

The silver lightning bolts on the guy's collar looked like twisted daggers. He returned the documents at last, then ordered, "On your feet." Jake stood and stepped into the aisle. "Spread your arms." Jake then got thoroughly and roughly frisked. The dumb shit, he thought. I'm not stupid enough to be carrying a gun.

"Your baggage." The satchel held only clothing, but Jake handed it over. Refusing could cause no end of trouble. The SS man took it and without a word stalked down the aisle and left the coach.

Jake sat, his arms and shoulders trembling. He hugged himself to get it under control. To his surprise, the gray-haired old woman next to the window, clutching a big wicker basket, whispered, "Those fools." Jake gave her a tiny nod.

The SS man came back fifteen minutes later and shoved the satchel at him as if it were garbage. "Here." Jake was sure the clothing would be in rumpled disarray. The man continued down the aisle and repeated the whole procedure with a frightened little man who said he was Hungarian.

In his hotel room in Freiburg that night, Jake found the clothing in his satchel as messed up as he'd expected. Refolding them, he discovered that a spare scarf was missing. He slammed a fist against the arm of a chair. That damned SS man had stolen it, the *Schwein. Schwein*? Gee, now he was even *thinking* in German.

Jake slept badly that night, even though he lay in a cozy bed beneath a warm goosedown comforter.

He reached Stuttgart in the morning. Being here in *O for Oliver*'s target city gave him an uneasy feeling.

The Bahnhof hadn't been bombed, but he saw some damage nearby as he walked the streets during an hour's wait between trains. The top floors of what had been a four-story sandstone building had been blasted to rubble. Workers had roped it off and were clearing jagged chunks of ruined stone from the sidewalk. He smelled smoke and singed fabric. Jake had covered fires for the paper and knew the harsh, damp smell of smoke lingered for days in ruined buildings.

He could see into blackened, ravaged rooms through a gaping hole where a wall and windows had been sheared away. He hoped that hadn't been the handiwork of *O for Oliver*, although, come on Jake, what difference did it make?

Many more policemen and soldiers walked the streets here than in Freiburg. Jake took a seat on a bench beside a fountain in a small public square and rested for a moment.

He moved on and found a grocery, where he bought a thick loaf of pumpernickel bread and a slab of Münster cheese to take with him on the train. This time he'd have a compartment and he planned to share the food with whoever his traveling companions might be.

Back in the Bahnhof, the sound system was playing *Stille Nacht*. As passengers lined up beside the waiting train, cops eyed them all closely, Jake included, but he was able to board without being hassled.

Soon the train rocked along through rolling hills and valleys, passing several vineyards, their grapevines winter-naked. His compartment mates were a beshawled woman and a couple who looked to be in their sixties.

Jake sat deep in thought as he gazed at the scenery. An old farmer stopped pushing his hand plow and watched the train rumble past. The last address Jake had for Rolf was from before the war broke out, more than three years ago. He had no idea if Rolf still lived there, in the Dahlem district. He decided to go instead to the *Deutsche Zeitung*. But what if Rolf wasn't there and he had to leave a message? He couldn't say Jake Weaver had stopped by, nor could he leave the name Hans-Karl Vogel, which would mean nothing to his friend. He'd just have to ask what time Rolf started work and come back later. A stranger not leaving a name would attract attention and people would talk—he knew how newsrooms were—but it couldn't be helped.

He thought about the lovely women of Berlin and one in particular, the one with whom he'd had a little fling back in 1930. A three-night stand with Winifrid, a beautiful communist. Jake had told himself it didn't matter, that he was a communist sympathizer only between the sheets. Jake the bedroom Red. Ass was ass, after all, at least before Valerie.

He hoped that his fiancée, from thousands of miles away, couldn't read his mind at this moment.

The train jerked to a stop, steam billowing around the windows. The passengers looked at each other, puzzled.

"*Was ist los?*" the old man said, getting up and leaving. Soon he was back with the news: A bomb had hit the tracks up ahead. They might have to wait an hour or so while repairs were made.

Jake opened his grocery sack to share his bread and cheese with the other passengers. The old guy gave the wheel of cheese a long look, then reached into his bag. Jake shuddered. A shiver sluiced along his spine. What was this guy reaching for?

The man's hand emerged holding a bottle of wine. He smiled and showed it to Jake. *Spätburgunder*. Jake knew that as pinot noir. He let out the breath he'd been holding. Good show, he thought in mimicry of Colonel Freeborn.

Bread and cheese were sliced and the bottle opened. The wine was good. When Jake thanked him, the man said he was celebrating.

"Celebrating what, sir?"

"I am a master cabinetmaker. I just received a nice contract from the government to fabricate tail-section patterns for fighter planes." This blabbermouth obviously took Jake for a German.

"Really?"

"*Ja.* The Ministry of Armaments plans to use subcontractors in small, dispersed shops so the bombing of big factories cannot disrupt war production so very much."

"That's clever," Jake said. "If parts are made in small shops scattered here and there before final assembly, they'd be almost impossible for enemy reconnaissance planes to identify."

"Just so."

Jake had been in Germany less than a full day and already he had some important intelligence for FDR. "Congratulations," he said.

The man raised his glass to Jake. "*Danke*."

The train eventually started up and rattled onward, making stops in Nuremberg and Bayreuth. Half an hour out of Bayreuth, Jake endured another obnoxious encounter with the SS, although this time his bag wasn't searched. Just the usual rude questions, fired like bullets, and another pat-down.

The hours dragged. Jake dozed a little. After stops in Hof, Leipzig and Potsdam, the train, about midnight, finally clanged to a stop at Berlin's Anhalter station. Stiff and weary, he planned to find a hotel, then search out Rolf Becker in the morning.

An ambulance train was unloading on the next track, scores of litter cases being carried off. The words *La Compagnie Internationale des Wagons-Lits* caught his eye. These were confiscated French rail cars.

Jake's throat caught at the sight of burned and bandaged soldiers, some with hands, arms or legs missing. Doctors and nurses hovered around them in muted light—only one in five overhead lights illuminated—presenting a ghostly scene. There's a reason they bring ambulance trains in the dead of night, Jake thought. Sights like this wouldn't do morale on the home front any good at all.

"Move along," a policeman demanded, startling Jake. He must have stared too long and too hard. He hadn't even seen the cop. Have to be more careful.

Wet snowflakes swirled in the near-dark as, tired and edgy, he stepped out onto the blacked-out street.

Well, here he was back in Uncle Dieter's city for the first time in a dozen years. He twined his muffler tight around his neck and looked around warily. Jake realized that, unless he was at his field headquarters in East Prussia, Adolf Hitler was less than a mile away.

CHAPTER TWENTY-SIX

Jake spent what was left of the night at the Adlon, *the* hotel in Berlin. Pricey, but what the hell, Hearst would reimburse him. Maybe. The elegant Adlon was in the middle of everything, close to the Chancellory, the government offices on *Wilhelmstrasse*, and the Brandenburg Gate, with the Goddess Victory and her four-horse chariot perched on top.

In the morning, the bread and cheese from the train a distant memory, he helped himself to a hearty breakfast. Wartime Berlin might be short of food but the Adlon seemed well supplied with eggs, ham and sausages. Probably plunder from Polish farms. Everything tasted good but the coffee. The Germans obviously hadn't invaded Brazil.

A horde of uniformed officers and chubby, prosperous-looking businessmen filled the dining room. Was anyone sneaking glances at him? Did he look out of place? Was he using his fork properly in the left hand? Valerie's parting words popped into his mind again. "You'd damn well better come back to me, Jake. I'll be waiting for you."

He thumbed through the *Deutsche Algemeine Zeitung* as he ate, searching for a Rolf Becker byline. He didn't find one, but a story on the second page caught his eye.

Tomorrow would mark one year since Japan's attack on the American Fleet in Hawaii. The Führer was quoted as praising his gallant ally for striking a courageous blow against the USA, which had been strangling Japan's economy with illegal and immoral trade sanctions.

What a load of crap, Jake thought. The article did one thing, though, it reminded him of Pearl Harbor. He'd forgotten that tomorrow was December 7th.

Back in his room, he searched the Berlin phone book. It listed five Rolf Beckers and four R. Beckers, but none with the Dahlem address that was the last he'd had for his friend. No point in calling any of those numbers. He'd go to the paper instead.

He turned to his map of Berlin and saw that Unter den Linden University was not far, at number 6 of its namesake boulevard. This was closer than the *Deutsche Zeitung*, so he decided to stop there first before going on to find Rolf.

Jake dropped his key at the desk and left the hotel, wondering if his room would be searched while he was out. A foreigner here in wartime—it was a real possibility.

He thought about that, his nerves jangling, as he walked east on Unter den Linden. He couldn't see any bomb damage, although he knew the RAF had raided Berlin a few times. Then he noticed a roundish patch of fresh asphalt where the broad boulevard had been repaired. Lower-floor windows of several buildings were sandbagged for protection.

He saw more bicyclists than cars and assumed that gasoline was almost impossible for people to get. Red, black and white Nazi banners rippled in the breeze along the street, which he knew Berliners claimed was the equal of Paris' Champs Élysées. But to Jake, between those arrogant flags and the winter bareness of the famous linden trees in the median, the boulevard looked grim. He walked on under thin sunshine, warily alert. A few people were on foot, their breath steaming in the morning air. Patches of snow appeared here and there on an otherwise impeccably clean street. Not a speck of trash, not even a cigarette butt.

Jake soon reached *Universität Unter den Linden*. "My name is

Hans-Karl Vogel," he reminded himself. "I am a Swiss businessman." He paused at a huge statue of Alexander von Humboldt, and read that he was the university's founder. He then hiked up the broad steps and entered, glad to be out of the cold. At the reception desk, a pretty blond woman gave him directions to the Physics Department. It was in the next building, connected by an enclosed breezeway. Arriving there after walking along a stately hallway of—what, marble? travertine?— Jake met a white-haired man carrying a stack of papers.

"Excuse me, do you know where I can find *Herr Doktor* von Braun?"

"He is at Peenemünde," the man said, then quickly added, "*Ach,* I should not have said that. He is in the field. We expect him back in two days' time." His brows arched. "You know our young genius?"

"I'm an old friend." *Peenemünde*? Jake wondered.

"I am sure when he returns he will be happy to see you. He has been working much too hard these days."

"*Ja,* I know. He was always a fiend for work." Jake smiled, gave a slight head bob, and said, "*Danke schön.*" He was getting better at playing the role of a German, or at least a Swiss who knew his way around Germany. He hoped. He turned and tried to look nonchalant as he strolled back to the exit, thinking: Have to look up Peenemünde, wherever that is.

Out on the street a gray stake truck rolled by, the back filled with soldiers, some wearing helmets, others in field caps. One of them waved and Jake returned the gesture. Wehrmacht morale was high, at least on that truck.

He passed a synagogue he remembered from 1930. It looked sad and abandoned now, its doors chained and padlocked, the lower windows boarded up.

Several blocks farther along, the *Deutsche Zeitung* occupied a building of dark red brick. Jake found the city room, or whatever Germans might call it, on the second floor. He glanced around but didn't see Rolf.

What he did see looked about the same as any city room: desks, typewriters, telephones, reporters and editors. A pneumatic tube ran from the copy desk through an opening in the wall. Jake knew this shuttled copy to typesetters in the composing room. There was one big difference, though, between this and an American city room—it was tidy.

"*Kann ich Ihnen helfen?*"asked a doughty *Hausfrau* type sitting at a reception desk.

"I am looking for Rolf Becker." Better be careful here. Jake mustn't reveal that he knew Rolf from America.

The woman said, "Who?"

"Rolf Becker, one of your reporters."

The woman's brow scrunched for an instant. "Becker? He does not work here." What the hell? Jake thought. The woman seemed to fidget, then, glancing down at what looked like a work schedule, she scanned a note paper-clipped on top, and said, "That is, he is not working here today."

"Will he be back tomorrow?"

" *Ja, um zehn Uhr.*" Ten a.m.

"*Danke* . . . Oh, please tell him Herr Weber"—pronouncing it Vay-ber—"will stop in to see him. Jacob Weber." Jake had told Rolf the origin of the Weaver name, that it had been Weber two generations back. Rolf would remember that, and then he'd know his cryptic message about Uncle Dieter had gotten through and realize that Jake was now in Berlin.

He left and spent a couple of hours walking and looking at the sights. Gray sky hung over the city like dirty dishwater. He saw the Brandenburg Gate, its simple scale more pleasing than Paris' mammoth Arch of Triumph. The Kroll Opera House, where the Reichstag, now a sham assembly of Hitler's puppets, had been meeting since the Reichstag fire. The Pergamon Museum, perched on an island in the River Spree which wound through the heart of town like a ribbon. Jake hoped the war could be won without *O for Oliver* or some other Allied bomber ruining these fine buildings.

He found himself passing Number 8 *Prinz-Albrechtstrasse*, a stone building he recalled from 1930 as the cheery Folklore Museum. With a shock, he saw the words *Geheime Staatspolizei* in black Gothic lettering on the facade. The words were small, as if the occupants didn't want to advertise themselves but were so arrogant they just had to. A little. He shuddered. That organization was better known by its abbreviated name: the *Gestapo*. It was all Jake could do to keep from running as he moved on. As far as he was concerned, *O for Oliver* could bomb the hell out of *that* place.

Unlike London, not many people were about. It felt eerie, like a town in the Old West when the residents hid out as the bad guys rode into town. In Nazi Germany, where people informed on one another, where you kept your mouth shut if you didn't support the dictator, staying home seemed to be the norm.

Jake found that powerfully sad. The highly visible Berliners he'd seen in 1930 were lusty, gregarious and full of song, despite their economic woes.

Back at the hotel, he collected his key, went to his room and examined it closely. Everything looked just as he'd left it. Wait. No. He'd left his maps rightside up, hadn't he? Now they lay face down. His spine shivered. The bastards had been in his room. But *what* bastards? There wasn't anything here that could give him away, was there?

Trying to be calm, he sat and unfolded his map of Germany and began looking for someplace called Peenemünde. It took quite awhile because he wasn't sure how it was spelled. At last he found it, in small type, on a Pomeranian island just off the northeast coast. With his index finger, he traced an imaginary rocket launch several miles out over the Baltic from this tiny town.

And the rocket man, Wernher von Braun, was expected back from there in a couple of days. Then, if he could arrange to meet him, he'd have a real test of his acting ability. As Hans-Karl Vogel, he'd have to convince von Braun that his company could supply some items he could use. He'd try to persuade him that he was pro-German and charm him into giving away some details on his A-4 rocket. Sergei Prokofiev had said von Braun was an affable guy, that he liked to talk, and his city editor always said Jake had Alan Ladd charm to call on when he wanted to. Well, he wanted to.

Jake went to the movies that night in an ornate theater a block off Unter den Linden that reminded him of the Pantages in Hollywood. As the lights went down, strident patriotic music played and the screen flashed footage of a big Nazi Party rally in Nuremberg, thousands of troops massed in perfect formation before an adoring Hitler. Then a newsreel pictured smiling, confident German soldiers hiking into Russia's Caucasus, while others were shown, grim but heroic, battling the British in North Africa. No mention of Stalingrad.

The main feature, *Ohm Krüger*, turned out to be an anti-British film heavy on propaganda, light on dramatic style. It was directed by Hans Steinhof, once highly regarded in the international cinema, now obviously a tool of the Nazis. Some in the audience, perhaps the more sophisticated Berliners, didn't seem to appreciate it. Others ate it up, guffawing and sneering at the English caricatures. Jake was both disappointed and amused. He'd take Frank Capra any day.

CHAPTER TWENTY-SEVEN

W hen he returned to the *Deutsche Zeitung* the next day, Jake scanned the city room but didn't see Rolf. He also didn't see the receptionist, so he waited just inside the doorway for a couple of minutes. He was about to go over to the nearest desk and ask a reporter when Rolf flung open the door and burst in.

"Hey Jake!" he exclaimed in plain American. He caught himself and added in German, "How nice to see you, old *Freund*. It was a wonderful surprise when I heard you were here yesterday." They shook hands warmly. For just an instant, the nearby reporter shot a queer look at Rolf which Jake almost missed.

"Come on, let's have a cup of coffee." Rolf led Jake down a hall, clapping him on the back and giving him a warm, sidelong look. They reached a nearly deserted lounge and poured themselves cups from a tall coffeepot. "This is awful stuff," Rolf said quietly in English.

"Auf Deutsch," Jake whispered. "We must always speak German."

"Still bossing me around, are you? Just like in L.A." Fortunately, he said this in German. "But you are right, sometimes I get too lazy for my own good." He scowled at his cup. "We cannot get real coffee, you know. They brew this *Kacke* out of acorns or chicory, something like that. One can only get the real thing on the black market."

Rolf tossed a wave at the room's only other occupants, two men at a far-off table, who didn't seem to notice. He and Jake took seats that would be out of earshot. "Those guys are in the circulation department," Rolf said.

Jake took a sip and made a face. Remembering the so-called coffee he'd had at the Adlon, he wasn't surprised. "You're looking well, Rolf, and we've lots to catch up on. But first, tell me about Dieter."

"Slow down. We will go into that soon enough. Now what about *die Frisur* of yours." Meaning hairdo. "Real pretty. First thing I noticed."

"Tell you later. But Dieter, Rolf. That's why I'm here."

"I know, but not here, not now." There was a hardness in Rolf's eyes that Jake had never seen before.

"Why?" Jake said softly. He stole a glance at the two men in the corner. They were deep in their own conversation.

Rolf ran a hand through his wavy yellow hair. "There's a lot you won't understand. I will give you the whole story, count on it. Be patient." He brushed a strand of hair back in place. "It is *so* good to see you. I knew you would turn up here one of these days, clever old you. You know, your German is still quite good. How are things at the *Express*? How is old Aggie Underwood?"

Frustrated, Jake said, "She's fine. Covering the police beat now."

"The cop shop, eh?"

"Yes, and good at it. She'll be the next city editor."

"Really? Well I'll be damned." Rolf lit a Liebig cigarette and offered the pack to Jake, who shook his head. "Still not smoking, eh? Well, you have plenty of other vices." Jake grinned. Fair enough—although that was before Valerie.

"How is *Opa* Hearst?"

"Grandpa Hearst is still meddlesome, but he's mellowed a lot. Remember what an isolationist he was? He's on board now, lock, stock and barrel, after Pearl Harbor."

"Is everyone like that?"

"Oh yeah, the whole country's united now, determined to see

this through."

"I am sorry to hear that. I was hoping there was still a chance for a peace settlement before this little fracas got much worse."

Fracas? Jake thought. He calls this worldwide firestorm a little fracas? "You really thought there was a chance of that?"

"Of course, I am German after all."

"Times have changed a lot, Rolf. Say, today's the anniversary of the Japs' attack on Pearl Harbor."

"I know. We have a story on that."

"A very slanted one, too."

"Well, this *is* Germany, you know. The Japs would have helped us more by going against Russia instead of you. That would have tied up the Siberian troops in the Far East and made Stalingrad a cakewalk. Then the Wehrmacht could have swept down through Iran to the Persian Gulf."

What was Jake hearing? Rolf sounded in favor of Hitler's war.

"Yes, of course you're German, but not a Nazi."

Rolf paused and drank some of his synthetic coffee. "No . . . not a Nazi." He idly turned the cup in his hands. "After the fall of France, Churchill still had a chance to make peace, you know."

Jake was stunned but tried to understand. Rolf *was* German and it would be natural not to want a fight to the finish that could be devastating for his country. Jake looked around and said quietly, "How could Churchill do that? After the rape of Poland, then Norway and France."

"Rape? That's a bit strong. Remember, it was France and Britain who declared war on Germany."

"Honoring their commitments to Poland, Rolf."

"*Ach*, you are German too. Your parents were born here. Surely you would like to see this end before we have another bloodbath like last time."

Jake didn't answer, didn't like this conversation at all. He was an American. Period.

The other men got up and left. Rolf said *"Guten Tag"* as they passed, looking as if they weren't sure who Rolf was.

"Say, I have a swell idea," Rolf said when they were gone. "Goering is hosting a dinner for newsmen at *Karinhalle*."

"Hermann Goering, the Reichsmarshal?"

"Ja, the fat man himself. A lot of foreign journalists will be there. French, Italian, Spanish. He loves to entertain, show off his big place, and show these guys what swell fellows the Nazis really are." That *was* sarcasm, wasn't it? "I can take you along."

Jake had heard about Karinhalle, Goering's lavish hunting lodge in the Schönheide Forest north of here. What a story! *Always the reporter*. What an opportunity to gather information. *And now also a spy.*

But it didn't make sense, the Luftwaffe commander-in-chief back here throwing parties while his air force was embroiled in a desperate war deep in Russia. "That'd be good," he said, "but will Swiss guys be there too? That could be a problem."

"Swiss? Why?"

"Oh, right, you don't know. I snuck in here through Switzerland. My papers say I'm a Swiss businessman." Maybe he shouldn't have said that. Rolf seemed so different from the guy he'd been in L.A.

"Ach so. I knew you would come up with something clever like that. It explains your dye job. Anyway, I am sure it will work. Every newsman doesn't know every other newsman, you know that, even in Switzerland. We will say you're from a small-town weekly. It will work."

"Okay, maybe so." The idea was appealing. Jake looked around the empty room. "Are you still living in Dahlem?"

Rolf frowned slightly and pushed that misbehaving lock of hair off his forehead. "No." He didn't elaborate.

What the hell was going on? Rolf keeping secrets, backing Hitler's war.

"Where are you staying?"

"At the Adlon."

"I always liked your style, Jake."

"Yeah, but I'd better move. The old expense account has its limits, you know."

"I'll find you something. There are lots of inexpensive hotel rooms these days."

"Tourism a bit off, is it? Now damn it, tell me about Dieter."

"You haven't seen—"

"Your message meant the SS killed him, right?" Jake persisted.

Rolf consulted his fingernails, then gazed around the room as if inspecting every light fixture. Finally he cleared his throat and said, "Yes, I am afraid so."

"Why, when?"

"Writing your story already? Don't forget the 'where.' As I said before, Jake, there is a lot you do not understand. You will learn everything in due time."

"Why all this damn stalling? What's the deal?" Jake wanted to get this over with. Find out who killed Dieter, do something about it, and get the hell out of this creepy country.

"The party at Karinhalle is in two days." Another damn change of subject. Jake made a fist. "I will drive you out there. *Benzin* is rationed like crazy, but the *Zeitung* still has some. By the way, German chemists are coming up with some synthetic fuel, using alcohol and oil extracted from coal. Many Wehrmacht vehicles are being converted so they can run on it."

Artificial gas. Now there was a story. Jake knew Germany was dependent on oil from Romania. Thank goodness, with the vast oil fields in Texas and Louisiana, the U.S. would never need foreign oil.

Rolf looked at his pocket watch. "I must get back to work, Jake. Let me take you to dinner tonight. We will go to Horcher's. I've got an expense account, too."

"Horcher's?"

"*Ja*, real high on the hog. I'll pick you up at seven."

Walking down the street, Jake thought how bizarre that had been. He hadn't even been able to ask what beat Rolf was covering or what kind of assignments he was getting. He'd gone half a block when he looked back at the *Zeitung*'s brick facade. There was Rolf, coming down the steps and walking off in the opposite direction. He hadn't seen Jake.

I thought he was going back to work, Jake mused. Well, maybe he's running down a story. He thought about following him, see where he was going. Why had he thought that? His natural suspicious reporter instinct? No, he decided, following Rolf would be dumb. He walked on in the direction of the Adlon. A cop approached, wearing the odd headgear of the Berlin police that looked to Jake like an overturned coal bucket. The man gave a quick little salute as he walked on past and a sense of relief swept over Jake.

The iron hands on the big clock read 7:15. No Rolf. Jake sat waiting in an overstuffed chair in the Adlon's lobby, drumming his fingers on the arm rest, looking at troubling thoughts about his old friend. Why had Rolf stonewalled him on Uncle Dieter? And where had he gone after leaving the paper? Maybe he should have followed him after all.

No, he just needed to relax, quell his impatience and let Rolf explain in his own good time. Anyway, what choice did he have? Speaking of time, back in L.A. Rolf had never been late. Jake scanned the lobby. Was anyone looking at him? Peeking from behind that marble pillar?

Tapestry, the British agent who lived in Schöneberg, crossed his mind. Would he need to look her up one of these days and ask her help? An attractive young war widow with a broken nose and a loathing for Hitler, Colonel Freeborn had said. How attractive? Jake wondered, and felt a twinge of guilt for wondering. He was deeply in love with Valerie, for goodness' sake. Sure, he'd been in and out of quite a few beds after his ill-fated early marriage in Texas—including his fling here in Berlin back in 1930. He smiled, remembering how he'd combined a memorial service for a beloved aunt with some strenuous rolls in the German hay. But all that had stopped when he'd met Valerie, his captivating tool designer. Still, no harm in wondering. Just harmless curiosity, right?

"Herr Weber," a familiar voice called. Jake looked up and there was Rolf. "Herr Weber" was much better than the "Hey Jake" Rolf had blurted this morning. "I hope you are hungry."

Jake said "*Ja*, starving," and got up.

Fortunately, Rolf carried an umbrella large enough to shelter them both, for they walked to Horcher's through an icy rain.

Jake looked around the blacked-out city and wondered how you could tell which shops and cafés were open, with their signs unlit and blackout curtains drawn? Rolf seemed to know, though, and soon had them at the restaurant.

Inside Horcher's, Rolf shook out and furled the umbrella, which he checked along with their coats and hats. The maitre d' called Rolf by name and showed them to a leather-upholstered booth. Jake took in the rich furnishings, maroon brocade wall coverings, small lamps on the tables. And the people. There weren't many.

Rolf ordered peach Schnapps, Jake just a beer.

"*Spaten-Bräu*?" asked the waiter.

"That'd be fine."

Rolf looked tense as he scanned the menu, fingers beating a tattoo on the edges.

"What do you recommend?" Jake asked.

"The leg of lamb is excellent. Fine lamb from Dutch farms. They have connections here, get good cuts of meat ordinary folks can only dream about . . . So, you came in from Switzerland, did you? Tell me how you pulled that off."

"Nothing much to tell. You know what I want to talk about."

"Later, after we have had a drink or two. I must toast my old friend's good health."

The drinks came and Rolf did that, adding, "How are you, Jake, really? Tell me all about yourself."

Jake did, reluctantly at first, but the words flowed easier when he told about Valerie.

"So the Casanova of L.A. has fallen hard. Congratulations. She must be quite a woman."

Rolf said he had a girlfriend himself, a secretary in one of the government offices, a Bavarian beauty with great *Kiste*. Tits. Rolf hadn't completely changed, Jake thought. Still chasing the fuzzy doughnut.

"You going to marry her?"

"Probably not." Nope, Rolf hadn't completely changed.

The waiter returned. Jake ordered the leg of lamb, not to be polite but because it sounded good. Rolf asked for Sauerbraten.

Jake spoke quietly, even though the adjacent booth sat empty. Few diners were here on this winter night.

He took a drink of his lager, much better than the room-temperature pub brew he'd had in London. "I know you'll tell me about Dieter when you're ready, Rolf, but at least tell me where he's buried. They did bury him, didn't they?"

"Of course, but you mustn't go and see the grave. The caretaker would inform on you, on anyone visiting that grave, and next thing you know, you've got the SS tailing you."

"Christ, this country of yours has gone completely nuts, Rolf." Damn, he'd have to keep his voice down.

"It is a phase we're going through. After the war everything will moderate. You'll see."

"This war will be long and bloody, Rolf." Almost whispering.

"If so it will be very bad for everyone, you and the *Tommis*, not just Germany."

Jake didn't know this guy. Not anymore.

Their meals came, and Rolf asked for a chilled bottle of Gewürztraminer. When the waiter left he said, "Dig in, Jake. Enough war talk."

The lamb was delicious. Jake wished he could enjoy it more. They ate in an uneasy near-silence, broken only by some small talk. The wine helped Jake's mood a little.

Later, after they both declined dessert, Rolf lowered his voice and said, "Do you know the name Putzi Hanfstaengl?" Stunned, Jake shook his head. Time to play dumb.

"The way you cover that military beat, I thought you might. Well, he is a German. Prominent Munich family. Used to be part of Hitler's inner circle, but now he is in Washington. He is under Roosevelt's care, I understand."

This turn of the conversation couldn't have surprised Jake more. "How do you know that?"

"That is not important. Like you, I find out things. Anyway, he knows too much about Hitler. Over there, he is a danger to the regime."

Jake stared hard into Rolf's eyes. "You don't even work for the *Zeitung* anymore, do you? Party member or not, you sound like part of the regime yourself."

"Call it survival. I am a loyal German, I have told you that. I also told you there are things you would not understand. Now then, Putzi Hanfstaengl, are you sure you've never met him?"

"I'd never even heard of him."

"Never talked to him?"

"How could I?"

"Never discussed possessions of his he might have left behind in Germany?"

Oh-oh, Jake thought. Rolf knows something. He sat mute, waiting to see what this guy would say next.

"Well, you've got connections, Jake. You probably know people in the White House." He leaned forward. His voice dropped to a whisper. "I want you to find Putzi Hanfstaengl and kill him."

CHAPTER TWENTY-EIGHT

Kill Putzi Hanfstaengl?

Jake felt the blood drain from his face, spilled what was left of his wine. He started to mop it up but the waiter materialized as if by magic, took care of it, and brought him another napkin. "Something more to drink, gentlemen?"

Rolf nodded.

Jake looked at Rolf's glass and said, "I'll have Schnapps this time, too." When the waiter left, he gazed at his knuckles but they had nothing to offer. Finally he managed, "That's a very bad joke, Rolf," knowing in his gut that it hadn't been a joke.

In both hands, Rolf clutched his glass in front of him like a poker hand. With a direct gaze, he said, "It is not a joke. I shocked you just now, I know, but listen. You could handle it yourself or have someone else do it. You know some shady characters in the States, I daresay even members of the Mob."

Rolf was right. Jake had watched a Stars' game in June with Raymond Chandler and the gangster Mickey Cohen, and he'd once had a drink with Carlo Gambino.

"Before you say no," Rolf went on, "consider this. We will place a substantial sum for you in a numbered account in Switzerland. And I do mean a substantial sum. Only you will know the number of the account. When the war is over, you go there and quietly collect it." An evil grin. "You know how to get in and out of Switzerland . . . don't you?"

Jake sat silent as the Sphinx.

"The Third Reich shows its gratitude in ways such as this to friends who lend a hand." Rolf put his glass down. "I cannot emphasize enough that we are talking about a considerable amount of money."

Jake had trouble catching his breath. His fingers drummed on the tabletop. What could he possibly say to such madness? The drinks arrived, buying him a moment. He gulped some Schnapps and felt the heat as the strong Dutch gin worked its way down to his stomach.

"Don't answer right now, Jake. Sleep on it. And while you're sleeping, think on this: You *are* capable of doing this. After all, you came all the way here to kill someone . . . didn't you?" Rolf held up a hand, palm outward, indicating "Don't answer."

Jake didn't. He took another drink.

"Five hundred thousand Reichsmarks," Rolf said, "in case you were wondering. They can be converted to Swiss francs and then into U.S. dollars. That would be approximately a quarter of a million dollars. You and your Valerie will be well set up, very well indeed."

Jake figured this offer held about as much water as Hitler's non-aggression pact with Russia, or his guarantee of Czech sovereignty. Even if such a deposit were made, once the Germans were defeated, Reichsmarks could be worthless. *If* the Germans were defeated, that is. The Nazis could still win if they made peace with Russia and threw all their might against England before America's growing power could take effect.

Jake took another sip and then spoke into the silence. "You won't get an answer out of me, Rolf, not till you tell me what happened to Dieter."

"You are right, Jake." Rolf studied his glass a moment, then looked up. "Okay, here is the story. Dieter was involved in a resistance group which the Gestapo uncovered. They executed three of the leaders as enemies of the state."

"Dieter and two others?" Jake mumbled.

"*Ja.* I am very sorry, old friend. I had nothing at all to do with it, you must believe that."

Sure I must, Jake thought darkly. "Who did it?" Staring daggers at Rolf. "Who ordered him killed?"

"I do not know."

"But you can find out."

"I doubt it. For your own good, Jake, don't ask me to, and do not try to find out yourself." Rolf took a drink, set the glass down and fiddled with his fork. "You would only get yourself killed." He reached over and touched Jake's arm. "Leave it alone. For your Valerie's sake, if not your own"—he pulled his hand away—"leave it alone."

Jake slowly shook his head. "Are you SS, Gestapo or what?" he said at last.

"Let's just say that I know how my bread is buttered. As I told you, it is survival . . . Now, just sleep on this. Tomorrow I will move you to the Hotel Eden. Very comfortable, yet less expensive."

And with hidden microphones in the rooms, Jake thought. He drained the rest of his Schnapps in one long swig.

They parted shortly after that.

Back in his room, Jake paced around and around like a mule tethered to a grinding wheel. He'd been in plenty of bad fixes before, but never anything like this.

Instead of a helpful friend, Rolf had turned out to be some sort of government agent, and one who'd pointedly asked whether Jake had ever met or spoken to Hanfstaengl. That was troubling enough, but worst of all was the fact that he was at a dead end on who killed Dieter. Had Jake come all this way for nothing?

At breakfast the next morning, the Berlin papers reported that the Russians had broken through north and south of Stalingrad to surround Germany's Sixth Army. Jake's lips made a whistling shape. This was big, for the state-controlled press to make such an admission. The Wehrmacht was in trouble in Russia. Jake glanced around the room, trying hard not to smile.

This development was blamed on the failure of the Romanian army to hold back the Reds. These inept "allies" had been covering the Germans' left flank.

Of course the papers claimed the setback was only temporary. General von Kleist's Fourth Panzer Army would crash through and relieve their encircled comrades. Meanwhile, Hermann Goering's Luftwaffe would keep them well supplied by air. The Third Reich's gallant soldiers would not want for food and ammunition.

And while the German air force now faced its greatest challenge, its commander was back here throwing parties for newspapermen. It was plain crazy.

Pushing the papers aside and taking a bite of a rich egg dish, he pondered Rolf. They'd been good friends back in L.A. How could a man change so much in a few years, go from a typical, cynical journalist to some kind of Nazi operative? Had Jake been this bad a judge of character?

Rolf had mentioned possessions Putzi Hanfstaengl might have left behind. Could he know about the Hindenburg letter? An even bigger question was: How should Jake deal with this grotesque offer to kill the man? Should he play along?

He'd come here to find out about Dieter's murder. And, if possible, do something about it. Maybe Rolf was right. Maybe he *had* come here to kill someone.

CHAPTER TWENTY-NINE

Rolf came by the Adlon the next day and Jake checked out. They walked along the Kurfürstendamm to the Hotel Eden under a drab sky promising snow. An S-bahn streetcar rumbled past.

Lugging his satchel as he trudged, Jake felt smothered by a sense of being swept along in this tide of events. He was no longer in control of anything. He hated the feeling. Should have stayed home . . . or in London; great town . . . Basel had looked nice, too. In fact, right now anyplace looked better than Berlin. He told himself to confront Rolf. Soon. Today.

Although smaller and less grand than the Adlon, the Hotel Eden was nice enough. Clean, and decorated in an art deco style.

Jake registered and put his things in his room on the third floor. He wondered if it was bugged. The notice on the back of the door, besides listing the checkout time, said ominously that guests were to proceed rapidly to the basement shelter in case of air raid.

After they took a corner booth in the hotel bar, Rolf went to the counter and collected two steins of *Spaten-Bräu*. He sat again, lifted his colorful earthenware mug and said, "Prosit."

Uneasy moments passed. Fiddling with a napkin, Jake decided to break the silence."You've got to give me more on Dieter, on his execution. Don't tell me the only reason I'm here is so you could hire me to kill someone I don't even know, this Putzi person."

Rolf grimaced and pursed his lips.

"What's his last name again?" Jake asked.

"Hanfstaengl. Putzi Hanfstaengl."

"That's a mouthful. How do you spell it?" Although Jake knew very well.

Meeting Jake's eyes again, Rolf spelled it out, letter by letter, then added, "I've said all I can say about your uncle. Stay away from it, Jake. Stay away from it."

Nothing was clear to Jake anymore, nothing except that this one-time friend had turned out to be a real worm. Jake felt like leaping across the table and . . . what, punch him in the face? Choke the living daylights out of him?

Calm down, Jake told himself. Control your breathing. He took a gulp of his lager.

"Have you been thinking?" Rolf asked, doing the poker-hand thing with his stein.

"Thinking?"

"Don't play dumb, Jake. Thinking about Putzi Hanfstaengl and the Swiss bank account."

"I'll tell you tomorrow."

"On the way to Goering's?"

"Or on the way back."

That night Jake checked the lamps, picture frames and bottoms of drawers for hidden microphones. He didn't find any, but he was no expert on such things.

Rolf was at the wheel of a black Audi with running boards and big fender-mounted headlights as they drove north the next day. Outside of Berlin, the road to Karinhalle ran through flat country dotted with small lakes and streams and lots of trees.

It had snowed during the night but the smooth blacktop already had been plowed clear. Snow stood in mounds at the side of the road and clung to tree branches. Jake was glad the Audi's heater worked.

Suddenly Rolf played his hand. "Might as well level with you,

Jake. You deserve to know. I was a government agent the whole time I was in L.A."

Jake choked back a gasp. He shot Rolf a hard look.

"I was sent to learn what I could about Walt Disney, see if we could infiltrate his studio, maybe slip some propaganda tidbits into his movies and cartoons."

Holy smoke.

"We knew he was a political conservative, anti-labor and anti-Roosevelt. When that didn't pan out, I was told to find out how hard it might be to kidnap him, since Hanfstaengl by that time had bolted."

"Kidnap Disney so you could swap him for Hanfstaengl?"

"Exactly."

So Jake had pegged that right after all, the kidnapping plot. He should have been pleased at his sagacity. He wasn't.

"You know what first put you onto that, Jake, the notion of Germany kidnapping Disney?"

God, the things Jake was hearing. No point in even answering.

"I did. We were at the Continental after work. I'd had a couple too many and let slip a wrong word or two. Biggest mistake I ever made in this business."

That wasn't true. Dieter had tipped him off to the Disney thing with his cryptic cable from Denmark. Why was Rolf doing all this lying?

"But then it rather amused me, the way you tried to dig into it, this horrible Nazi plot to nab your great American icon. Snooping around in L.A.'s German restaurants and all. You know, Jake, I always loved to watch you work. Always the bulldog. Anyway, I was also checking on the other studios, other producers, finding out who might be inclined to see things our way. Newspaper publishers, too. Grandpa Hearst looked like a fine candidate—back then.

"But there wasn't anything fake about our friendship, Jake, you must believe that. I've always liked you. All those good times we had? Totally on the up and up. Now here you are, and still the bulldog. You might get some good stuff out here at Karinhalle." He glanced over at his passenger. "Don't worry, you are still a great friend. I owe you much. I will not blow your cover. Swiss reporter, then?"

"Yes."

"By the way, what is your name? I will have to introduce you around."

No point in ducking it. Jake would probably be searched and have to show his passport. "Hans-Karl Vogel."

Rolf chuckled. "I like it. Well, Hans-Karl Vogel, I hope you will still think of me as a friend, and that you'll try to understand our point of view. Just as Britain has the right to profit from its empire, Germany should be the economic master of continental Europe. It makes sense."

No it doesn't, Jake thought. You could have been the economic top dog without invading and occupying all those countries. And you'd have been even stronger economically if you'd left your Jewish business leaders and bankers alone to do what they do. No, your point of view stinks.

Jake also thought about Rolf quizzing him on possessions Putzi Hanfstaengl might have left behind in Germany. That scared him.

"A *Pfennig* for your thoughts," Rolf said.

"You'd be getting cheated. I was only thinking what pretty country this is."

"Liar." Rolf slowed as a line of field gray military trucks passed in the opposite direction. One big vehicle carried an artillery piece. "That is our 88-millimeter," he said. "Great weapon. Shot the hell out of the British tanks in Africa."

"Not all of them," Jake pointed out.

"No." Rolf's brow pinched. "Not all of them." A long pause. He looked worried. "You said you'd give me your answer today."

"And I will. Be patient."

"Jake, I am under the gun here." His composure slipping now. "Can't stall them much longer. They want Hanfstaengl badly."

"Why? Because he knows Hitler had his niece bumped off after she got tired of shacking up with him?"

"Geli Raubal committed suicide."

"Did she?"

"Of course."

"A beautiful young woman with her whole life ahead of her? Sure, and I'm Clark Gable. Rolf, you're a fool, a bloody fool."

"Bloody fool? Ha. That's a Limey term. You came in through England, didn't you?" Rolf's spirits rising again, if only for a moment. "Switzerland by way of England. Bloody fool indeed."

A small, russet-colored deer sprang across the road in front of them, leapt nimbly over the plowed snow at the shoulder, and vanished among the trees.

Rolf glanced in that direction. "Well, since you appreciate this landscape, this batch of woods we are coming to is the Schönheide Forest. Karinhalle is not far now."

They passed through checkpoints at two perimeter fences before the grand place appeared out of the trees, part hewn stone, part stucco and part half-timbered in the north German style. Jake thought its ostentatious scale was all wrong for the pastoral surroundings. He knew that Hitler had named Goering, among his other titles, Grand Master of the Hunt. Comic opera absurdity; the Third Reich abounded in it.

A guard in a sky-blue Luftwaffe uniform checked their papers against names on his clipboard but, to Jake's surprise, didn't search them.

At the massive wooden doors, a butler took their hats and overcoats and led them into a huge reception room lined with suits of armor and scores of paintings. Probably stolen. A tall Christmas tree bright with ornaments stood in a corner.

Jake knew that Karinhalle was named for Goering's first wife, the Swedish Baroness Karin von Something or Other. Goering had met her in Sweden, where he'd worked as a civilian pilot and parachute salesman after the First War. The baroness died of tuberculosis, which had broken Goering's heart, or so the story went. A decorated fighter pilot in the war, he had returned to Germany, fallen under Hitler's spell, and also remarried. Jake couldn't remember the name of Wife No. 2.

At the end of the room a garish, oversized painting of the Reichsmarshal, dressed like a Teutonic knight, caught Jake's eye. One hand rested on the hilt of a long sword. Jake had to stifle a laugh at the pomposity.

Seven or eight men walked about, examining the decorations, either more impressed than Jake or pretending to be. Rolf called some of them by name and introduced Jake as "Hans Vogel of the Swiss press." Happily, that raised no questions. One lone Luftwaffe military policeman stood guard along the wall, eyeing the guests. Others gradually arrived and soon the room held about twenty-five men, all wearing suits and ties.

Six attractive women entered through a side door carrying filled champagne glasses on silver trays. Jake had half expected Bavarian-style serving wench outfits, but these ladies wore cocktail dresses of varying styles and colors. Jake noticed—of course—that two of them wore low-cut necklines revealing ample German bosoms. The women looked to be in their mid-twenties to early thirties. "Professional hostesses" described them better than "waitresses." Jake thought of another, much older, word.

Soon everyone was sipping good French champagne—Jake wondered what brand—conversing with one another or flirting with the women.

A muted sound system piped Christmas carols and light classics into the room. Jake recognized some Strauss waltzes. The music suddenly stopped and—honest to God—a fanfare rang out, rich with brass, and Goering swept regally into the room, his fat body encased in a tailored uniform bristling with gold braid and medals. The word buffoon sprang into Jake's mind. Goering's large, strong-jawed face, now puffy, retained a shade of its youthful handsomeness. A *Pour le Mérite*—the Blue Max, Germany's Medal of Honor—hung at his throat.

"Members of the international press," he announced, his arms sweeping out grandly, "I bid you welcome to Karinhalle."

Jake's throat caught. *Jesus, I'm really here.*

A couple of men took out notebooks. Goering noticed. *"Nein, nein,"* he boomed. "I will have some official remarks for you later, my friends, over dinner, but first we must get acquainted, *ja?"*

Rolf moved to Goering's side, an apparent signal, for a couple of other journalists lined up behind him. Rolf gestured for Jake to join the queue. God, Jake thought, I'm about the meet the No. 2 Nazi of them all. He hoped he wasn't sweating. "My name is Hans-Karl Vogel," he drilled himself. "I am a Swiss journalist. My name is Hans-Karl Vogel. I am a Swiss journalist."

Soon, like a king granting an audience, Goering was taking individual introductions.

"Rolf Becker, *Deutsche Zeitung.*" Rolf clicked his heels. Pathetic, Jake thought.

"Ja, Rolf my friend, good to see you again." Shaking hands.

"Konrad Hirsch, *Der Angriff.*"

"Delighted, Herr Hirsch. *Willkommen.*"

"Maurice Devereux, *Le Progrés*, Lyon."

"Bienvenu, monsieur." When Jake's turn came, he said, "Hans-Karl Vogel, *Oltner Tagblatt*, Switzerland." This was a paper Jake had read at breakfast the morning *O for Oliver* had landed.

"A *Schweizer*, how grand." Blue eyes sparkling with charisma. "*Willkommen.*" His handshake was firm.

When everyone had met the great man, the guests drifted back into small clusters. Like a fat bumble bee, Goering buzzed from one to another, making small talk.

As the ladies refilled glasses, a group of young men burst in, dressed in Bavarian costumes with suspenders, short pants,

Lederhosen and little Tyrolean hats. They paraded to the center of the room and launched into a leg-kicking, heel-slapping folk dance as oom-pah music gushed from the speakers. The guests formed a circle around them and tapped their feet to the music. Some tried to clap along as best they could with champagne flutes in their hands. Others whistled.

While hairy knees flashed, Jake saw Goering, still working the room, approach. Jake told himself, "In for a penny . . . I *am* a reporter, after all."

"Your excellency, I wonder if I might interview you? My country values its friendship with Germany but there are concerns about the relationship now that the war has been on for three years."

"And which country is that again?"

"Switzerland, sir."

"*Ach so*, you are the *Schweizer*. I had a splendid ski holiday at St. Moritz many years ago, 1912 perhaps. No, '13 I believe. It is still in good repair?"

"Of course, sir, in fact the resort has been enlarged."

"Good. So you wish a private interview with the Reichs-marshal?"

Maybe, using all the reporter charm and guile he was said to have back in L.A., he could wheedle something useful out of Goering, like how to meet Wernher von Braun. It would be tricky but maybe he could.

"Well," the fat man said, "I should be delighted to impart a few words to the good people of Switzerland. After dinner then."

CHAPTER THIRTY

When the folk dance ended, Goering led his guests down a corridor to a long dining hall that screamed hunting lodge. Mounted trophies of deer and bear heads lined rough wooden walls along with pith helmets and antique rifles arranged in crisscross fashion. Heavy oak beams. Wainscoting of a darker wood hugged the walls' lower halves. Trestle tables were set up in a narrow U-shape.

Goering took his place of precedence at the center of the U's base. Jake saw no place cards and Goering said with a sweep of his big arms, "Sit wherever you like, gentlemen."

Rolf quickly took a seat close to the host, and Jake sat next to him. Waiters appeared bearing pitchers of beer and steaming platters of beef, pork, venison and warm fresh bread. Side dishes included sauerkraut and potato salad. Hunting lodge meets Bavarian beer hall.

Goering speared slabs of meat for himself and, after his plate was filled, the others helped themselves. A man on Jake's left, early twenties with slicked-back hair and a trim mustache, introduced himself as Federico Fellini of Italy's *Il Popolo di Roma*.

"*Buon giorno*," Jake said. "Jake, er, Hans-Karl Vogel, Switzerland." Stupid damn mistake. Can't ever slip like that again, he scolded himself. He prayed that Goering, chattering away with a man at his elbow, hadn't noticed.

Goering stood, lifted a beer stein and proposed a toast "to all of the Third Reich's splendid European friends." The guests rose and drank to the toast, though Jake detected fake enthusiasm in some of them, including the Italian kid at his side. Jake knew a lot about faking.

Fellini leaned toward him and said, "I am a reporter now, but what I really want to do is write screenplays and perhaps even direct. I have lots of ideas for films."

"I hope it works out," Jake said. "Good luck with that."

When the guests sat again, the Italian bit into a sauce-covered potato and said softly, "Wretched food. No wonder so many Germans are fat as battleships."

Jake flashed him a small sidelong grin.

"So you are Swiss?" Again, little more than a whisper. "I love Switzerland. I wish that my country too was neutral."

Jake glanced about, making sure everyone was deep in their own conversations before answering.

"You don't support the Axis cause then?"

It looked as if Fellini almost laughed. "Nor do ninety percent of my countrymen. We have no quarrel with Britain or America." He cupped his hand at the left side of his mouth to foil any lip readers at his end of the table. "*Il Duce* has made a grievous mistake."

Jake didn't answer. He knew Italian divisions had been decimated at El Alamein. A couple of others were supposed to be in Russia, poor devils.

He also knew there was no one in this room he could trust, including this innocent-sounding kid. "Actually, *amico*," he said, "I find the sauerkraut rather good."

When the meals were mostly finished, Goering pulled his bulk to his feet and announced, "Now for the official remarks I mentioned." Notebooks and pencils appeared, including Jake's.

"We are grateful for the help our European friends have supplied to the Third Reich, raw materials, civilian workers and so on. German industry is redoubling its efforts. In addition to being commander-in-chief of the Luftwaffe I am also Minister of Armaments, you know. Soon our powerful offensive will be resumed."

In the deep Russian snows? Jake asked silently. He'd heard the adage that the Soviets' best commander was General Winter.

"We will see this through," Goering went on, "to a successful conclusion, and then the New Order in Europe will enter into a long period of peace and prosperity for all of us."

Someone raised a hand and said, "But what of England, sir?"

Irritation flashed across Goering's face. "If the *Englanderen* know what is good for them, they will wise up and make peace." He made a chopping motion with his hand. "Otherwise we will crush them. Now, no more questions until I have finished." He droned on for several minutes, spouting more propaganda, but losing steam as he went. It seemed to Jake that he was bored with himself. Goering's eyes began to look glazed.

When he finished, he took questions. There were only three or four lame ones, which Jake figured had been planted. None was as bold as that first one.

Remembering the cabinetmaker on the train, Jake wanted to ask about dispersing aircraft production in small shops but knew he mustn't.

Then *Signore* Fellini asked when the Italian troops on the eastern front would be allowed to go home. Goering snapped back into focus and fixed him with a stern look. "When their mission has been completed."

The dinner broke up shortly after that and the guests were herded into another room with chairs, love seats and small tables positioned around a blazing fireplace. A string quartet played Bach.

The women in their take-me dresses magically reappeared, carrying trays of brandy snifters and boxes of cigars. Before Jake could accept either, a butler approached, bobbed his head and said, "You are the Swiss gentleman?"

Jake nodded and the man said, "If you will come with me, *bitte*, the Reichsmarshal will see you now."

Jake followed the man up a stairway into a large upper room. Goering was there, admiring an intricate model train network that filled most of the room. A locomotive pulling eight or nine cars chugged through a tunnel and up a hill, sending off a tart ozone smell.

Goering turned from it, shiny-eyed, and said, "My hobby. *Wunderbar*, no?"

"Certainly," Jake said, trying to hide his stupefaction. The head of the Luftwaffe and German armaments production playing with toy trains while the army faced disaster on a frozen battlefield half a continent away.

Goering spent several minutes describing the layout, the switching mechanisms, signal lights, trestle bridges, an elaborate coach which he said was a perfect model of his own special railroad car.

He was on something. Not heroin. Jake had seen heroin addicts in L.A. Cocaine then? No, he wasn't euphoric enough for that. He was just kind of floating. Maybe morphine. At last he motioned Jake to a chair and sat opposite him, sinking onto a leather sofa that groaned under his girth.

"So, Herr Swiss reporter, what is it you wish to know?"

Jake asked several innocent questions. How were Germany's relations with Switzerland? Excellent, Goering said, although he was aware that many Allied spies operated there. Was there any chance of trade interruptions? None in the least. Germany needed Swiss electrical equipment, precision instruments, dairy products—"Ah, the delectable cheeses you have"—and the Swiss economy needed German marks.

Time to cross a line, Jake decided. "How do you think the war will go, Reichsmarshal?"

"We will win, of course. But"—he stopped and inspected his beringed fingers—"it is more difficult now. We have . . ." Goering's eyes lost focus. He sat mute for at least a minute as if he were all alone. Jake, tense, didn't move, wondering what, if anything, was going on in the mind behind that large face.

Then Goering shook himself and said, "Will you excuse me for a moment?" He stood and left the room.

What a truly strange man, Jake thought, staring at the elaborate model-train setup. Strange, and stripped of the arrogance of power, which he surely radiated a couple of years ago. Because his Luftwaffe was in trouble, so was his standing with Hitler, and Goering knew it all too well.

Jake caught sight of a small, leather-bound book on an end table next to the sofa Goering had occupied. Could be a journal or a book of appointments—or anything. Might contain something revealing. Should he steal a peek? He wouldn't take long, just a quick look. Goering would be gone another minute or two, wouldn't he? Did Jake hear any sound from the other room? No.

Well, okay then, this is what reporters do. He pulled himself to his feet, walked over softly, glanced behind himself once, and put a hand on the cover. A gold Maltese cross and swastika were embossed on the rich, chestnut-colored leather, along with the word *Ullr*. Jake didn't know much about pagan German mythology, but he recalled from something he'd read that Ullr was the ancient god of something, the hunt, maybe.

He'd just begun to raise the cover to peer inside when he heard a door squeak and the "huh-umph" of a throat clearing. He pulled his hand away from the book, turned, and found himself looking at the butler who'd led him up here a little while ago. Trying to look casual about it, Jake walked slowly toward his chair, while the man gave him a cold stare. Then he allowed a miniscule bob of his head and said, "I came to see if you would you like something to drink." Speaking coldly and not adding "sir."

"Thank you, no, I'm fine." Jake took his seat.

The man's stare lingered a moment before he said, "As you

wish," and left as quietly as he'd appeared.

Jake wiped his forehead with the back of his hand. He'd learned nothing at all but felt as guilty as if he'd read five or six pages.

Goering reappeared. Jake turned his attention from the book to this big man. He was floating again—he'd taken something while out of the room. Jake found it hard to picture this enigma as a dashing fighter pilot twenty-five years ago.

"Yes," Goering mumbled, his corpulence challenging the sofa again. "The Swiss are our good friends. I have funds in Zurich, in the Federated Bank of Switzerland." He fixed Jake's face with a hard stare. "You know it, of course."

The Federated Bank of Switzerland? Jake nodded. He decided not to pursue the war difficulties Goering had started to mention. After asking a couple of harmless questions and getting mundane answers, Jake took a different shot, a risky one. "Do you know Magda Goebbels?"

But it seemed to be all right when Goering, though looking surprised, said, "Of course, the poor, dear woman."

"Poor woman?"

"Her husband has had many blatant affairs, right out in the open. Film actresses and the like. Humiliated her shamefully. She sought a divorce, but the Führer forbade it. Bad for appearances. He ordered them to make it up, or at least pretend to. And he told Goebbels 'no more affairs, absolutely none.' "

Goering must really despise Goebbels, Jake thought, for him to be telling me all this. There must be a hell of a power struggle at the level just below Hitler—a power struggle that Goering could be losing to Goebbels and Himmler.

The big man scratched his nose, then looked straight at Jake. "All of that is just between us, eh?" He waved a hand in a big sweeping gesture. "But enough of that sorry business."

Jake found these wild mood swings—from hard-ass Nazi to buddy buddy—unnerving.

Goering fell silent. Time dragged. Then with a sudden steely gaze he blurted, "You are not Swiss!"

Jake froze.

"There is something about your face, your eyes, your manner. I saw it at dinner. You do not have the typical reserve of the Swiss. One could quite easily take you for an American."

Jesus. Cold fear iced Jake's veins. Suddenly he couldn't breathe.

"But of course it is quite impossible that you could be American." Another long pause, then, "You are Irish!"

"Irish? I assure you, sir—"

"You do not know the Federated Bank in Zurich. That was quite apparent on your face."

Jake wondered if he would leave here alive . . . or in chains. "But there are many banks," he countered. "I'm from a small town, Olten, many kilometers from Zurich and its banks."

"Bosh. You are Irish. But that is all right. I do not mind." Surprising Jake. "You hate the English as much as we do. Your neutrality is admirable, but it would be so much more helpful if you would cooperate with us, allow us to establish bases. Our warplanes and U-boats could make good use of bases in Ireland."

"I'm sure that's true, but as a Swiss newspaperman, there is nothing—"

"Are you IRA?"

"IRA? I assure you, sir, I am not—"

"I had thought that we had friends in the IRA." Jake wondered about Goering's use of the past tense. Maybe the Irish were resigned to the belief that in the end the Germans would not defeat Britain, and Goering realized it.

"Never mind." The fat man waved a hand, swatting away the whole matter. "You are here with Rolf Becker, a good man, so I will pry no further into your situation." His eyes lost focus again and he sank against the back of the sofa as if surrendering to sleep.

Jake sat mute as interminable minutes passed.

Then Goering mumbled to himself, as if sleep-talking, "Why oh why did the Führer ever march into Russia? I told him . . ." His eyes closed. "I told him . . ." Silence overcame him. Time dragged in the hushed room. Jake could hear his own breathing.

He could see that this man was weighed down by his failure in the fall of 1940 in what was being called the Battle of Britain. This fat bankrupt seemed to be hiding here, in denial of the enormous problem of supplying the beleaguered troops in Stalingrad, and of his obvious loss of stature with Hitler. Pathetic.

Goering stirred, opened his eyes, leaned forward and stared hard at Jake. "What I just said—about Russia—you will forget that." The tough Nazi again. A moment passed uneasily, then the big man said, "If there is nothing more, Herr O'Connor or whatever your name is"—a wicked laugh—"I will bid you good night. And tell Herr Becker that your secret is safe."

Coming down the stairs a bit unsteadily, Jake wondered how much, if any, of what he'd just experienced had been an act. Was this doper a complete buffoon or had he been trying to throw Jake off? Suspicions had surely been raised. Even high on drugs, Goering had spotted that there was nothing very Swiss about him.

Would Goering order someone to keep an eye on this nosy companion of Rolf Becker's? Quite possibly. Asking for that private meeting, Jake knew, had been the mistake of a too-eager reporter. And he never should have mentioned Magda Goebbels. *Damn, you go waltzing in there, hoping to get a story, plus some info Roosevelt could use, as if that was some American major. That's one of the two or three most powerful men in Germany, you idiot.*

As he reached the downstairs hallway, Jake's skin felt clammy, his stomach queasy. He thought he might have to duck into a restroom and throw up. He leaned against a wall and fought it off. Over-eagerness had poisoned his judgment. He wondered what the hell that creepy butler might be telling Goering about his snooping visitor.

When he finally got his nerves back in check, Jake made up his mind about something.

As the Audi pulled onto the road back to Berlin, he said, "I'll do it, Rolf."

"How did it go with Goering?"

"Did you hear what I said? I said I'll do it. I'll kill this Hanfstaengl person."

CHAPTER THIRTY-ONE

Surprise spilled across Rolf's face. The car swerved for a moment, the shielded headlights dancing dimly across the road, before he could straighten it out.

"I'll kill him on one condition," Jake said. "You introduce me to Wernher von Braun."

"Wernher who?"

"Wernher von Braun, the rocket man."

Jake figured if he could get home with something on von Braun's rocket, the White House would owe him big. Hanfstaengl was already in deep hiding; maybe Jake could get Steve Early to issue a false story to the wires that somebody had killed him. Rolf would be none the wiser. Roosevelt liked ploys like that. Appealed to his taste for trickery.

"I know nothing of such a man," Rolf said unconvincingly.

"The hell you don't, Rolf. The guy who's building rockets for the old Fatherland, firing them off into the Baltic. Don't play dumb with me."

Rolf frowned, thought a moment. A shadowy suggestion of trees whirred past in the darkness. Finally, he said, "*Ach*, that is top secret. Very top. You've always been full of surprises, Jake, but this time you blow me right out of the water. How did you ever dig that up?"

"Never mind that. Do we have a deal or not?"

"Even if I could do this, I would have to do some checking around.

Be very dangerous. If Himmler got word that I was nosing—"

"Start with Unter den Linden University."

"Jesus, you are good." Rolf hit the steering wheel with the flat of his right hand. "If you go home and write a story on that—"

"I won't," Jake said, knowing that he *would*, unless FDR told him not to.

"If you are *not* going to write a story, why do you want to contact him?"

Good question. Jake thought a moment. "Okay, I admit, if I get something good I will file a story, but only if the rocket becomes a weapon and you people use it. Once it's in use, the Allies will know about it and my piece can't hurt you. Before such a thing's deployed, my story would be seen as wild speculation, a non-story."

"Hmm," Rolf said. A moment lengthened before he blurted, "But no, it is out of the question."

"Oh? You said you were getting desperate, Rolf. Had to get this done. Well, you do something for me, I do something for you."

"I am getting you half a million marks. Isn't that enough?"

Jake didn't answer. He still believed that offer was as worthless as bows and arrows to a Panzer corps.

"Look, Jake, no one trusts anyone here anymore. Himmler is probably having von Braun watched, not sure he is totally on board. Forget about him. If you don't eliminate Hanfstaengl, or if you write something about von Braun, it will be very bad for you—and for your lovely fiancée."

Yeah, there were Nazi agents in the U.S., Jake knew that. "Man," he snarled, "what the hell's happened to you? You've gone from being a friend to being a Nazi creep who blackmails people, threatens loved ones, shit like that."

"It's the craziness here in this country right now. I told you, I'm under the gun here. If I can't get this done—"

Rolf took a hand off the wheel and made a slashing motion across his throat.

Jake stared at this now-stranger. "Okay then, we don't have a deal." Jake leaned back in his seat and looked out at a road sign that flashed past in the dark. BERLIN, 10 KM.

"Risky shit," Rolf muttered to himself.

Long minutes elapsed, the silence broken only by the drone of the motor, the whine of tires on macadam. Jake's thoughts strayed darkly back to Uncle Dieter, as they did several times a day. Had Rolf told the truth about his death? Finding out who'd ordered Dieter murdered, and why, wouldn't bring him back, but Jake still needed to *know*, and maybe exact some kind of retribution. That's why he'd come here, damn it.

Eventually, as the blacked-out suburbs of Berlin began to appear, Rolf spoke again. One word. "Okay."

"Okay?" Jake had almost forgotten about von Braun.

"Yes, okay. You drive a hard and dangerous bargain. But I will find out about von Braun, and tell you tomorrow. But if you write a story *before* the rocket is used as a war weapon, if it ever is, our people will find your woman—"

"Shut up, Rolf." A frigid silence filled the car. Soon they were in city streets.

"How are you going to do it?" Rolf said at last. "Kill Hanfstaengl."

"As you said, I know some bad characters in L.A. Once I'm back home, three-thousand miles from Washington with alibis galore, I'll hire somebody to bump him off."

Rolf stared at him. "Good," he said softly but sounding unconvinced.

Jake woke from troubled sleep several times that night. In the morning, he found a folded note had been slipped under the door of his hotel room. He picked it up and recognized Rolf's printing. "BISMARCK 1272, VON BRAUN'S FLAT."

He showered, dressed, and gulped down a cup of the hotel's

mock coffee. Then he stepped out into a clear, frigid morning and found a phone box down the street. Jake wasn't going to make any calls from his room. He took out a handful of German coins, read the instructions, dropped a five-*Pfennig* piece in the slot.

"*Telefon Fräulein,*" a woman said.

Jake gave her the numbers and was told to deposit, "*Zehn Pfennig, bitte.*"

Soon he heard a phone ring. After three quick double buzzes, a strong male voice answered.

"*Herr Doktor von Braun?*"

"*Ja.*"

"This is Hans-Karl Vogel of Schätzen Products of Zurich, and—"

"That is most interesting," von Braun jumped in. Jake couldn't imagine why.

"—and we have some electrical instruments, timers and so forth that I'd like to tell you about."

Von Braun laughed, again catching Jake by surprise. "Yes, certainly. I am always interested in precision instruments from Switzerland. Do you know *Universität Unter den Linden?*"

"Yes, I do."

"Come at 6 p.m. then. Physics Department. My office is Room 12."

"Thank you, Doctor. I'll see you at six."

Jake put down the phone, his hand shaking. That was easy, he thought. Too easy. And what the hell had the man been laughing about? Had Rolf contacted von Braun? Blown his cover? Had Jake mentioned von Braun to anyone else? Goering? God, he hoped not. He tried to remember.

Back in his room, he couldn't have felt more alone. Or futile. Uncle Dieter dead, and no leads whatever on that. Rolf a damned Nazi. All the time they'd palled around in L.A. he'd never picked up on any clue, any character trait, that would suggest he might be a Nazi agent. So here was Jake, bereft and friendless in the enemy capital. And stupidly calling attention to himself with the loopy but dangerous Hermann Goering.

He thought about Tapestry, the British agent in Berlin. Colonel Freeborn had told him to contact her only in an emergency. Well, he needed a friend. Rolf wasn't a friend. Jake was alone and frightened. Didn't this constitute an emergency?

He puzzled over it for half an hour, pacing round and round the room, before making his decision. Finally, he said, "Okay, what the hell."

CHAPTER THIRTY-TWO

Hours later, having used Berlin's subway and then five blocks of foot power, he found himself on *Marburgstrasse* in the Schöneberg district. Number 84 was one in a long line of attached two-story, red-brick rowhouses with steep slate roofs. He scanned the street as he approached and saw no one about.

At exactly 3 p.m. as instructed, his heart flittering, he went to the maroon-lacquered door and pushed the button. He heard no footsteps but, as seconds ticked by, he felt himself being scrutinized through the tiny peephole.

He heard the clunk of a lock being thrown, then the door opened about three inches, enough to see a wide-open green eye and—*Jesus!* —the snout of a pistol, both leveled at him.

Following Colonel Freeborn's instruction, he said, "Excuse me, I am looking for the *Volkspark*. Can you direct me?"

"The one on *Lessingstrasse*?" the woman said, and opened the door wider. She gave a come-in jerk of her head, which Jake obeyed. He noticed that she scanned the street in the brief flash of time before snapping the door shut.

Tapestry stood about five-four, wore a navy blue woolen skirt, a white blouse buttoned at the neck, and was barefoot. Beneath dark blond hair tied back in a bun and those green eyes, she indeed had a broken nose, but Jake didn't find it unpleasant. In fact, he thought, the twisted bridge added character to a lovely face. Slug Irene Dunne across the snout and here's what you'd have.

She'd lowered the gun, a Luger, to her side. "About the pistol I ham sorry," she said in accented English, and went to a narrow table against a wall and put it down beneath a lamp. "One cannot be too careful."

Jake still hadn't uttered a word. He stood there, taking in a large sitting room. A patterned sofa with a gooseneck lamp at one end, two overstuffed chairs, a wind-up Victrola sitting atop a walnut radio console, hardwood floor partly covered by a Persian-looking rug, and a Christmas tree in one corner.

Wiring leading to the light switches was attached to the walls, indicating this old place pre-dated the age of electric lights.

"Your name I do not know," Tapestry said with a cautious smile, "only that you are an American agent."

"And I don't know yours. Are we supposed to leave it that way?" It felt rather good to be speaking English again after several days of nothing but German.

"I haff no instructions on that," she said, "from our Colonel Freeborn. And how is the dear man?" A dash of sarcasm there?

"He was fine a few days ago."

"Good. Well, I am Gretchen Siedler. Would you like some tea? One cannot get real coffee anymore."

"Sure. Thanks."

"I will put the pot on then." She motioned toward a chair. "Please sit, make yourself comfortable. Tell me your name only if you wish."

Why not? Jake thought. If Colonel Freeborn trusts her, I guess I should, too. "It's Jake. Jake Weaver."

"I am pleased to meet you, Mr. Weaver." She offered her hand and he took it. Long, slender fingers grasped his with strength. She released the grip and headed toward an arched doorway. "I will be only a moment."

Jake sat in the chair she'd indicated. While he heard kitchen noises and water running from a tap, his eyes fell on a gold-framed photograph on an end table. A young man's smiling face in a peaked Luftwaffe cap and a uniform tunic fastened at the neck. Her late husband, Jake surmised.

"My late husband," said Gretchen Siedler, suddenly back in the room.

"I heard about him. I'm very sorry."

"Thank you." Her face clouded. "Such a waste. A senseless waste, serving these fool Nazis. But let us not speak of that." She settled in the chair opposite him and crossed her bare legs at the ankles. Nice ankles, he noticed.

Most women he knew wouldn't have gone barefoot in the presence of a stranger. He admired Gretchen's self-confidence. The shape of her ankles, too. Come on Sweets, he thought, thinking of Valerie. Don't be reading my mind.

"I feel I must tell you something," Gretchen said. "I was against the Nazis at the start. I was nineteen and at university when they came to power, nine, ten years ago. I disliked their strong-arm tactics, the torchlight parades, their hateful treatment of the Jews. I was married a year later and my Friedrich felt the same. But gradually I saw the people regaining their pride, and we got caught up in it, though I am ashamed to admit it now. It was intoxicating, the economy growing strong, great highways being built, the glory of the Olympic Games."

"And your husband joined the Luftwaffe," Jake said.

"He did not join," she said firmly, her face hard for a moment. "Friedrich was conscripted by the army. He had been in a sport flying club; he loved to fly. When they learned he was a pilot, he was placed in the Luftwaffe. He had no choice. Since my husband was serving, I felt I should also. I had a friend in the Abwehr, military intelligence. I spoke English, so I was sent there, to our London embassy, to find whatever low-level intelligence I could."

"And the war broke out," Jake put in, "you were caught, and

your husband was killed in the Blitz. I am very sorry about that," he added softly.

"One moves on, but thank you, Mr. Weaver. You must be a kind man."

"Colonel Freeborn assured me that you're anti-Nazi."

"I am *very* anti-Nazi. My eyes have been opened. I hope you believe me. I had been seduced by all that false glory. My Friedrich died in vain. So stupid, bombing London. So many people killed, and for what?"

A sharp whistling sound chirped from the kitchen. "Excuse me, the water, it is ready."

She got up and disappeared through the arch. "Do you require cream?" she called. "I have no sugar. It is difficult to get sugar."

"No, plain is fine."

She returned carrying two steaming mugs and handed him one, then sat in her chair.

"I do believe you, about your being anti-Nazi," Jake said. "So what about the name Tapestry?"

"I have no idea. They make a game, the British, of thinking up odd code names for their agents. Old Freeborn runs someone in Hamburg known as Dandelion," she said with a small laugh. "The English sense of humor is so different from that of the German. It is subtle; ours is coarse. Crude sexual jokes are common. Now, will you tell me something of yourself?"

Jake sipped some tea. It was good. He was hesitant, but he did need a friend, and he felt, *hoped,* he could trust this woman. He'd grown cynical during his years of reporting, developed a keen sense of when he was being lied to. What Gretchen had said had the ring of truth. Either that or she was a hell of an actress.

"Okay then. I'm a newspaper reporter in Los Angeles. My parents came from Germany. My uncle—I was very close to him—remained here, in Berlin. German was spoken in my home when I was little, so I know the language. I learned that my uncle was murdered by the SS, so I vowed to come here."

Loathing darkened her face. "The SS are bastards," she hissed. "But even with the war on you would come?"

"Even with the war on. I have some contacts in the White House. President Roosevelt agreed to help, and he put me in touch with MI6 and our Colonel Freeborn. And . . . here I am."

"Yes, so here you are." She smiled. "You are either very brave or very reckless; I think perhaps some of both. You must have loved your uncle very much." She crossed her legs, then re-crossed them the other way. "Well then, brave and reckless Mr. Weaver, what is it that I can do for you? Are you having difficulties?"

"For starters, you can drop the Mr. Weaver. Just Jake will do."

"All right . . . Jake."

He liked the sound of her voice. And the look of sad friendliness in those green eyes. Eyes like Ginger Rogers', whom he'd once met.

"Difficulties," Jake said. "Well, yes. I have two aims here. One, to learn about my uncle and, two, to find out about Germany's rocket program, to see if they're developing a rocket weapon that could attack Britain or maybe even the United States."

"I know nothing about either, but I am most sorry about your uncle." Her face tightened in a scowl. "The SS are savages."

For the first time Jake grew aware of a clock ticking behind him. Recalling that he'd been in Berlin five days and hadn't got very far, he thought of it as a metaphor. He drank more tea, then put the mug down on an end table.

When he didn't speak, Gretchen said, "I know how to move around in Berlin without being seen by the prying eyes of the Gestapo."

"Is the Gestapo on to you?"

"No, and I must be most cautious to keep it that way." She leaned forward. "I know how to get messages to Colonel Freeborn"—Jake wondered how she got messages out—"things I have seen, troop movements, anti-aircraft defenses in the city, such things as that.

But I know nothing about rockets. If Germany has them, it is quite secret."

"Actually, I have a meeting later today with the scientist who heads that up. It was—"

"What?" Gretchen blurted, eyes wide, spilling some tea.

"Yes, a Dr. Wernher von Braun. It was about my uncle where I hoped you could help."

"Let us come to that in a moment," she said, wiping at the drops that had fallen on her skirt. "How on earth did you arrange a meeting with the leader of this rocket business?"

"Called him on the phone. Got his number from a source."

"A source? Here? My, you are a better spy than I. You do not need *my* help, Jake."

"Well, I thought the 'source' was a friend. A German I used to know in the States. Turns out he's no longer a friend. Turns out he too was seduced by the Nazi hoopla—except he still is."

"Then why would he give you this man's number?"

Jake ran a hand across his chin. "Well, we sort of blackmailed each other. He needs something from me."

"And I will not ask what this is."

"Yeah, that would be best."

"Well, if you learn something important about rocket weapons, tell me and I will pass it on to Colonel Freeborn."

The clock behind Jake began to bong with sharp, clear notes. Jake turned and saw a beautiful, wall-mounted pendulum clock doing its thing. Four o'clock.

When the last note finished chiming, Gretchen said, "Are you hungry? Have you taken lunch?"

"No, I skipped that."

"Then you must be hungry."

"Is there some place—"

"No, we must not be seen together. Come, I will fix us something." She casually touched his shoulder as she walked past.

Jake followed her into the kitchen. A thick chopping block above heavy wooden legs served as a table. Brass pans and steel carving knives hung from hooks above a gas range. Sitting on clawed feet of iron was a wooden icebox with a nickel-plated handle.

Gretchen opened a tin of soup, poured it into a sauce pan, added water and lit the gas range. The sudden whoosh of the gas flaring up startled him. Then she took some cheese from the icebox. Jake watched as she cut thick slices of bread. Her quick thrusts with a sharp butcher knife were also unsettling.

"I'm just a curious old reporter," he said as Gretchen busied herself making sandwiches. "If you don't mind my asking, can you tell me what happened to your nose?"

"No, I do not mind. It was in December of '40, during the Blitz. I was down in the Russell Square tube station with hundreds of other people sheltering there while the bombs exploded up above. I fell into conversation with three women I was crammed next to. Big strong girls. They worked in a munitions factory." Gretchen put the sandwiches on plates and set them on the table, then poured soup into shallow bowls.

"When the all-clear sounded and everyone returned to the street, they called out to me. Those cows shoved me into an alley and proceeded to beat the *Scheiss* out of me. Apparently my accent had labeled me. One of them called me a dirty Kraut and hit me with a punch Max Schmeling would have been proud of. Besides my nose, I think also that my cheekbone cracked."

"That's awful."

"I got in a few good licks, too. Isn't that your American saying? Dug a deep gouge in one of their faces."

"Good for you. She deserved it."

"I forgive them. Blood runs hot in wartime. Tempers flare. After all, their city was taking a fearful pounding." She offered an ironic smile and took a small bite of her sandwich.

"What an amazing attitude. And yet, after that beating, you still help the British?"

Gretchen's eyes turned steely cold. She put down the sandwich she'd been holding. "Yes. As I see it, it was Adolf Hitler who killed my Friedrich, not an RAF pilot. And he's killed thousands of other good men, many of them dying in Russia at this very moment." Her jaw hardened in a scowl and she looked away. "That devil is the worst thing that could have happened to my country." Her voice hard as stone. "To save its soul, Germany must rid itself of him."

This emotional outpouring was so genuine that Jake, moved by it, was tempted to put his arms around her. Instead he leaned forward and touched her hand. "I'm glad I came here."

She turned toward him again and slid her gaze into his eyes. "I am also." Her fingers twined around his for just a moment. "Eat. The soup, it is growing cold."

Jake liked this woman. He liked lots of women. Don't go doing something stupid, he told himself. He took a bite of his sandwich and said, "Say, this is good."

Gretchen smiled. They ate in silence for a few moments. Then Jake asked, "How do you manage? Do you have a job?"

"Curious reporter again, yes? I receive a pension from the Luftwaffe. Also, I still work part-time for the Abwehr, Wednesday through Friday, in the decoding section, although the pay is small."

And you glean information there for the Brits, Jake thought.

The wry look Gretchen gave him seemed to confirm that notion. She put her spoon down and said, "Your uncle, when was he killed?"

"Probably in the last few months. I heard about it four or five weeks ago when a letter came through from Sweden."

"From your 'source,' your supposed friend?"

"Yes. No telling how long it took for it to make its way from Berlin to Stockholm, then on to me."

"What do you know about his death?"

"My source told me he was caught in a resistance group and

executed along with two others."

"They like to publish those as heroic state acts, as a way of warning others not to get treacherous ideas," she said. "I can go to the library and look at the back editions of the papers. Perhaps I can find it. What name shall I look for?"

"Dieter Weber. And thanks. Knowing the date and place would be a start."

"The place is usually an enclosed courtyard at the Gestapo building on *Prinz Albrechtstrasse*. Your poor, poor uncle." A look of grief swept across her face. "I am sorry to say a firing squad shoots them at night against a brick wall. That is not made public but people talk, you know. The gunshots echo around the neighborhood."

Jake put his half-eaten sandwich down on his plate. He'd lost his appetite.

Before he left thirty minutes later, Gretchen asked him to return the next day, after she'd done some research at the library. Should he? Jake wondered. Was he making a dangerous mistake here? He had to trust *someone*.

As he walked in the direction of the U-bahn station, remembering the touch of Gretchen Siedler's hand, he caught himself thinking about the affair he'd had in this town in 1930.

CHAPTER THIRTY-THREE

The door stood open and inside he saw a man in shirtsleeves, with shoulders like Bronko Nagurski's, seated at a long desk. Jake knocked on the door jamb and the man looked his way, put down some papers, got to his feet and said, "Please, come in."

Wernher von Braun was more than six feet tall, maybe two hundred pounds, with a round, intelligent face. Jake knew he was only thirty and had headed Germany's rocket program for the past six years. He had an aristocratic bearing.

As he walked into the cluttered room, Jake said, "I am Hans-Karl Vogel and—"

Von Braun laughed the way he had on the phone. He stepped around Jake and closed the door. Jake felt trapped.

"What is this game?" the scientist said, blue eyes alight with mischief. "I know Vogel, have had some dealings with him, and you are not he."

Damn! Jake's breath caught. He knew his face hadn't concealed his shock.

"So, who are you?"

What could Jake say to that? Yeah, Colonel Freeborn, he thought, in this game there's always the unforeseen.

As if he'd smelled something bad, the joviality vanished from von Braun's face. "Are you one of Himmler's boys? If so, just leave me alone. Tell your Reichsführer SS for the hundredth time that I am a loyal German and a member, that I accomplish my work better and faster without his meddling."

Jake wondered if he should string along with that, play the role of an SS man, keep von Braun on the defensive. He decided not to. Too risky. Improvising, he said, "No, I'm not SS. I happen to be acquainted with Vogel. I knew my own name would mean nothing to you, so—"

"And what is your name?"

"Erich," Jake contrived. "Erich Weber." Combining his original family name with the first name of the Hitler Youth kid who'd driven him to Lorrach. Best he could do on short notice.

"And are you, Herr Weber, giving information to the British as does your friend Vogel?" Jake's heart jumped past a beat or two. Wouldn't Freeborn have told him if Vogel had been working for the Brits?

"I don't know what you mean, *Herr Doktor*."

"Bah. I know what you are. SS. Okay then, yes, I am in contact with scientists from other countries, I admit it. Science is international, a communal search for truth." His arms swung wildly, his face reddened. Jake took a step back. This big palooka could really wallop him if he wanted to.

"Science does not know political boundaries. But since the war, my contacts have only been with men in Scandinavia, Italy and occupied France. I am a German, not a fool. Tell that to your Himmler." Von Braun slammed a fist on his desk. A slide rule jumped.

Maybe Jake *should* have played along. Himmler obviously was a burr under this guy's saddle.

"And while you are at it, tell him Hitler is very anxious for the A-4 to proceed. He would not look kindly on anyone who delayed it, not even Himmler. So go and look for traitors somewhere else. You will not find them here, not in my project."

Jake backed off another step. This was one of the damndest impasses of his life. What could he say? The only ID he had was

Vogel's, and von Braun knew he wasn't Vogel. He wondered if Gretchen Siedler could get him some fake papers, but even if so, it couldn't help him right now, not this very minute.

Von Braun laughed. "*Mein Gott*, I love to tell you people off. You could do our cause more good by finding me a cheap source of liquid oxygen—or by picking up a rifle and fighting our real enemies, instead of trying to find them here, where there are none." He slumped into a chair and rubbed a large hand across his forehead. "*Ach*, I have been working too hard, day and night. Sometimes I need to let off some steam. It builds up, *nein*?"

The steam expended, he rubbed his eyes, lowered his hands and stared hard at Jake. "But before you take your pathetic ass out of here, tell me why you used Vogel's name. What kind of trick was that? Have you got the poor devil locked up or something?"

Jake felt sweat on his brow. "I don't know what to say."

"And why not? It is a simple question. Why did you use Vogel's name?"

"I . . . ," Jake groped. "I am not SS. I'm not from Himmler. And I am not German. I am Swiss, and an acquaintance of Vogel, as I said."

Then, an idea. "I know Professor Goddard." It was a middling lie. Jake had met Robert Goddard once, for a few minutes, after the American rocket pioneer had given a talk at Cal Tech. "I was hoping I could speak with you." Jake prayed von Braun wouldn't ask for identification.

"You know *Herr Doktor* Goddard?" von Braun said eagerly. He opened a drawer and produced a bottle of Johnnie Walker Black Label. Jake wondered where he'd got it. A pre-war gift, maybe?

"I have some glasses around here somewhere," von Braun said, rummaging through the clutter on his desk. He found a coffee cup and then a highball glass, half hidden behind a fat notebook. He wiped them with a handkerchief and poured a couple fingers of scotch into each.

Handing the glass to Jake, he said, "Robert Goddard, the rocket scientist, is a genius. All that we know about rockets started with him."

Von Braun raised his glass, said, "*Prosit*," the traditional toast, and they drank.

Von Braun put his cup down and said, "I corresponded with him when I was at university, ten years ago or so. He was good enough to reply and answer my questions. This great man must be more than sixty years old now. I still have his letters. I cherish them. How I wish I could correspond with him again. I should ask him many things, about gyroscopic guidance controls, for instance."

"He wouldn't give you any straight answers now."

"No." Von Braun took another drink. His eyes filled with regret. "It is a pity that war must make enemies of scientists."

"What did you mean a moment ago," Jake asked, "about Vogel passing information to the British?"

"A calculated guess. Many Swiss and Swedes who deal with both sides are tempted to trade information. The opportunity to make extra money is always enticing. For example, we have learned much about British radar from a Swedish firm that supplies them with optical equipment."

"Well, old Hans-Karl might have been doing some of that," Jake contrived, "but not me. I'm just a humble journalist. I haven't even been to England, not during the war."

"A journalist? Where? What are you doing here?"

This is make-it-up-as-you-go time, Jake told himself. "I'm a reporter for the *Oltner Tagblatt*, and I write stories on the side for a scientific journal. That's *my* way of making extra money."

"And you used Vogel's name, thinking it would make it easier to get in to see me."

"Exactly."

"And so it worked. Well then, Erich, what is it you wish to know?"

Jake sipped some scotch, but not too much. Had to keep a clear head here. He'd told some whoppers in this country, but now he'd just scored the hat trick, being first Hans-Karl Vogel, then a friend of his, and now a reporter moonlighting for a scientific magazine. Any Detroit Red Wing would be proud.

"The kind of propellant you are using," he answered, "and the range of your rocket."

"A liquid propellant. It is not much of a secret; Swiss scientists may be aware of that. Solid is too unstable, difficult to control ignition and thereafter the direction in flight. Range I will not discuss."

"Liquid propellant then?"

"Yes. I mentioned liquid oxygen before. I find that a composite of liquid oxygen and alcohol works best."

This guy is so proud of his work he can't help but blab about it, Jake thought. Maybe Swiss scientists know about that propellant, he reflected, but the American Army doesn't. *Thank you, Dr. von Braun.* "And you won't—"

"Discuss range? Of course not." Von Braun's eyes hardened. "We are at war. And I caution you strongly not to quote me on the propellant or even to use my name. I forbid it. If you write about the propellant, say it is only conjecture, speculation from Swiss chemists."

"You have my word," Jake said, and held up his glass. Von Braun clinked his cup against it.

Jake wanted to ask about the rocket's warhead but knew he'd pressed his luck far enough.

"Are you married, *Herr Doktor*?"

"Wernher, please call me Wernher, but no I am not. I have a young lady friend who wants very much to marry, but she grows impatient with my heavy work schedule. It is not possible to see her often. She says that I am married to my work, and in that she is correct . . . And you, Erich?"

"I am engaged."

"To a lovely Swiss maiden?"

"Er, yes."

"Good. I advise you to see as much of her as you can."

Jake, who was said to have a knack for winning people over, raised his eyebrows playfully and gave a sly grin intended to convey that he'd seen *all* of his fiancée, many times.

Von Braun laughed heartily and raised his cup. "To your good eyesight, Erich."

Jake returned the toast and they drank, their faces enjoying the moment. Men will be men—everywhere—Jake thought.

After several minutes of conversation about nothing vital, while the level in von Braun's bottle shrank, Jake took another shot. "You said you missed your contact with Dr. Goddard. Maybe I could get a message to him. I know people who fly from Zurich to neutral Lisbon."

Von Braun seemed to think for a moment. "This is possible?" he said at last.

"Probably so. What would you say to him?"

Jake could see debate whirling behind von Braun's astute blue eyes. At last he said, "That my interest is not war, but scientific advancement. That I am certain we will one day break the bonds of Earth and send a rocket to the moon."

"The moon?"

"It is entirely possible, in fact inevitable." His eyes blazed with enthusiasm. "Once a rocket has pierced the Earth's atmospheric envelope, reaching the moon will not be difficult, largely a matter of good mathematical calculation. But we are many years from that. It will take a much larger rocket than we now possess, an engine with far greater thrust." He stopped abruptly. At last he said, "You must not write of this."

"I know, you forbid it," Jake said with a conspiratorial grin. "Wernher, I never double-cross a source."

"That is good. I would also assure Professor Goddard that my rocket could not possibly reach America. London, perhaps, but not America."

Yes, although this guy knew better, he couldn't help but talk about his work. Jake knew other scientists like that. He'd hit paydirt here. FDR would be thrilled. But even back home, should Jake write this? He liked von Braun, wouldn't want to imperil him with Hitler. "London you say?"

"Yes. I am not a soldier. I have no wish to harm people, but my government finances my work, makes it possible to achieve much, to amass new knowledge. In a year or two, if our tests work out as I hope and the war has not ended, my rocket—the Luftwaffe uses the term 'ballistic missile'—will be capable of reaching London. Two months ago, it attained an apex of eighty kilometers with a range of three-hundred kilometers." He pursed his lips. "But I have said too much."

Fifty miles up and two-hundred out, Jake thought, doing a rough computation in his head. He was too smart to go further, to bring up payload, launch platform or any of the U.S. Army's other questions. That would blow the small rapport he'd established here.

Von Braun glanced down at his slide rule and a piece of paper filled with equations. "We have talked enough of these things. You will be in Berlin tomorrow? If so, come back then and we will speak further of a message to Professor Goddard."

CHAPTER THIRTY-FOUR

The wail of sirens swept into an already mixed-up dream, which had something about rockets, a barefoot woman and a bullet-scarred brick wall. This was different. Jake's dreams didn't usually come with sound effects. Seconds later, when the distant hammering of explosions joined that insistent siren shriek, his eyes jerked open. *Air raid!*

He leaped out of bed and slipped into pants and a shirt. He stuffed his wallet into a back pocket, glanced at the air-raid notice on the door, and left. Knowing the iron-gated lift would be slow and probably crowded, Jake loped toward the stairs at the end of the hall and joined a parade of anxious people pushing downward as fast as possible. Some wore robes, nightshirts and slippers. Others were buttoning shirts and fastening belts on quickly assembled clothing. Women clutched purses to their chests. Others held the hands of frightened children.

As they reached the basement, Jake glanced at his watch. Two-thirty. He followed the crowd into a big room where he was quickly impressed by the efficiency of the setup. Folding chairs lined three of the walls and others filled the center, auditorium style, before tables set with coffee urns and steaming pots of what, soup? A furnace, a thicket of ducts and pipes, and rows of electrical meters lined the fourth wall. The floor was bare concrete.

Uniformed women and young bellboys helped the elderly to find seats. Jake took a chair in the fourth row. A banner adorned with the ubiquitous swastika hung on the wall behind the tables, black Gothic letters proclaiming, "Vigilance and steadfastness will assure Germany's victory."

Down here the explosions were distant, muffled thunder. Jake wondered if *O for Oliver* was somewhere up above, trying to dodge searchlights and flak.

The room was less than half full, reflecting, Jake figured, the hotel's low occupancy rate on this wartime winter night. Even so, this was the most Berliners he had seen in one place since 1930, the streets now so thinly populated whenever he'd been out. Though not laughing and boisterous as they'd been back then, they were orderly and resolute, a handsome people determined to control their fears.

Some people hugged one another, others sat mute, and the old man next to Jake clutched Rosary beads and whispered Hail Marys. A young mother tried to hush her crying baby.

The lights flickered and dimmed, and many people gasped. But the power loss didn't last and soon the lights blazed at full strength again.

A policeman entered the room wearing that bucket-shaped topper. Thank God he's not Gestapo, Jake mused. He was S*chupo*, regular police. Most of those he'd seen were in their late forties or fifties, too old for the military. This one, stocky with a bit of paunch, fit that pattern. He walked around the room, scanning faces. Jake made sure not to make eye contact.

The cop stopped at his row. Jake could feel the man's eyes on him. The sensation soon passed and before long Jake saw him talking with one of the uniformed women. "*Alles hier ist gut,*" he said, and left the room. Jake stifled a sigh of relief.

The building didn't shake and plaster dust wasn't showering down from the ceiling, as he'd seen in the movies. Apparently no bombs were hitting close by. Maybe it was a small raid.

A few people wandered about, some filling coffee cups, but Jake wasn't interested. After awhile it grew quiet outside, and then after several more minutes, the long straight note of the all-clear signal could be heard, though only faintly. A bellboy opened the door and everyone began to leave.

Jake joined the file of people but as he passed through the doorway, the cop was there, staring at him. Pouches sagged below each of his brown eyes. "Come with me," he said, jerking his head toward a quiet spot away from the crowded stairway.

Jake's stomach went cold. *What now*? He remembered his promise to Charlie Root, the Hollywood Stars' manager, to attend the season opener in April, and wondered if he'd ever be able to keep it. Wondered if he'd even be able to get out of this country.

"Your identification, *bitte*." Not harsh and rude like the SS man on the train, but still the cop's words were more demand than request.

Trying to keep his hand from shaking, Jake got out his wallet and handed him the laminated card. The cop studied it and compared the photo with Jake's face. He also seemed to stare at his hair for a long moment, adding to Jake's uneasiness. Was something wrong with it? Was the dye washing out?

The cop handed the card back. "Passport, *bitte*."

"It's up in my room. I didn't take the time—"

"All right then. Why are you in the Third Reich, *Schweizer*?" Spoken as if a Swiss was an inferior being.

Jake wondered why he'd been singled out. There must have been other foreign hotel guests in that shelter. But he wasn't going to ask.

"I am here making sales calls"—trying to sound calm—"for my company, Shätzen Products."

"And what sales calls did you make yesterday?"

"Just one. At *Universität Unter den Linden*."

"That is correct. You were observed there." Jake was stunned. Was that blond university receptionist informing the police about visitors? God, what a country.

"*Danke*, Herr Vogel. That is all. You may go now."

Whew. Jake gladly complied. He managed to keep his body under control till he reached the landing at the first floor, well out of the cop's sight. Then his teeth started chattering and he shuddered all over. He grabbed the handrail to steady himself.

Finally in control, he stepped into the lobby. He was tempted to go outside and see what damage the raid had caused, but the streets would be crawling with firemen, repair crews—and *police*. Besides, he was exhausted. He looked at his watch. Three-ten.

He went up to his room and looked out the window. Nothing much stirred nearby, but he heard distant sirens and a saw a glow in the eastern sky. The air raid must have targeted the industrial section over in that direction. He stripped off his clothes and fell across the bed, willing himself not to think about cops, the SS or rocket bombs. Somehow he succeeded.

CHAPTER THIRTY-FIVE

He woke up at nine, bright sunlight slanting into the room. Remembering the way the Berlin cop had stared at his hair, he went to the bathroom mirror for a look. Damn, there were small traces of his natural red at the roots and in his sideburns. Back home he'd gotten haircuts every two or three weeks. His hair's quick rate of growth was something he hadn't considered. Neither, apparently, had MI6.

As he walked toward Gretchen's house in Schöneberg, Jake thought about the fact that she was still working for the Abwehr. That made her a double agent. She'd been awfully convincing yesterday, and Colonel Freeborn had insisted she could be trusted. So why was there a pinprick of suspicion in the back of his mind?

He was pretty sure he'd reached her street without being tailed or observed. But there were lots of windows along this block, with who knew how many curious eyes peering from behind curtains.

Gretchen opened the door to Jake, quickly closed it behind him, took his hand with her right hand and touched his arm with her left. She said, "I am so glad to see you," then added, "I could find nothing in the newspapers about your Dieter Weber. I even looked back an entire year. Perhaps they do not publicize all the executions." Her belted lavender dress, dotted with white flowers, fell several inches below the knee. She wore a cameo brooch and was barefoot again. "But I picked up something for you," she said with a wry smile, handing Jake a bottle. The label read, "*Vorgesetzt* Hair Dye. Ginger/ Brown."

"Colonel Freeborn had your hair dyed to match that of some other person, your cover, I presume."

Jake nodded.

"Yesterday I noticed your natural color beginning to peek through," she said.

Man, he was impressed. She'd spotted his hair problem even before he had. How could he not trust this woman? "You don't miss much," he said.

"I tested some of it on a small white cloth and it is quite close to what you have now."

Soon, she had draped a towel over his shoulders and was trimming his hair with comb and scissors, prior to giving him a new color job. The touch of her fingers on his scalp sent pleasant tingles rippling through his head and down his spine.

While she worked, Jake told her about the cop who'd questioned him.

"The *Schupos* are not as bad as the *verdammte* SS," she said, "but still they keep an eye on all the sensitive buildings. The university apparently qualifies because of the presence there of your rocket engineer. You are not going back there?"

"I have to."

"Be most careful then, now the police know of you. I like you, Jake, I would not want . . ."

When she didn't finish the sentence, Jake said, "I know. I hope this isn't the last time I see you, either."

"Mmm," she said.

After she finished the trim, Gretchen began shampooing his hair, Jake sitting on a kitchen chair in front of the sink. He felt even more warm tingles. As her fingers worked the lather in, he asked himself if Gretchen's thoughts were similar to the ones he was having. He believed he knew the answer. I love Valerie, he told himself. I love

Valerie. He hadn't realized until now just how full of loneliness he'd been for the last several, tense days.

Gretchen washed off the shampoo, donned rubber gloves and began rubbing in the dye. When she was finished, she said, "We will let that sit for half an hour, then give you a rinse."

When he got up from the chair she peeled off the gloves and removed the towel. Then she took both his hands and gazed into his eyes. "It is a good job, I think."

"But you're not looking at my hair."

She leaned forward and planted a fervent kiss on his lips. Somehow Jake wasn't surprised. His arms found their way around her back and pulled her tight against him. She was lightly perfumed with a violet-like scent.

Lust is the enemy of logic, Jake told himself. He pulled back and said, "Gretchen, I'm engaged to be married."

"I know."

"You know?"

She kissed him again, a quick one this time. "I knew that you were married"—a melancholy smile—"or spoken for."

Women, Jake thought. They seem to know everything. Well, except for Dixie Freitas, the waitress he'd married back when he was young and stupid. She hadn't known much.

While waiting for the rinse, as if nothing unusual had just happened, Gretchen asked about his meeting with Wernher von Braun. Jake described it, how he'd been accused of being SS, but had finished by drinking the scientist's scotch and learning about the rocket's fuel. They sat in chairs at the carving-block table.

Had he been wrong to tell her all that? he wondered. Having knowledge of von Braun could be dangerous if she were ever picked up for questioning.

"Perhaps you should have let him continue to believe you were SS," she said. "You could have kept him on the defensive, gained some control."

Women are so sly, Jake thought. "I considered it. That could work with some people, but not von Braun. He doesn't fear Himmler. He berated me good before I convinced him I was a Swiss reporter and the conversation turned pleasant."

"You are a disarming man, Jake," she said with a coy smile that said many things. "And clever."

As she got up and put the kettle on for tea, Jake asked, "Do you know the name Magda Goebbels?"

Gretchen lit the gas beneath the kettle and turned. "Of course, the wife of that big-mouth clubfoot." Jake liked that; it said much about the true thoughts of astute Berliners.

"Do you know where she lives?"

"At their estate near Lanke in the northeast suburbs, I believe, but why ever do you want to know about that?"

When Jake explained about the Hindenburg letter and Putzi Hanfstaengl, Gretchen said the name sounded vaguely familiar, that maybe she'd read it in the newspapers some time back. He told her about Hanfstaengl's desire to get the letter back.

"A deathbed letter to Hitler, asking him not to rule by decree?" she said. "How interesting. Ten years ago that could have done some good."

It still could, Jake thought. Making the letter known could arouse in Germans a sense of betrayal and possibly weaken Hitler's hold on them.

The tea now ready, Gretchen filled two mugs and took her seat. "You must not even think of going to *Frau* Goebbels," she said, her brows furrowing above her eyes. "It is far too dangerous for you. If you were observed at the university, just think—"

"I told Hanfstaengl I would try."

"And you are a man of your word, but this is asking too much. That would be going too far."

Jake sipped from his mug. "I don't want to go back home and say I tried and failed, if I hadn't even tried."

"But you must not," she insisted. "Perhaps I can do it."

His eyes widened.

"I could approach her house looking like a cleaning woman, or a repair person. Women are doing much work now for the power and gas company. Woman to woman, I could gain her confidence and perhaps get this letter for you."

She must be playing straight with me if she would do that, Jake tried to convince himself.

"No, Gretchen, that's—"

"It is time for your rinse." Gretchen took his elbow and steered him back to the sink. As she ran warm water through his hair, her fingers again stirred up his hormones. Jake told himself this was the second-most exciting woman he'd ever met, Valerie popping into his mind. Again. Of course.

When he stood, Gretchen lifted the towel from his shoulders and tossed it toward the chopping block. She'd undone the bun at the back of her head and let her hair fall to her shoulders. She touched his cheek, her hand still warm from the water. "I wish for you to undress me," she said. When she took his hand and led him toward the bedroom, Jake knew he should find the will to resist, to pull his hand away.

CHAPTER THIRTY-SIX

Before going to Unter den Linden University the next day, Jake took a long walk around central Berlin. He saw bomb damage in several places. A couple of craters were roped off in the big park, the Tiergarten. One two-story building had been reduced to a tangle of brick and stone rubble, and crews with wheelbarrows were already at work removing some of it. He was shocked to see that some of the workers could only be slave laborers, hollow-faced, skinny, sad-looking men shivering in black-and-white striped pajamas. The stuff he'd heard about Nazi concentration camps must be true.

Streetcars juddered along, sparks fizzing above them from overhead wires. As always, he saw more bicycles than cars. Everywhere he went, he looked around carefully for cops or anyone who might be watching him. As he walked, he couldn't help thinking about what had happened yesterday in Gretchen's bedroom.

He remembered every delectable moment. Her creamy skin, how her nipples came erect at the touch of his tongue, the way her body had trembled at that moment. Her moans of pleasure that more than matched his own when he entered her, the urgency of their lovemaking as their bodies moved together. The explosive release of all that had been building up.

Afterward, her head snuggled on his shoulder, a leg draped over him, she'd murmured, "I hope you understand how much I needed you. Your closeness, your warmth, your tenderness. I know we can only be together for a brief moment. When you go home, you will give your woman all the love that will never be mine. But Jake, I hope you will never forget your friend in Berlin, your friend who will always be grateful to you."

"How could I ever forget that?" he'd said. He kissed her crooked nose, thinking, *How could I not trust a woman who sees so clearly, who says things like that?*

And yet that newspaperman's cynicism lurked in the back of his mind. At the end of the day, could he really trust her?

As the university came into view, Jake, whose mind had always been able to travel two avenues at once, thought also about Uncle Dieter. Why hadn't Gretchen been able to find anything on his execution in the newspapers? What did that mean, if anything?

He entered the building and exchanged nods with the blond receptionist. He wondered if she was the one who'd "observed" him for the police.

Reaching von Braun's office, he saw a woman standing there with the engineer. They were deep in conversation. Von Braun spotted Jake and said, "Erich, *bitte*, come in." He handed the woman a folder and said, "Get back to me with these performance figures as soon as you can then, Hanna. I leave for Peenemünde tonight."

The woman was small and athletic with short-cropped blond hair and inquisitive blue-gray eyes. Those eyes stared at Jake for a moment as if memorizing his face. She made him think "cop." Suddenly he knew who she was. He'd actually met her at an air show five years ago in Glendale. His spine tightened. Did she recognize him? Was she puzzling over the color of his hair?

She gave a small nod, turned, and left.

Jake was still shaken by the encounter as von Braun motioned him to a chair and said, "*Guten Tag*, Erich. You will please forget what I just said. About my destination."

"I didn't hear a thing," Jake said, trying to manage a trust-me smile. "Just something about figures." He noticed a day-by-day calendar on von Braun's desk. It showed *Viersehnt Dezember*. December 14th.

Conversation quickly turned to Robert Goddard. "I have written him a letter," von Braun said. "Almost exactly what I said yesterday, that I am not a soldier and that he mustn't think badly of me, whatever might occur in this war. My conviction that a rocket can reach the moon in the next ten or twenty years and that I would be pleased to work with him toward that end, after the war, if that should be possible . . . How will you get this to him?"

"I'll have a trustworthy friend mail it in Lisbon, inside a larger envelope addressed to a technician at the California Institute of Technology, who can forward it to him."

Von Braun leaned forward. "And you can assure me that no one else will see this message?"

"Yes," said Jake. "I met this California technician in Geneva before the war and we spent an evening drinking. We developed a rapport. He said he would be glad to help me at any time. I'm sure I can count on him to see that it gets to Goddard unopened." The only lie was that the evening of drinking had been in Pasadena, not Geneva.

Jake noticed two models on top of a credenza. One was of a bullet-shaped rocket standing upright with Buck Rogers fins at the base. The other looked like some kind of small strange plane without a propeller.

Von Braun followed his eyes, then walked over and put a hand on the rocket. "This is my A-4; the rocket I have told you about. Goebbels wants to call it the V-2, the 'V' standing for 'Vengeance.' This other is a very different kind of weapon, a pilotless jet plane, radio-controlled, carrying a ton of explosives. Goebbels wants to designate it the V-1."

Jake knew of jet planes. In great secrecy, Bell Aircraft was developing a jet fighter. "A flying bomb, then, that can be guided to its target without a pilot?"

"If it succeeds, yes. Preliminary tests have only just begun. It is not my design. My interest is only in rockets, but one of my colleagues gave me this model. You must not write of this."

"Of course I won't."

"Good."

Thinking again of the woman he'd recognized and who'd given him such unsettling scrutiny, Jake said, "Who was that lady, if I may ask?" He already knew the answer.

"That was Hanna Reitsch, the acclaimed aviator and test pilot. She is an old friend. *Ach*, I should have introduced you. I apologize."

"No need." Jake knew about Hanna Reitsch. At the time of Amelia Earhart's disappearance over the Pacific, the German flier had said that the American woman wasn't much of a pilot and that her ill-fated round-the-world flight had been a foolish stunt. He hoped like hell that Hanna Reitsch hadn't remembered him. He also wondered what kind of performance tests she was running for von Braun.

The scientist returned to his desk. He seemed rushed—the clutter of papers and blueprints was bigger than the day before—and the chat that followed was brief, though pleasant. Von Braun mentioned that an air force plane would fly him to Sweden in a few days to see a supplier there.

At the conversation's obvious close, he showed Jake his letter to Goddard. Jake read it and handed it back. Von Braun folded it and slipped it into a *Universität Unter den Linden* envelope. "I thank you for doing this for me," he said.

Jake looked at the envelope and said, "You keep this for now. It will be safer here with you. I'll come back for it before I leave Germany."

"All right. I will return to Berlin in two days' time."

"Fine. *Auf Wiedersehen* then."

After Jake left, von Braun gazed on the model of his rocket for a moment.

"Ha. I should very much like to strike at England with my rockets," he thought. "Are they not bombing hell out of *us*? It would be validation of my life work. My interest is outer space, not war, but I am German and war is what I have. I would never say these things to *Herr Doktor* Goddard, of course, nor to that little Swiss, although I do find the man likeable. *Ach*, if I can use him for my purposes, I shall."

CHAPTER THIRTY-SEVEN

Rolf Becker stopped by the hotel the next day and gave Jake a number to a private account at the *Schweiz Commerzbank* in Zurich.

"Get this done for me," Rolf said over a cup of tea, "and the money will be there, old friend." The last two words rang phony as hell. Rolf seemed preoccupied and uncomfortable. Jake knew *he* was.

Rolf didn't say much while fiddling with his cup, but his gaze wandered around the room as if searching for something. They didn't talk long and Rolf soon left. Jake was glad to see him go.

Pushing his former friend out of his mind, Jake was soon walking along *Schillingstrasse*. He felt about as good—make that less bad, he corrected himself—since arriving here. Although he'd gotten nowhere on Uncle Dieter, Tapestry, aka Gretchen Siedler, had proved to be a comfort—in more ways than one. He knew that she'd be working today at the Abwehr. His instinct told him he could trust her—*couldn't he?*—and that her loathing of the Nazis was real. From Wernher von Braun he'd gotten some good information. However, leaving this madhouse without achieving any retribution over the murder of his uncle left a raw sense of failure.

These thoughts bounced around in his head as he strolled along on a clear, chilly day, still alert for cops or others paying attention to him, but overall not feeling too bad.

Gretchen Siedler knew the Abwehr's voluminous files included a complete roster of SS personnel. She often perused it, looking for various names that might be of use to her. She'd found that she could do this with ease. It was accurately said that Admiral Wilhelm Canaris, the easy-going director of military intelligence, ran a loose ship. Unlike MI6, Gretchen knew. *Or the Schutzstaffel*. The SS didn't like or trust Canaris.

Seated at a long cedar table at the rear of the file room at Abwehr headquarters on *Wilhelmstrasse*, she was scanning the SS list again during her lunch break. She took a bite of her sandwich, salami and cheese on pumpernickel. French mustard.

She thought about Jake Weaver and his uncle. She'd been thinking about Jake a lot the last two days. She had to remind herself that he'd be leaving soon and that what they'd done was just a fleeting satisfying of needs.

Suddenly she saw something on the list that made her eyes jump.

Jake bounded down the stairs at a subway station and boarded a train to the northeastern suburbs. He'd memorized the address Putzi Hanfstaengl had given him for the Goebbels estate in Lanke and he wanted to take a look at the place, just ride by on a bus.

Even though Hanfstaengl had told him Joseph Goebbels usually stayed downtown near Hitler's Chancellory and was seldom out there with Magda, Jake was curious. He'd made a careful study of the Berlin transit map and to reach Lanke he had to switch to a bus at the end of the U-bahn line at Bernau, a bus that ran past the Goebbels estate. He hadn't come up with a scheme for approaching the woman and was not going to. Not today, anyway.

Besides, Gretchen had said she might be able to handle it, woman to woman, and get the Hindenburg letter for him. He still didn't like the sound of that. It could be dangerous for her. Or, what if Gretchen was up to something else? Like warning Frau Goebbels?

The bus was not crowded. He took a seat to himself about halfway back and automatically began to scan his fellow passengers. The backs of the heads in front of him belonged to two soldiers, three women, and an elderly man traveling with a small boy.

A horizontal rack above the windows carried advertisements and strident Nazi slogans, such as "Victory Requires Vigilance," "The Führer Expects Everyone to Do His Part," and "Please Donate to the Soldiers' Home." Substitute Uncle Sam for Führer and he could be on the Pico Boulevard bus to Santa Monica.

Thoughts of home and Valerie flooded his mind, along with a stab of guilt about Gretchen Siedler. He knew that he'd allowed her to seduce him. That was a twist. He was usually the one doing the seducing. He tried to convince himself that their lovemaking hadn't meant anything, that it was a behavioral anomaly, a transgression he would not repeat.

He also thought about Hanna Reitsch, the test pilot who'd been in von Braun's office. He was still shaken by the way her intense eyes had scrutinized him.

The bus reached Lanke. In a pricey neighborhood near the Lieptnitszee lake, he scanned the house numbers and found he was close to the Goebbels home. A sudden impulse. Why not get out and walk by? Just a quick recon, then he'd catch the next bus and be on his way. He tugged on the cord.

Before long, he was approaching the stone-and-stucco estate, his breath issuing wispy puffs of steam. He didn't stop and stare, but gave it a good sidelong look as he drew near. Huge arched windows looked out from the ground floor, and chimneys reached for the sky at each end of the two-story building. Wispy smoke drifted from one of them. The place reminded him a bit of oil baron Edward Doheny's Greystone Mansion in Beverly Hills.

The large front door suddenly sprang open and a rosy-cheeked boy of six or seven, well bundled up against the December cold, ran out, and then a girl, a little older, chased after him. They darted past Jake, laughing. Mufflers flapped around their necks. The boy looked back over his shoulder and called, *"Guten Tag, mein Herr."* Jake smiled and nodded.

The boy ducked through a hole in a hedge and his big sister followed. Jake smiled again. Just a couple of kids playing games, probably well-shielded from the horrible war in which their father was so deeply involved. Something pathetic about that.

He heard a female voice call, "Hilge, Helmut," and saw a tall blond woman in the doorway, cradling a fur coat against herself with both arms. Magda Goebbels had probably been beautiful ten years ago, he supposed, but her face looked faded somehow, and a bit puffy. Sad, too, the face looked sad. Her eyes met his for a moment and she nodded. Without breaking step, he dipped his head in acknowledgment and touched the brim of his hat.

He strolled on by, wondering what bleak thoughts might be filling the mind of that lonely, betrayed woman. He wondered too how much comfort Putzi Hanfstaengl had given her. At least she had her children around her.

Well, he'd met Magda Goebbels—in a way. Their eyes had mutually said good morning. For an instant, each had been aware of the other.

Jake was half a block away when an unmarked black sedan squealed to the curb just ahead of him. The doors flew open. What the hell was this? Two beefy men in Gestapo uniforms bolted from the car and rushed him. His heart hammering, Jake took a step back. They grabbed his arms. He struggled but couldn't break free. They held his arms like vise grips. His biceps hurt.

They dragged him toward the car. As he was thrown into the back seat, his right foot caught on the running board and twisted. A hot stab of pain throbbed in his ankle. The goons piled in on each side, their big shoulders pressing against him.

Shit, Jake thought. Holy damn shit. "What are you doing? I am a Swiss national—"

"Quiet," the monster on his left snarled. "No talking."

Two more Gestapo men occupied the front seat. The driver began to pull away while the doors were still closing.

Through the window, he spotted the Goebbels girl staring at him. She grabbed her scarf and jerked one end of it above her head as if hanging herself. She let her head loll to the side, her tongue dangling from the mouth, and she crossed her eyes.

CHAPTER THIRTY-EIGHT

As the car headed back toward central Berlin, Jake thought his aching ankle might be broken.

The goon on his left leaned forward and caught the eye of the guy on his right. "This one was easy, eh?"

"Oh, *ja*." The second guy flashed an arrogant smirk at Jake, this helpless little fish that he'd netted.

Jake was swallowing needles of panic. I'm a dead man, he told himself. Who did I mention Magda Goebbels to? The answers came fast. Rolf Becker, Hermann Goering and Gretchen Siedler. Which one fingered him? Goering? Probably. Rolf? Maybe. Did it even matter now? How could he have been so stupid? Stupid and sloppy. He remembered Marion Davies saying, "Promise me you'll be as careful as you possibly can." *Right, Miss Marion.*

Suburban homes began to give way to bigger buildings. He was surprised he was allowed to see them, surprised he hadn't been blindfolded. The sky looked like putty, the buildings drab, the occasional swastika banner hanging limp as wet laundry. The car passed a flak tower, a high, ugly concrete blockhouse with anti-aircraft guns poking up from the roof. They were on a broad boulevard now. They passed a café where Jake had had his lunch just the other day.

He remembered Gretchen saying that sensitive buildings like Unter den Linden University were likely being watched. The Goebbels estate would fall into that category. How stupid could he have been, going there? You don't grow old in this world by making mistakes, Mickey Cohen had once told him. His mind's eye saw that Goebbels girl again, mocking him with her make-believe hanging, her scarf jerked tight around her neck, tongue dangling.

When Jake saw the Brandenburg Gate appear in the west, beneath the Quadriga, the four-horse chariot, he knew they were close to Gestapo headquarters. Which probably was his destination.

He wished with all his heart that he could turn the clock back a few years to a time before the Nazis were in power, to the time when the Gestapo building housed the Folklore Museum.

Soon, damn it, the fears about his destination proved right. An icy chill walked his spine as the car made a right turn onto *Prinz-Albrechtstrasse*. At Number 8, the driver down-shifted, wheeled into an alley and jerked the car to a stop at the rear entrance. They don't unload prisoners out in front where people can see them, Jake realized.

The doors opened and Goon One grabbed his arm and hauled him into the alley. When the guy let go, Jake told himself, I might get shot, but I've got to try this. I can probably outrun these apes. He'd been a sprinter at Catholic High in Baton Rouge, years before.

He made a quick pivot, took a step—and buckled. He'd forgotten about the ankle. The goon grabbed him, spun him around, and threw a haymaker into his gut. Pain exploded. A geyser of vomit retched from his mouth. Dizzy, his vision blurry, he heard a voice snarl, "Haul this bag of *Scheiss* inside."

"Should have handcuffed him," said a different voice.

Before long, half-conscious, Jake was shoved into a chair. He heard a door slam, then receding footsteps. Through a veil of pain, he gradually discerned that he'd been placed at a wooden table inside a small room, a room that smelled very foul. No, *he* smelled very foul, he soon realized, seeing ribbons of upchuck trailing down the front of his shirt. The room had bare, whitewashed walls and a large mirror. Two chairs besides the one he was in.

He was all alone. And in more misery than he'd ever known.

And to think that two hours ago, or however long it was, he'd been feeling pretty good about himself. About his German language skills, his meetings with Wernher von Braun, his ability to move around in this enemy capital without attracting attention. Ha. He hadn't known jack shit. All the time he'd been a mouse surrounded in a pit full of vipers. Until now, he'd never really known the meaning of the word "alone."

Again he noticed the wall mirror he was facing, a large one. He'd seen one-way glass like this at the Wilshire precinct in L.A. Some Gestapo guys were probably behind it, watching. He stifled the urge to give them the old middle-finger salute. Instead, he put his arms on the table and laid his head on them. Everything ached, not just his ankle. He might have a broken rib.

After a long while, he didn't know how long, the door opened and a small man came in, placed a drinking glass and a ceramic pitcher on the table and left without speaking.

Well good, his throat was parched. He could use a glass of water. He picked up the pitcher but it felt too light. He peered inside. Empty. He scanned the room looking for a sink, a faucet, a spigot, but there was no source of water to be found. What kind of lousy joke was this?

He put his head back down on his arms. Time passed like continental drift. Occasionally he opened his eyes and peered at the empty pitcher. It only made his thirst worse. These creeps must consider this persecution, he thought. Hell, it *is*. An insidious damn form of torture.

He dozed off a time or two. When he snapped awake the second time he wondered, could those goons behind the mirror possibly enjoy watching a man slowly die of boredom . . . and thirst?

He reached down and felt his throbbing ankle, then decided to get up and test it, the hell with whoever was behind that glass. Let 'em look all they want.

He pushed the chair back, stood up gingerly, turned his back to the mirror and took a hobbling step, then another. It hurt like hell but he could put a little weight on it, very little. Maybe it wasn't broken, just a bad sprain. He took one more limping step, then turned back. They could see his face now. Thank you, he imagined his ankle saying in relief as he sat.

Jake slipped in and out of alertness.

Hours must have passed. He was surprised that he hadn't been searched, that he still had his passport, wallet and wristwatch. He checked his watch. Three-thirty. Hours *had* passed. Just as he was about to doze off a third time, he heard the door open. He raised his head and took a look.

A man was coming in, surprisingly not in uniform. The guy wore a gray double-breasted suit and wire-framed glasses. Not very tall. Professorial looking. A small gold lapel pin bore a swastika, as did his armband.

"*Guten Tag,*" he said, not unpleasantly. "May I see your identification, *bitte*?"

"Why have I been kept here so long? What's going on?"

"I am sorry for the inconvenience. Your identification, *bitte*."

Jake produced his identity card.

The man's nose twitched slightly, no doubt at the smell emanating from Jake's fouled shirt. But he said nothing about it, just scrutinized the card, comparing the photo with Jake's face. Then, "Why are you in Berlin, Herr Vogel?"

Jake repeated his oft-told story, here on business for Schätzen Products.

"I see. And may I ask what you were doing at the Goebbels home?"

"I wasn't at anyone's home. I was just taking a walk." Maybe *nobody* finked on him, Jake thought, clutching at a mental straw. Maybe they just watch sensitive homes like that one, and routinely haul in strangers. After all, there aren't many pedestrians out in this wartime winter.

"Just taking a walk?" the man said. "Many kilometers from the Hotel Eden?"

Rolf! Jake thought. *That bastard*. Only Rolf knew where he was staying.

"The Hotel Eden?" he said, his ankle and ribs still barking with pain.

"Yes, the lodgings of all foreigners are made known to us. We must be most careful in wartime. So, perhaps you were just taking a stroll after all," the man said politely. "Let us move on then. Four days ago, you had a private meeting with Reichsmarshal Goering."

Rolf! It had to be Rolf. That bastard was definitely informing on him.

"How did you find the Reichsmarshal?"

"How did I find him?"

"Yes, his manner, his comportment."

"He was cordial. A gracious host."

"Did he seem distracted? Did his mind wander?"

"No, he seemed quite normal."

"Alert, would you say? Not lethargic?"

"Alert, yes."

"You saw no indication that he was using, shall we say. . . narcotics?"

Jake saw what was going on here. The head of the SS, Himmler, wanted to show that Goering was on drugs so he could discredit him with Hitler. It was part of the power struggle inside the Nazi hierarchy. Jake wasn't getting into that.

"No, nothing at all like that."

"The Reichsmarshal did not look drowsy or unfocused?" the guy suddenly asked in English, very good English. The sneaky creep.

In German, Jake said, "What did you say? My English is not so good." The man gazed into Jake's eyes, then laughed.

At last he said, "Very well then, Herr Vogel." He handed Jake his identity card and turned away.

"Am I free to go then, or what?"

The man didn't answer. Instead, he reached beneath his jacket and pulled a riding crop from a back pocket. What the hell? Jake thought. With a quick movement, the man slashed it hard across Jake's face. Hot pain seared deep. He knew his cheek was cut.

"*Auf Wiedersehen* then," the man said cordially and simply left the room, shutting the door behind him.

"You damn bastard," Jake tried to shout at the door, but it came out as a weak croak. He could feel tears mixing with the blood on his cheek.

He stared again at the mirrored window. His reflected face wore a thin red gash three or four inches long.

The damned glass looked larger now, seemed to be growing, or else the rest of the room was shrinking. He could feel the eyes behind the glass, staring, penetrating, maybe laughing. Oh Valerie, he thought. What have I done, Sweets?

He hadn't eaten for hours, but oh the thirst. His mouth was sandpaper.

It had been about eleven when he'd reached Lanke. He'd been here more than four hours, the worst four hours of his life.

Two months ago, on assignment from Hearst, Jake had lived through the roughest night of the Guadalcanal campaign. It was the night the Imperial Navy had sent battleships into Ironbottom Sound and blasted the U.S. perimeter with fourteen-inch shells for more than an hour. Forty-one Marines were killed that night. Jake spent it cowering in a slit trench, a borrowed helmet on his head, mosquito bites everywhere, and convinced he would never see another sunrise.

He would gladly live that night over in exchange for the day he was having now. He realized his teeth were chattering uncontrollably.

CHAPTER THIRTY-NINE

It smelled dank and stale, like the root cellar at his cousin's farm at Opelousas. Jake couldn't remember being moved, must have passed out. He looked around and saw two walls of water-stained brown brick leading into a corner, and a third wall of new-looking concrete cinder-block. Standard jail-issue iron bars formed the fourth, with an inset gate of more iron bars and a heavy lock.

He found that he was lying on a cot with a thin mattress, and not handcuffed. He saw an open toilet and a porcelain sink. A dim light bulb in an enameled metal cone hung from a ceiling of rough-cut boards. This must be one corner of the basement. That would account for two old-looking walls and a newer one. The Folk Museum probably had once used this cellar as storage space. Now it was a dungeon—no other word for it—sectioned off into small cells.

The last Jake could remember was that man slashing him across the face. He'd been in that room with the one-way glass and the empty pitcher.

Besides the knifing pain in his ankle and ribs, plus a roaring headache, he felt as if his face had been attacked by a swarm of bees. He put a hand to his cheek. Raw and swollen. He listened for sounds. Somewhere a cell door rattled. Then a deathly silence settled in.

Through a fog and pain and despair, he drifted back to other troubles, times when he'd found himself in a bad fix.

In '37, he and Vern Hatfield had been flying down to Tijuana to do some gambling—and gamboling—at Agua Caliente. Vern, a pilot, had rented a Taylor Cub at little Fletcher Airport on Rosemead Boulevard and off they'd gone, into the wild blue yonder. Everything went fine for the first forty minutes or so, skimming along over the sprawling orange groves and bean fields around Santa Ana and Tustin, then looking for girls on the beaches at Dana Point from a thousand feet.

But south of San Clemente the engine started to sputter. Vern, wearing a worried look, said,"Something wrong with the fuel mix, or the sparkplugs are fouled, something like that."

Somewhere above the Santa Margarita Rancho, the engine quit altogether. Vern looked desperately for a place to set it down. There were lots of citrus and avocado trees down there, and ragged fields strewn with boulders, but he spotted a dusty road running between two big groves. Without any power he had only one shot at it. Vern made his approach and soon the road rose up to meet them.

It was an almost perfect landing. Almost. The road wasn't quite wide enough and the right wingtip caught a tree. The plane did a handstand, mangling the prop and leaving the tail sticking straight up in the air. Then it slowly nosed over and came to rest upside down. Jake cut his forehead on something in the cockpit and Vern broke a wrist.

A ranch hand drove them to the Oceanside hospital in a pickup truck. Jake received eight stitches and Vern got a plaster cast. Jake would never forget the Santa Margarita Rancho. Uncle Sam later bought the place and was building a big Marine Corps base there.

Then there was the earlier time when he was arrested on a drunk and disorderly after a fight in the café and bar in Longview where Dixie Freitas waited tables. The fight was over who would win Saturday's big game, Texas or TCU. Jake's money was on the Horned Frogs. He hadn't started the fight, but he sure as hell got into it, along with eight or nine other guys. Fortunately, Carl Estes, the *Morning Journal*'s publisher, had a lot of pull, and Jake was released the next day, charges dropped. Estes made the arrest report disappear. The night spent in that small stinking cell with three guys he hated had been harder to take than the tongue-lashing from his editor and being docked two days' pay.

None of those experiences were as bad as this. Not even close.

He gazed around his cell and wondered how long he'd been here, and that's when he discovered his watch was gone. Sitting up and slapping at his pockets in panic, he found they'd also taken his wallet, passport and identity card. His belt, too.

He got up and hobbled over to the sink, turned the tap and a paltry rivulet of water dribbled out. He cupped his hands and scooped some into his mouth, then did it again. It tasted faintly of rust. Then he slapped some on the front of his shirt and tried with little success to scrub away some of the dried vomit.

Shaking his head at the mess he was in, he shambled back to the cot, lay down and put a hand over his eyes. He'd been in Germany how long now? Seven days? Nine? His brain wasn't working very well.

He tried to sum up. He'd learned very little about the murder of his uncle, nothing at all about the Hindenburg letter, a little something about Germany's rocket weapon . . . and had gotten himself locked up in a Gestapo prison. No one in the whole world knew where he was. That's what he'd call the biggest failure of his life. And probably the last. How could he have been so stupid as to go and take a look at Magda Goebbels' home?

Heavy footfalls broke the silence. Sounded like jackboots on the concrete floor. Maybe someone was coming to bring him some food. Or to whip him, more likely. Jake tensed, but no one appeared beyond his bars, and soon the sounds faded and were gone. Some guard making his rounds, probably.

His thoughts drifted to Winifrid, the lovely Marxist he'd taken to bed back in 1930. That had been a far better trip to Germany than this one. He should have folded his cards then and never come back to this damned place.

He closed his eyes and let his mind turn to the best woman in his life, Valerie. He recalled her exact words. "You'd damn well better come back to me, Jake."

"Twenty to one against, Sweets," he murmured despairingly. Sleep overtook him again.

CHAPTER FORTY

Jake had a blurry memory of the iron door opening, strong hands grabbing him, and hauling him to his feet. Had that been dream or reality?

He woke to find he'd been moved yet again, to another part of the cellar, the *real* dungeon this time. He was strapped down onto a cold tabletop. Whatever bound him cut tight against his wrists and ankles. A hot floodlight beat down on his face.

A slender, bespectacled man stood before him in a black uniform, the tunic partly unbuttoned. A cruel grin on a weasel-like face. Jake looked away from him and took in a nightmarish scene. Hooks and chains hung from rough gray walls, and steel tables bore heavy leather straps and stirrups, the kind that had shackled the Frankenstein monster. Cables and pulleys dangled from the ceiling. Ominous red wires snaked out from large storage batteries.

He wished he could just blink away these visions. He was drowning in hopelessness. Why had he ever agreed, what felt like a lifetime ago, to do some spying for President Roosevelt? Or told Putzi Hanfstaengl he'd see what he could do about Hindenburg's letter? *Jesus*, the pain. His face throbbed where he'd been slashed, and his ribs and ankle ached.

Could that be a severed hand on the floor? Leaking blood into a drain? Ragged wrist bones and tendons exposed? My God, *it was*. Jake's wrists seemed to shrink in fear. He jerked his head away from the horrific sight.

The Earth had orbited the sun for five billion years, but now for Jake it had stopped dead. He was in hell. He'd often thought he might go to hell for some of the things he'd done in his life but the truth was, he was already there.

The man was leering at him. "I am supposed to ask you some questions," he said. "So, *Ihr Name, bitte.*"

Jake answered with his well-rehearsed story. "I am Hans-Karl Vogel. I am a Swiss businessman."

"They tell me you are not Vogel, but I really do not give a damn. *Wiederholen.* Let us try that one again."

"But I am Vogel."

"What are you doing in the Third Reich?"

"Making sales calls."

"Wrong answer." Weasel Face actually giggled. "Once again?"

"Representing my company."

With each response, the man laughed and gazed around longingly at the torture devices. "Tell me you are a spy. That is what I want to hear. What British agent runs you?"

The floodlight burned hot on Jake's face. In desperation, he took another tack. "Look, I know Wernher von Braun. I've been bringing him supplies for his rocket program. I've done nothing wrong."

"Von Braun? Never heard of him." The man slapped Jake hard across the face. *Damn.* Needles and pins stabbed. If the wound on his cheek had begun to scab up, it was broken open again for sure. He thought of the Goebbels girl, taunting him with that make-believe hanging.

"You're all mine," the nut case said, and glanced down at the dismembered hand. "My little toy. Oh the fun I am going to have with you."

Drowsy with hurt and fatigue, Jake drifted in and out of alertness. He didn't know how much time had passed when he suddenly realized the Gestapo creep was attaching electrical wires to his arm and ear with some kind of a spring clip. Felt like a pliers pinching hot into his flesh. *If only I could wake up from this nightmare*, he thought, *and find myself at home with Valerie's welcoming arms around me. Fat chance.*

Weasel Face bent over a storage battery and put his hand on a toggle switch. With a demented grin, he said, "I do not really give a damn who you are or what you say."

Jake's tongue felt fat and spongy, but he managed to croak, "My name is Hans-Karl Vogel. I am a Swiss—"

The guy threw the switch. Jake's body bucked against his bindings. Jolts of scalding pain shot through every nerve ending. A hundred times worse than any electrical shock he'd ever felt.

"Now, give me something, anything, my little toy."

"Look," Jake managed, spluttering. "Look . . . I have a wife . . . and kids . . . in Zurich. Have a heart."

"Well, isn't that nice." The man pushed the floodlight aside, bent over and glared at Jake from close range. "You are going to tell me what I want to know. I will make you talk. And not about your *Frau und Kinder* . . . Oh, how I love this." His wild laugh echoed around the room. Peter Lorre couldn't have played it any better. He walked over and threw the switch again.

Jake convulsed in even greater agony. Felt like his whole body was on fire. "*Nein, bitte*," he whimpered, begging in spite of himself. *Another shot or two of this heat lightning and I'll be dead*, he told himself. *If I show up at the Stars' opener it'll be as a ghost.*

The shining sea that was to be the second half of his life had become nothing more than a tenuous little drop of water.

The man leered. "It took seven hours for the last one to answer me, but he did. Oh yes, he surely did." The slimy devil reached down and began to unbutton Jake's fly. *Jesus God*, he was going to clip a wire to his testicles. *Please, just shoot me.*

He thrashed against his bindings, but the cord or rope, whatever held him, stayed tight as ever. *Let me die, God*, he prayed. *Please, take me now.*

Jesus, the creep had a hand on his balls.

"Stop!" a voice shouted. "I will take charge of this prisoner myself. Remove those wires and untie this man."

"Oh, just when it was getting good. Why don't you watch the fun, sir?"

"I said *stop*, you fool!"

"Oh, but *Hauptsturmführer*—"

"Obey me or I will have your damned head."

"*Jawohl.*"

Did Jake hear heels clicking in obedience? His senses had all but deserted him, but somehow the new voice had sounded familiar. His feverish mind must be playing tricks.

He forced his burning eyes to look at the interloper. Through a mist of pain, he thought he saw a big, aging, gray-haired man in an SS uniform, a silver death's-head on his peaked cap.

"Say nothing, you damned spy," his Uncle Dieter said. And Jake fainted dead away.

CHAPTER FORTY-ONE

J ake is floating in cold space, as chilled as if he were atop Mount Baldy in January. Somehow he's aware that his teeth are chattering.

Now he's entering a hospital room, carrying a bouquet of daffodils and tulips, and lays eyes on Valerie Riskin for the first time, lying there in her bed. The aircraft tool designer, possibly the only woman in her profession in the United States, had saved some lives the day before when explosions had rocked her factory. Jake is there to interview her for the *Herald-Express*.

"I look awful," Valerie says, "but if you really want to ask this old wreck some questions, fire away."

"Prettiest wreck I ever saw," Jake answers, hoping that hasn't come across as pathetically shallow. Within minutes he knows this is the woman he wants to marry.

Now the bartender at the Continental stands before him. "Gimme an Eastside, Shaker," Jake tells him. He hears the clack of a cue ball from the pool table. Bob Wills and the Texas Playboys are belting *Take Me Back to Tulsa* on the jukebox.

Suddenly he's out on the track at Catholic High, doing his stretches. The coach blows his whistle and says, "Sprinters, to the starting line." Jake digs two small holes in the cinder track for his push-off, then crouches into position, his outstretched fingers pressing against the ground in front of him.

He's at Gilmore Field, standing at his front-row seat just above the Stars' dugout, hat held over his heart. Jeanette MacDonald is singing the National Anthem. Jake is crying. Funny, he loves the anthem but it's never made him cry.

Next, Uncle Dieter has a hand on his shoulder as they stand in line for the Ferris wheel at the Louisiana State Fair. This must be 1935, Dieter's last visit to the States.

Jake is weeping even more, his face and chest wracked by deep sobs. Weird. Why would he cry at a fair?

"I am so very sorry, my dear Jacob," Dieter is saying.

Jake's eyes fly open. He's not dreaming. Not anymore. His Uncle Dieter really stands there. Warm tears on Jake's cheeks.

Dieter still wore that damned black uniform. "I never knew something like this would happen," he said. He held a tiny red bottle and was applying something to the cut on Jake's face. It stung. Must be iodine.

Jake realized his wrists, ankles, ribs and face all hurt. His heart felt dried-up, empty. "Dieter?" he managed in little more than a whisper. "You of all people? It's not possible."

"Shh. Save your voice. Let me do the talking. No one can hear us here."

They were in a small room with beige wallpaper, Jake slumped in an upholstered armchair. Some framed certificates hung on the wall. His ear and arm burned where the electrical wires had been clipped on. As he wiped tears from his face, he noticed that his shirt had been laundered.

Remembrance of the past few hours drifted sluggishly back into his brain. He knew some cops and the terms they used. "Grievous bodily harm" came to mind.

"You're supposed to be dead," he muttered.

"Fortunately, I am a rather lively corpse. I have much to tell you."

"That uniform tells me plenty."

"Please, hush now. When I summoned you—"

"*You* summoned me? But Rolf—"

"Yes, I had Rolf Becker send you the letter. I knew he could get it through. I trusted Rolf. *Then.* It was only later that I learned I should not have, and found where his loyalties actually lay. I should have known one can trust almost no one in these times." Dieter grimaced. "Rolf will receive his just rewards, I assure you."

Once the tactic had worked and he'd showed up in Germany, Jake wondered, why had Rolf still lied through his teeth about Dieter having been executed? "But—"

Dieter silenced him with an upraised hand.

"Do not let the uniform deceive you, Jacob. I am not one of *them*," he said, his mouth curling with distaste as he pronounced the word. "I found that joining the *Schutzstaffel* was the way I could do the most good."

"Like I could do Duke Ellington some good by joining the Klan?"

"Please, Jacob, you must try to understand. From the inside, you see, I have been able to save a few people—do you remember Dr. Rosenbaum?—and to obtain better treatment for certain good Germans in the camps. There are a few others like me in the SS, but too few, I am sorry to say."

It was too much for Jake. "I can't deal with all this right now," he muttered. He shook his head; closed his eyes for a moment.

Two Jakes seemed to be debating.

"Why was I crying my eyes out? I don't cry."

"It was probably a reaction to what you'd just been through."

"But I was bawling like a baby."

"Well, you'd never been tortured before."

"Why did I ever get off that bus?"

"You've always been an irrepressible reporter."

"Now my uncle's standing here in an SS uniform, telling me to trust him."

"Maybe you should. He's never lied to you."

"I will have a doctor examine you," Dieter was saying, "a man we can trust. I did not know where or if you would arrive, my son, but I never expected you to be caught and . . . *mein Gott*, tortured. How can I ever forgive myself? *Gott im Himmel*, what you have been through. It is lucky that I check the Gestapo's arrest reports each day."

"God damn it, Dieter—"

"Even half dead, you swear like a sailor—eh?—or a news-paperman . . . My compliments on your German, by the way. It is good."

Jake tried to focus. His head throbbed. "But . . . in that letter, why did you have Rolf say you'd been killed?"

"Because it was the one thing that would make you come here. You would not have come otherwise, would you? If, for instance, the message merely said I had something important to tell you?"

"No . . . I guess not."

"Do not tell me how you managed to reach Switzerland. It is best that I not know."

"Switzerland? You know—"

"I saw your papers while you were unconscious."

"I see. So what's the important thing you have to tell me?"

Dieter put a hand on Jake's shoulder. "Later. Let us first get you some medical attention and then a little food."

CHAPTER FORTY-TWO

The room had a chemical smell, maybe ether. "Where are we?" Jake asked.

"This is an anteroom at a medical clinic in Grunewald. The doctor is one of us, a member of the resistance."

Dieter handed him three pills and a glass of water. "Aspirin. Good German aspirin. Take them," he instructed.

Good. Jake had a headache that hit like Joe Louis. As he swallowed them, he wondered why the hell he'd been put through all this. "Dieter, why would they turn that wrecking crew loose on a foreigner they know very little about?"

"Before the war, they would not have, but paranoia grows and grows. Sadly, now that Hitler has burned his bridges, mistreatment of suspicious strangers runs rampant."

Jake noticed a gray and white cat, perched on top of a file cabinet, eyeing him languidly. He realized it was the first animal he'd seen in Berlin, cat, dog or even horse, for that matter.

A door opened and a balding, middle-aged man in a white smock stuck his head in, a stethoscope hanging from his neck. "Ready?" he said.

"*Ja.*" Dieter took Jake by the arm and led him into an examining room, Jake hobbling on his bad ankle.

A mirror hung on a wall and Jake saw himself for the first time. Pale, in need of a shave, and with a three-inch laceration across his cheek, he looked like a rail-riding hobo who hadn't slept for days. One earlobe was blistered an angry red.

The cat had hopped down from its perch and was rubbing itself against the doctor's ankle. The man put Jake in a chair and applied salve to the cut and the burns on his ear and arm. Then he had him limp to an X-ray machine, where he took exposures, first of his ribs and then his ankle.

After the doctor went off with the film, Dieter handed Jake a paper sack. It contained his wallet, passport, identity card, leather belt and wristwatch. Everything seemed to be there. Although he couldn't recall exactly how many marks had been in the wallet, the amount seemed about right.

Jake climbed on a stand-up scale and slid a couple of weights to the right. "Seventy-three kilos."

"That's about one hundred-sixty pounds," Dieter said.

"I've lost five pounds then, thanks to the damned Gestapo . . . Awhile ago, you said you'd rather not know how I got here, but you should at least know about my cover."

"I know about your cover. Hans-Karl Vogel. I saw your papers while you were unconscious, remember?"

Soon the doctor returned, carrying the X-rays. He clipped them to a light bar on the wall and pulled a toggle. The light snapped on with a sharp click. Jake jerked as if he'd been shot. Damn, he'd had enough of toggle switches. Would that sound unnerve him the rest of his life?

The doctor examined the illuminated negatives, then pointed. "You have a crack in your third rib, see? There is nothing to be done for that; it will heal by itself. On your ankle, I see no bone break. What you have is a severe sprain. I believe that a ligament is badly stretched or even torn. I can put a cast on it. It will take about an hour."

"No," Jake said. "No cast. It would slow me down too much."

The doctor looked at Dieter for backing, but Jake's uncle merely shrugged.

"All right then, I will wrap it tightly, though it is against my better judgment. You should immobilize this area"—pointing at the film—"as much as possible for many days." He went to a cabinet and began removing some supplies.

The doctor wrapped Jake's swollen ankle, gave him a bottle of pain pills, a small jar, and a walking cane. "Take two of these tablets three times a day," he said, "and apply this salve to your burns for the next three or four days. Stay off your feet as much as you are able, but when you must walk, put very little weight on that foot. Use this cane."

"Thank you, Horst," Dieter said. "Can you lend our young friend a razor? I think he should like to shave before having a bite of dinner."

When Jake's face looked more presentable, Dieter rubbed his ample belly and said, "You must be hungry, Jacob. We must put some of those five pounds back on you, eh?"

Jake hadn't eaten in a long time—appetite had been the least of his worries—but yes, he realized now that his stomach was in want of some food.

"A car is waiting. Let us go then."

Jake limped along behind him, through a rear door, where a small gray Volkswagen stood in the alley. It was nighttime. Jake had lost all track of time. A few snow flurries drifted down. A handsome woman of about fifty sat behind the wheel.

"Ask no questions," Dieter whispered to Jake. Then, louder, "*Guten Abend, Liebchen.*" Who the hell is this woman? Jake wondered. He didn't trust anybody anymore.

"You sit in front, your ankle," Dieter said, and then proceeded to work his large body into the back seat. When he was settled in, Jake took the passenger seat beside the driver. "*Guten Abend,*" he said, noticing high cheekbones and a nose Monet would have appreciated.

She answered with a wry smile, turned on the windshield wipers, shifted into first, and off they went.

No one spoke as they drove, but Dieter reached forward once and touched the driver's cheek. Aha, Dieter's got a girlfriend. You dog, Jake thought, you sixty-three-year-old dog. He must have grinned, for the woman shot him a coy glance. The snow flurries stopped and she switched off the wipers.

She soon pulled up in front of a small café on a quiet, tree-lined street. "Here we are," Dieter said, and Jake fumbled for his cane, opened the door and said "*Danke*" to the woman. When Dieter got out, he and the driver exchanged smiles laced with intimacy, and she drove off.

"Is that—"

"I said no questions. She is a friend, a good friend." Dieter gave him a worldly smile.

"It's good to know you have a woman friend here in Berlin."

The clouds were scudding away from the blacked-out city and the night was turning clear and cold. Jake gazed up at the stars, impersonal pinpoints of light billions of years old that didn't know or care that on a tiny, faraway planet a great nation of music, art and science had been taken over by cruel, immoral thugs. "Look, Dieter, there's Orion the Hunter. Remember when you first pointed out that constellation to me?"

"I believe so. It was sometime in the Twenties, was it not?"

"Right." Jake turned toward the café. "This place is okay?" he asked.

"*Ja*, come, it is cold," and Dieter opened the door for him. Jake had trouble getting the cane in sync with his hobbling steps.

It was a small place and only two tables were occupied. Dieter exchanged good evenings with a man Jake took for the proprietor and led the way to a private rear room where a table was set for two. Dieter closed the door behind them.

"God, I need a drink," Jake said as he dropped himself into a chair, resting the cane against the table. His ankle ached.

"I am sure you do. I will get you something good and strong."

"Will I be able to go back to my hotel?"

"No. I will have your things collected, your bill settled, and move you into a secure apartment in District Wilmersdorf, southwest of the city center." Dieter took a drink from a filled water glass. "I could issue orders that you have been cleared of suspicion, but that might direct distrustful eyes toward me. Instead, I will just make it known that I am personally handling this suspect prisoner."

"You can do that? I heard you called *Hauptsturmführer*. That means major, doesn't it?"

"SS major, yes. I have complete authority in the small surveillance section of which I am in charge. I can make a few people disappear, Jews, other good people. Disappear into places like Switzerland or Spain. My authority and methods are not questioned, but I must not do this to excess. I must be careful not to raise suspicions." Dieter leaned closer across the table. "In great secrecy, Jacob, I assist an old friend, Carl Goerdeler, the former mayor of Leipzig, who heads a resistance group."

The proprietor came in and presented two paper menus. "We are short of everything, as you know, Dieter, but I believe I still have a bit of the stuffed ham. Also, some goulash."

"The stuffed ham, Albrecht, if you would," Dieter said," but first some Schnapps. Also, some beer, anything cold and dark." The man nodded and Dieter handed Albrecht the menus unread. When the man was gone, Dieter stared intently into Jake's eyes for a moment.

"Now, let me tell you the real reason I summoned you." His fingers drummed on the tabletop for a moment. "You have a daughter here in Berlin."

Jake tried to catch his breath. "A daughter?"

"Yes, a lovely twelve-year-old child, and she needs your help."

CHAPTER FORTY-THREE

Jake shook his throbbing head. Had he heard right? "A daughter?" he murmured.

"You will recall that the lady you met here in 1930, Winifrid"—Jake flashed on that woman, pictured her slender face—"was the niece of a friend of Marta's and mine. She became pregnant and gave birth nine months after you left."

Jake gasped. "My God, you should have told me."

"Winifrid asked me not to. She did not wish to leave Germany and she did not want you to feel obligated or trapped. I told myself," Dieter went on, "to keep an eye out for them. Sad to say, Winifrid died of influenza when the girl, Ilse is her name, was four."

Jake bit his lower lip. "Winni's dead? Man, that's . . . ." His fists clenched. "I really liked that woman."

"Unfortunately, yes. If my dear Marta had been alive, we would have taken the girl in and raised her. But as an older man and a widower, I felt I could not do this by myself. Now I wish that I had. Ilse was placed in a state-run orphanage, where she received the full Nazi indoctrination. At nine, she became a member of the *Bund Deutscher Maedel*, the girls' section of the Hitler Youth."

Jake sighed, then made a mental calculation. He'd met Winifrid at the memorial service for his Aunt Marta and had first slept with her that very night. That had been in February, so the girl would have been born the following November. She'd have turned twelve just last month.

Winifrid had been a communist. What a bizarre turn, Jake thought, for her daughter—hell, his daughter too, maybe—to become just the opposite, a Nazi. *His daughter*? He had trouble taking this all in.

"For crying out loud, you should have told me, especially after Winni died."

"But, my son, a single man far away in America, you would have been even less able to care for her than I, here in Germany."

Jake stared at Dieter and said, "Winni died of the flu? That doesn't add up. The big influenza outbreak was over long before then, by the early Twenties."

Dieter shrugged his shoulders and pursed his lips. "That is the story. She died in a state hospital. Influenza was given as the cause of death." His face wore a these-things-happen look. "She was a Marxist after all."

Jake made a fist and blurted, "You should go with me."

"With you?"

"Back to the States. Away from this madhouse. You like America."

"No, not while I have work to do here. Every little bit helps. When xenophobic love of country and blind veneration of the military transcend respect for your fellow man, bad things happen. There are good people in Germany, many of them, but they stood by while the government gained broad powers over their rights. In regard to Jews and other 'undesirables,' they struck a Faustian bargain. Now they are cowed, afraid to speak out. If I can help, even in a small way, to make Germany whole again, here is where I belong."

This is why I love this man, Jake thought. This is why I came to this cuckoo land, because killing this good man would have been an unforgivable crime. "I can't tell you how glad I am to know you're alive," he murmured.

"It was a terrible trick to play on you," Dieter said, frown lines playing on his brow. "But you also can help the nation of your parents' birth, by helping your daughter Ilse. By saving her."

How the hell could I do that? Jake thought. I don't even know the kid. "So I really have a daughter? Holy smoke, tell me about her."

"Ilse works at a *Flakturm*, helping with the artillery shells."

"A child?" Jake tried to picture twelve-year-olds on top of a flak tower during the terror of an air raid. Explosions, flares, searchlights.

"Yes, many Hitler Youth do that, boys and girls both, in love with their uniforms. She has been quite propagandized. You've much work to do, you must set her mind straight. Save her, you see?"

Save her? Me? Jake wondered again how he could possibly do that. Even if he could somehow get the little Nazi out, could he and Valerie raise a twelve-year-old girl in L.A.? Would his fiancée even try? She had a kind heart and was compassionate, but she was also dedicated to her career. Would she say 'Okay' or would it be 'You and your love child can take a hike.' She wouldn't do that. Would she?

Albrecht returned with a tray bearing two glasses and large steins of beer, which he placed on the table. "I have just enough stuffed ham left for two."

"Excellent," Dieter said. "And some of your splendid dumplings, too."

When Albrecht was gone, Dieter raised his glass and said, "*Prosit.*"

Jake clinked the glass and tossed down some of his Schnapps. "Ah, that helps," he said. "You're still in touch with her? Ilse?"

"Yes. She knows that Marta and I were friends of her mother. She respects that I am in the SS, so I see her every now and then. I try to give her the occasional subtle suggestion that the Nazis might not be right about everything, that she needs to open her mind."

"And?" Jake prompted, taking another drink.

"She resists. Doesn't want to hear that. Children of her age can be very serious, but I have planted a seed or two."

What an emotional riptide I'm caught in, Jake thought. Dieter alive . . . and me a *father*.

The stuffed ham and dumplings arrived shortly after that and they dug in with gusto.

Slicing off a piece of ham, Dieter said, "There is a serious food shortage, but"—with a laugh—"thank God Germany has many pig farmers."

"This is good," Jake said. "Didn't realize how hungry I was." The ham rolls were stuffed with celery, red and white cabbage, and another item or two Jake wasn't sure about.

Jake finished his Schnapps and took a sip of beer. It was good. He hadn't been able to communicate with Dieter for more than three years, not since the war broke out in Europe, so he brought him up to date. He was now the *Express*'s military writer and he'd been to Guadalcanal for Hearst's International News Service. He also told about Valerie, the terrific woman he was going to marry. "Her voice can melt your heart."

"Like my Marta," Dieter said, his eyes watery. He raised his stein and made a toast to Valerie.

Jake took a bite of dumpling, chewy and tasty.

"Have you heard the name Hanna Reitsch?" he asked.

"*Ach*, she is a famous pilot, gliders and regular airplanes both. Before the Luftwaffe came out into the open in '36, she was a leader in the flying clubs. She set many records. Now she test-flies new aircraft types for Heinkel and Junkers."

"Anything else?"

"Only that she is admired by Hitler. I do not know if she is a party member. Why do you ask?"

"I ran into her in Wernher von Braun's office. She's running some kind of performance numbers for him. I met her before, years ago at an air show, only for a few minutes but she might have recognized me the other day. I didn't like the way she looked me over."

"Let us hope you will not see her again," Dieter said, and asked who this von Braun person was. Jake gave a brief explanation that included Sergei Prokofiev and President Roosevelt.

Dieter looked stunned. "You were always getting yourself into things, Jacob," he said at last, "but here you must be very careful."

"After what just happened, you bet."

When the meals were finished, Dieter said, "Tomorrow you will meet your Ilse."

Oh crap, Jake thought.

CHAPTER FORTY-FOUR

Dieter installed Jake in the apartment at the safe house in Wilmersdorf. They talked for an hour, still catching up, Dieter describing the craziness that had invested Germany in the past decade and asking about Jake's work and his Valerie.

"Who else is lodged in this building?" Jake asked.

"Just one other at the moment, an old deaf clergyman who is wanted for protesting from the pulpit. You will never see him.

"We all have many purposes in life," Dieter went on. "Mine at this point is to do what good I can for my country and to save some lives. Yours is to continue writing the truth for your American readers, to become a good husband . . . and to be a good father. You must redeem Ilse, take her to a good life in America and bring fresh air into her mind. I know you will find a way, somehow, to do this."

How? Jake thought. I might not get my own ass out of this shit-hole country, let alone take a kid I've never met. But expressing that would hurt his uncle, so he said, "I know you regret not having children of your own, Dieter, but you've been a good father figure to me. A great example."

Dieter hugged him, which didn't do Jake's ribs any good at all.

Before leaving minutes later, Dieter said, "Answer the door to no one but me. I will give the door two quick knocks, wait two seconds, then rap twice more."

That night Jake swallowed some pain pills and looked at his

face. The swelling had gone down some and the cut on his cheek was scabbing up but would it leave a scar? Jake sure as hell didn't want a damn Prussian badge of courage on his face. He swabbed salve on his burns, iced down his swollen ankle for several minutes, and went to bed.

The two-room flat was warm and the bed snug. As he lay there beneath its goosedown comforter the enormity of all this overwhelmed him. *Dieter alive*—after all Jake had been through in the last four weeks to come here and avenge his death. Now he wanted to avenge *himself*, beat the hell out of that slimy little bastard who'd tortured him. Though his memory was foggy on some of the details, Jake was pretty sure the guy had reduced him to actually begging for his life. Achieving some payback would be fantastic, but impossible—he'd never be able to find the man.

Tears came. Unwanted. What's wrong with me? he thought. I don't have crying jags. He held a pillow to his face and sobbed. Damn, he hadn't cried himself to sleep since he was a little kid.

In the morning he heard the two quick double raps at the door and let his uncle in. "*Morgen*, Jacob," Dieter said, and handed him a cardboard cup of tea and a bag containing two rolls. "In a few minutes I will take you to see Ilse. It is all arranged."

Jake's stomach tightened. "You can't tell her I'm an American."

"No, of course not, that will take time. You will still be Herr Vogel from Switzerland but she must be told that you are her father."

Jake took a bite of a roll. "Is that wise?"

"*Ja,* she is curious to know about her father. I have told her that her mother was a good woman who loved her, but of course nothing about her having been a communist. We will see how she reacts to you, how the conversation goes, and then, how do you say it, improvise?"

"Play it by ear."

"Yes, play it by ear. I love some of your American sayings."

Jake had never had the least problem meeting new people, but he found himself growing nervous at the prospect of encountering his own daughter, a stranger. So the kid had some of his genes. She was an ardent Nazi; why not leave all this alone? "What have you told her about her father?" he asked.

"Only that I know him, nothing about his nationality."

"She must have asked."

"I've said that you were European but not German, and that you one day might come here."

Jake finished the first roll, took a bite of the second, and changed the subject. Remembering that Wernher von Braun had said he'd be back in Berlin in two days, he asked, "What's the date today? I've lost track of time."

"It is the fifteenth. Your, ah, visit to the Gestapo building took only one day."

"Seemed like a week."

Before they left, Jake told about Rolf Becker's desperate request that he kill Putzi Hanfstaengl and the offer of half a million Reichsmarks.

Dieter made a sound somewhere between a laugh and a growl. "The poor fool has really got himself in deep this time."

"Of course I would never do anything like that, but I might be able to fake it, plant a story in the papers saying Hanfstaengl was dead. Roosevelt might go for something like that."

"When the war is over," Dieter said, "you might find nothing in that Swiss account or perhaps a few counterfeit marks. You would never be able to prove you had made an agreement, a deal."

"And, Dieter, if Germany loses and the Nazis fall, Reichsmarks could be worthless anyway."

"There is that, too, *ja*."

"Does Rolf even work for the *Zeitung* anymore?"

"No, he is a functionary for Goebbels' Ministry of Propaganda and Enlightenment. He visits all the papers to make sure they are toeing the line, saying the proper things. There are many like him, former newspapermen."

"That makes me sick," Jake said. "Rolf used to be a good reporter."

Dieter said, "I have heard rumors that he is in Goebbels' doghouse."

As they left the building, a bundled-up woman was sweeping and scrubbing the sidewalk in spite of the cold. The gray Volkswagen sat at the curb, Dieter's *Liebchen* at the wheel.

Jake still wasn't introduced to the woman as she drove them toward Spandau in the western suburbs. He got only the occasional coy smile from her, but it was obvious that she and Dieter were lovers. Good for them, Jake thought. Everyone, no matter their age, needs comfort and affection. Gretchen flashed across his mind. So did Valerie.

When they arrived thirty minutes later, their destination turned out to be a curious complex of classroom bungalows and stone barracks. Jake said "*danke*" to the woman, got a "*bitte*" in return, and got out, cane in hand. He and Dieter approached the barracks, where two boys who looked about fifteen stood guard. Their Mauser rifles looked almost as big as they were. Jake found the heel-clicking and the "Heil Hitlers" depressing. Dieter's SS uniform obviously carried a lot of weight. No pun intended, he told himself. Even here, what Valerie called his sick humor had surfaced.

Dieter led the way down a corridor, Jake doing his best to keep up. He was getting better at using the cane. They entered a small, empty office, where the wall bore a clock and a scowling portrait of the Führer, and sat on chairs near a wooden desk that had seen better days. Jake put his hat on the desk.

"We have complete privacy here," Dieter said. "No listening devices."

Jake hoped he was right. His fingers drummed on the arm rest. What the devil am I doing here? he wondered. If I wasn't nervous meeting FDR, why am I nervous now?

Before long the door opened. Jake caught his breath. A brown-eyed girl in a khaki uniform entered hesitantly. Blouse, Sam Browne belt, long skirt, red and black swastika armband, a long-billed field cap on her head.

He and Dieter got to their feet, Jake unsteadily. *Holy cow. This is my daughter? This toy soldier?* Her ear-length hair, Jake saw with a shock, was brownish-red, the exact color of his own, before the dye job. He'd been completely unprepared for the impact of this moment.

She was slender, average height for her age, her face nicely shaped though pale, but then it was wintertime.

"Heil Hitler," the girl said and gave the Nazi salute.

My God, Jake thought, these people have made a fawning vassal out of this young girl. Young girl? No, *my daughter*, he corrected himself.

Dieter didn't return the salute, pleasing Jake, who stared at this creature, his flesh and blood, the product of his little fling with Winni.

She returned Jake's gaze with curiosity. It was a long and awkward moment. The child obviously wondered why the SS *Hauptsturmführer* had summoned her, and who this strange man was. Say something Dieter, Jake urged silently.

"Please sit, Ilse my dear," Dieter said at last, waving her to a chair. "I have a surprise for you. May I introduce Herr Vogel?"

Ilse, who had sat for only a second, jumped to her feet and extended her right hand, dropped her head in a slight bow and said, "How do you do."

Jake took the hand, saying, "You are a lovely young woman. A pleasure to meet you." Gazing at his girl's face was like looking into a mirror.

"Please sit, my child," Dieter said. Her brown eyes, deferential and cool, rested on Dieter as she sat, but stole a sidelong glance at

Jake, curious about this stranger in civilian clothes. Weighing no more than a hundred pounds, this still-developing girl would grow into an attractive woman, Jake thought.

"Ilse my dear," Dieter began, "Herr Vogel comes here from Switzerland."

"I hope your journey was pleasant," she said without emotion.

"There is no way to edge into this slowly," Dieter went on, "So I will just say it. Herr Vogel"—he paused for a beat—"is your father."

Her mouth dropped open, her eyes wide as saucers. Jake thought, *Smooth, Dieter.* Are we supposed to get up and hug? Ilse made no move to do so. Jake didn't either.

Instead, she crossed her arms. "Well, *Vati,*" not hiding the sarcasm, "where have you been all these years?"

That hurt. What could he say? "I didn't know about you until yesterday. Had I known I would have come to you long ago."

"Humph. And what? Taken me to Switzerland? I should not have liked that." The arms crossed tighter across her little chest.

Damn, this was off to a bad start. "I would like to get to know you," Jake said, trying for a friendly grin.

"Humph," again. "Well, my curiosity has been satisfied. *Danke.* If there is nothing more, *Hauptsturmführer,*" and she began to get up.

"Do not leave, my dear," Dieter said. "There is much more."

"*Jawohl.*" As she resumed her seat, she looked at the cane and said, "You are injured, Herr Vogel? Did this happen in an air raid?"

"No, I sprained my ankle getting into a car faster than I wanted."

"And the cut on your face?"

"Part of the same accident. I was having a bad day."

"I am sorry," she said, though not sounding like it. She let a moment pass, then, "I remember my *Muti* a little, but I have no memory of you. Where were you when she passed away?"

"If I had known about you back then, I would have come."

Would he have?

"And taken me off to live with the milk cows, and to take flügelhorn lessons? Were you and my mother married?"

Jake wondered if she knew about the facts of life. "No, we were not, but I held her in great esteem. She was a good woman." I'm a lying bastard, he told himself. I didn't know Winifrid very well. "If I'd been aware of you—"

"So you created me and then ran off." Again, the hurt. But, okay, she knew the facts of life. Savvy kid.

"Left me to an orphanage. Well, the Third Reich is my father, a very good father at that."

"Ilse," Dieter cut in, "you mustn't talk to your father like that. He is a kind man. He wants to help you." How can I? Jake asked himself for the tenth time.

"I apologize, *Hauptsturmführer*," Ilse said.

"As I have told you before, everything is not as it seems. You are a bright child. By questioning and challenging, one learns the real truth of things."

"Dieter," Jake said, "she was questioning and challenging *me*. I like that." He turned to Ilse. "It's what I do also."

"And what is it that you do? What is your occupation?"

"I'm a newspaper reporter . . . in . . . Switzerland."

"I like to write." Some of the chill lifted from her. "Perhaps one day I could write for a newspaper. How was it that you became a reporter?"

Jake told how he'd started as a cub reporter on a small paper—not mentioning that it was in Texas—gained experience, and then took advantage of an opening on a larger paper in a big city. "I'd love to see you become a reporter, but not for one of today's German papers. They mostly print what the government wants them to say, propaganda."

At her look of protest, Jake added, "Surely you know that. This is understandable in wartime, but think about it. Have you ever seen any negative comment printed about the government?"

Ilse's hands became fists. "The Third Reich is protecting all of Western civilization from the scourge of Bolshevism and yet instead of helping, the British and Americans only interfere." She seemed to be quoting Goebbels word for word. "That is not propaganda, that is the truth."

"It's a viewpoint, Ilse, and just possibly not the whole truth."

"Your *Vater* could be right, Ilse," Dieter said. "Open your mind to the possibility."

"If you were not a good SS man and very kind to me"—turning to Jake—"and if you were not my *Vater*, I might say that you are both traitors."

"Neither of us is a Judas," Dieter said.

"A Judas? And what is that?"

"A man in the Bible who—"

"I have not read the Bible. It is *verboten*. This Judas, he was a Jew?"

"No, he was not," Dieter lied, "but the word means betrayer. Neither of us is that."

"Then I believe you, *Hauptsturmführer*. Ilse looked at the clock and said, "I must go. I have mathematics class. There is no school tomorrow. Shall I see you then?"

"I suggest that you see your father alone tomorrow. You have much to talk about."

She crossed her arms again—had that scared her?—and looked at Jake with trepidation. But she said, "I enjoy the zoo. Ours is one of the world's finest. Perhaps I could show it to you?"

"It would be my pleasure," Jake said, not sure that he meant it. With reluctance, though, he made arrangements to meet her in the morning in front of the zoo.

Back in the apartment, Jake told Dieter about Gretchen but not *everything* about Gretchen. He told him that her husband had been killed while bombing England and that she now worked for the Abwehr as well as the British.

"This troubles me," Dieter said. "I know the British have agents here, as do we in England. One must be very careful these days. I hope she is truly on your side."

"She's okay, Dieter. I trust Gretchen."

"I pray you are correct."

Jake had rewrapped his ankle before going out to the barracks. It still hurt but not as much. "I want to see Gretchen again, let her know I'm no longer at the hotel. But she lives several blocks from the U-bahn station."

Looking at the cane, Dieter said, "Then I will drive you. You must not walk that much. I would like to meet this woman."

CHAPTER FORTY-FIVE

A daughter! Here in Berlin. Jake paced painfully around the apartment that afternoon. Sure, the ankle was killing him, but he could think better on his feet, so the hell with it. A vortex swirled in his mind as he struggled to come to grips with this biggest surprise of his life.

Maybe the kid wasn't even his. How could Dieter be sure? Winifrid must have had other lovers. Oh, but who was he kidding? Ilse's eyes and hair were dead-ringers for his own.

After being footloose all these years, to suddenly find he was the father of an almost-grown girl was a crushing revelation. And, biggest question of all, how would Valerie deal with this? God, she might really flip.

Jake tried to think of something else, like some persuasive and disarming things to say to Ilse tomorrow at the zoo. But he knew that in the end he'd mostly wing it.

At the wheel of a big blue Daimler sedan, Dieter drove Jake to Gretchen's neighborhood in Schöneberg that night. When his uncle made no mention of his woman friend or her Volkswagen, Jake decided not to pry.

"What happened to your sweet little Porsche?" he asked. "I loved that car."

"As did I, but I sold it to a general whose goodwill I needed.

Also, he offered a generous sum."

Dieter took a circuitous route through blacked-out streets and doubled back a time or two. On *Marburgstrasse* at last, he passed Number 84 twice, then, satisfied that he hadn't been tailed, parked two doors down.

He had told Jake that he wanted to meet Gretchen, to form his own opinion of her, and that Jake should prepare her for this surprise before he came in. So he stayed behind while Jake made his way to her door, using the cane and moving slowly.

Jake knocked. Seconds passed while Gretchen no doubt checked the peephole before opening the door. Her mouth dropped open when she saw the cut on his face and that he was leaning on a cane.

She gasped, shut the door behind him, and hugged him tightly.

"Ouch," Jake cried and pulled back. "Not so tight. Broken rib."

"*Mein Gott*, what has happened?" she said, taking his hand and leading him to the sofa. Jake said he'd been arrested by the Gestapo. She brought him a snifter of cognac and sat next to him wide-eyed to hear the tale.

While Jake described his ordeal, she twice interjected, "Those *Schweinehunde*." When he finished, she said, "You should not have gone to the Goebbels', even for a look." She laid a hand gently to his face. "I told you that I would handle that." He nodded in grim affirmation.

"When everything looked its worst, and I thought my, er, genitals were about to be fricasseed, I was rescued."

"Rescued? How? By whom?"

"You'll find this hard to grasp, Gretchen, but it was my Uncle Dieter. He's alive."

"Really?" she said, sounding less surprised than Jake had expected. He told her Dieter was trustworthy, that though he was in the SS he was not one of their cruel sadists. Remembering Dieter's note of suspicion, Jake said nothing about his uncle slipping a few condemned people out of the country.

Gretchen asked many questions about Dieter and about Jake's injuries. This was so much to load on her that Jake didn't mention his daughter.

At last she seemed to accept that his uncle could be trusted. So Jake, with one last surprise, said that Dieter was outside and could he come in?

Jake knew Dieter could be grandfatherly and charming, and tonight he was at his best. He drank some of the cognac Gretchen offered and said kind words of sympathy while admiring the photo of her late husband. He volunteered little about his work, spending more time filling her in on Jake's last two days. Jake sensed that he was testing her, sizing her up.

"Gretchen, do you know the name Hanna Reitsch?" Jake asked.

"Yes, I know Hanna."

"You *know* her?"

"Yes, Heinrich was a flight instructor in her Luftwaffe cadet school. We got to know her quite well. Why do you ask?"

"I met her in von Braun's office. Scared the hell out of me the way she looked me over. Is she SS or something?"

"Hanna Reitsch is not in the *Schutzstaffel*," Dieter threw in.

"Nor is she in the Luftwaffe," Gretchen said. "She doesn't much like Hitler, but she is passionate about her duty to Germany. I took lunch with her just last month, and we argued about this. 'But surely not to *this* Germany,' I said, but to little avail."

"Hmm," Jake said, feeling no reassurance.

The conversation turned to Magda Goebbels and the Hindenburg letter she supposedly was holding for Putzi Hanfstaengl. "Aha, so that is how you knew about Hanfstaengl when Rolf brought his name up," Dieter said, "and why you were found out there at Lanke." He turned to Gretchen. "Jacob was always an impetuous boy."

"Impetuosity slew the feline, or something like that," Gretchen said, making her guests laugh.

Dieter said, "I will make an appointment and then take us there tomorrow and settle the matter, how is that?"

"What?" Gretchen gasped. "Us?"

"The SS provides her protection and I am SS. I could be paying a courtesy call on Himmler's behalf to see that her security is being properly handled. It would not be difficult. I could introduce you as my assistant, to take notes if necessary, and Jacob as Herr Vogel, who is visiting me on business."

"It sounds most risky," Gretchen said.

"Less risky than you going out there alone pretending to work for the power company," Jake responded.

Her face wrinkled. "Perhaps." She took Jake's hand and held on warmly. Dieter noticed that, Jake saw.

"I understand that she is lonely out there," Dieter said, "while her husband plays big shot in the city center. She might be pleased to have the company of three such charming people as we." He winked at Gretchen.

Later, when the conversation began to lag, Dieter put his empty snifter down on an end table. "It is settled then. Tomorrow night, if the lady is available," he said, getting to his feet. "Perhaps you two would like a little time alone. I will be outside, Jacob." He took Gretchen's hand, kissed it gallantly, and left, twining his muffler around his neck.

Minutes later, after he'd said his private goodbye with warm kisses, Jake began to realize that Dieter wasn't driving toward the safe house in Wilmersdorf. They were actually downtown. In the blacked-out streets, he noticed with some icy fear forming in his chest that they were near the Gestapo building. What the hell was Dieter up to?

They passed what appeared in the gloom to be a tavern. Half a block beyond, Dieter pulled over to the curb. "I thought you might like to say hello to someone," he said.

"What? Say hello—"

"A *friend* of ours"—Dieter glanced at his watch—"will be

coming out of that place before long." He pointed back toward the tavern. "He pours a lot of Schnapps down his miserable little throat every night at this time before crawling home to his equally miserable little apartment."

The coin dropped. Jake understood. The tavern door soon opened and he saw a man and a woman come out. She clung to his arm as they strolled off. The man was too tall to be the weaselly little sadist who'd tortured him.

Five or ten more minutes passed glacially.

Jake had done some boxing in the Navy years ago—until the day he ran up against a Mexican kid with lightning fast hands.

The door swung open and a little man emerged and shambled off in the opposite direction. Leaving his cane behind, Jake stepped from the car and quickly crossed the street, trying not to limp. His ankle hurt, but what the hell. In a few moments he fell in behind Weasel Face, trying to step lightly and quietly. He followed him around a dark corner into a side street.

Weasel Face must have sensed or heard something, for he turned and looked straight at Jake. Even in the dim light recognition struck. His eyes widened, his jaw dropped. "You!"

"Howdy," Jake said in Tex-English, and drove a left hand into the little man's chest. He followed by snapping a hard right to the jaw. Weasel Face grunted in pain and staggered back against a brick wall. Then, almost gagging on adrenaline, Jake was all over him, body-punching like a crazed maniac, which at that moment he was. Left right left right.

"*Nein, bitte,*" the man gurgled as if he had a mouthful of marbles. Sunk to begging, just as Jake had been.

"*Eins mehr,*" Jake said. He reached back, put all he had behind it, and drove his right fist into the man's face. The nose exploded in a gush of blood. A couple of teeth tumbled from his mouth like little hailstones bouncing off a roof. The guy crumpled to the sidewalk and curled up in the fetal position.

It was all Jake could do to resist kicking the bastard. He'd better get his ass out of here before someone came along. He straightened up, inhaled a deep breath, said, "*Guten Abend*," and walked off. His hands ached like hell but he was filled with rich satisfaction.

Back in the car, Dieter said, "I hope you told him hello."

"And goodbye, too."

"Most appropriate. That one will be drummed out of the Gestapo tomorrow, and then go into the Wehrmacht. In a few months he will be on the eastern front."

"Perfect," Jake said.

CHAPTER FORTY-SIX

Back at the safe house in Wilmersdorf, Dieter went to the little icebox and chipped off some chunks. He wrapped them in towels and swaddled them around Jake's aching hands. The two talked awhile, but it was late. Dieter didn't stay long.

Jake had trouble falling asleep. Beating the crap out of that torturing little bastard replayed over and over in his mind. Too bad he couldn't have fried Weasel Face with some of his own electricity. Thoughts of Gretchen also swirled. And Valerie back in L.A., of course. But most of all he thought about his daughter Ilse, the biggest surprise of his whole life. What the hell had he gotten himself into? Finally, despite ankle and hands throbbing, he drifted off.

In the morning, Jake was leaning against an iron gate at the entrance to the Berlin zoo, waiting for Ilse. He was glad that warm gloves were hiding his swollen hands. He wondered why he'd agreed to this outing. He'd almost made up his mind to not even try to take her out of this country. Instead, he could just come back and see her after the war.

But precisely at ten o'clock as they'd arranged, there she was and he felt somehow pleased at the sight of her, this little woman with a military greatcoat of field gray reaching her ankles. They'd each come by public transportation.

Once inside, Ilse said, "We can use a wheelchair. There is no charge. I can push you about."

"No, I'd rather just walk along with you as best I can. Just don't go too fast for the old man."

The *Zoologischer Garten* was huge and first-rate, Jake thought, far superior to L.A.'s Griffith Park Zoo.

Ilse was polite but reserved as they strolled the landscaped grounds. Her breath blew gray and wispy in the cold air as she pointed to an enclosure. "I love the elephants. They are so big and strong. Intelligent also. They come from Africa, you know."

A few Berliners were about, well bundled up against the chill. Some of them, noticing Jake's limp and his cane, smiled and gave little salutes, taking him for a wounded veteran. Little do they know, he thought.

He noticed a grotto-like enclosure boarded up with plywood. Part of the steel handrail in front of it was blackened and torn. It must have been bomb damage. Jake wondered if any animals had been killed, or had gotten loose.

A woman herded two little girls along the pathway. Seeing them, Jake suddenly knew what had bothered him about Dieter taking Gretchen and him to meet Magda Goebbels. Frau Goebbels had seen him and, even worse, so had two of her kids. One, the girl who'd taunted him, had had a very good look indeed.

Ilse led him to an enclosure that held a pair of American bison. "I wonder what America is like," she said, gazing at the shaggy beasts. "Before the war, I saw some of their motion pictures. Tom Mix, Johnny Mack Brown. I wonder if the savage Indians still attack the white men."

"No, that ended a long time ago."

"How do you know this? You have been to America?"

"Yes, once, a few years ago. I liked it very much. The people were nice."

Ilse's face clouded defiantly. "Nice? In Chicago they shoot each other with Tommy guns, and they make war on Germany. They cannot be nice, these American gangsters. They are the enemy."

"There are nice people and bad ones in all countries, Ilse."

"We are ridding ourselves of the bad ones here. We are building a strong, racially pure society."

"I find that having all kinds, the good and the bad, various religions, several races, is what makes a society strong." Jake, ashamed, didn't mention that racial segregation still held sway in the American South.

"Several races together, *nein*! It must not be. My teachers say—"

"Your teachers say what your government tells them to say."

Ilse stalked a few steps away. The look of scorn on her face cut like a razor. "My teachers speak the truth."

"Do you really believe that most Germans support Hitler, Ilse?"

"Of course, what a silly question."

"If that is so, why are there thousands of paid informers to spy on people? And fifty-thousand Gestapo officials? Two million policemen? That's one for every forty Germans."

Ilse's brow furrowed. "Who told you such things?"

"*Hauptsturmführer* Weber, and he should know."

She crossed her arms tightly.

"It's something to think about, Ilse, but let's not spoil the day talking about these things." He pointed with his cane. "Look at the lions over there."

"Yes, they came from German East Africa, before the colonies were stolen from us by the hateful Versailles Treaty."

Jake stifled a sigh. He steered clear of politics for the next hour.

At a bear enclosure, three frisky little cubs romped and played. Ilse clapped her hands, her ash-brown eyes bright with glee. "See how cute they are. I should like to pick up their warm, furry little bodies and cuddle them."

There's still some little girl in this young soldier. The thought warmed Jake.

When they stopped at a small café near the giraffes, he bought a hot chocolate for her and a *Glühwein* for himself. He took a sip of the spicy wine punch. He wanted to tell her it "hit the spot," but couldn't translate that into German so he simply said, "*Schön warm.*"

Ilse nodded. Gazing at her face, Jake couldn't help but add, "Say, your eyes look just like mine."

"I suppose they do, *Vater.*"

Had the little Nazi actually called him father? And without sarcasm?

"Your mother," he probed, "do you have any memory of her being sick?"

Ilse's face scrunched in thought. "I do not think so. It was a long time ago, but no. One day they took her to hospital and me to the orphanage. They told me she was very ill, but I cannot recall her acting unwell. But she must have been, mustn't she?"

The bastards, Jake thought. "I'm glad that we're getting acquainted, Ilse." Jake recalled Wernher von Braun saying that he was going to fly to Sweden to see a supplier. Maybe . . . "Say, have you ever ridden in an airplane?"

"*Nein*, never. I should like to very much, of course. The Luftwaffe has the finest planes in the world."

"Maybe I could arrange that."

Her lips parted in a happy little-girl smile. "You could do that?"

"Possibly," he said. She had actually smiled at him. First time! Was she starting to like him? And was he truly thinking he could fly her out of here with von Braun's help? No, no, forget that, he told himself. But he had to admit her smile had warmed him.

"I must be back by four," Ilse said later when they had seen just about everything in the zoo.

"Can you get a pass tomorrow?"

"Perhaps. Our schedules are more flexible in the afternoon, after classes. We cannot leave the post overnight. We must always be ready should the *Tommi* air raiders come."

He thought about her and other children like her, in harm's way on the flak tower during those attacks. "Are they frightening for you, the raids?"

"A little of course, but it is a grand show, in a way. All the bright colors. The parachute flares drifting down like Christmas trees, the tracer shells going up, the sight of an enemy plane when it is caught in the searchlights. You cannot imagine."

I can imagine very well, Jake thought. I've been up there among those flashing lights and exploding shells.

"If it were not so harmful to my city, one could grow fond of it."

Jake had heard things like that before from veterans, but never from a veteran who was *twelve*.

"You're quite the little soldier, aren't you?" And that's exactly what she looked like in her greatcoat.

"I merely do my duty."

As they headed toward the exit, she said, "I hope you liked our zoo."

"I did, Ilse. I've enjoyed this day."

"As have I, *Vater*." Ilse moved her hands in mimicry of an airplane banking in flight.

They passed under a glowering Nazi flag and walked toward the U-bahn station. Had she really called him father? Twice?

CHAPTER FORTY-SEVEN

Dieter had made an appointment with Magda Goebbels for eight o'clock. He collected Jake at six-thirty at the safe house and drove to Gretchen's in the Daimler, again making sure he wasn't being tailed. As they drove through mostly empty streets, Dieter said Frau Goebbels had been quite willing to see them, and that she'd added with a little laugh that her "social calendar was not terribly full these days."

Jake told of his uneasiness about all this, that he'd been seen by Frau Goebbels for a brief moment and even more by two of her kids.

"Perhaps just Gretchen and I should go then," Dieter said. Jake didn't like the sound of that, but why? Would his own uncle, whose age hadn't kept him from taking a lover, hustle Gretchen? Or because Dieter didn't trust Gretchen and thought he could control her better without Jake around? Or was it that Jake, ever the curious reporter, just didn't want to miss out on an eventful evening? Yes, that was it. Or so he wanted to believe.

On arriving, they found Gretchen appropriately dressed for her role as Dieter's note-taker in a simple high-necked white blouse, black skirt and black patent-leather pumps.

When Jake told of his misgivings about meeting Magda Goebbels, Gretchen produced a disguise: a false mustache, a pair of horn-rimmed specs with plain glass in them, and a dark brown hat with a band of burnt orange. Vogel's hat, the one Jake had been wearing, was gray.

"Where did you get these things?" he asked.

"I am a spy after all. I know about disguises. The hat was Friedrich's." She placed it on Jake's head, stood back and exclaimed, "My, it looks good on you." Jake grinned stupidly. He watched her open a small ceramic jar, scoop out something gummy on her fingers and affix the mustache to his upper lip. Man, it felt strange.

Before leaving for the Goebbels home, they spent several minutes deciding how to broach the subject of Hindenburg's letter, what would be said and by whom. Jake related that Putzi had said to mention Magda's nickname for him, "*Jucken*," which meant "itch." Gretchen chuckled at that.

To Jake's surprise, Dieter told her about Jake having a daughter here in Berlin. Gretchen's mouth dropped open and she gave Jake a look he couldn't decipher. "How ... surprising," she murmured. "And the mother?"

"Is dead," Jake said. "Ilse was raised by the state."

"*Wunderbar*," Gretchen uttered with a grimace.

Why had Dieter broken this bit of news? Jake wondered. Was he testing Gretchen again?

"She is twelve years old," Dieter said, "an indoctrinated little Nazi but a good girl underneath. She has a fine mind, a mind Jacob must find a way to enlighten."

Yeah, right, Jake thought, but then he proceeded to tell about their day at the zoo.

"That is good," Gretchen said, "that you had time alone together. You must try to take her out of here if it is at all possible. She belongs with you and your woman."

"It won't be easy but I'll try," Jake said. Did he really mean that?

Dieter looked at his watch. "We had best be going."

They walked to the Daimler and piled in, Gretchen between

them on the roomy front seat. Jake felt an odd guilt wearing her late husband's hat.

"My surveillance section includes Lanke and Bernau," Dieter said as he drove. "That is how I learned so quickly that you had been apprehended, Jacob."

"Almost not quickly enough. That creep was having too much fun at my expense."

"*Ja,* fortunately I was not five minutes later. Anyhow, I told the night patrol on Goebbels' street that I am personally taking over until midnight. We will not be bothered."

They reached Lanke, found the right street and pulled into the wide circular driveway. Jake left the cane in the car, telling himself to try not to limp.

At precisely eight o'clock—ah, German efficiency—Dieter rang the bell at the mansion's front door and a maid answered.

"*Kommen Sie herein,*" she said and took their coats. "This way, *bitte,*" and she showed them into a richly appointed sitting room. Jake took in two plush sofas of a deep maroon fabric, armchairs, two gooseneck lamps, a grand piano, crystal chandelier, paintings on the walls, burning logs crackling in a stone fireplace, decorated Christmas tree, and a sideboard stocked with liquor bottles, decanters and cocktail glasses.

The maid took their drink orders, Gretchen and Jake asking for cognac and Dieter a Schnapps.

Then Magda Goebbels appeared, wearing a long satin dress of dark blue, high neck and half-sleeves. "*Guten Abend und Willkommen,*" she said, still looking a bit washed-out to Jake, a few steps past pretty. Her blond hair was pulled back into a severe bun and her blue eyes were full of friendliness.

"I see you have drinks. I believe there is some eggnog in the kitchen if you would prefer something Christmasy."

"*Danke, nein,* dear lady," Dieter said. "This is fine."

Without asking, the maid poured some clear liquid—gin?—into

a glass, dropped in two ice cubes with a tong, spritzed in some seltzer, and handed it to her mistress with a tiny curtsy.

"Thank you, Gerda." Turning to her guests, Magda Goebbels said, "Make yourselves comfortable. Please sit."

Dieter said, "I am *Hauptsturmführer* Weber, Frau Goebbels. May I present Herr Vogel, a business acquaintance from Switzerland, and my assistant, Gretchen Schmidt." Although the phony name hadn't been rehearsed, Jake approved. No point in revealing Gretchen's real name.

Magda Goebbels nodded at each of them in turn. Jake, uncomfortable in his glasses and mustache, prayed there'd be no sign of recognition as they looked at each other. Apparently there wasn't, and she sank into a plush chair with cabriole legs near the fire.

Gretchen pulled a notepad and fountain pen from her purse, playing her role.

"Before we talk of security," Magda said, "what brings you to Germany, Herr Vogel?"

Jake said he was supplying products to Wernher von Braun.

"And who is that?"

"Oh"—Jake was taken aback—"he is a scientist working on weapons development."

"I see, good. And how do you find Germany these days?"

"Steadfast and doing her utmost for the war effort."

"Oh please," she offered with a sardonic smile. "You are not talking to my husband. Do you not find the people uneasy and worried?"

"Mostly I see businessmen and weapons specialists and I find them the same as ever."

"Is that so?" A small laugh. "Well, I find my neighbors here anxious, especially about the fighting in Russia. You have had dealings with Russians?"

"No I have not, Frau Goebbels."

"Well, they are a hard, dogged and impudent sort, and there are so *many* of them." She leaned forward. "Have you heard this little story that is going around? A Hitler Youth lad standing at a large wall map, says, '*Kapitan*, where is Russia?' and his commander points out the Soviet Union, spreading across most of the map. 'Goodness, and where is the Fatherland?' The captain points out little Germany. 'Oh, *mein Gott,*' the boy cries, 'has the Führer seen this?'"

Magda laughed heartily and the others joined in. Then Dieter took a drink and said, "Yes, the Soviet Union is very large, but I am sure the Reich will triumph over these primitives . . . Now, if I may, about your security here." He launched into a description of the patrols in the area. "Have you been satisfied?" Gretchen's pen was poised to write.

"I feel quite safe, although Hermann Goering called the other day and warned me that an Irishman had been asking about me."

A chill crawled on Jake's neck. Damn, he never should have met with Goering.

"An Irishman?" Dieter said. "How odd. We will keep a sharp lookout. Do you suggest any changes?"

"No, your people are quite thorough. Just the other day they dragged off a man who was taking a walk on my street." Did she glance at Jake? Man, he felt weird in that false mustache. "I understand the new laws allow them to do that," Magda added, "without recourse to due process."

Jake noticed a definite look of distaste as she said that. He knew the woman was well-bred and had been a socialite before this marriage, her second, to Goebbels.

"Difficult times call for certain measures," Dieter said.

"I hope the difficult times will end soon." Magda then launched into a reminiscence of the happy times that used to be, the glittering parties, the friends she enjoyed but saw so little of now. Her world, Jake knew, was gone with the wind, just like Margaret Mitchell's Old South.

The maid returned and said the children were ready for bed

and would like to say good night. Oh-oh. Jake's stomach tightened. *Please don't parade the kids in here.* But to his relief, Magda rose and said, "Excuse me, I will be back in a moment, after I tuck my darlings in."

The maid stoked the fire, added a log, and also left.

Dieter put a finger to his lips and motioned them toward the covering sounds of the fire. "This room is unlikely to be wired," he whispered, "but say nothing that could compromise us." Jake and Gretchen nodded.

When Magda returned moments later, Dieter said, "I believe Frau Schmidt would like to have a word with you. Might she?"

Magda turned to Gretchen, looking puzzled.

"*Jucken* requested that I see you, if possible," Gretchen said.

Magda blushed deeply and put a hand to her throat. Composing herself, she shot a suspicious glare first at Dieter, then Gretchen. At last she said, "I see. Very well, dear, come with me," and motioned for Gretchen to follow her.

They left the room and Jake put his hands up, palms out, in a gesture that said to Dieter, "Let's hope this goes well." They had stood as the women left, but now they slumped into their seats in anxious silence.

Magda led Gretchen into an imposing library, explaining that it was her private study.

Gretchen looked around at a mahogany desk and shelves full of books and said, "Very nice. I enjoyed your story of the boy and the map of Russia."

"Then here is another. A man asks his friend if he still believes Germany will win against the Russians, the English, the Americans, the Canadians and the Australians all together. He answers, 'I would rather believe in that than go running around with my head chopped off.'"

Gretchen laughed.

"These are circulating among those of us," Magda said, "and there are many, who think the war against Russia is a dangerous folly and that Hitler's honeymoon time with the people is over. Now then, you mentioned *Jucken*." She stared hard at Gretchen. "Are you one of Putzi's lovers, too, or is blackmail your game? Is this a threat of going to my husband?"

"No, nothing like that. I do not even know this man Putzi."

"Good, but in any case it would not have worked. I do not give a damn what my husband knows about me or my friendships. But now then, what of Putzi? You have seen him?"

"No, but one of Admiral Canaris' agents has." Gretchen explained that in addition to her services for the *Hauptsturmführer*, she worked for Canaris in the Abwehr. Then she told the story that she'd rehearsed about the letter. "Supposedly Herr Hanfstaengl left it with you for safekeeping and he should like to have it returned," she concluded.

"This is possible, to get it to him in America?"

"Yes, through one of the admiral's agents," Gretchen lied.

"I see, well then, this was five or six years ago. Putzi was very kind to me when I was having a bad time. He gave me an envelope addressed to Adolf, the wax seal broken. It was very nice paper, a woven linen I should say." She put a hand to her cheek. "Now wherever could it be? I put it somewhere. We shall have to look."

Ten minutes later, the women reappeared in the sitting room with disappointment on their faces.

"I could not find it," Magda said. "The envelope must be here somewhere but I cannot recall where I put it. We searched everywhere. I am so sorry."

Gretchen raised her eyebrows at Jake in a "what can you do?" look.

The hell with it, he thought. At least he tried. He was going to leave this madhouse very soon, some way, somehow, and that'd be that.

A door flew open and in came a small, rat-faced man in a Wehrmacht uniform, carrying a leather briefcase and limping on a foot that wore an oversized platform shoe. It was Joseph Goebbels.

CHAPTER FORTY-EIGHT

J ake and Dieter jumped to their feet, Jake numb with dread. "Minister Goebbels," Dieter said, giving the Nazi salute and clicking his heels."Heil Hitler."

Joseph Goebbels' return salute was a lazy little wave. "Who are you people?" he demanded.

"Excellency, I am Group Leader Weber, commandant of security for this district. This is Frau Schmidt, my assistant, and Herr Vogel from Switzerland."

Jake thought this runt, his ears too large for his small face, couldn't weigh more than a hundred and twenty pounds. But the guy had power and he knew it, radiated it. Jake tried not to visibly shake as Goebbels stared at him.

Finally shifting his gaze to his wife, the runt said, without warmth, "Hello Magda. What are these people doing here? Having a bridge party, are you?"

"We were about to remove our clothing and have an orgy." Jake had seen unhappy marriages before and this one seemed particularly sad.

Goebbels turned his gaze on Gretchen—whose wedding ring was quite visible on her left hand—and said, "I should like to see the clothes removed from this one."

"Excellency, Frau Schmidt is a war widow," Dieter said. Putting an end to that crap, Jake thought. He was very proud of his uncle at that moment.

Goebbels' leer vanished.

"I have been sent by Reichsführer SS Himmler," Dieter went on, "to check on security, to ascertain that we are doing all we can for the protection of your home and that of your neighbors."

"You may tell Himmler I believe it to be satisfactory. I have no complaints, do you, Magda?"

"I do not. Why are you here, Joseph? I was not expecting you."

"I have work to do, a speech on the Stalingrad situation to prepare. The damned Russians refuse to admit they are beaten," he said, but sounding as if he didn't believe his own words. "There are so many damned interruptions at my office, so many people hounding me about this and that, I chose to do it here in peace and quiet. So if you would kindly cancel the orgy."

"I will give you all the peace and quiet you require, my darling." Dripping with sarcasm.

Goebbels' bitter little eyes turned again on Jake. The scrutiny in that stare made him feel guilty and exposed. His mustache and glasses felt like obvious fakes. "What is your purpose here, Herr *Schweizer*?"

"My company is selling supplies to Professor von Braun."

"And charging the Reich exorbitant prices, are you?"

"The standard rates, Dr. Goebbels, I assure you."

"Herr Vogel had a late meeting with me," Dieter put in, "and I suggested he ride along with us tonight."

Goebbels' gaze bore into Jake for another few seconds, then, suddenly looking very tired, he said, "I will bid you all *Guten Abend* and retire to my study." He clomped off carrying his briefcase.

"You might want to look in on your children," Magda called after him.

"Yes, I might," he said without glancing back.

When he was gone, Jake thought, well, I've met the propaganda minister. Pompous twerp.

"He is all bark and little bite, that one." Magda said. " Another drink, my friends?"

Suddenly the twerp reappeared. "I would like a word with the *Schweizer.*" Jake's knees went weak. *What now?* "Come with me, please."

His head heavy with foreboding, Jake followed Goebbels down a hallway and into a small office.

Goebbels set his briefcase on a baize-covered desk next to a typewriter. The office was sparsely decorated. Steel file cabinets lined one wall. A large portrait of the Führer hung on another.

"It is most unusual for an SS official to have a foreign visitor accompany him at night like this. Show me your identification."

Jake reached into his jacket and handed over his identity card.

Goebbels glanced at it and said, "I see you have grown a mustache since this photograph was taken."

Jake tried to keep from trembling. The damn mustache never felt more fake. Was it still on straight? "Yes," he said, "I thought I would give it a try."

"I do not much like it."

"To tell the truth, neither do I. I'll get rid of it soon." *Real soon.*

Goebbels returned the card and said, "What is your business, Vogel?"

"I am a wri—"

"Writer?" Goebbels stiffened, his eyes widened. "I thought you were selling supplies to our rocket man."

Don't flinch, Jake told himself. He'd made a bad mistake. Damn it, he'd been talking too much with von Braun about his writing. "That too. It is my main job, but I also write articles for various Swiss newspapers. One must feed his family."

"A salesman and a writer." Goebbels paused in thought. "Yes, I suppose there are certain parallels at that. One might even say that I also am both a salesman and a writer. What is it that you write?"

"General interest things for newspapers, occasionally a wire service."

Jake tried not to sweat while Goebbels seemed to mull something over.

"Hmm, well then, Herr Writer, perhaps you could help me. I am searching for something new and encouraging to tell the German people about our temporary difficulties at Stalingrad. I have already told them that help is on the way, that the army there will persevere, that the air force will keep them supplied."

"Yes, I have read the newspapers."

"They have heard it all. Ideas, I need fresh ideas."

Jake was bowled over by the direction this conversation had taken. He thought about this stunning request. Come on, man, he prodded himself, you're supposed to be a great military writer.

At last he answered. "Well then, you could say that Stalin has made a strategic mistake pouring so many resources into that city so far from Moscow." Jake hated himself for this but his life could be on the line here and besides, damn it, Goebbels had challenged his creativity.

The juices were beginning to flow. "Yes, and many Russians are dying through petty vanity, just to prevent Stalin's disgrace at having his namesake city captured."

"That is good," Goebbels said.

"And in doing, so," Jake went on, "Stalin—"

"The brutish Bolsehevik dictator," Goebbels interjected, getting into it himself.

"Yes, in doing so, the brutish Bolshevik dictator has pulled reserves from other fronts, Moscow, Leningrad and so on—you would know those better than I, Dr. Goebbels—making other German victories all the more possible."

"Yes, that is a good slant."

"Therefore," Jake went on, "the historic struggle at Stalingrad is worthy of the German nation. The heroic efforts of the people at home to support your soldiers is in the finest tradition of your great nation."

"Yes, yes, weakened other fronts, Moscow could fall. A vainglorious gamble by the pig Stalin just to save his own name, a gamble that will backfire on him and lead to his certain demise. That is a good approach, Herr Vogel. I will take it from here."

Goebbels took a step toward his desk. "Good night, then." But turned back and said, "Say, would you like employment in my ministry? Writing for me?"

Jesus! "That's very flattering," Jake managed, "and tempting, but no thank you all the same."

"You would not like living in the Third Reich?"

"I love my own country, just as you do yours." *Asshole.*

Goebbels squinted. "I could force you to remain, you know."

Enough groveling, Jake told himself. "That, sir, would cut off a flow of essential precision tools to your rocket program."

"Hmm . . . All right then, get out of here."

Goebbels scowled and plopped himself in the chair in front of his Kanzler typewriter. Over his shoulder he said, "A word of caution. Tell no one of our discussion here."

"Of course not." Jake left. Gladly.

Walking down the hallway, he shook with both relief and self-reproach. *Damn you, you just helped write some bullshit Nazi propaganda.*

CHAPTER FORTY-NINE

Jake removed the glasses the minute they got in the car. A block away, he peeled off the mustache and rubbed at the residue of the adhesive.

"What happened in there?" Dieter asked. "What did Goebbels want?"

"Nothing much. He offered me a job."

Dieter laughed. To Gretchen he said, "Jacob was always making the jokes." Dieter laughed again and shook his head. "Offered him a job," he muttered to himself.

"Well," Gretchen said, "he's a horrid, stupid man."

"The lame little creep is drunk with power, Gretchen, but he's not stupid," Jake said. "He has a Ph.D. and is a brilliant communicator."

"That degenerate may be smart in that sense, but he is stupid in many ways. Did you see how he leered at me and made a wisecrack about seeing me naked? I thank you for putting him in his place, Dieter." Gretchen reached over and touched his arm. "The way he treats his wife is stupid also. She sees things clearly, knows that Germany is on a very wrong course."

"Goebbels probably knows that, too," Dieter said, "but has to go along, he is in so deep. He has hitched his star to Hitler and there is nothing he can do but string along with him."

"Out there in the snows of Stalingrad," Jake said, "that star has begun to set."

"You may be right," Dieter replied, "but Hitler is very lucky. He keeps pulling rabbits out of his hat. If he could still somehow take that city, Stalin could fall, and then he'd turn his full power on England."

"That's a possibility," Jake said. "This war is not close to being over. But Dieter, be careful of Goebbels. Watch your back. That little bastard won't forget the way you squelched him."

"I know and I will . . . What will you do now, Jacob?"

"I'll be leaving in a day or two if all goes well."

"Oh?" Gretchen exclaimed, sounding sad. "How?" she added, but must have thought better of it. "No, do not tell me. It is better that I do not know. And what of your Ilse?"

"I hope to see her tomorrow. She'll call you, Dieter, if she can get another pass."

"I will see that she gets a pass."

Gretchen said, "I do not mean to pry, Jake, but what can you tell me of her mother?"

"She was someone I met here almost thirteen years ago. I was here for the memorial service for my Aunt Marta." Jake saw Dieter wince at the mention of his late wife. "Winifrid was a communist and I suspect the Nazis had her done away with. I never knew she'd got pregnant until the other day when Dieter told me. It was quite a shock."

"I am sure that it was. I am sorry for being curious."

"Don't be. Curiosity is my business." An unwelcome thought sprang into his mind. What if *Gretchen's* pregnant? *Please, no.*

When they reached the safe house, she asked, "May I come in for a moment? I need to use the *Toilette*."

"I will wait here," Dieter said, and Jake and Gretchen went to the apartment.

Inside, Gretchen looked around briefly at the spartan quarters and Jake, pointing, said, "It's in there. It adjoins the bedroom." His satchel lay in there on the bed. He'd packed most of his things, hoping to make his getaway the next day.

Carrying her handbag, Gretchen closed the bedroom door behind her.

Jake sat in a chair, trembling at the memory of the fear that had seemed to throb inside his skull at the moment he'd come face to face with Joseph Goebbels.

Ever the reporter, he organized his mental notes. Okay, he'd met three powerful Germans, Goebbels, Goering and von Braun, all smart and clever men. Goebbels, brilliant, depraved and dangerous. Goering, a good mind dissipating in drugs and defeatism. Von Braun, visionary scientist, an enemy by virtue of his birth but a vigorous young man who might one day send a rocket to the moon. What stories Jake would have to tell, *if* he could get out of this mad place. That "if" was weighing heavily on his mind as he heard the toilet flush. Still Gretchen didn't return. Maybe she was freshening her makeup.

When she reappeared a couple of minutes later, she put down her purse, gave him a melancholy look and leaned against him. Jake didn't resist, the hell with the cracked rib. She laced her arms around him and kissed him. "You know, it made me a bit jealous for a moment, hearing about your Winifrid and your child." She gazed into his eyes. "I will miss you."

"And I'll miss you, Gretchen. You've been a great help to me." At her coy smile, he added, "In many ways."

She leaned close and placed a hand on his belt buckle. "Is there time—"

"No," he said with reluctance. "We mustn't, Dieter is waiting."

An unhappy look crossed her face. "I will always cherish the memory of what we've shared, Jake."

"I will too, Gretchen. December 13th is a date I'll never forget."

"Perhaps when this war is over," she said, "I might visit you in

California."

As Jake struggled to find a reply, Gretchen said, "No, that would not really be such a good idea, would it?" She looked wistful for a moment. "Well then, should you run into any emergency before you leave and need more help, phone me. When I answer, say, 'Sorry, wrong number' and I will meet you by the duck pond at the *Volkspark* in fifteen minutes. You know where the park is?"

"Yes, two blocks south. I've seen it."

"Goodbye then, dear Jake." Gretchen kissed him again, opened the door and started down the steps.

He watched till she reached the car. Then he closed the door, threw the bolt and let out a sigh.

Later, in bed, like metal filings to a magnet, his thoughts were drawn to Gretchen and Valerie. What had developed with Gretchen was electric, a wartime nexus where both parties' needs were met. Fleetingly. That brief union had given him strength and hope in the darkest moments of his life, but his connection with Valerie was far more vital, a deep bond more fulfilling than anything he'd ever known. So, lock this up somewhere, he told himself. On to Valerie and a new, better life. *If I can get my ass out of here.*

Jake didn't know how long he'd been asleep when he was jarred awake by strange sounds in the apartment. What the hell? A shiver sluiced through him. He heard drawers opening and closing in the kitchenette, then footsteps on the hardwood floor in the little parlor. No one had knocked on the door. Was it Dieter? A burglar?

A moment later, in the murk of the unlit rooms, a figure appeared in the bedroom doorway. Just a silhouette but it looked like Rolf Becker.

"Who are you? What do you want?"

"Where is it? Where the hell is it?" It *was* Rolf.

"Where is what?"

"You know, *Verdammt Mist*, you know." Screaming. "The

letter."

"Come on Rolf, take it easy. I don't have any letter."

The black outline raised an arm. A gunshot fired. Jake saw the white muzzle flash, felt the air pulse beside his head, a breath from taking off his ear.

He rolled off the bed and hit the floor. He reached up for something, anything, on the nightstand. His hand found the alarm clock. He hurled it at Rolf as another shot fired. The bedside lamp exploded.

Jake had won two fights in the Navy. He'd never been one to take any crap and being shot at was the worst possible kind of crap. He scrabbled fast across the floor. Another shot fired. He body-blocked Rolf in the knees. Rolf staggered and fell. Jake pulled himself up, adrenaline running wild, and kicked. Hit an arm or a wrist. Heard the pistol skitter across the floor.

Choking on blind anger, Jake kicked again, then again. He found the wall switch by feel. Flipped on the overhead light. Rolf was scrambling on all fours toward the gun.

Jake snatched his cane, which he'd left leaning against the wall. Just as Rolf picked up the gun, Jake drove a punishing blow to the wrist. The gun fell. He struck with the cane a second time, hitting the lower arm. And again. Something cracked and it wasn't the cane. He hit the neck this time.

At last controlling his rage a little, he leaned down and picked up the pistol. "Rolf, you bastard, you've finally snapped. Gone right off the deep end."

Rolf stared up at the gun, leveled now at his face. "I knew you wouldn't do it," he croaked. "I *knew*. You don't have the guts to kill Hanfstaengl for me."

"It's not a matter of guts. It's common sense, you idiot, you fucking bastard." Jake realized he was speaking English. *Shouting* English. "What the hell were you looking for?"

Rolf didn't answer.

"I don't have anything you could possibly want."

A hand on his neck, his face wincing in pain, Rolf murmured, "I'm finished, Jake. You were my last hope. That letter could have got me off Goebbels' shit list. Would have fixed me up with Hitler."

Jake had never seen such a miserable, defeated creature in his life. "I don't know anything about some fucking letter you want."

"Kill me, please," his former friend pleaded. "I'm done for anyway. Finish me off. I'm begging you."

Jake fired.

Rolf jumped and whimpered.

Jake, his ears ringing, saw a jagged bullet hole in the plaster beside the doorjamb. He'd missed on purpose. "Get your ass out of here."

"Jake—"

"Get the hell out. Tell them I'll do it if you want, maybe it'll buy you some time. But I won't. You were right about that. I'll never kill anyone, not Hanfstaengl, not you. Get out!" Screaming again.

Rolf pulled himself to his feet. Angry red welts already appeared where Jake had kicked and cane-whipped him. One arm hung limp. His yellow hair was a mess. He gazed at Jake with an empty, pathetic look of ruin, then turned and staggered toward the front door.

Before he closed it behind him, he murmured, "But we had some good times in L.A.," and stumbled into the night, holding the arm Jake had thrashed.

Good times! Maybe I *should* have killed him, Jake thought. The stupid bastard tried to kill *me*. Dieter could have covered it up and got rid of the body.

Stop that, he told himself, murder is never the answer.

How the hell did he ever find me? he wondered as he slammed the door bolt into place. And find out about Hindenburg's letter?

Jake reeled into the bedroom, closed the door, propped a chair against it, and looked at the bullet holes and the shattered lamp. He picked up the alarm clock—its glass face splintered—and wondered how deaf the old clergyman who shared this building really was.

Rolf's pistol was a small Walther PPK. Three bullets remained in the clip. Jake placed it under the pillow and crawled into bed. He tried to slow his breathing, but his adrenal glands were still jangling. Hours passed before an edgy sleep could overtake him.

He dreamed he stood against a bullet-pocked brick wall, wearing a polka-dot clown suit, a round spot of orange rouge on each cheek. An SS firing squad faced him, rifles raised. They fired and lines of fat red bullets swam toward him like slow crimson tadpoles.

CHAPTER FIFTY

In the morning, after a few hours of sleep that was more tiring than restful, Jake cleaned up the remains of the murdered lamp and dumped them in the kitchen trash. Then he left, scanning the street more carefully than ever. His rib hurt something awful, even though he'd swallowed two pain pills before leaving. The crack must have worsened during that fight.

It had been three days since his last meeting with Wernher von Braun. He walked without the cane toward Unter den Linden University, still limping but not as badly. If the rib was worse, at least the ankle wasn't.

He found von Braun in his office, his hair uncombed and bloodshot eyes revealing a lack of sleep. He was jotting something on a notepad. At first he didn't seem to know Jake.

"Yes? . . . Oh, Erich, it is you. Good. I was just looking at my letter to Dr. Goddard and thinking of you." He motioned Jake to come in and sit.

"You look tired, Professor. You should take a break from your work now and then."

"It is frustration more than fatigue. The Führer! First, it is full speed ahead on the rocket, give von Braun all the materials he needs. Then it is, no, tanks must have top priority. More tanks for the eastern front." He swept aside a pile of papers. "Then, no, fighter planes.

Goering must have more fighter planes to defend against the air raids. Back and forth it goes. There is only so much steel and aluminum and oil, and only so many technicians. It is a great tug of war between industry, branches of the military, and the Führer."

"And I must not write of this," Jake said with a grin.

"Yes, I forbid it," and they laughed at what had become their shared joke.

Then von Braun said, "Erich, you do not look so well yourself. Your face, what has happened?"

Jake touched the cut now healing on his cheek. "Oh nothing, just a little accident."

"Hmm." Von Braun's brow twisted. "Not with one of our zealous policemen, I hope . . . Well then, Erich, I fly to Sweden tonight to meet with a supplier."

"Tonight?"

"Yes. The Luftwaffe prefers to fly across to Sweden at night. RAF planes have not appeared over the Baltic at night. It is safe, at least so says the Luftwaffe. I leave Tempelhof at five."

"Would it be possible for me to go with you?" Jake figured he could find a way to reach England from neutral Sweden.

Von Braun, taken by surprise, stroked his chin.

Jake jumped into the silence, saying, "You see, I could mail your letter to Dr. Goddard in Sweden myself and avoid using a third party. This would be much safer for you."

"*Ja,* it would at that. All right then, you can meet me there at half past four at what is still called the Lufthansa Foreign Departures desk, even though Lufthansa makes no international flights these days. The air force has taken over the airport."

Jake had reached a hard decision. It would be criminal to leave Ilse behind. "Would there be room for one more? I know it's a lot to ask, but I have a young friend, a Hitler Youth girl, who has never flown in an airplane."

Von Braun hesitated. His hand went back to his chin. At last he said, "A young girl, you say? Yes, I suppose that would be all right. No passengers were expected, besides myself, but the crew will do as I say. They are at my disposal. I am afraid the girl would be bored, though. My business will take several hours before I could fly her back."

"I'm sure she would be honored to tag along with you, Professor; she is a bright girl."

"Very well then, have her with you at Tempelhof at half past four and we will give the girl her plane ride."

"I know we have developed some trust," Jake said. "I'll have more to tell you tonight on the plane."

Von Braun didn't look surprised. "Yes, I will look forward to that. I have sensed that you have been holding something back."

"*Auf wiedersehen* until tonight then," Jake said, and took his leave.

Jake had been back in the apartment no more than twenty minutes when he heard two quick raps on the door, a pause, then two more. He opened the door and Dieter came in, carrying a cloth sack.

"What have you got there?"

"A photostat of Ilse's birth certificate, a stuffed animal she likes to sleep with, and a few of her civilian clothes. Assuming you have something cooked up for her today, I collected these from her barracks while she was in class . . . *Mein Gott*, you look unwell. Did you not sleep last night? Meeting Joseph Goebbels must have been distressing."

"It wasn't Goebbels. Let me show you some fresh bullet holes." Jake led him into the bedroom and told him about Rolf Becker's attempt to murder him. He handed Dieter the pistol. "Here, this was Rolf's."

"*Gott im Himmel*. The fool has completely snapped. Thank God you fought him off."

"Rolf's bigger than me and I have a bum ankle, but he's a lousy shot and darkness is a great equalizer. Plus, I had the cane. I may have broken his arm."

"*Sehr gut*," Dieter said unkindly. "I am sure that Rolf will be taken care of."

"Executed? Thrown in prison?"

Dieter shrugged his shoulders. "I should like to place him in a mental institution. A few of them are still legitimate with real psychiatrists, not Nazi quacks. But I dare not. It would be too dangerous for me. Himmler will decide."

"Rolf was after that letter," Jake said. "How could he have known I'd met Hanfstaengl?"

"Germany has agents in Washington. Conceivably someone in Lafayette Square with binoculars keeps tabs on who comes and goes from the White House."

"Even if I'd been seen, how would they know who I was?"

Dieter shook his head. "Perhaps someone inside the White House sees the guest list and reports on it."

"God, I hope White House security is better than that. But the letter, how could he know about the letter?"

"When did Rolf first arrive in Los Angeles?"

"Early '38, I think."

"Hanfstaengl's affair with Magda Goebbels took place before then. You say Rolf was a good reporter, perhaps he discovered that relationship."

Jake shrugged.

"Now then," Dieter said, "what are your departure plans?"

Jake told him about Wernher von Braun, and that a flight to Sweden would take place today. "I'm to meet von Braun at Tempelhof at four-thirty. I want to take Ilse."

"I knew you would come up with something. That is good. I will drive you. I will pick up Ilse and have her here by a quarter to four. I will see that she has a pass."

"That's swell. I won't tell her what I have in mind till we reach

Sweden."

"I was about to suggest that. Be gentle and let her enjoy her first airplane ride. She will be very unhappy, rebellious even, when she learns what you are up to."

"Don't I know it. This will be the hardest job of persuasion I've ever had."

CHAPTER FIFTY-ONE

Jake had never seen an airport as big and splendid as Tempelhof. Its large, half-moon-shaped terminal building, glistening in a cold rain, was an architectural gem. And big. You could put Glendale's Grand Central and L.A.'s Mines Field in here with room to spare.

He and Ilse got out of the Daimler. He left the cane in the car. Dieter could return it. Jake put down his satchel and the cloth sack containing Ilse's things and put a hand on his uncle's cheek, saying, "Thank you for everything. I will see you again one day, after this war mess is over."

"Yes, count on it."

Regret that he'd failed to articulate his feelings years ago still churned inside. "I love you, dear Dieter," Jake said, and gave his uncle a hug. Ilse's eyes widened. She looked surprised and somehow impressed at the same time.

Jake pulled back, gazed warmly into Dieter's eyes, then picked up his satchel and the sack, managing to clutch both with his left hand. With his right, he took his daughter's hand and led her out of the rain and into the terminal at the best pace he could manage.

Just inside the door, out of the cold, stood a Luftwaffe guard, shouldering a rifle. Looked to be in his fifties. They walked past him, heading down a curving marble corridor.

Eight or nine soldiers, lounging and smoking, were huddled around a counter. One of them gave Ilse a good going-over with his eyes.

Farther along, Jake spotted Lufthansa International Departures and saw von Braun approaching from the opposite direction. When they met, von Braun took Ilse's hand, said it was a pleasure, and she answered with a shy smile. He pulled an envelope from a jacket pocket, looked around carefully, and handed it to Jake. "This is the letter we have discussed." Jake slipped it into an overcoat pocket.

The three walked together to the counter, where a uniformed Customs agent saluted von Braun and said "Heil Hitler." The professor said, "*Ja, ja.*"

Jake tried not to look worried. He hadn't expected Customs, only an airline employee.

"These two will accompany me on the flight," von Braun said. "This is Herr Erich Weber and his young friend." At the mention of that name, Ilse shot Jake a startled look.

The man noted Ilse's Hitler Youth garb and said, "You are obviously a German citizen."

She straightened. "Proudly so, yes. Heil Hitler."

Jake forced back a scowl.

"And you, sir?"

Jake said he was Swiss.

"*Ihre Pässe, bitte.*"

Damn, Jake thought, if only von Braun hadn't introduced him as Erich Weber. "Surely that's not necessary. I'm leaving the country, not entering."

"It is required." The agent extended a hand. "Now, please."

Jake stood motionless for several seconds, then slowly reached into his jacket. What could he do? He finally drew out the passport, handed it over, and told himself not to look concerned.

The agent studied it for what felt like a month, while Jake sweated it out.

"It says here," the man said at last, "that your name is Vogel. Can you explain this?"

"Erich, why," von Braun demanded, "are you still using Hans-Karl's name?" His large face stippled with a fury Jake had not seen there before.

"I, uh . . ." Jake faltered, shifted his feet. "I was keeping this for a friend," he told the agent. "I must have mistaken it for my own. Careless of me."

"Using a false name for a journey outside the Reich is a crime. I must detain you."

"I'll just go and get the correct one," Jake countered. "I can be back here in twenty minutes."

"*Nein.* I must detain you here. The police can determine whether you have a proper passport."

"Oh, come on now, you look like a reasonable man."

"*Nein!*"

I'm so close to getting out of here, Jake thought, *now this*. The hell with it. "Look here," he said, "I'm getting on that plane." He stared defiantly into the man's eyes. "I am a businessman with a very full schedule. I have an important meeting to get to. I told you I made an honest mistake, and that's that."

"I will not allow it. You have violated Reich law."

Jake snatched the passport back. "I'm going!"

"*Nein!*"

Jake took a step away from the counter. He thought maybe he'd made a mistake turning Rolf Becker's gun over to Uncle Dieter.

"You are under arrest," the agent roared.

"He is *not*," Ilse said quietly but firmly. Jake couldn't believe his ears. "Come, *Vater*."

"Father?" the agent blurted. "Did you say 'father'? Then you are under arrest too, *Fräulein*."

It was hard to tell who took whose hand first, but Jake and Ilse turned and bolted toward the entrance, Jake's limping gait a hippety-hop trot.

"Stop," the agent's voice boomed behind them.

Von Braun, standing there, cried, "My letter!"

The cluster of soldiers, aroused by the shouts, eyed Jake and Ilse closely as they approached. "They need you down there, hurry," Jake said, and pointed to where the agent gesticulated madly and von Braun stood open-mouthed, arms akimbo, his face crimson. Several soldiers took off down the corridor, but an older one, wearing sergeant's stripes, put up a hand. "Halt! Where are you going?"

"I am a Swiss journalist," Jake said, "with a diplomatic pass. On my way to your commanding officer to get a story. You don't want to be a part of that story, do you?"

The sergeant lowered his hand. His face wore a question mark.

"Esteemed *Unteroffizier*," Ilse said, standing with military bearing in her uniform, "I have been ordered to accompany this gentleman and see that he has no difficulty in keeping his appointments. We are running late, but I will show you the orders if you insist." She reached into a coat pocket that Jake assumed was empty.

"*Nein.*" The soldier stepped aside. "Go ahead."

At that moment the guard from the entrance clomped past in his jackboots, toward where soldiers were getting entangled with von Braun and the Customs man, slowing their progress. With a quick backward glance, Jake saw something besides anger on von Braun's face—panic—as the big man tried to push through the knot of people in his path. His letter to Robert Goddard, incriminating in the wrong hands, was getting away to God knew where.

Jake had problems of his own. He and Ilse rushed outside, Jake still juggling his satchel and the sack of Ilse's things in one hand.

She was doing her best to walk steadily, but Jake saw her biting on her lower lip. A tear bled down a cheek. Poor kid has to be devastated, he thought. She knows what it means to be in trouble with the authorities in this country. She's probably wondering why the hell she stood up for me—I wonder too—and picturing herself in a concentration camp.

"Don't worry, Ilse," he said. "This will come out all right." He gave her hand a warm squeeze. "Nice work back there. Good thinking."

"I—." Ilse didn't finish the thought, whatever it had been.

They reached a corner and turned. Now beyond sight of the airport entrance, he urged, "Come on, *Liebchen*, pick up the pace." And she did, obviously as eager as Jake to put distance between themselves and Tempelhof.

Jake's ankle was throbbing again. He wished he'd kept the cane. They kept moving fast, though, and turned left or right at every intersection. The rain had stopped but the sidewalks were still wet. Jake kept looking around for cops or slow-moving cars. And taxis. Because of the gasoline problem, he'd seen very few cabs in Berlin.

They came upon two girls in civilian clothes, both about sixteen, Jake thought. One was tall and full-bodied and was smoking a cigarette. The other was petite, not much bigger than Ilse. Jake noted her woolen coat.

"My daughter would like to trade coats with you," he said.

"I do?" Ilse muttered.

"It would not be a fair trade," the girl said. "Such a fine army coat." She fingered the sleeve of Ilse's wrap admiringly. Her friend puffed on her cigarette and looked amused.

"Yes, *bitte*," Ilse said. "That is a lovely shade of blue."

The girl looked down at her coat as if to say "It is?" Shaking her head, she said, "All right then, if you are really serious." She removed her coat and the exchange was made.

As they hurried on, Ilse said, "That was good thinking, too. They will be looking for a man and a girl in uniform, won't they?" She removed her field cap and stuffed it in a pocket of her new coat.

They came to a dim café, pinpricks of light escaping through a frayed blackout curtain in the window. Jake saw five bicycles near the door, two leaning against a brick wall, the others perched on kickstands. He took one and looped the carry strap of his satchel over the handlebars. "Come on," he said.

"We are stealing bicycles?"

"No, we're buying them." Jake took a ten-mark bill from his wallet and stuck it partway beneath a litter can next to the bike he'd selected.

Mounting his new conveyance, he clutched the sack to his chest with one hand, and was about to start off when the door swung open. A shiver wormed down his spine. A big man emerged. Late forties, black watch cap, heavy coat that had seen better days. He smelled of gin and tobacco. His hard stare took in the bike Jake was holding, then worked its way up to the face.

The moment dragged. Again Jake thought that maybe he should have kept Rolf's pistol. Finally, though, the man said, "*Ach*, I thought you had my bicycle, but I see that mine is the *Lanzer* over there." His gaze held for another couple of seconds, then he turned, boarded his bike and pedaled into the darkness.

Jake figured his sigh of relief could be heard in Poland. He placed a foot on a pedal and pushed off, holding the sack against his chest and steering clumsily with one hand.

Ilse picked a bike and soon caught up to him. "Where are we going?" she asked.

"To Schöneberg. Do you know how to get there?"

"No."

"Well, it's northwest of here. It will take us awhile, but we'll find it." Jake heard the whine of a siren, sounding a few blocks away. *Don't come any closer*, he begged.

CHAPTER FIFTY-TWO

They rode along empty sidewalks, staying close to buildings, Jake wobbling less as he began to get the hang of one-handed steering. Ilse had to go slowly not to leave him behind. A waning moon looking like a lopsided lemon spilled faint light on the blacked-out city. They wheeled along for several minutes in what Jake thought was the right general direction, turning often. A cab came by. "*Now* he comes," Jake muttered. The driver slowed, looked them over, then drove on. Another siren wailed in the distance.

When the sound died away, Ilse said, "I saw how you said goodbye to the *Hauptsturmführer.* He is more to you than a friend, is he not?"

"Well, yes, actually… he's … well, my uncle."

Ilse's bike swerved for a moment. "*Mein Gott.* Your uncle? Then . . . if this is so, I too am related to him. He is my—how do you say it?—great uncle, *ja?*"

"That's right, Ilse." Even in the dark, Jake saw her lips part in a smile. "*Grossonkel Dieter,*" she murmured, trying out the words.

After three miles or more, a broad plaza and an imposing building loomed up out of the gloom. Jake saw the sign, *Rathaus Schöneberg.* The town hall for this district. "Hey, the old navigator did pretty good," he said.

Three blocks farther on, they found *Lessingstrasse* and Jake saw the *Volkspark* in the distance. Spotting a phone box, he stopped and went in to call Gretchen. Through the glass, he saw Ilse's face clouded with bewilderment and fear, her breath blowing little fogs of steam.

Gretchen answered in the middle of the second double-buzz. Thank God she's there, Jake thought.

"Hallo."

"Sorry, wrong number." He hung up.

"We're going to meet a friend of mine," he told Ilse. "Someone we can trust"—couldn't he?—"someone who can help us. Leave the bikes here. They'll be our gift to some needy Berliner."

He clutched Ilse's hand and they set off on foot for the *Volkspark*. The sleeves of her new coat were only slightly too long. They reached the park and even though their eyes were now fully adjusted, it was difficult to see under the trees. They took a few wrong turns before finally finding the duck pond, the still, flat surface of the water like an ebony tabletop.

They stood in silence, in moon shadow, Ilse staring at Jake. The moment lengthened. He wondered what she was thinking. Slowly, timidly, she reached out with a trembling hand, stopped, then reached again and touched his arm. Then, as if some invisible barrier had given way, she pressed herself against him. He put an arm around her and pulled her closer, her body transmitting her anxiety.

"You're a swell kid," he said. "I . . . well . . . it dawned on me that I loved you when we were looking at the little bear cubs at the zoo. And you're strong. It took real courage to tell that man he couldn't arrest me."

"I do not know why I did that. I hardly even know you, but something . . ." Her shaky voice trailed off.

Jake felt deeply moved. He had twelve lost years to make up for.

Minutes later, he saw a woman's shape appear from the shadows. She wore a floppy hat, long overcoat and boots. Even though she was bundled up, he knew it was Gretchen by the way she moved.

When she reached them, Jake whispered, "Gretchen, this is my daughter Ilse. We've run into a problem. I hope you can help us."

"Happy to meet you, dear." Speaking softly. "So here you are again, Jake, like a bad penny. Isn't that the saying?"

"Afraid so."

"Well, it is cold here. Come back to my place. It is dark, we can enter through the alley and not be seen."

Soon they were in Gretchen's kitchen. Ilse looked about, her eyes as wide as silver dollars. Gretchen prepared a steaming mug of hot chocolate for her while Jake explained their predicament. How they'd planned to fly to Sweden with von Braun but that a Customs agent at Tempelhof had detained them and then surely called the Gestapo.

"And you made a run for it?"

Jake nodded. Ilse looked bewildered and frightened.

"Thank goodness you got away." Gretchen's lips pursed. "I learned something disquieting today at the Abwehr. Von Braun is a member of the SS."

"He's what?!" Jake felt an icy chill. All this time he'd been cozying up to a member of the SS?

"Yes," Gretchen said. "Perhaps he is not active, perhaps it is self-preservation, but his name is on the roster. I saw it."

"I will be drummed out of the Hitler Youth," Ilse jumped in, almost sobbing, tears on her cheeks. "I will be arrested."

Gretchen hugged her trembling body and said, "No, you will not be arrested. Do not worry. I think a friend of mine can help you." She turned her head away from Ilse. "Jake, I will call Hanna Reitsch. She owes me a big favor. She got into a mess with the Gestapo, something about a supposedly Jewish great-grandmother. It was not true. I used my Abwehr connections to straighten it out."

Gretchen gave Jake a peck on the cheek, which poured surprise across Ilse's face, and went to the phone in the front room. She could be heard giving the operator some numbers.

"What is to become of me?" Ilse pleaded. "Must I leave the

Fatherland? Will you take me to Switzerland?"

"I don't know all the answers right now, Ilse. I promise you this, though, you won't have to live with milk cows and flügelhorns."

Jake heard only bits and pieces of Gretchen's half of the conversation taking place in the other room. "They are good people. . . . *Ja* . . . Trust me, Hanna . . . ."

Soon Gretchen was back in the kitchen. "Hanna will help you. I will drive you to the airfield at the Heinkel Works. Come, we must leave. Are you finished with your chocolate?"

Ilse nodded and Gretchen led them out the back door to a small garage facing the alley. Jake hadn't seen the garage before, nor the black Volkswagen parked there.

Jake stuffed the bags in the boot in the car's nose and soon they were driving through dark, wet streets.

Gretchen said, "Hanna was to test a new fighter for range and night-flying characteristics in the next few nights. I convinced her to do it tonight. She said, 'Well, all right then, as you know, I do love adventure.'"

"Where are we going?" Jake asked. "You said Heinkel."

"Ernst Heinkel's company field in Orianenburg. It is not a military base. Hanna will meet us there."

"I don't like that. By now, probably every airfield, train and bus station have been alerted to look out for a man and a girl."

"Hanna mentioned an auxiliary gate, one used by ground crews only."

Jake knew the risk was great. He wondered what was going on in Ilse's mind as she sat silent in the back seat. "I didn't know you had a car," he said.

"I drive very little. I am permitted just nine liters of *Benzin* a month and that only because of the Abwehr. Most people get none."

It took thirty minutes to reach the airfield in the northern suburb. In the gloom, Jake could just make out the control tower and beacon, both eerily dark.

Gretchen drove past the main gate and guard shack, then down a side road that angled along a concrete wall topped by coils of barbed wire. Soon, through the dimness of Gretchen's hooded headlights, they came upon a figure in a military flight suit. The apparition held up a hand and Gretchen stopped. She switched off the engine and lights and the three climbed out.

"Well, here are my two passengers," Hanna Reitsch said as Jake retrieved the bags from the little trunk. "Come with me, quickly."

"Thank you, Hanna dear," Gretchen said.

"*Bitte*. This will settle my debt to you."

"I'm most grateful." Gretchen gave Hanna a hug, then kissed Jake on the lips and said, "Well, *auf Wiedersehen* again, Herr Bad Penny. Do not forget." Ilse and Hanna watched, bemused.

"I won't," Jake said.

"Come, quickly," Hanna Reitsch said, and Jake and Ilse followed her along the wall for about twenty yards to a recessed tin door. As she produced a ring of keys and began unlocking the door, Jake heard the rattly sound of the Volkswagen starting and driving off. *Godspeed, Tapestry*, he said to himself.

Inside the airfield Jake caught the smells of dry grass and machine oil in the chill air. He saw three Heinkel 111 bombers parked on a wide apron, looking like tethered eagles. Large factory buildings covered by camouflage nets stood in the gloom across the field.

Reitsch walked beside Jake across dormant, frost-covered turf grass that reminded him of the rough at El Rancho Golf Club. Reitsch gave him a sidelong gaze as penetrating and unnerving as when she'd studied his face at von Braun's office.

"So it is you. Have we not met somewhere, I mean before the other day at the university?"

His mind spun and his ankle ached. "No, I'm sure we haven't."

Reitsch offered him a curious little smile.

They reached a trimotor plane that Jake recognized as a Junkers 52. Reitsch said, "Wait here a moment, both of you. Stay close to this plane. I do not want the ground crew to see you." She strode off.

Jake studied the plane they stood beside, with its boxy fuselage. Affectionately called the "Iron Annie," the Ju52 was the Luftwaffe's workhorse transport, the German counterpart to America's C-47. Ilse leaned against him and he hugged her. "You mentioned that you like to write," he said. "I can help you with that."

In the distance, he saw Reitsch arrive at a black, twin-engine plane that resembled the British Mosquito. She and a couple of men with flashlights began to examine it. The lights probed the undercarriage, tires, wing surfaces and two or three radar rods jutting from the nose.

One of the men turned and looked toward Jake and Ilse. He seemed to be squinting. "Don't move," Jake whispered. "Stay perfectly still." It was hard to tell, but the stare seemed to be directed straight at them.

Reitsch finished inspecting the engine cowlings, went to the rear, put a hand on one of the twin tails and moved the trim tab up and down. At last she slapped the shoulder of the man who'd been looking toward Jake. He turned. A few nods and words were exchanged, and the two walked across the field toward a dark shed.

When they had entered the shed, Reitsch called, "Come."

Jake and Ilse walked to the plane.

"Did they see us?" Jake asked.

"I do not think so. They said nothing." She turned to the plane. "Now, this is a two-place fighter. It will be crowded but we can manage." Access was through a hatch on the bottom of the fuselage. Reitsch went in first, then helped Ilse climb up. Jake followed. Soon, wide-eyed, Ilse was stuffed into a small space behind the seats, along with the sack of her belongings and Jake's satchel.

As Jake strapped himself into the copilot's seat, Reitsch cautioned, "Do not tell me about yourselves or what you are up to." She fastened herself in, strapped a clipboard on her lap, and put a hand on the oval wheel known as a yoke. There was another in front of Jake.

Despite Gretchen's assurances about Hanna Reitsch, Jake was anxious, remembering Gretchen saying this woman was fervently devoted to the Fatherland.

Reitsch ran through all her preflight checks, then cranked the engines into life. "The Luftwaffe," she said, "is trying to determine whether this He219 should replace the Junkers 88 as our primary night fighter." Jake well remembered the Ju88. One of them had shot the bomber behind *O for Oliver* right out of the sky. "This plane is a rabbit," Reitsch added.

She keyed her hand mike and said, "Test pilot Reitsch, Special Air Detail. Heinkel 219. Request permission to take off on Runway Two-Seven." She listened a moment, then snapped, "*Scheiss*, I'm never asked for that."

"What?" Jake asked.

"There is a problem."

Reitsch eased the throttle forward and began taxiing the plane. It bounced a bit on the rough sod before she wheeled it onto a wide swath of concrete.

A man in a black leather coat, frantically waving a big flashlight, blocked their path at the head of the runway. The beam swept across Jake's face for an instant. *Damn, he might have seen me.* Reitsch eased the plane to a stop, throttled the engines down to idle and slid the canopy open.

The man came closer and shouted, "Where is your flight plan? You must have a flight plan. And do you have a passenger?"

Jake reached back and put a hand on Ilse's shoulder. "No matter what happens," he whispered, "stay down."

"I never have a flight plan," Reitsch called back. "Do you know who I am?"

"*Ja*, of course, *Fräulein* Reitsch. But the Gestapo has ordered us to check any departing planes tonight."

Yes, Jake knew, Hanna Reitsch had a problem. The problem was Jake Weaver.

CHAPTER FIFTY-THREE

I never file a flight plan," Reitsch repeated. "When I test a plane I go where I please."

"I must ask again," said Flashlight Man, "do you have a passenger? I think you have a passenger."

Reitsch didn't answer. Flashlight Man moved close to the left wing and stared at the cockpit. Only the purring of the idling engines disturbed the silence of a long, tense moment.

Jake saw indecision on Reitsch's face. He wondered how much she was really committed to the favor she'd promised Gretchen. He knew he had to do something. Well, he thought, a bluff worked on that sergeant at Tempelhof. Here goes. *Again.* "Keep down," he repeated to Ilse.

He unbuckled and stood, showing himself. His heart hammered as something—surprise? satisfaction?—spilled across Flashlight Man's face.

"I am *Sturmbannführer* Richter," Jake called out. "I am on the staff of Reichsmarshal Goering. This test flight has been ordered by the Reichsmarshal himself. This plane is very important to him."

"Well, I," Flashlight Man stammered. The propeller wash rippled his trousers.

"The Reichsmarshal," Jake went on, "will want to know why this important flight has been impeded. What is your name?"

Flashlight Man shifted his weight from foot to foot.

"Your name!" Jake demanded.

"I, I . . ." Flashlight Man seemed to shrink. He held a hand on his hat to keep it from flying away. "I see," he said at last, "in that case, you must surely proceed. I am sorry to have troubled you, *Sturmbannfürer*." He gave the Nazi salute and backed off a few steps. "Have a safe flight, *Fräulein* Reitsch." The man gave a small bow, then flashed his light three times at the control tower. Three flashes answered from the tower and a moment later two bright rows of runway lights popped on, piercing the blackness.

"Bravo, *Major*, well done," Reitsch said as Flashlight Man scampered off. "Where did you study dramatics?"

Jake's only reply was to let out a huge breath of air. Ilse hadn't said anything, must be puzzled as hell, he thought.

Reitsch lined the plane up between the rows of lights and gave the engines more power.

"Where are we going?" Jake asked.

"To Göteborg, Sweden. About five-hundred kilometers from Berlin. We will arrive there in little more than an hour."

"Good." He prayed she wasn't lying. He didn't trust anyone anymore. He thought about the trick Luftwaffe fliers had played on Putzi Hanfstaengl, pretending to take him into the Spanish Civil War but actually landing in Germany. Would she pull something like that on him tonight?

Reitsch revved the engines and shoved the throttle forward. The plane bolted down the runway—it was a rabbit all right—and was quickly airborne.

Jake felt a hand on his shoulder. He turned and saw Ilse sitting up and gazing with bright eyes through the back of the canopy. As the landing gear came up and thumped into their wheel wells, the flare path blinked off. The lights had been on less than a minute.

"This is wonderful," Ilse shouted to be heard. "We took off so fast."

"This plane has a top speed of more than six hundred kilometers per hour," Reitsch said. Whew, around four hundred miles an hour,

Jake figured.

Reitsch checked the various instruments on the panel in front of her as they climbed, her face alert and intent in their glow. They soon leveled off, Jake marveling at the plane's rate of climb.

"Daimler Benz engines," Reitsch said, sounding proud. "Very powerful, rated at one-thousand horsepower."

"Göteborg, you said." Jake tried to picture a map of Sweden. Where was Göteborg? Close to Stockholm? "You can land there?"

"*Ja.* I have done so before. Sweden does much business with the Third Reich. They allow us access to the Göteborg aerodrome."

Before long Reitsch began taking the plane through a series of maneuvers. Sharp banks to the left and right. Some climbs and stomach-wrenching dives. Ilse squealed and bounced around as if she were riding the Cyclone Racer at the Pike in Long Beach.

At the end of each maneuver, Reitsch made a notation on her clipboard. Jake was awed at her ability to control this jackrabbit with one hand while writing with the other.

"I would like to do a snap roll," she said, "but the girl could get hurt. I will save that for another time. *Mein Gott,* I love to fly."

Jake saw that his yoke danced along with hers, duplicating its every move. He glanced at the instrument panel. The gyrocompass read slightly west of true north. He blew out some air. They were heading toward Sweden.

Awhile later, Reitsch said, "We are near Copenhagen, but there is nothing to see. The Danish towns are blacked out."

Jake looked back and saw that Ilse had curled up in a little ball, asleep with her head nestled against the sack. She used it as a pillow. He thought about the stuffed animal in that sack. Next time she falls asleep she'll be holding her little friend, he told himself. It was cold. He hoped his daughter wasn't freezing.

He leaned back in his seat and summed up this crazy journey of his. Mostly successful. Too bad about the Hindenburg letter, but Dieter alive! That was the main and best thing. He prayed his uncle would be okay. That was a dangerous game he was playing.

Jake had some important things to tell Roosevelt—and they'd make great stories for Hearst's papers. Von Braun's rocket—and himself a member of the SS. Synthetic gasoline made from coal oil. Small, dispersed, hard-to-bomb shops building aircraft parts. Slave laborers clearing air-raid damage. He also carried a message for Professor Goddard. He tried not to think about Rolf Becker.

Maybe I'll get to the Stars' opener after all, he thought. I'll have to teach this girl sleeping behind me all about baseball.

The plane purred onward. Jake checked the gyrocompass again. The direction was still right, thank God.

A moment later, he followed Reitsch's eyes toward a light far below. "We are now over the sea, the Kattegat. That must be a ship down there. With running lights on, it would be Swedish."

When they were well past the ship, Reitsch pushed the plane into a dive and fired the guns. Orange tracer shells hammered from the wings and formed a cone of light, converging several hundred yards in front of the nose.

"What the hell," Jake muttered. "Are we under attack?"

"No, no, just testing the guns." She pulled the plane back to level and made another notation.

Minutes later, to Jake's total surprise, she reached over, touched his thigh for a moment and said, "So you kept Gretchen's bed warm, did you?"

Jake didn't answer.

"Well, she is a good girl. I am very sorry that she lost her husband. He was a fine pilot."

Jake still said nothing.

Ten minutes later, the plane slowed and Jake saw lights.

So did Ilse. Awake again, she cried out, "Oh, look at all the lights, the twinkling lights down there."

"We're over Sweden," Jake said. "Neutral Sweden, a country at peace, happy to light up its cities at night without fear of attack.

That's nice, isn't it, Ilse?"

She didn't answer. Jake knew the girl was being pulled away from all that was familiar and comforting to her.

Maybe a mile or two in the distance, Jake made out an airfield beacon, its alternating shafts of bright green and white light flashing through swirls of snow.

Reitsch suddenly banked the plane in a wide turn and reversed course.

Jake saw the gyrocompass indicator swing around to *south*. "What are you doing?" he blurted.

"I have kept my promise to Gretchen. I have taken you to Sweden." Reitsch glanced over at him with a cold, thin smile. "And now we are going home."

"Back to Germany? You can't—"

"Oh, but I can. I do not know precisely who you are and what is your mission, but I could be shot for taking strangers out of the country."

"Then why fly all the way here?"

"I promised. I gave my word."

"That's nuts. You're crazy!" Is she armed? Jake wondered. Would she pull a pistol if he tried something? He hadn't seen a sidearm. He jerked on his yoke. The plane banked hard to the right and plunged.

"Do not touch that," Reitsch shouted. "What are you—"

"We're not going back." Jake maintained his grip on the wheel. The plane wobbled, lost more altitude. His stomach reeled. Pressure hammered at his eardrums.

"I'll wreck this damn plane if I have to."

A shrill sound came from behind them, Ilse screaming or crying.

Jake's and Reitsch's hands fought for control. She tried to counter his every move. It became a battle of muscle and will: his masculine strength against her desperate intensity. The plane bottomed out of its dive and shot upward at a sharp angle. Jake was pushed hard against the back of his seat—blood drained from his head—but he kept his grip on the yoke.

"Stop," Reitsch shrieked. "We will stall." She slapped at Jake's hands. "You will destroy this airplane."

"Damn right. Unless you land here."

Reitsch managed to force her yoke forward a bit, lessening the climb, reducing the risk of stall.

Next Jake stomped on the rudder pedal. The plane spun off its center of gravity like a bee-stung pony.

"You will kill us," Reitsch shouted, breathing hard.

"If I have to." Jake pulled his hands away, letting Reitsch think about it. She got the plane in level trim, bit her lower lip and looked as angry as a scalded cat.

"Do as he says," came a voice from behind them. *Good girl, Ilse*, Jake thought.

Seconds passed. "I mean it," Jake said. "I will wreck this plane before I'll let you take us back." He stabbed the wheel with the butt of his hand and the plane pitched off center once more.

Still panting, Reitsch trimmed it up again, stared hard at Jake, and shook her head ruefully. The moment dragged. At last, slowly, she said, "All right. I am not ready to die tonight." She swung the plane around to a northerly course. "You are mad!" she hissed.

Soon the airport lights reappeared. "Tell no one of what I am doing for you tonight."

"I won't."

"I mean not ever."

Jake knew if Hanna Reitsch got in trouble over this, she'd take it out on Gretchen. "I won't," he repeated.

Reitsch began her descent. Jake saw dim landing lights through powdery snow flurries. Without calling the tower, Reitsch made a smooth touchdown on a sod runway and brought the plane to a rapid stop. "Leave quickly," she said. "Göteborg crawls with British agents."

Ilse climbed down through the hatch first. Jake collected their things and tossed them down. Despite bitter cold rushing through the opening, Jake was sweating. He wanted to tell this bitch off with some choice words, but decided not to. That might bounce back to harm Gretchen.

Reitsch looked directly into his eyes and said, "It was at the 1937 air show in Glendale, California, was it not?" She paused for a beat, then laughed. "Get out of here, you dangerous fool."

"Glendale?" Jake said. "Where is that?" He jumped down, picked up their things, and took Ilse's hand.

Frozen grass crunched beneath their feet as they walked off. "That was most brave of you," Ilse said.

"Not really. Had no choice. We couldn't afford to go back." Jake saw two buildings, one obviously a hangar. He steered them toward the other.

"What was that about California?" Ilse asked.

"Do you know of Mickey Mouse?" Jake evaded.

"Oh yes, he is quite funny. I saw some of those cartoons before the war. I—" She stopped herself midsentence.

Jake thought she'd been about to say that she missed them.

"And do you know the name Walt Disney?"

"Yes, he created Mickey Mouse. I also saw *Snow White and the Seven Dwarfs*. I liked Bashful the best. I hated the wicked old queen."

"I did too. Would you like to meet Herr Disney?"

"Of course, but that is quite impossible. You mustn't tease me, *Vater.*"

They heard the whine of the He219 taking off. They turned and watched it climb and vanish into the darkness.

Realizing that he was walking on free Swedish ground, Jake felt as if a great weight had been lifted. Even the air felt better to breathe than it had in Germany. His ankle seemed to hurt less and somehow the snowflakes even looked whiter.

They entered a building that turned out to be a small, spartan terminal. Christmas carols were being piped in.

Reaching a row of benches beside an empty departure gate, Jake said, "Let's rest a moment." He sat, rubbed his aching ankle, then opened his satchel. "I want to make sure my things are okay."

He began to check the contents. Underwear, shirts, socks, all possessions of a dead man he'd been impersonating for two weeks. He couldn't wait to get rid of them, put on his own clothes, let his reddish hair grow out, and get back to his typewriter. And Valerie. Buy that house she had her eye on. The Louisiana Kid was going home. A wonderful thought. Hell, he even longed to see that winged red horse on the sign above his local filling station.

Wait. What was this? He'd come across an elegant envelope, maybe ten inches by four, light tan in color, the paper stock a fine linen. It was hand-addressed in good calligraphy, simply to "Herr Hitler." A maroon seal on the back was broken.

Jake took a deep, satisfied breath. Here at last was Hindenburg's letter! Gretchen must have slipped it into his bag when she'd gone into his bedroom last night. Ilse was watching him closely, curiosity etched on her face.

He opened the envelope and, to his surprise, pulled out a small note on powder-blue stationery. Could this odd little piece of paper possibly be the Hindenburg letter? He unfolded it and held it up. "Frau Goebbels did have the letter," he read, the words appearing in a neat, feminine cursive. "She knew exactly where it was all the time. By the time you read this, I will have burned it."

What the hell?

"I am German after all. My country has enough world embarrassment without this. Years ago, the letter might have done some good. Not now. It is too late for that. Hitler will be in control until the end. Please find it in your heart to forgive me, and please try to keep me there, in your heart, as I will you. Your faithful friend in Berlin, Gretchen."

His heart? She had destroyed the letter, and without his ever having laid eyes on it. She must have written this little confession last night. He shook his head and wondered if he'd ever begin to understand how women thought.

He put the note back and closed the satchel.

"What will we do now?" Ilse asked, a tear glistening on her cheek. "What will happen to me?"

"Good things, I promise you. Come on, let's go."

Ilse got up, took her *Deutscher Maedel* field cap from the pocket of her new coat, stared at the swastika a moment, then tossed the cap in a trash can.

Outside, a light snow fluttered down and Ilse held her coat tight against herself as Jake waved to the driver of a waiting cab. As the man stowed the satchel and sack in the trunk, Ilse asked, "Where are we going?" Her breath steamed. White flakes began to collect in her reddish hair.

"So you'd like to meet Herr Disney," Jake said.

Her face scrunched in anxiety, Ilse climbed into the back seat. Her father followed, and the driver pulled away from the curb.

"*Sprechen Sie Englisch?*" Jake asked him.

"Yes I do, a little."

"Good," Jake said in English. "American Consulate, please."

Ilse shot him a look of astonishment. It was eight days before Christmas.

EPILOGUE

The Associated Press, Aug. 10, 1945

BALTIMORE—Dr. Robert Goddard, noted scientist and the father of modern rocketry, died here today, just hours after President Truman received the Japanese government's offer of surrender.

Although he was America's pre-eminent rocket scientist in the 1920s and '30s, he was not called upon by U.S. weapons developers during this war.

In England, Wernher von Braun and other German rocket specialists, now in U.S. Army custody, expressed amazement at learning this.

"His was the greatest rocket mind in the United States," von Braun said. "Our early work in Germany was made possible by Dr. Goddard, from whom we learned virtually all we knew."

One of Goddard's early inventions became the bazooka, which U.S. forces have used to good effect against the Germans and Japanese.

Goddard was 63. He will be buried in his hometown of Worcester, Mass.

Los Angeles Herald-Express, Nov. 13, 1947

SANTA MONICA—Ilse Weaver was crowned homecoming queen last night at Santa Monica High School, one day after her 17th birthday. The auburn-haired beauty was crowned by last year's queen, Sarah Gilchrist, at halftime ceremonies of the football game between Santa Monica and Dorsey high schools.

Miss Weaver's parents, Mr. and Mrs. Jake Weaver, were among the cheering crowd. Jake Weaver is assistant managing editor of the *Herald-Express* and Valerie Weaver is an aircraft designer at North American Aviation.

Their daughter Ilse wore a long-sleeved gown of white satin, gathered at the waist, and a huge smile as she waved happily toward the stands at the moment of her coronation. Ilse, who hopes to attend UCLA, is a member of the Glee Club and the German Club, and is on the school newspaper.